To Luna —
Enjoy.

# DAUGHTERS OF FIRE & SEA

BOOK ONE

HOLLY KARLSSON

DAUGHTERS OF FIRE & SEA
(Daughters of Fire & Sea Book One)

Copyright © 2019 by Holly Karlsson

All rights reserved.

Cover design by Maria Spada
Ornamental break design by Lisa Kaplan-Salgado

Developmental Editing by Kendra Olson

Ebook ISBN: 978-1-7330998-0-6
Paperback ISBN: 978-1-7330998-1-3

www.byhollykarlsson.com

*For Kent, who always listens to my ideas even when I talk loud enough to be heard from space. Passion and enthusiasm in all things.*

*;)*

# PROLOGUE

## ELAINA

ELAINA WAS EXCELLENT AT HIDING. It was a skill she'd mastered as a small child, evading her nurse and older brothers when she wanted to be alone. She'd hid from her mother as well before Queen Arina had died and left her.

Her vibrant red hair was always a mess, her dresses constantly in need of soap and needle, and her pale skin perpetually smudged with dirt and ink. When Elaina wasn't hiding in the numerous, dark tunnels that filled the old keep or terrifying her nurse by climbing the castle's walls, she was ensconced in the library, pouring over ancient manuscripts on magic. She'd even managed to blackmail her brothers' fencing tutor into teaching her on the sly, one of her proudest achievements.

Elaina was, if her father had bothered to pay attention, the worst possible princess, or best if her opinion mattered at all.

"I'm going to join the infantry," she'd told her brother Raendar on her seventh birthday.

He'd laughed at her and shook his head, his good humor remaining even as she hooked the back of his legs and unbalanced him, driving him to the ground.

"There are women in Father's army," Elaina had argued, glaring at her brother, as she caught him in an armlock.

"Yes, but Father will never agree."

"We'll see," she'd said.

Now, fifteen years old and a near echo of her dead mother, Elaina had caught her father's attention, but not in the way she'd hoped. He hadn't stopped her from fencing or studying magic in the library — in fact, he'd demanded she do more. Elaina was expected to best a man with both her wit and a dagger. She was expected to speak multiple languages and to argue politics in the Scorched Court. She was supposed to draw the eyes of suitors for political alliances, and yet be seen as unattainable and untouchable, loved and feared by men and women everywhere.

Elaina was supposed to be everything, and need nothing. It was exhausting and alienating and had driven her to hide more and more. In stolen moments in dark hallways, she'd allowed herself to breathe, cry, and scream silently unobserved.

On one such day, when she'd slipped away to pound her fists against the wall, she'd ended up inside a secluded passageway off her father's study, the doorway concealed by a heavy tapestry. She'd been standing just inside it, taking deep, shuddering breaths in the unused space, trying to calm her racing heart when she heard the door open. Back pressed against the slick stone behind her, Elaina could see a sliver of the large room and the bookcase of massive, leather-bound tomes against the far wall. Willing her breath to slow, she watched as her father stepped into view.

King Rakarn was a large, imposing man, with broad shoulders and a barrel chest. His thick, dark brown hair was clipped short, military style, and tamed with oils. His pale skin was coarsened and tanned by the harsh ocean winds, and scaly red patches marked his cheeks and neck. Elaina's father was a man of rough, blunt edges and dangerous power, and whether he chose to smile or not, which was rare, there was always something threatening in his brown eyes. She'd once overheard her nurse say that her father's eyes were his worst and best feature, terrifying with their fierce focus, and yet beautifully edged by thick, black lashes.

Elaina's father turned, and she wondered if he'd seen her behind the tapestry, but he merely stepped deeper into the room. "Why did you come here?" he asked, his voice both harsh and indifferent, a tone Elaina knew well.

An unknown woman answered his question. "You owe me a favor," she said.

The woman's tone was nearly as severe as her father's, and Elaina craned her head curiously, trying to see who it was. Shifting sideways along the wall, she caught sight of a woman standing in front of the door, now closed, her hand on the shoulder of a young boy.

Elaina smothered a gasp. The woman had wings tucked behind her back, the feathers black like a raven's. She was tall, taller than her father, with long blond hair and bright blue eyes, and skin so pale that Elaina wondered if she'd ever seen the light. Her arms, bare from wrist to shoulder, were long but muscular and covered in tattooed runes that glinted an unsettling green. Armor covered the rest of her, a combination of black leather and scale, and a coiled whip hung from a belt around her waist.

*She's a Daughter of Valen*, Elaina thought, her heart pounding in her chest. She'd only read of them in the old histories in the keep's library, never seen one. What was she doing here? The Daughters lived inside the Veil, ushering the souls of dead warriors to Vaelnorn.

The boy shifted, catching Elaina's eye. She'd been so fascinated by the woman she'd forgotten he was there. Was he related to the Daughter somehow? The boy shared the woman's features, with the same blue eyes and blond hair on the edge of becoming brown. His feet were bare, which Elaina thought was odd, and he was wearing a simple tunic of white cloth over trousers. He was silent and reserved, immobile as a statue, with a calmness Elaina's brothers were incapable of. If not for his curious eyes, taking in the room, she'd have thought him frozen, perhaps magicked by the woman behind him.

Elaina's father was silent for a long moment, and then he answered, his voice thin, not quite resigned but without its usual force. "What do you need?"

"You must take my son," the woman said.

"Your son?" There was a note of disbelief in her father's voice.

Elaina's eyes widened. The Daughters of Valen did not have sons, only daughters. Her tutor, Gaila, said no male could handle their power and were therefore killed to spare them torment and protect the souls in the Veil.

"He's been bound, his wings ... removed," the woman said. Her voice tightened, and a muscle rippled in her cheek. She looked like Ryker, one of Elaina's brothers, when he was trying not to cry, not to show emotion. "When I leave here, he will not remember me." Her fingers shifted on the boy's shoulder, and he looked up at her.

"What do you expect me to do with him?" Rakarn asked.

It sounded like he was sneering, and Elaina could picture the expression on his face well. Her father did not like to fix problems that weren't his own. He saw it as a sign of weakness.

"You must hide him for me. Place him with a family. Maybe in Thenda. Don't keep him here." The woman's eyes narrowed, and she clenched her hand, igniting the runes on her arm. "Be careful how you treat him," she said. She looked again at the boy, her face softening with a genuine, loving, heart-broken smile that Elaina had seen on her own mother's face.

Chest tightening, Elaina pressed her fists against her mouth as tears filled her eyes. The boy didn't cry or beg; he merely stared into his mother's face with quiet focus. He didn't seem to understand she was leaving him, that this might be the last time he saw her.

"He's bright and curious," the woman said. "It should not be hard to find someone to care for him."

Elaina expected her father to voice some argument about why he, of all people, should not be tasked with such a simple thing, why it was beneath him, beneath a king. She expected him to demand an apology for the insult. But her father did none of those things.

"We are even, then, if I do this for you?" Elaina's father asked. It did not sound like a question.

The woman laughed, a harsh, joyless sound. "We will never be even, *Vel'kah*. You are a scourge on my soul."

"As are you, on mine," her father growled back.

*Vel'kah? What did that mean?* Elaina wondered. She looked back at the boy's calm face. What was wrong with him? Could he not hear his mother's words to her father? They were deciding his life right in front of him, and he wasn't raging or yelling or feeling the fury and agony that Elaina felt on his behalf. She couldn't understand it.

Confused, Elaina looked at his mother. What had she meant about binding him? And what did her father owe her, this Daughter of Valen?

"He is not yours," the woman said, perhaps prompted by some unseen expression on her father's face.

Elaina bit down on her lip, eyes widening. Had her father bedded this fearsome woman? She was not so naive that she didn't know her father had mistresses since her mother's death, and she wouldn't have been surprised if he'd had any before. Possible though it was, the boy looked nothing like her father. He was leaner, more delicate in his features. He didn't have the Raendasharan fierceness.

"I'll send word where I've placed him," Rakarn said.

"No," the woman said sharply. "I can find him if I need to." She looked down at her son. "I hope I never do." Fixing her eyes on Elaina's father again, the woman frowned. "He won't age for seven years," she said. "An effect of the Veil. You'll need to prepare the family. Make up an explanation; threaten them if you have to."

Elaina's father barked an incredulous laugh. "And after that?"

"He'll age as any human." The woman crouched down and gently turned the boy around, putting her hands on his arms.

"You are loved," the woman said, her voice soft. "Never forget that. Never lose your curiosity for the world." She squeezed his arms, an affectionate gesture, and began to speak in runes, the magical language of the dragons, the Old Ones, long dead. Her arms glowed as she spoke, the runes igniting in a rush of color.

Elaina felt magic fill the room, a stifling pressure that made her sweat. She knew elemental spells, but the woman was talking too quickly, too quietly, for her to hear. She was activating something connected to her son, and as Elaina watched, she saw the boy's eyes glow.

He cried out, curving forward, and Elaina saw blood darken the back of his shirt. The woman grimaced, back arching like the boy's, but she didn't stop speaking. Her eyes shimmered, wet and dark and anguished.

Elaina smelled blood and charred flesh, and her stomach flipped in revulsion. She wanted to scream, she wanted to run, but the terror of her father finding her here, thinking she'd spied on him, kept her frozen in place. He wouldn't believe it'd been an accident.

Abruptly, the boy sagged in the woman's arms, and her words cut off as she hugged him to her chest. Then, she pushed him gently back and stood up, releasing his hands.

The boy looked up, his face puzzled, recognition gone. "Who are you?" he asked.

The Daughter smiled sadly. "No one important." Looking back at Elaina's father, she gave him a sharp, dangerous look, and then she turned and left.

Elaina stood trembling, watching from the dark passageway, as she listened to the door open and close. The boy turned with a confused expression and looked at her father.

Stepping back into view, Elaina's father placed a hand on the boy's shoulder. His face looked ... almost sympathetic, and Elaina's heart ached. She couldn't remember him ever looking at her that way.

"Come," her father told the boy. "Let's get you back to your family."

Together, they walked out of sight. Elaina listened for the heavy thud, as the door closed again, and then she scrambled down the passageway to her room wiping tears from her cheeks.

She never saw the boy in the keep again.

# 1

LYRIC

LYRIC HELD A STEAMING cup of tea beneath her nose for warmth and stared up at the shingled roof of her front porch. The dead branch, dropped from one of the onyx-bark trees arching overhead, had smashed a hole through the old gray wood. It'd have to be repaired.

She squinted as the sun slid free of the scattered clouds overhead. Light bounced off the pearled glass of the attic's round window, momentarily blinding her as it shimmered like a dragon's eye.

The sun was warm on her head, and Lyric tilted her chin towards the sky. She closed her eyes, appreciating the unexpected warmth, and breathed in the sweetened air, smelling the tall grass of the prairie at her back. As she inhaled again, letting her worries slip, just for a moment, she detected an older, earthier smell, wood and dirt and dampened moss, the scent of the Umberwood forest.

"You'll have to go up there," Runa said, jarring Lyric from her thoughts.

Lyric cracked open an eye and spotted her twin sister's slim shape on the shadowed porch.

The sun, perhaps startled by Runa's brusque tone, slipped back behind the clouds.

"Yes," Lyric said, sighing. She shivered, tugging her shawl closer and brought her cup to her lips.

Runa stepped down the stairs and joined her on the grass. She planted her hands on her hips and looked up at the damaged roof with a cross expression.

Though she'd become familiar with Runa's wraithlike state the past six months, it still unnerved her to stare straight through her sister's body. Looking at Runa as she was, Lyric could see the wandering border of the forest and the distant mountains beyond.

"Stop that," Runa said without turning her head.

Hiding a smile, Lyric looked back at the house. "It's a shame Mr. Torenson is too scared to come out here now," she said. "Remember how he repaired our door last autumn? It doesn't get stuck anymore when the rains come."

"We're capable on our own," Runa said, crossing her arms. "We have nails, a hammer, extra wood from the shed."

"Yes, I'm *capable* of climbing up the ladder and fixing it, but that doesn't mean I want to. It's cold, and my shin still hurts from when Mrs. Laelan's son kicked me." Lyric made a face. "Your fault by the way."

Runa chuckled, her sharp face softening at the memory. "I was checking to see if you'd set his arm yet. I felt like a bandit, skulking beneath the window in the dark." She grinned. "That boy's a little monster."

Lyric laughed, and freed a hand from her shawl, placing it on Runa's arm. She didn't understand why she could still touch her. Her sister was dead, a ghost, at least she seemed to be. Lyric could feel the shape of Runa's arm beneath her fingers, but there was no familiar warmth of living skin, no real sensation or texture.

She'd wondered, more than once, if she could only touch

Runa because they were twins and connected in some way, soul to soul, that transcended death. It was a theory, and one she couldn't test. No one in Elae's Hollow would enter their house now, much less touch her phantom sister.

Sighing, Lyric tucked her hand back into her shawl. They should probably be grateful that their neighbors were only avoiding them, and that no one had attempted to burn their house down. Kalizans were not exactly welcoming of anything weird or magical.

Runa tucked a lock of red hair behind her ear and squinted up at the trees around their house. "What tree did this come off of anyway? I don't see any broken branches."

Lyric shrugged and turned around. "I'll find the ladder." Her eyes passed over the prairie, and she paused, seeing movement in the tall grass. Someone was walking towards them.

"What is it?" Runa asked, following Lyric's gaze.

As the person drew closer, Lyric saw it was a young woman, her hair covered by a pale blue handkerchief. Her shoulders hunched, her posture bent, as though she was forced forward by a strong wind, unable to turn back.

"It's Tora," Lyric said, a smile lifting her lips. "She's come back."

At odds with her flash of happiness, a sour feeling seeped into her stomach, and Lyric glanced sideways at Runa. Her sister's mouth had tightened, and her eyes had grown dark.

Frowning, Lyric shoved aside the unwelcome emotion, recognizing it as something outside herself, but it took several breaths before the lightness in her chest returned. She didn't always mind the slip of her sister's emotions into herself — the invisible, emotional tide connecting them had been useful more than once — but sometimes it was downright irritating.

"I'll be inside," Runa said, walking up the steps into the house.

Lyric watched her sister leave, and then looked back at the

prairie. Tora was alone, which was good. She doubted Runa would be pleased if Dalen had chosen to accompany his future bride.

Pretty and plump, Tora had pale blue eyes, and rounded shoulders. She was eighteen, one year younger than Lyric and Runa, and was to be married the coming week. She'd forever been a bright-eyed and animated girl, always ready with a smile and a quick word.

Within the shade of Lyric and Runa's house, Tora was not her usual self, her face pale and pinched, her eyes shifting around, as though danger lurked in every shadow.

"Hello, Tora," Lyric said, smiling encouragingly. "What brings you by? How's your arm?"

"Much better," Tora said. She nervously licked her lips, and darted a glance at Lyric's face, before looking back at the ground. "T-thank you for helping me."

Lyric swallowed a sigh and tried to keep her face relaxed and friendly. Honestly, their neighbors' fear was ridiculous. Had they ever seen Lyric or Runa turn someone into a toad? They asked for help if their need was great enough, but no one would meet their eyes or share a cup of tea when they visited the village.

Lyric almost preferred the derisive whispers that had chased her through childhood to this eerie silence. She hadn't thought she could feel more isolated, and yet now with Runa's bizarre death and ghostly body, it was like she'd died alongside her sister.

In all honesty, it stung. She'd grown up with them, had helped them for years. She'd been born in the valley, in this house, even if her mother, Elaina, had not. Elae's Hollow was their home. Lyric could still remember playing with Tora when they were children, chasing each other across the prairie, and stealing apples from Malen's farm.

"Of course, Tora," Lyric said. "I'm glad I was able to help. If you're still experiencing pain, I have more of the rosewater and lavender tincture I gave you, to apply to your arm. Did you run out of the calendula tea?"

"Yes," Tora said. She offered a relieved, half-smile. "Can I bother you for more?"

"Of course."

"I brought you something," Tora said abruptly. "To thank you." Opening her shawl, Tora removed a small, leather-bound book from the belt at her waist. The book was old, with a reddish-brown cover, water-stained and torn on one corner. "A traveler left this, at the inn," she said. "My father won't miss it. It's filled with old stories about a Blood Queen and lands outside the valley. I know you like to read."

Lyric's pulse quickened, and it took effort not to snatch the book from Tora's hands. "Yes, thank you, Tora. I do." She slowly reached forward, skin prickling and smile widening, as Tora handed her the book. Reverently Lyric ran her fingers over the cover.

Their valley was isolated, their village small, so hardly anyone came across their mountains, and though their mother had taught her and Runa to read, books were few and far between. This book was a treasure.

Pressing it against her chest, Lyric looked into Tora's face. "I'll get the tincture and tea for you. Would you like to sit on the porch, have something to drink?"

"No," Tora said quickly, shaking her head. She rewrapped her shawl around her shoulders and stepped back as if worried Lyric would force her inside.

Tora's reaction wasn't a surprise, but a lump still formed in Lyric's throat as she walked into the house. Swallowing her disappointment, she headed into the kitchen, passing the large, wooden table in the center of the room, where Runa was sitting. She set down her cup and Tora's book and started hunting for the burn tincture in a tall, wooden cabinet.

"Won't come in?" Runa asked scornfully.

Lyric sighed. "No." She selected two small bottles, of dark glass, from the assortment of remedies inside the cabinet.

"You shouldn't care what she thinks," Runa said. "Or what anyone thinks."

Bottles balanced in one hand, Lyric turned to face her sister. She didn't want to argue about this again.

Runa was leaning across the table, vibrant red hair spreading across the scarred wood like diaphanous pools of fire as she studied the book's cover.

"This is our home," Lyric said. "We belong here."

"Mother wasn't from here, and neither was Father."

"We grew up here," Lyric said, narrowing her eyes. "How can we help them if they're afraid of us?"

"They're never going to accept us," Runa said. She leaned back in her chair and crossed her arms. "You should leave, Ly. Go somewhere where you can start over. Where people will appreciate you."

Lyric arched an eyebrow. "And leave you here?"

"I'm a ghost, Ly. Mother kept you here, kept us here, and she's gone. I'm not going to bind you here too."

Lyric shook her head. "They need me, need us. What would they do if I leave? If we're not here to help? No. We can't leave anyway, Ru. We still don't know what happened to you. Who did this.

"And where would I go, anyway? You know what Mama said, how dangerous it is out there. The bandits, the damaged roads ..." Lyric lifted the bottles and gestured towards the door. "I need to take this to Tora."

She walked away before Runa could respond, passing quickly through the sitting room to the porch beyond, followed by her sister's irritation.

Tora still waited at the base of the stairs, her head swiveling. She jerked as the door slammed shut in Lyric's wake.

"Here," Lyric said, holding out the bottles. "Same instructions as before."

Tora nodded vigorously and grabbed them, quickly tucking the bottles under her shawl. She turned to go, then paused, looking back at Lyric. Eyes meeting, her gaze shifted to somewhere below Lyric's ear, perhaps focusing on the tangle of brown hair draping over her shoulder.

"There's a songsmith in the village," Tora said.

Excitement sparked inside Lyric's chest. "Oh?" she asked. The last time one had passed through their valley, Lyric had been nine or ten. Elae's Hollow did not often draw the eye of world travelers. They were barely noticed by Nitana, their capital.

Lyric thought about Runa, and the symbols on her chest, and hope flared bright and hot.

"You love stories, so ..." Tora met her eyes again, tentatively smiling.

"Do you know how long they're staying?" If the inn was dark enough and crowded, maybe Lyric and her sister could see the songsmith without someone noticing Runa in the shadows.

Tora shook her head. "No. He's only been here a day. Well, I need to get back."

Lyric nodded. "Thank you for the book, Tora, and the news. I would love to hear him sing."

Tora nodded, her cheeks turning pink.

"If you need anything, stop by any time," Lyric said.

Tora nodded again and then dipping her chin she turned and began to walk away, back towards the village.

Lyric watched her leave, eyes slipping over something in the darkening field ahead of Tora — a deer most likely — then she turned and skipped up the stairs into the house. Yanking on the iron handle, she let the door bang open against the wall. She rushed into the kitchen, giggling as Runa eyed her suspiciously.

"There's a songsmith at the inn!" Lyric said.

"Really?" Runa made a face. "Why?" she asked. "Are they writing an epic about farmers?"

"Hah hah," Lyric said, rolling her eyes. "Who knows why, but if one is here, we can ask him about the symbols. They travel, don't they? They know all kinds of stories, myths, things about magic. He'll know what it is. Runa, we can figure out what happened to you!"

Lips twisting, Runa leaned back in her chair and dropped her hands into her lap. She was calm, too calm, and Lyric stared at her in disbelief.

"How are you not excited about this?" Lyric demanded.

"It's been six months, Ly," Runa said. "I want to know what happened just as much as you do, more than you, but don't get your hopes up. We don't even know if we can talk to him, or if we can get inside the inn where he is." She gestured at herself, at the chair beneath her, visible through her body. "Maybe he won't know what the symbols mean. Maybe he'll be scared off when he sees me. Maybe this is related to the old gods and—"

Someone knocked on the door.

Lyric jumped, spinning towards the sound. It was a firm knock, not a tentative rap of knuckles, but confident and measured.

"Tora?" Runa guessed, though her expression suggested she didn't believe it.

"I have no idea," Lyric said. Her thoughts jumped to whatever she'd seen beyond Tora in the field. Had someone else decided to call? Smoothing a hand over the front of her dress and adjusting her shawl, that'd slipped from one shoulder in her excitement, Lyric calmly walked to the door and opened it.

A man stood on the porch wearing a wide, brown hat and holding a gnarled walking stick. He looked young with a fine-boned, beardless face. When their eyes met, he smiled, and it made Lyric think of an unfurling sail, slow at first, then snapping with a brilliance that stole her breath.

"Miss Graymorn?" the man asked. He stared straight into her eyes, not dropping his gaze to her mouth or chest, yet Lyric was aware of every inch of her body.

Her toes curled against the wood floor, as her hand strayed to the collar of her dress. He was tall, and she had to tilt her head back to look up at him. "Um, yes," Lyric said finally, flushing as his blue eyes sparkled. "Lyric Graymorn. Who are you?"

"I'm Kell Layreasha, Songsmith of the Emerald Tones, by way of the Radiant Hall of Corsicayna."

Lyric blinked.

"That's a mouthful," Runa said over her shoulder.

The man, Kell, looked past Lyric's left ear and grinned.

Lyric shifted to the side, so Runa could join her in the doorway, and tried to draw back her mind from wherever it'd fled. "The songsmith," she said. "You're staying at the inn?"

"I am," Kell said, nodding.

"Then what are you doing here?" Runa asked. She peered around him, perhaps to see if he was alone.

"Ah, well." Kell cleared his throat. "I've heard a few stories about your house, Miss Graymorn. I admit I was curious."

"So it was the opportunity to see a ghost, was it?" Runa asked.

Kell's eyes crinkled at the corners. "One should never turn down the opportunity to meet a ghost."

"Would you like to come in?" Lyric asked, nudging her sister. Kell's arrival was serendipitous. The songsmith was here, on their porch, they had to take advantage of this opportunity.

Runa was eyeing him suspiciously, but Kell gave them both an enthusiastic smile. "Yes, thank you," he said.

"Wonderful," Lyric said. She nudged Runa out of the way and opened the door wide, letting Kell enter.

Smiling at her, Kell removed a worn pack from his shoulder and placed it beside the door, along with his staff, and walked into the house. He smelled like a cool mountain breeze, skipping across the surface of a deep lake, and for a moment, Lyric thought she heard the call of birds.

Lyric led him into the kitchen, Runa trailing, and gestured to a chair at the table. She cleared away her cup and the book and set about reheating a pot of water on the stove. As she busied herself with preparing fresh tea, Kell sat down and removed his hat, placing it on the table. Runa, sitting in a chair opposite him, stared at him intently.

Lyric eyed Kell anxiously, worrying he'd be unnerved by her sister's brown-eyed stare, but he merely smiled and looked around the room. She noticed his eyes linger on the three wooden Trinity statuettes that sat upon the windowsill, which she'd draped in flowers.

"A neighbor carved them," Lyric said over her shoulder.

"They're beautiful," Kell said. "Your neighbor is very skilled."

Pouring fresh tea for herself and Kell, Lyric brought their cups to the table, setting one down in front of him. She gave Runa an apologetic look, who shrugged, unbothered, and then she sat down in the remaining chair.

Kell lifted his cup to his mouth with ink-stained fingers and inhaled, smiling appreciatively over the clay rim.

"I'm sorry," Lyric said after a flash of realization. "I never asked if you wanted tea. We don't have any beer or birch sap. We do have water..."

"This is wonderful, thank you," he said. "It was a chilly walk from the village."

"Yes," Lyric said, nodding. "I wouldn't be surprised if we get snow before too long."

"What did they say about us that made you come out here?" Runa asked. "Why are you in Elae's Hollow anyway?"

"I'm traveling south down to Raenborschia," Kell said. "Your beautiful valley happened to be on my way."

"On the way?" Runa said, raising an eyebrow. "We're in the middle of nowhere."

"It's true, we are," Lyric said.

Kell chuckled. "Last night when I arrived, one of the locals at the inn mentioned the witches at the forest's edge."

Runa snorted and rolled her eyes.

"A woman shushed him," Kell continued, smiling, "and eyed me warily, and my curiosity was piqued. A song and several free drinks, and bits of a story started tumbling out."

"Drunken boors," Runa growled. "I suppose Dalen Pell was the loudest of the lot."

Kell raised a curious eyebrow. "I don't believe I met anyone named Dalen."

"They're calling us witches now?" Lyric asked. Hurt, she avoided Kell's knowing eyes and looked down into her tea, taking a long sip.

"Let me guess," Runa said, her voice dry. "We'll steal your bones, and whistle away your soul and give it to the Thrice-Buried Hag in the woods?"

"Naturally I was intrigued by being able to whistle away a soul," Kell said.

Lyric looked up at the merriment in his voice and found herself mirroring his smile. "We're not all that interesting, in truth," she said. "Well, except for the mystery around Runa's death."

"Don't mind the ghost in the room," Runa said.

"Would you mind if I asked what happened?" Kell asked. He smiled at Runa. "You're the first ghost I've met."

"Perhaps we could trade?" Lyric asked, sitting straighter in her chair. "Our story for information?"

"Information?" Kell asked, looking between Lyric and Runa with a wide, curious smile.

"I'd like to know more about you first," Runa said, interrupting.

Lyric eyed her, then returned her gaze to Kell's face. Runa was right, of course. She'd been so focused on what they needed, what they could get from him. Who was this man in their kitchen? Could they trust him? Did it matter? They'd found no answers in their village.

Kell smiled. "Of course," he said. "What do you want to know?"

"What is that mark, around your neck?" Runa asked, leaning forward.

Lyric blinked, her eyes dropping to Kell's open collar. There it was, a thin, tattooed line of blue across the base of his throat. She hadn't noticed it. She'd been so distracted by the light in his eyes.

Kell's sea-blue eyes dimmed, like a sky darkening with storm clouds. "I'm bound," he said. His hand shifted on the table, as though he wanted to lift it and touch his throat.

"Bound?" Lyric asked, frowning. "What does that mean?"

"I'm from Thenda," Kell said. His face was tight, the mask of someone hiding emotions they didn't wish to share. "Or as it's known today, The Tainted Shore. There are things I ... I can't speak of." He swallowed, hands clenching around his cup of tea.

Lyric was captivated by the play of emotions across his face. Pain, anger, and frustration fought for control until one by one, they slipped away. Kell seemed lighter again, untroubled. It was a performer's face, slipping on a mask.

It felt wrong, intrusive, to voice her question aloud, but the words tumbled out before Lyric could stop them. "Thenda," she said, "the country where everything died?"

"Yes," Kell said. "I was a child when it happened."

"And someone won't let you speak about it," Runa said. It

wasn't a question, but a statement. She was angry for him; it was there in her voice.

"That's the short of it," Kell said. "After I left, I went to the Radiant Hall in Corsicayna and studied there for eight years. Then I traveled with another songsmith who mentored me, until I officially earned my colors." He gestured at a small, emerald pin of two crossed flutes, fixed to the collar of his shirt. "I've been traveling across Erith ever since."

"Corsicayna," Lyric said, "they have big libraries there, don't they? Books on magic?"

"Yes," Kell said, a smile returning to his face. "As a songsmith, I gather pieces of stories wherever I go, and what doesn't already exist in the records in Corsicayna, we add. Together we ensure our histories aren't lost to the winds of time. The libraries there are truly treasure-troves of information."

"I'd love to visit sometime," Lyric said. She tried to imagine entire buildings filled with books and her heart skipped inside her chest. Perhaps if Kell couldn't help them, she would travel there with Runa.

"You'd love it," Kell said. "It's a beautiful city."

"What does it mean to be an Emerald Tone?" Runa asked, eyeing the pin on Kell's collar.

"It refers to my skill with storytelling and instruments. As an Emerald Tone, I can play every known instrument." There was pride in his voice, but it didn't sound like arrogance. Smiling, Kell glanced between Lyric and Runa. "Do you have family here in the valley?" he asked.

Runa narrowed her eyes. "Why?"

"Just Runa and I," Lyric said, giving her sister a look.

"They said your mother wasn't born here?" Kell asked.

Lyric pursed her lips. How much about her and Runa were their neighbors willing to give away, to strangers no less? "Yes, that's true," she said. Perhaps if she gave Kell their history, he'd feel sorry for them and want to help. It couldn't hurt. He didn't seem dangerous.

"We don't know where she came from, but our mother said we don't have family anywhere else."

"Ly ..." Runa growled. Lyric ignored her.

"Your father?" Kell asked. "I'm guessing he's ..."

"We don't know," Lyric said. "He was a sailor who passed through the village. Runa and I were born after he left."

Runa made another annoyed sound, deep in her throat, but Lyric continued.

"We don't know his name," Lyric said, "only that his eyes were green as springtime, and his laughter could cause an avalanche. Our mother's words." Lyric smiled, remembering how their mother's face lit up when she'd spoken of him. She'd said nothing else, given no reason why he'd left or where he might be. Lyric and Runa had tried multiple occasions to get it out of her, but they'd never managed to learn more. It was a mystery in itself how a sailor had ended up in their land-locked valley.

Lyric glanced at Runa. Her sister was staring at the table, her face unreadable, and her arms crossed.

"Mama raised us, on her own," Lyric said, "and trained us to be wise women. That's what she was, for our village, until we took over." She saw the unspoken question in Kell's eyes. "She disappeared when we were fifteen, during the Winter of Kreshan."

"Disappeared?" Kell asked. "You don't know what happened?"

"Wolves, probably," Runa said. Defiance sizzled along their bond.

"I don't believe that," Lyric said, shaking her head. "No creature would harm Mama."

Runa sighed, and Lyric shot her an irritated look, knowing what she'd say.

"Lyric likes to think our mother was called away on some grand mission, some secret purpose," Runa said. "But if that's true, she abandoned us without a word and hasn't attempted to contact us since. I prefer thinking it was wolves."

Something howled off in the distance, and Runa settled back in her chair.

"Is that what happened to you?" Kell asked. "Wolves?"

Lyric glanced at Runa, catching her eye. Runa's story was what was important here, the story that led to the symbols.

"No," Runa said. She sighed. "It happened six months ago."

"During the Harvest Festival," Lyric added.

Runa gave her a look, and Lyric grinned impishly.

"Yes, the Harvest Festival. Anyway, it was our birthday, and we were supposed to go together."

"People are usually nicer to us during the festivals," Lyric said. "It's like they forget who we are." A memory of tasting mead and candied apples, and looking at old books on the tinker's cart came to her mind. Her eyes must have lit up with remembering for Kell looked at her with a bright, knowing smile.

"Supposed to be together, but weren't?" Kell asked.

"The blacksmith's wife went into labor right when we arrived," Lyric said, "and I left to deliver her baby. Both of us didn't need to go, so Runa stayed." She grinned sideways at her sister. "Besides, she was supposed to meet up with D-"

"I stayed," Runa interrupted. She shot Lyric a dark look. "I wandered the village for a while, and then after a couple of hours, walked to the bridge by the abandoned mill."

"Lovers like to meet there," Lyric said.

Runa glared at her again, and Lyric hid her smile behind her cup of tea.

"I was standing on the bridge, *alone*, when I heard a screech, like a nail dragged across metal. The sound filled my ears, my head. I thought my skull would break apart. Then the bridge shook violently, and I fell. It felt like a mountain was crushing me, and I ... screamed." Runa made a disgusted face. "Then I felt pressure expand inside my chest and ..." She gestured with her hand. "I was here, at home."

"She simply appeared," Lyric said, "right over there." She gestured behind Kell's chair. "I'd just gotten home from Jaeyn's house."

Kell, listening quietly, looked over his shoulder, as if imagining what Runa looked like in that moment. "You appeared back here, dead?" he asked. "A ghost?"

"Yes," Runa said. "We went back to the mill, to find my body, but nothing was there. No evidence of anything. I half expected to find the bridge ripped into pieces, but it looked untouched."

Kell frowned, a curious look in his eyes. "You heard a screech, you say?"

"Yes," Runa said.

"And that's not all," Lyric said, impatient. "Show him, Runa."

Runa gave Kell a long look, then lifted both hands to the collar of her dress and began to unhook the top three buttons. She snorted, when his brows raised, and pulled apart the fabric with a quick flick of her wrists, baring the pale skin of her upper chest.

"Whatever happened, marked me," she said.

Kell leaned forward, staring hard at Runa's exposed skin. "Those are dragon runes," he said, surprise in his voice. "Mage runes."

"As in the language of magic?" Lyric asked. Excitement flared inside her stomach, and she leaned forward to stare at the intertwined symbols marking Runa's chest in vibrant blue. It still looked like an unfamiliar tangle of coiling lines.

Years ago, Lyric found an old, moss-covered stone in the Umberwood, covered in shallow etchings she thought might be ancient runes, but they'd been too worn to copy, and she hadn't known anyone who could decipher them. Lyric felt a thrill that she'd been right.

"Magic?" Runa asked. She scowled and looked down at her chest. "You're saying someone used magic on me?"

"Do you know what it means?" Lyric asked, looking at Kell. Leaning across the table as they were, her face was right next to his, and when Kell looked at her, Lyric's breath caught in her throat. Up close his blue eyes had flecks of green and gold in them.

Clearing his throat, Kell looked back at Runa. "Well, I'm not entirely sure, but I think that this one means 'soul seek' and that means 'heart.' I've seen runes before, heard them spoken, but written like this ..." He smiled apologetically. "It can get complicated." He leaned back in his chair.

"Can you use magic?" Lyric asked.

Runa seemed disturbed by her question and shot Kell a sharp glance.

"I tried once, in the Radiant Hall," Kell said, "but I wasn't very adept at casting." His cheekbones flushed slightly, and Lyric wondered if he was embarrassed. "Music is more my strength," he said.

"You mean you can just try?" Lyric asked. "Anyone can try?"

Kell looked at her. "Casting? Of course." He smiled. "You know the old stories, I'm sure. Magic is in all our blood. It's the creative force or energy that the Trinity wielded to give us life, and the use of it ... well, that's just manipulating its flow."

"So someone used magic on me," Runa repeated. "To kill me?"

"I don't know," Kell said, his expression earnest.

"But why me?" Runa asked. "We don't know anyone who uses magic. We're in Kaliz. I'm sure you know the general attitude here about mages."

"Magic, I can't believe it," Lyric said. She supposed it made sense. What other explanation could there be? It wasn't a normal occurrence for someone to die and walk back into their house, as though nothing had happened. And where was Runa's body? Bodies didn't vanish into thin air. "Someone must have taken it," she said aloud.

Kell and Runa looked at her, confused.

"Your body," Lyric said, looking at her sister. "Someone used magic on you, and then took your body."

"For what possible reason?" Runa asked. "It's not like I—"

A loud popping sound drowned out her words, and Lyric jumped in surprise. The air became heavy, charged with static.

Runa yelped, her hair frizzing wildly out from her face, and Lyric felt her curls lift off her shoulders.

Kell stood up, his eyes wide with alarm.

There was another pop, louder, and the smell of burnt cinnamon flooded Lyric's nose. A woman flashed into existence beside Kell, her boots thudding as they hit the floor.

Runa cursed, falling over, and Kell, still in the motion of standing, caught himself on the back of his chair.

The woman's red hair, streaked with white at the temples, frizzed around her face, obscuring her features. She was wearing trousers, and a leather jacket, buckled across her chest in a style Lyric had never seen before.

Raising her hand, the woman shoved hair out of her face and surveyed the room with bright, hawkish eyes.

"Mama?" Lyric gasped. There was no mistaking their mother's face, or her gold-green eyes. They were still as keen as ever, but she looked older and grimmer than Lyric remembered. There were lines on her face, and a new scar on her right cheek.

Confusion, surprise, relief, and joy flared inside Lyric's chest, and she shoved her chair back impatiently.

Their mother, Elaina, looked between Lyric and Runa with a confused frown. "You're both here," she said, her voice disbelieving.

## 2

RUNA

RUNA STARED at their mother with a mixture of anger and elation. Elaina was here, alive, not rotting in the woods somewhere or bones at the bottom of a stream. She was *here*.

Glancing at her sister, Runa saw joy and love lighten Lyric's face. She was crying, tears rolling down her cheeks and dripping off her chin onto the floor. Everything was forgiven. Mother was home.

Runa bit the inside of her cheek and the sudden pain cleared her head. No, everything was not forgiven. Where had she been? Why had she come back? Runa picked herself off the floor and rose slowly, staring at their mother. She didn't smile, her teeth clenched behind her lips, when Elaina's face shifted from stern confusion to relief, to happiness, a mirror of Lyric's.

Runa frowned. What was it their mother had said? You're both here?

"Marleena?" Kell asked, his voice confused. There was recognition in his face.

Runa narrowed her eyes, glancing between them.

"Elaina," their mother said quickly. A warning replaced the

unrestrained emotion on Elaina's face, as she eyed Kell carefully.

"You know each other?" Lyric asked. Her giddy smile slipped, as she tried to understand. Then she gasped and rushed at Elaina. "Your arm!" she said.

Runa looked at Kell, searching his face for clues. He knew her mother, likely them as well. Why had he pretended not to know who they were? Anger flared, then faltered as she smelled burning flesh. She looked at Elaina, stepping towards her despite the tangle of emotions constricting her chest.

"Oh," Elaina said absently, lifting her arm. "Yes."

"You're on fire!" Runa said, eyes flaring in alarm. Could Elaina not feel the heat on her skin? The pain?

The sleeve of their mother's jacket was shoved up above her right elbow, and across the top of her forearm danced a line of blue flame. Runes were tattooed beneath it, its shape distorting as the flesh burned. Elaina slapped at it with her free hand, mindless of injury to her fingers, until Lyric threw a towel over her arm and smothered the fire.

"Thank you, Lyric," Elaina said. She removed the towel and examined her burned arm. The skin was a horrible red, blistered and blackened, her tattoo gone.

Kell, eyes wide, stared at Elaina as if madness had taken her.

Grabbing bandages and ointment from the cabinet, Lyric backed their mother into a chair and began to clean and wrap Elaina's arm. She shot a worried look at Runa.

"This will scar," Lyric said, uncertainly.

Elaina nodded, whatever pain she might be feeling absent from her face. "I had to hurry," she said.

Anger, familiar and deep, boiled up from inside Runa's chest, and she glared ferociously. "Where have you been?" she demanded. "We thought you were dead!"

"I'm sorry for that," Elaina said, her eyes shifting from regret to impatience to something not unlike fear. She looked at Runa's face, as though it was the first time she'd seen it. "I wasn't expecting you to be here."

Elaina might as well have stabbed a knife into her chest. "Sorry to disappoint you," Runa growled, "but I would never abandon her too."

"Ru," Lyric said, her voice chastising.

"No, that's not ..." Elaina rubbed her head. "They said they'd kidnapped you."

"They?" Runa asked.

Elaina stood up, waving away Lyric's ministrations and finishing the wrapping of her arm. Her eyes dropped to Runa's open collar, to the runes on her skin.

"Runa died, Mama," Lyric said.

The tone of Lyric's voice made Runa look at her. Her sister's eyes were full of worry and fear. It was always so easy to see what she thought and felt. Even if Runa didn't have the constant sensation of her twin's emotions brushing across her skin, she'd always know what was in Lyric's mind and heart. It was something she loved about her and something she hated. Some day, Lyric's compassion would hurt her in ways Runa would be unable to prevent.

"No," Elaina said.

Runa looked back at their mother, frowning as Elaina shook her head.

Stepping back, Elaina angled her body away and ran her hands over the bottles attached to her belt; several were broken. She cursed, then strode out of the kitchen to one of the windows that faced the prairie.

Runa glanced at Lyric, who met her eyes with confusion. What was going on?

Marching back into the kitchen, Elaina stepped up to the

stove and reached for the fire poker, hefting it in her hand before returning it to its place against the wall. "You're here," she said, looking at Runa, "so you're not dead. They must have your body." She looked at the runes again on Runa's chest and blew a breath between her teeth. "Obviously they bungled things." Her eyes sharpened accusingly. "You learned how to ... no." Elaina shook her head. "That's not possible."

Baring her teeth in frustration, Runa gestured with her hands, her fingers clawing the air. "Damn it, Mother! Learned how to what? What's not possible? Who are you talking about? Who did this to me?"

Elaina scowled, likely not appreciating Runa's cursing. "You're alive, Runa," she said. "Your soul has been pushed out of your body."

Kell bumped the table, drawing Runa's eyes. He opened his mouth, maybe to ask a question, then he shut it again. Was he afraid of Elaina?

Runa narrowed her eyes. How did Kell know her? *Why* did he know her?

Her eyes moved back to track their mother. Elaina moved around the kitchen, restless, looking out windows and staring into corners as if she expected something to jump out from the cracks in the wall. She shoved up the sleeve on her undamaged arm and checked a device strapped around her wrist. It was a timekeeper. How had she earned enough money for one of those?

"We need to go," Elaina said, addressing the room. "They'll be coming here."

"Who are they?" Runa demanded. She slammed a fist into the table, her hand passing through the wood without a sound.

Elaina lifted her head, her eyes disapproving.

"Perhaps—" Lyric began, always the peacemaker.

"We're not fifteen anymore, Mother," Runa said, interrupting her. "You can't keep things from us and order us around. We've been living on our own for *four years*."

"Yes, I realize that," Elaina said. Her eyes blazed, but her voice remained cool, controlled. "I will answer what I can, but first we need to leave. Go somewhere safe. Someone dangerous is trying to draw me out, and they'll be coming here. They'll know I've arrived by now. Just ..." Their mother closed her eyes and pain flickered across her face. "Please, trust me." Opening her eyes again, Elaina looked at Runa imploringly. Their mother seemed tired, worried, stretched thin.

Runa's anger faltered as she watched their mother's eyes. Perhaps Elaina's life had not been easy since leaving? Maybe something or someone had prevented her from coming back. What if she hadn't left because she wanted to, but because she'd been forced?

A crack opened in Runa's heart and for a moment she wanted to forgive everything. She wanted to rush over to their mother and hug her. She wanted to feel small again, protected. She wanted—

No. No, Elaina had to first explain if she desired absolution. A mother didn't just walk away from her children. A mother didn't abandon her family.

Runa looked at Lyric and stared into her sister's wide, conflicted eyes. "Fine," Runa said. "Where do we need to go?"

Relief washed over Elaina's face, and she stepped forward, holding out her hands.

Lyric, dropping the bandages, immediately grabbed one hand.

Runa frowned, staring at the callused palm of their mother's other hand, and reached for it slowly.

"Kell," Elaina said, "grab my shoulder." She waited as he shifted forward and rested a hand on her.

Kell looked at Runa, catching her suspicious frown. He flushed and looked away.

"This is going to be unpleasant," Elaina said cryptically. "Don't let go."

The air charged unnaturally, and the last thing Runa heard was Kell.

"Wait, my staff!"

# 3

RUNA

THE WIND HOWLED like an otherworldly beast, ripping through Runa's hair as she stared out at an ocean of dark blue water. She was standing on a large platform of jagged, black stone, that jutted over crashing waves. The sea felt angry, not at her, but at the stone beneath her. The water pounded again and again against the cliff, and vibrations hummed against the soles of her bare feet.

*Wait, how did I get here?* Runa frowned at the unfamiliar landscape. She'd been at home with Lyric and with ... with the songsmith, Kell, that's right. They'd been talking, and she'd shown him the runes on her chest and then ... Mother? Their mother had arrived.

A memory of their conversation drifted back to her, and Runa turned around, looking for Lyric and Kell and Elaina. Where were they?

There was a castle behind her, a massive structure of spikes and night-black stone, rising into a sky that was — Wait, where was the sky? Something else rippled overhead, gray and filmy, like fabric.

She should feel afraid, shouldn't she? Was it odd that she didn't? Runa was ... comfortable. All the frustration and anger and hopelessness of the past six months was softened, watered down, like her emotions were on the other side of a deep pool of water, and all she felt was their echo.

Runa stepped backward, her heel scraping against a sharp edge of stone. She looked down, surprised by the sensation. She could feel. It hurt.

"You're a small thing, aren't you," a sharp voice said, disapprovingly.

Runa turned around, surprised but not alarmed, and found an old woman standing between her and the edge of the cliff. She was small, like Runa, and had a cross expression on her face, her lips twisted and thin. Her eyes were dark, almost black, and they glared out from beneath graying brows that slashed down over them. She had a presence that made Runa feel like a small rodent frozen in the shadow of a hawk's sharp claws.

This woman commanded and expected to be obeyed. Her thick white hair hung in three braids over her shoulders, the snowy strands twisted around small, blood-red gems. She was wearing a black dress, long and fitted, with a high collar. Pinned over her throat was a silver dragon, its wings outstretched, giving the impression that she had spikes jutting out from either side of her neck.

Runa felt a combination of unease and awe, but the emotions were distant. She knew she needed to be cautious of this woman, but not fearful.

"Who are you?" Runa asked. She was proud of how clear and strong her voice was. No one would bully her, not even this strange woman with dangerous eyes.

"I am Elenora," the woman said. She eyed Runa with disdain, sniffing as she noted her simple dress of gray wool and her unbound hair. Her eyes lingered on Runa's bare toes, then lifted back to her face.

"I don't know where my shoes went," Runa said, feeling like she had to explain. "I haven't thought about my feet much. No reason for it. I haven't felt any sensations in a long time." She frowned. Why was she confiding in this stranger?

"You're a shade," Elenora said, as though excusing Runa's indecorum. Then she sniffed and folded her hands. "But appearance always matters, especially for a princess of the Scorched Court."

Runa frowned, eyeing the woman's arrogant face. Was she making fun of her in some way?

"I'm the daughter of a village wise woman," Runa said.

Elenora laughed, a harsh and discordant sound. "A what?" she asked. "A soldier, perhaps, or a pirate. That girl was always a handful."

"That girl?" Runa asked. She eyed Elenora. Clearly, the woman was confused.

Elenora sighed, disappointed. "Your mother, Elaina'delaina. Really, child, she never told you?" She sighed again and sent a look skyward towards the strange, rippling grayness. "I see this will take longer than expected." Her eyes narrowed, and she refocused on Runa's face.

"You are not from some backwater village, girl," Elenora said. "Your blood is the blood of dragons, of Raendashar. You are a Burner, a Raendasharan mage!" The old woman pursed her lips. "At least you will be once I'm done with you."

"A ... what?" Runa asked. What in Hel's name was she talking about? She'd heard of Raendashar before. It was a harsh, coastal country, as far east as you could get from Kaliz without walking into the Sea of Screams. Raendashar was at war, wasn't it? With the Sireni? They bordered the Tainted Shore.

Abruptly the small woman loomed in front of her, and Runa bit her tongue in surprise. Her heart thudded in her chest, and she nearly reached up and covered it with her hand, marveling at the sensation. She could feel her heart again. What was going on? She was still a ghost, still unmoored from her body, but something was changing here. Runa felt solid, more alive.

"I'm going to help you," Elenora said. She smiled a fierce, dangerous smile. "I'm going to teach you."

"Teach me?" Runa asked.

Elenora sighed. "Find your head, girl," she said. "I'll quickly tire of you if you're going to echo everything back at me. I'll talk to you again, after—"

Everything disappeared.

RUNA BLINKED, her eyes trying to adjust to the lack of light. She was cold, and the air stank like something was rotting nearby. "Ugh," she said, staring into the dark.

The ornery old woman was gone. Had she dreamed it? Their conversation had felt real. As real as … whatever this place was.

Who was Elenora and why did she think their mother was from Raendashar? Had Runa just spoken to one of the old demigods, who'd disappeared from the world? She was clearly not one of the Trinity, but perhaps—

"Runa?"

She spun at the sound of her sister's voice. Lyric stood behind her, her shape barely visible in the gloom.

"Just a moment." That was Elaina's voice, their mother. She said something else that Runa didn't understand, and then dim light flared overhead.

Looking up, Runa saw an orb of light about the size of an apple. There was another above Lyric's head, who stared up at it with undisguised wonder, another over Kell, and a fourth above Elaina.

"There," Elaina said, running her fingers over something on her belt. She lifted her head and looked around expectantly.

Runa, following her gaze, saw nothing but endless darkness in all directions. The inky ground, empty and featureless save for the occasional edge of white rock illuminated by their light, was slick beneath her feet.

Taking a step away from her, Lyric bent down and touched one of the rocks, half-embedded in the ground. "It's pitted, like old bone," she said, surprised.

The light above Lyric's head followed her as she moved, and Runa stared up at the one above her own head again. It was magic, wasn't it? Their mother had done magic. She shot Elaina a suspicious look, which their mother accepted with a raised brow.

"Where are we?" Lyric asked, before Runa could voice the question herself.

"This place has many names," Elaina said, "but the most common name is the Veil. This place is what separates the living world from the dead."

Old stories filled Runa's head, as her imagination conjured unseen specters in the dark. "Where ghosts go," Runa said. She wet her lips, her skin growing cold. Was it dangerous for her to be here? Bodiless as she was, what would happen if she accidentally crossed over into the Underworld? "Why bring us here?" she asked, feeling a small needle of panic.

Elaina eyed her, concern and something else filling her eyes. "It's the perfect place to stash a body and hold it in stasis," their mother said. "Your body's here, somewhere.

"When I learned they'd kidnapped you, I started looking. I was afraid they'd take Lyric next, so I decided to get her and ... and I found both of you." She looked at Lyric and Runa, and then Kell. Something inscrutable passed between them before

Elaina's eyes returned to Runa. "We're together now, so we can focus on reuniting you with your body," Elaina said.

Runa narrowed her eyes, observing Kell and their mother. She opened her mouth to ask how they knew each other, but Lyric spoke into the silence.

"How did you bring us here, Mama?" Lyric asked. Her face was puzzled, her green eyes filled with questions.

Runa thought back to her strange conversation with Elenora. Why had the woman focused on her? Why not Lyric? Should she tell their mother what had happened? She looked at Elaina's impassive face and felt resentment rise in her throat.

"She's a mage," Runa said, her voice flat. "A Burner." She watched their mother's face and caught a faint flicker of surprise.

Lyric blinked rapidly, her brows knotting over her eyes. "A what? No ... I mean ... how do you know?"

Runa shrugged one shoulder, earning an irritated huff as Lyric crossed her arms.

Her sister looked at their mother and tapped a finger against her lips. "The tattoo, the lights ... us coming here ... when did you learn how to do this?" She frowned, perhaps unsure if she should be impressed or annoyed. "Is that what you've been doing? Learning magic?" Lyric asked. "Since you left?"

"I think she's always been one," Runa said. "You're from Raendashar."

Again, there was no denial in their mother's eyes.

"Ru, how do you—" Lyric said.

"Can we talk about this later?" Elaina asked. "They can follow us here."

"They," Runa said flatly. "Again with the mysterious 'they.' No, Mother. I think it's time you tell us what's going on, and who *you* are. Can we even trust you anymore? I'm not sure."

Kell, an uncertain smile on his face, stepped forward. "I think your mother is just trying to protect you," he said.

"We're not children, Kell," Runa said.

"No, no, of course." Kell awkwardly stepped back. He scrubbed a hand through his hair, looking chastised.

Runa resisted the urge to roll her eyes as Lyric laid a hand on Kell's arm and smiled reassuringly. *He's not one either*, Runa wanted to say.

"My father is King of Raendashar," Elaina said. There was a challenge in her eyes, one that Runa met with a firm-eyed stare of her own. Thanks to Elenora, whoever *she* was, this was not as shocking as it would have been.

Kell's eyes snapped back to Elaina's face. Was that something he hadn't known?

"King?" Lyric breathed, dropping her hand from Kell's arm. "You're a …" She stopped speaking, head tilting. "Hasn't Raendashar been at war for hundreds of years? With the Sireni?"

*Why was Lyric asking about the Sireni?* Runa thought, looking at her sister. About sailors?

"Yes," Elaina said, her lips thinning.

"Why?" Lyric asked. "Over what? I've heard stories…"

"About Serith and the Three?" Elaina asked. "Yes, that is likely why the war began. Raendashar claimed Serith and her Sireni acted with cowardice in the Demon War, and the Sireni contended that it was the dragons and their human armies who abandoned Serith.

"Today, the war continues because of my father's aggression and the desire of some of the Sireni to reclaim land they believe is sacred."

"Land?" Runa asked incredulously. "What do they care for land?"

"There's a story that the ground beneath Rathgar's Hold, Raendashar's capital, was once a tideland where Serith held court. Those who want the land returned, believe Delbaeken the Black built the city there to spite them and Serith. Over the years, peace has been brokered and broken many times."

"Broken?" Lyric asked.

Runa studied Elaina's face. There was something in their mother's eyes. Disgust? Horror? Guilt?

"My father, under the guise of peace, invited the Sireni council, their Gales, to meet south of Rathgar's Hold. Understandably suspicious, they sent a Gale's daughter to represent them. My father killed her. Just because he could." Her eyes flashed, anger boiling inside them.

Runa stared at her. So their mother had lied about their family. They had a grandfather, and he was a murderer?

"She was young, like I was," Elaina continued. "After it happened, I left and tried to get as far from Raendashar as I could. I ended up in Elae's Hollow and met Mistress Ireina, and fell into the role of the village wise woman when she passed. Several years after that your father—" Her voice cut off, and she licked her lips, looking down at her hands. "Then I had you," she said. Their mother looked back up and offered a small, pained smile. "My girls."

Runa looked away, unsure of what to feel.

"Did your father, our ... grandfather, know where you went?" Lyric asked.

"No," Elaina said. "I didn't realize that my leaving would intensify the war."

"He used your disappearance to claim the Sireni retaliated," Runa said, clenching her fists. If he wanted the war to continue ... "He thought they killed you or said so."

"I was made aware of this, and was ... convinced to return home," Elaina said. She looked angry and sad. Her eyes glinted, and Runa thought she might cry. Instead, Elaina straightened. "I would never have left you if it'd been possible to protect you in Kaliz. There wasn't time to leave a note, and honestly ... I'm not sure what I'd have said. No child deserves that, to feel abandoned, and I know you must hate me, but ... but I truly thought I did the right thing. I still don't see a better path I could have taken."

Anger and pain warred inside Runa's chest. Her lungs were tight, and it hurt to breathe. Did their mother, *Elaina*, have any idea how they'd felt when she'd disappeared? How Runa waited, night after night on the porch, watching for her, wondering if she was injured or lost? Had she considered how long Lyric cried, or their terror when days stretched into weeks, into months, into *years*? Had she thought about how they'd try to find her?

Runa wanted to hate her, wanted to yell at her to leave them alone, tell her that they were better off without her, but she couldn't. After everything that happened, she still couldn't hate her. Before their abandonment, Runa had never doubted their mother loved them. Elaina had never been cruel, not once.

"You don't see a better path that you could have taken," Runa repeated back, her voice cold and flat. "Maybe if you'd stayed, we would have been prepared when they came for us. Someone tried to kidnap me, kidnap us, because you're the daughter of a barbaric, warmongering king. They're trying to flush you out. Why do they want you so badly? And if you were so careful *protecting* us, how did they find out about us?"

Guilt flashed across their mother's face, clear as day, and then anger rushed in to replace it. Did she know who'd betrayed her? Runa felt a heartless flicker of satisfaction.

"Are you the heir?" Lyric asked. "To the Raendasharan throne?"

Their mother's jaw tightened. "I am now," she said. "There were five of us ... two older and two younger. They're all dead now — casualties of war. The Sireni know I'm the only one left. They know I'm not with my father, so they're hunting me. I've evaded them—"

"Which is why they decided to grab us," Runa said.

Elaina dipped her head in acknowledgment. "Even without me, if the Sireni have you or Lyric then they have a legitimate claim to the Raendasharan throne and a seat in the Scorched Court. They could marry you to a Sireni captain. Or ..." She paused. "Or they could use you to persuade King Rakarn to cede the city in exchange for your lives."

Runa glanced at her sister. She couldn't feel Lyric's emotions here, not like at home, but as usual her thoughts were plastered all over her face. Lyric wanted to help their mother and get involved in the war. She never could stand the thought of someone dying, not if she could prevent it. Dangle a sad, bloody story in her face, an estranged grandfather, and Lyric wanted to rush off and fix everything.

Perhaps Elaina could still read her brown-haired daughter too, for she stepped forward and grabbed Lyric's shoulders. "I don't want to bring you into this," she said earnestly. She looked at Runa, including her. "I don't want this war, my father, to dictate your lives, your future. We'll recover your body, Runa, restore your soul and then we'll—"

"What?" Runa interrupted. "Skulk away to another little village? Hide in the forest? We can't go back to Elae's Hollow. The Sireni know we exist now."

"We can't walk away from this," Lyric said, putting a hand on their mother's arm. "We won't let you do this alone."

"Do what, Ly. Hide?" Runa asked. She smiled, a tight twist of her mouth, as fury flashed across their mother's face.

"Perhaps we should start moving again?" Kell asked, drawing everyone's attention. He cleared his throat as Runa stared at him. "I realize there's a lot here, a lot to go through, but if we are being pursued ..." He gestured at the darkness around them.

"Yes, you're right," Lyric agreed. Lyric looked at Kell for longer than was necessary and then stepped back from Elaina, hiding a slight blush by shoving her hair behind one ear.

Kell and Lyric were both right; it didn't make sense to escape whoever was after them, only to stand idly in one spot. It was a stupid move, and Runa was irritated at herself. There were still many unanswered questions, but they did not have to stand still for her to ask them.

"Yes," Elaina said, sounding relieved. She rummaged in a pouch at her belt and withdrew a round object. Lifting her hand, she held it flat in the center of her palm. It looked like a compass, with a thin, black shard fixed to the top.

"What is that?" Runa asked, curious despite herself. She moved closer, watching as the shard spun wildly, wobbling on a pocket of air beneath it, and then pointed fixedly over Kell's shoulder.

"That's a shard of demon bone," Kell said, his gaze tight to Elaina's hand. He looked up at her. "Where did you get this?"

"It's a compass," Elaina said. "To find the waystation."

"There are waystations here?" Lyric asked, her eyes widening. "You mean people come here regularly?"

"Often enough that you can find the services you need if you know where to look," Elaina said. She looked at Runa. "A friend of mine discovered that a pair of Sireni Screamers brought a girl's body into the Veil. It fit your description. We need to talk to her, find out if she's located where they are." Their mother looked between the three of them. "We need to buy food, supplies."

"Supplies?" Lyric asked. "How long will we stay here?" She stared away into the dark. "Does anything grow here?"

"Not a lot," Elaina said. She looked at the compass with a distracted expression. "Let's go. You can resume your interrogation later." She gave Runa a half smile, but Runa just stared at her until she looked away.

Lyric moved up beside her. "Be nice," she whispered. "She came back, Ru. Doesn't that mean something?"

Runa scowled. Did it? Could they move past everything?

Especially now, knowing their mother had been alive? Had Lyric forgotten how hard the past four years had been?

"This way," Elaina said, unaware of Runa's thoughts. She shot a glance backward, catching the three of them with her enigmatic eyes, and then without waiting for confirmation, set off at a brisk pace.

Runa had no choice but to follow.

# 4

LYRIC

IT WAS strange walking in the dark. Without the moon or stars overhead, Lyric couldn't shake the thought that they were deep underground, leagues of dirt and stone between them and the surface. The darkness surrounding her was absolute, and the weak glow of the light-orb over her head could not ease Lyric's sense of being trapped. She saw no outlines of trees or hills. No sign of life. Was there an end to the darkness? Would she find the unseen horizon if they walked far enough?

Lyric felt vulnerable and exposed, but there was also a curiosity inside of her, thready like the light, that wondered what the dark concealed. If the old stories were true, then the goddess Hel, one of the Trinity, had created the Veil and the Underworld and placed it into the hands of two demigods, Valen and Velaine. Were they here somewhere? Were the Old Ones, the dragons?

"What are you thinking?" Kell asked.

His voice was so close that Lyric squeaked, nearly jumping out of her skin. She flushed, hoping Kell couldn't see her face clearly in the dim light. "Dragons," she said. Her voice came out broken, pitched high, and she cleared her throat. "I was wondering if they're here somewhere." She looked up at Kell, who drew even with her, his long legs matching her stride.

He didn't look like the hale young men from her valley, all rough edges with broad, sun-browned faces and arms thick from felling trees and plowing fields. There was an elegance about him, as though an artist had sculpted his face. He'd looked made, not born or steeled by hours in the sun.

Kell smiled, his sun-lightened hair shifting across one eye. "Ah, your ancestors."

Lyric blinked. "My ... it seems so ridiculous." She laughed, unsure if she believed it. If their mother was from Raendashar, then Lyric also had dragon blood. Was that possible? Her blood was as red as anyone's, and she certainly wasn't immune to fire. A dragon would be invulnerable to flame, wouldn't it? Why not its kin? "I'd never considered it," Lyric said, shaking her head. "I can't do magic."

"How would you know?" Kell asked.

Lyric supposed Kell's question was a fair one. How would she know? Just because she wasn't shooting sparks from her fingertips, didn't mean that she lacked magic. She'd never actually tried a spell. Books on magic weren't accessible in Kaliz, especially not in Elae's Hollow. "True," she admitted, smiling. "Maybe Mama will teach me." Lyric glanced at their mother's straight back and watched her shoulder-length red hair sway across her shoulders.

No, it was unlikely that their mother would teach her. She'd kept her ancestry from them, told them they were alone in the world. If all her actions stemmed from the desire to protect her and Runa, she'd try to keep them as far from magic as possible.

"I think they are here, somewhere," Kell said, interrupting her thoughts. "The Old Ones."

"Really?" Lyric resisted the urge to peer off into the darkness around them. A dragon was not sitting out there watching them pass.

Kell nodded. "You know about the Demon War, right? How the demigods left to follow the Trinity to the Beyond?"

"Yes," Lyric said, "and then the Three, the dragons, created the High Council to maintain peace across Erith." Despite her isolation in Elae's Hollow, she had been taught the histories of their world.

"Yes, and after they ruled for several hundred years, they created the Human Council and left."

"Not to follow the Seven? Or the Trinity?" Lyric asked.

"No, they retreated to the Veil," Kell said. "They didn't desire to abandon Erith completely. They wanted to be able to return if there was a need." He smiled. "At least that's what the stories say. Sometimes we can't be sure what is a myth and what is true history."

"I wonder what would bring them back?" Runa asked, on the other side of Lyric. Her voice was muted, as though she hadn't meant to pose the question aloud.

"Not the Taint," Kell said, his own voice low, unsettled.

Lyric glanced at him. "The what?"

A faint flush darkened his cheeks. "The poison released during Thenda's destruction. Whatever happened, tainted the ground, the water."

Lyric's eyes dropped to the mark on his neck. "I knew everyone died, almost everyone, but the Taint is new to me." She looked at Runa, meeting her sister's frown.

"Maybe one country is a small thing to the Old Ones," Kell said, slowly. "Perhaps if it'd destroyed the entire eastern coast, or if the Taint had spread ..."

"Has it?" Runa asked.

Kell's jaw tightened. "I don't know. I've returned to Thenda only once. If the Taint has spread to Raendashar, or south to Oleporea, we should have heard of it. I've seen no signs in Chianseia or Jaina."

"It hasn't spread to Raendashar," Elaina said ahead of them.

47

Lyric glanced at their mother's back. At the house, Kell said his tattoo stopped him from talking about what happened in Thenda, but who had given it to him and why? What sort of mage was powerful enough to physically silence him? Powerful enough that no one even knew what caused the destruction or how to fix it? Why was it still a secret?

"What do you remember the day Thenda was destroyed?" Lyric asked Kell. She studied his face, watching as his jaw tightened and his eyes grew dark. He seemed frustrated and angry, but also sad.

"I remember the morning," Kell said. "I remember being with my mother in Salta. She was agitated, she wanted to leave, but my father ... my father wanted to enjoy the celebration. It was the seventh night of Daemonia and the capital was filled with people.

"I got lost, and ended up in the catacombs. I had some kind of sweet in my hand, my fingers were sticky, and I was calling for my mother. Then I ..." He stopped, the cords tightening in his neck, and put a hand against the side of his head.

"What's wrong?" Lyric asked, worried.

"I ..." Kell swallowed and touched his throat, fingers splayed over the skin. "It's blank, after that. I remember later, the chaos, the screams ... but I can't ..." He winced and shook his head. "What happened after ... I can't talk about what I remember, not without ..." His voice was tight, and Lyric put a hand on his arm. "Without pain."

"You remember before, and after," Runa said, "but not the actual event? Not what happened. Not who was there beyond your parents."

Kell looked ahead, at Elaina's back. "Yes."

"So someone caused it," Runa said. "Accidentally or purposefully. Someone is responsible."

Horror crawled across Lyric's back on spidery legs, and she shivered. She stared at Kell with sympathy and dismay, trying to imagine what it felt like surviving something so horrible. His family had died there. He was alone.

A fierce desire to punish whoever had hurt him burned inside her heart, and she reached for Kell's hand without thinking, twining her fingers through his.

He seemed surprised when she touched him, his eyes clearing, but he didn't pull away. Instead, Kell's fingers tightened on hers. His hand was cold, and there were calluses on his fingers.

Lyric's chest tightened, and her cheeks flushed as heat slid down her neck. She'd never held a man's hand before, not in this way. She wanted to smile, beam foolishly, but the horror still lingering in the air and the look on Kell's face brought her back to the moment. Lyric swallowed, and a chill settled inside her.

"Why Thenda?" Runa asked suddenly.

Lyric glanced at her sister's face. Runa was frowning in concentration. Mysteries always sparked her interest; especially if they involved someone being abused.

"I don't know," Kell said. He sighed angrily. "Thenda was peaceful." He glanced again at Elaina, and Lyric narrowed her eyes. What did their mother have to do with all of this? With Kell? She was so focused on her thoughts that she nearly plowed into her when Elaina stopped suddenly.

Kell prevented Lyric from stepping on her mother's heels with a tug on her hand. She looked up at him, lips parted, and he grinned sideways at her.

"Ow," Runa said. She bumped into their mother's shoulder.

Glancing back at Runa, Elaina smiled and shoved the compass into her belt pouch. "We're here," she said.

Lyric blinked, looking ahead of them. A shimmering, purple haze diffused the darkness. Rocks and sand were visible beyond the film, but they rippled, as though she were viewing the landscape through a veil.

"We're where?" Runa asked.

"The waystation," Elaina said. "Everyone hold on to me."

Lyric reached for their mother's shoulder, along with Kell.

Runa, surprisingly, accepted their mother's hand. Elaina seemed startled by it as well, and she looked at Runa longingly. Drawing in a breath Elaina nodded and took a step forward, carrying them with her.

The darkness vanished, and Lyric blinked in the sudden change in light. They stood inside a large room with paneled walls and a black wood floor polished to a near mirror-like sheen. The light was coming from lanterns, dangling on crystalline chains above their heads and along the walls.

"It's purple," Lyric said aloud. Fascination buzzed along her skin. "The flames are purple!"

Kell murmured something beside her, but Lyric was too distracted to hear what he said. She looked around, taking in the rest of the room.

The waystation was similar to the inn back home, with tables and benches, and a bar along the wall to her left. Shadowy, curtain-draped booths filled three of the corners, one currently being serviced by a dark-haired boy holding a tray. Sitting empty against another wall was a large stone fireplace beneath a trio of three, dented shields. Despite the lack of fire, the room was warm.

Less than ten people were scattered around the room in clusters of twos and threes. They were cloaked and turned their faces away so Lyric couldn't see their features. Who were they, she wondered? Why were they here?

Elaina walked towards the bar, and Lyric followed, distractedly letting go of Kell's hand.

A large woman, with a shaved head and a long, uneven scar puckering her left cheek, nodded at them as they approached. "Dandashara," she said, addressing their mother. "Good to see you again."

Lyric raised her eyebrows. Dandashara? How many names did their mother have?

"Galgosha!" Elaina said, her voice rich with pleasure. "Got any of that Fendriaken wine, I love so much?"

"I always keep a bottle or two around." The bartender, Galgosha, grinned, showing small, purple-stained teeth. She reached beneath the counter and withdrew a squat, ugly bottle, filled with a viscous liquid that looked like ink.

Lyric moved up beside their mother, eyeing the bottle and the large woman curiously. Standing next to Elaina as she was, she caught the grin that crossed their mother's face as she slapped an odd, triangle-shaped piece of iron on the bar top. It was a roguish grin, one Lyric had never seen on their mother's face before.

Galgosha palmed the iron coin and eyed Lyric, Kell, and Runa, then placed four glasses on the counter beside the bottle.

"Traveling with companions again, Dandashara? Did you tell them about what happened with the—"

"Always good to see you, Gal," Elaina said, cutting her off with a broad wink. "Did you find the location I asked for?"

Galgosha shook her head, looking regretful. "They're careful. No magic since they entered."

Elaina grimaced and nodded. "If the Supplier makes an appearance, can you send them over?"

"Will do," Galgosha said. She grinned and saluted.

Grabbing the bottle and two of the glasses, Elaina headed towards one of the curtained corners.

Lyric grabbed the remaining two glasses and shared a confused look with her sister. Based on the expression on Runa's face, if she'd started to soften towards their mother after their earlier conversation, that feeling had passed.

Hesitating, Lyric turned back to the bartender. "Excuse me," she said, "do you have any bandages or burn ointment? My mother's arm was burned."

Galgosha's eyes flickered, and she reached under the bar. "Here," she said, setting a small box on the counter. "Remind her a sick wolf is a dead one," Galgosha said, nodding at Elaina's back.

Lyric raised an eyebrow. "All right," she said, though she didn't understand. "Thank you." Smiling goodbye, she handed the glasses to Kell, and picked up the box, then followed their mother towards the booth she'd chosen.

Kell, moving ahead of Lyric and Runa, held back the curtain so they could slip inside after Elaina. Runa instead picked the curved bench on the left, but she didn't move far enough in for Lyric to sit beside her. Resisting the urge to pinch her sister, Lyric slid in on the side by their mother, scooting down to make room for Kell.

Smiling, he sat down beside her, laying an arm on the back of the bench, and Lyric tried not to get distracted when his leg pressed against hers.

Elaina made a noise and Kell shifted abruptly, breaking the contact.

"Here," Lyric said, sliding the box toward their mother. "For your arm."

"Dandashara?" Runa asked. A predatory glint shone in her eyes.

Their mother pursed her lips and, shifting the box to the side, unstoppered the wine bottle. She poured the thick liquid into one glass, then eyed Lyric and Runa, and filled the other three. Setting the bottle back onto the table, Elaina lifted her glass and emptied it. When she set the cup back down, the pressure of her fingers pressing against the bubbled glass created a soft popping sound.

"I've had to be many people these past four years," Elaina said. "Dandashara ..."

"And Marleena?" Lyric asked. She looked between Kell and her mother. "How do you know each other?"

"We met in Caynford," Kell said. "On the border of Raendashar and Chianseia." He looked at Elaina, as though seeking permission.

Elaina sighed. "I asked him to come here," she said.

Betrayal hit like a fist to Lyric's chest. She breathed in, the breath jagged and unsteady, and looked at Kell. His eyes were guilty, and she flushed as she looked away, angrily reaching for one of the filled glasses. Lyric knew it was ridiculous to feel anything about him. She didn't know Kell, but the idea that he'd found her because Elaina asked him to, and not because he'd been interested in her story bothered her.

Lyric flushed again and dumped the wine into her mouth. It burned, the taste sharp and strange, and she coughed, slamming the cup onto the table harder than she intended. She felt a cool hand on her back and knew it was Kell's and her face heated again.

Thankfully Runa spared her from further embarrassment and drew away Kell and Elaina's attention with a question. "Why?" she asked. "Why ask Kell to find us? Are you even a songsmith?"

Lyric looked up, eyes watery as she peered through her tangled hair. Runa was staring at Kell with a pointed, suspicious look.

"I am a songsmith," Kell said. He sounded honest, earnest.

"He is," Elaina said. "I asked him to protect you. I wasn't sure when I'd be able to come myself, and I knew the Sireni were looking for you." Guilt flashed across her face. "I thought you might trust him more easily than a sellsword."

Straightening, Lyric tucked her hair behind her ears. She risked a look at Kell. "Why come?" she asked.

"Did she pay you?" Runa asked, her voice sharp.

Kell angled his body towards Lyric. His eyes were bright, apologetic. "Your mother helped me, saved me actually, so when she asked for my help, I agreed," he said, speaking to

Lyric alone. It seemed important to him that she believed him, forgave him. "She thinks she can help me. I told you how I couldn't remember ..." His hand lifted to his throat, his fingertips brushing the tattooed skin. "I don't remember how my mother or my father died. If we remove the spell, maybe ..." His voice trailed off, and Lyric saw hope and desire spiral inside his eyes. The desire to know.

She resisted the urge to touch his face and looked back at Elaina. "You can do that?" Lyric asked. Could their mother remove a silencing spell? But if that were possible, why hadn't she already helped Kell?

"No," Elaina said, shaking her head. Her eyes caught on Kell's arm behind Lyric's back, and Lyric felt him pull it down into his lap.

"I can't, but my father ..." Elaina paused, her face tightening. "My family has collected magical tomes for centuries. Our private library is one of the finest in the world. If a record exists on how to remove Kell's spell, my father has it." A warning entered their mother's eyes. "You need to realize that your grandfather is a dangerous man." She stared at Lyric and Runa, her face tight and severe. "He's used dark magic before, releasing a plague on a Sireni ship. If he'd had more time, training, it might have spread; it might have ..." She pushed her cup away, reaching for the bottle. "He was involved with Thenda. I can feel it in my bones."

"You think he caused the Taint?" Runa asked.

Lyric gasped and looked at her sister. "You can't believe that he would—"

Runa shrugged. "We don't know him," she said. "If he's willing to lure and kill a young woman, what else is he capable of?"

Lyric jerked her eyes back to their mother. "Mama, do you honestly believe our grandfather destroyed Thenda?"

Elaina scraped the bottle across the table, balancing it on its edge, then met Lyric's eyes. "I don't have proof," she said, "but he's connected somehow. He knows people that—" She glanced at Kell. "He *is* involved."

"Is he who you learned that spell from?" Runa asked, pointing at their mother's bandaged arm.

"Blood magic," Elaina said. "No." Her voice was tight and fierce. "But he uses it. It's dangerous magic. Erratic. Exacting. Please, promise me you will never attempt it." She glared at them both, as though challenging them to defy her.

Lyric leaned back, feeling overwhelmed and out of depth. "I don't even know how we would learn," she said. She glanced at Runa and saw her sister's jaw set stubbornly.

"Who asked you to return to Raendashar?" Runa asked. "You said someone convinced you to abandon us. Was it our father?"

Their mother blinked, surprise flashing across her face. An exhalation of breath left her, not quite a laugh, but a startled, incredulous sound and she scrubbed a hand through her thick hair. "No, no it was my brother Raynard who asked me to return."

"Who is our father?" Runa asked. She leaned forward and placed a hand on the table, fingers tight against the scratched surface.

Lyric blinked. Despite the abruptness of the question, it was one she wanted an answer to as well. She looked at their mother, who seemed still a touch off balance.

"Girls," Elaina said, her voice tired. "Perhaps we could—"

"You said he was a sailor," Lyric said. Their mother was answering questions, maybe she'd finally tell them about their father. "Did he sail the Sea of Screams?" She thought about the Sireni, what little she knew of them. Of course, you didn't have to be Sireni to work on a ship, but if he was a simple sailor from Kaliz or Raenborschia, why would Elaina hide him? Why had she withheld his name?

Elaina looked past them, out into the room. She licked her lips, a distant look in her eyes. "They don't know," she said, finally. "The Sireni don't know."

"Don't know what?" Lyric asked.

"That your father is one of them."

Kell exhaled softly beside Lyric, but she didn't look over to see his expression. When Elaina had first told them about their connection to Raendashar, Lyric had found herself asking about the Sireni. She hadn't known why. Her father was Sireni and somehow ... somehow Lyric had known.

"Does our grandfather know?" Runa asked.

Their mother put a hand over her mouth and shook her head. "I don't know," she said. "If he did ..." She shook her head again. "I'm not certain he knows you exist. Your father's brother knows, and a few of his clan, but that's it." Elaina stared at Lyric and Runa, holding their eyes in turn. "This knowledge is dangerous. The Sireni already want you for being my daughters. If they discovered you share both Raendasharan and Sireni blood ..."

Lyric sunk back against the booth. She felt adrift as if her head had floated away. Everything she'd ever believed was a lie. Everything she thought she would become now seemed impossible, foolish.

Kell shifted, and his hand brushed against her knee. Lyric focused on it, drawing comfort from the accidental contact, trying to ground herself.

"What does our father think about this?" Lyric asked. "Is he still alive?"

Their mother looked down, lips pressing tight, and rubbed the knuckles of her left hand. "He's alive," she said. She looked back up, staring into Lyric's face with regret and concern in her hazel eyes. "I hadn't planned to tell you this way," Elaina admitted. "About your past, about me. Not like this all at once, all jumbled together."

"You didn't expect to tell us at all," Runa said flatly.

Elaina's hand slapped the table, her eyes flashing like something had caught fire inside them. "You don't know what it's been like for me," she hissed. "You don't know—" She cut off, staring wide-eyed at Lyric, who'd drawn back, heart pounding.

Breathing in, her hand clenching, Elaina leaned back, agonized eyes flicking to Runa.

Runa, spots of color high on her cheeks, was staring back with wet-eyed intensity. Her chest heaved, her emotions just beneath the surface. The translucent quality to her shape wavered, flickering opaque.

"Ru, you're changing," Lyric said, distracted.

Her sister looked down, mouth open, and the odd flicker went away. "I ... I don't know what that was," she said.

Elaina cleared her throat, face composed again, and clasped her hands in her lap. "We should rest," she said. "I've told you all I can for now. We need to do what we came here for." She looked at Runa, regret hollowing her face. "I need to think, decide what to do next."

Runa looked up, face and eyes cold, controlled. "Which we will discuss and decide on together," she said.

Their mother bristled, like a cat with her back up, then nodded. Weariness rounded her shoulders. She looked drained. "Galgosha will give us a room. We'll be safe here. We can sleep for a few hours, then decide what to do. Can we agree? Rest?"

Lyric stared at her sister, pointedly. The air was charged with emotion, and she wanted to cry and scream. She resisted the urge to grab Kell's hand and pressed her hands flat on her knees. *Hold it together*, she thought. *We're together. Everything will be fine.*

Runa broke off her stare with Elaina and looked at Lyric, nodding once.

"Fine," Runa said. She slid out of the booth, standing stiffly as Elaina moved past her.

Kell stood too, and Lyric scooted out after him. He reached for her, like he wanted to offer her his hand, but then pulled it back and stuck it in his pocket, eyes darting to Elaina's drawn face.

Not catching Kell's look, their mother signed with her hand to Galgosha, on the other side of the room, and the bartender signaled something back.

"This way," Elaina said. She led them along the wall, past the fireplace, to an unobtrusive doorway, which opened into a small hall.

Runa hung back, waiting to enter last, so Lyric followed Elaina inside with Kell on her heels. They walked to a staircase and headed down.

"This is strange," Lyric said aloud, breaking the tense silence. "Usually in inns, you climb up. Are we sleeping in the cellar?" She laughed. Exhaustion was making her feel silly.

"The waystation is more like a series of caves, than a building," their mother said.

The stairs ended at a long hallway filled with closed doors. Lyric eyed them as they passed; they all seemed uniform with nothing distinguishing one from another. Elaina paused at the fourth door on the left and opened it with a quick push.

Moving up behind their mother, Lyric peered inside the room. It was small, with two beds taking up most of the available space. The walls were empty of decorations, and there were no windows. Beside the door was a chair and table, upon which sat a lamp that emitted purple light. Covering the floor was a threadbare rug.

"Is that animal skin?" Lyric asked curiously. "What kind of animal has purple fur?"

"Let's get out of the hallway," Elaina said, ushering them inside.

They bunched together, as Elaina shut the door, and Lyric bumped against Kell. She tilted her head back, smiling brightly.

Kell stared at her, a mix of curiosity and pleasure lightening his eyes and for a breath, Lyric forgot where they were. Their shared moment was interrupted by Runa shoving past, and Lyric's chin slammed into Kell's chest. Lyric and Kell laughed, wincing, and she grabbed his arm to steady herself.

Runa flopped onto one of the beds. "I feel more solid here," she said aloud, addressing no one.

Lyric glanced at her, and it looked like Runa wanted to tell her something, but then her sister's eyes slid to their mother and her face shuttered.

"I wonder why that is," Lyric said, moving around Kell to sit beside her sister. She thought about how Runa's body had shifted in the common room upstairs, and glanced at her sister's face, raising an eyebrow.

"Later," Runa muttered. "Just ... have you seen anything?"

"Seen?" Lyric asked. "Like what?"

"Never mind."

"You should sleep," their mother said. "I'll keep watch."

Kell moved aside, allowing Elaina to sit down on the bed opposite Lyric and Runa.

Their mother rubbed a hand over her face, her eyes shadowed.

"You look exhausted, Mama," Lyric said. "Maybe you should sleep first." She gestured at the closed door. "Do we need to keep watch? We're in a locked room."

Elaina eyed the door, swaying slightly. "Old habits," she said. "We are as safe as we can be here. Galgosha is upstairs."

Lyric smiled. "She looks like she could take on a Sireni or two."

"Yes, she can," their mother said, chuckling.

"I'll sit in the chair," Kell said.

Lyric glanced at him in confusion, then blushed as she realized why he was picking the uncomfortable-looking chair. There were four of them in the small room and only two beds.

"I don't mind sharing," Elaina said to Kell. "Just stay on your side."

Kell cleared his throat and ran a hand through his hair. "It's fine," he said. "I've done this before. Fallen asleep in a chair that is." He sat down and stretched out his legs, crossing his ankles. Shifting against the back of the chair, he wrapped his cloak around his shoulders and chest.

Elaina shrugged and laid down. "The Supplier will be stopping by. We can trade then."

"Supplier?" Runa asked.

Elaina yawned and crossed her arms over her chest, shutting her eyes. "They'll have food and clothes for travel, and maybe ..." She began to snore.

Lyric grinned and looked at Runa, who snorted.

"Might as well sleep too," Runa said. She pulled her legs up onto the bed and rolled over, close to the wall.

Lyric glanced at Kell, who was reaching for the lamp.

"We'll be fine," he said, smiling at her.

"Of course," Lyric said. She stared into his eyes. She hadn't been thinking about the Sireni.

Kell tapped the lamp, turning it off, and Lyric blinked in the sudden darkness. She laid down carefully and listened to the sound of her sister shifting beside her, and their mother's soft snores. Something scuffed against the floor, probably Kell moving his foot.

Lyric's thoughts drifted to home. Had the Sireni found their house? What had they done after discovering Lyric was gone? Had their neighbors noticed that Lyric and Runa were missing? Had Tora come back for—

*Tomby & Runa*

SOMEONE WAS SHAKING HER AWAKE. Lyric opened her eyes and stared up at a purple sky. Where was the sun or the stars? Her head felt thick; her senses slow.

She sat up and stared at the rough wood beneath her. Was she on a ship? It wasn't rocking side to side. Had it run aground? Lyric didn't feel like she was moving at all.

Turning her head to the right, Lyric found an old woman kneeling beside her. The woman's square face was wrinkled and darkened by the sun, and her small blue eyes studied her with a bird's keen focus. Old tattoos curled down the sides of her throat and across her upper chest, the ink faded to a pale blue.

Flushing, Lyric realized the woman's chest was bare, and she jerked her eyes to the collection of chains that hung between her breasts. Crafted from delicate strands of metal and threaded with a variety of seashells, ocean-tumbled stones and pieces of carved wood, the necklaces shifted as the woman moved, catching the light.

A long white skirt covered the woman's lower body that she'd tucked beneath her knees. Sashes in blue, green, red and yellow wrapped her waist.

"Hello," the old woman said, smiling. Her face looked kind, her smile genuine.

Lyric immediately felt safe in her presence and returned the woman's smile. "Hello," she echoed. "I'm Lyric. Who are you?" Was she dreaming? What happened to the room where she slept? Where were Runa and Kell? Where was their mother?

"My name is Gandara," the old woman said. "You are wondering where you are?"

"Yes," Lyric said. She frowned and eyed the woman's face. "Am I sleeping?"

"Yes," Gandara said. "I am ... borrowing your dream."

"You're a ghost?" Lyric guessed.

Gandara smiled and inclined her head. "I lived many ages ago."

Lyric eyed the woman's unfamiliar clothes. "Are you Sireni?"

"Yes, I am your ancestor. Your blood sang out to me when you arrived." Her eyes filmed and she seemed to disappear inside herself. "I want to help you," Gandara said, her eyes refocusing on Lyric's face.

"Help me how?"

"You are untrained. Someone might take advantage of that."

"Like who?"

Gandara's face darkened, and she pointed a gnarled finger at the center of Lyric's chest. "The fire blood burns in you too. You must be careful you are not swayed by their bloodlust. Their desire for power, for destruction."

"I'm sorry," Lyric said uncertainly. "What are you talking about?" Was she referring to their mother? Lyric being half Raendasharan?

"You will call the winds," Gandara said. Her eyes grew distant again, and Lyric studied her with concern. The old woman seemed forgetful, her mind drifting.

"I can teach you the language of the ancients," Gandara said.

"Dragon runes?" Lyric asked.

Gandara grimaced, a look of distaste on her face. "Ancient runes," she repeated.

Lyric stared at her. Wasn't Serith, the Sireni's progenitor, still a dragon, even if she lived in the ocean? It seemed that the distrust between the Sireni and Raendasharans did run deep.

She considered Gandara's words. What was her true motive for seeking to guide her? Was Gandara's offer an attempt to ensure Lyric didn't train in Raendashar? Or was the old woman worried about her mother teaching her? Lyric sighed. That was about as likely as the old gods returning.

It couldn't hurt to accept Gandara's help, could it? There was nothing threatening about the old woman. She seemed amiable. Lyric usually got a good sense of people, and she didn't think Gandara wished her harm. And, if their mother wasn't going to teach her herself, Gandara might be her only option.

Making a decision, Lyric smiled. "I'd love to learn," she said aloud. Maybe it was all a dream. It couldn't hurt to accept help from her ancestor.

Gandara's face softened into a wide grin. She looked excited like they were two young girls sharing secrets. "I'm happy you came here," she said, beaming. "Now that we're connected, I can reach out to you again."

Lyric raised an eyebrow. "Because of the Veil?" she asked. She felt silly, asking yet another question, but Gandara seemed pleased by her interest.

"Your link to your sister," Gandara said. "Her presence has created certain ... holes."

"What do you mean holes?" Lyric asked, alarmed.

Gandara's smile slipped, eyes growing serious. "You need to be careful," she said. "She is more fire than water. She will destroy, not flow."

Irritated by the old woman's words, Lyric frowned. "Runa is a good person," she said.

"Perhaps," Gandara said, shrugging one rounded shoulder. "Be vigilant. Power corrupts."

"You don't know Runa," Lyric said, her voice sharp. She breathed in, trying to calm herself.

"Just be cautious," Gandara said soothingly. "Now, let me teach you the word for wind."

# 5

ELAINA

ELAINA WOKE TO DARKNESS. She blinked, staring at the unfamiliar ceiling, her nerves thrumming. She listened to the sounds around her, keeping still, orienting herself. Everyone was asleep, their breathing deep and slow.

Trying to pinpoint what awakened her, Elaina sat up slowly. Her back ached. She'd forgotten to remove her belt and fell asleep with a bottle pressed into her back. Shifting it down to her hip, she rubbed at the sore spot, fingers worrying the knot in her muscle.

Someone rapped softly on the door.

Had the Supplier arrived? Lowering her feet to the floor, Elaina stood up. She stepped over Kell's long legs to reach the door, briefly debating whether to wake him up and send him to the bed.

She decided against it. He was dead to the world, his mouth open and his head tilted backward in a way that had to be uncomfortable. Kell looked younger asleep, barely older than her daughters. He didn't look like the boy she remembered. How long had he lived in the Veil before his mother brought him to Elaina's father? Did Kell dream of her sometimes? He claimed he couldn't remember her or the day in the keep, but he should have. Had Elaina's father done something to him? Her lips twisted. How many marks had her father left on Kell's life?

The tap came again, and Elaina blinked, pulling back from her memories. She bent down to grab the dagger in her boot and reached for the door. Hand wrapping around the iron handle, she opened it and stared into the hall.

A short man stood in front of the door, and he touched the brim of his tall, purple hat as their eyes met. "Pem, Supplier of Bits and Baubles and anything else you may need," he said. He was shorter than Lyric and Runa by a full handspan and had bright orange eyes and curly, black hair that stuck out from beneath his hat in every possible direction.

"Hi Pem," Elaina said, smiling despite herself. It was impossible not to when faced with such a friendly, mischievous grin. "My companions are sleeping, but halls have eyes." She nodded at the walls. "Perhaps we can conduct business quietly inside the room?"

"Of course, not a problem," Pem said, bobbing his head and adjusting a long, canvas bag on his shoulder.

Elaina shifted sideways to open the door wider, and Pem slipped in through the gap. He found a place at the foot of the bed Elaina had slept on and watched her as she shut the door.

Darkness didn't fully return, despite cutting off the light from the hallway, and Elaina was surprised to see Pem's hat glowing softly along the sides and beneath the brim. Gleaming filaments crisscrossed the stiff fabric, as though he'd draped it in spiderwebs. The muted light illuminated his face and hands.

Elaina glanced at the beds, checking if Pem's presence had woken anyone, and was relieved to find everyone still asleep. She looked at Pem. "We need cloaks, warm enough to sleep in on the road, and boots for my girls if you have them. And food and water for at least several days."

Pem nodded and looked at Lyric and Runa. "I may have something that will fit the lasses," he said softly. He glanced at Kell. "The boy?"

Elaina eyed Kell's clothing. "He has a cloak already," she said. "He was a bit sad to lose his staff though."

"Ah," Pem said, grinning. He removed the bag from his shoulder and set it on the ground, loosening the cord around its neck.

"And," Elaina said, "we need a Soulworm." She'd fallen asleep wondering how to find her daughter's body, and a Soulworm had appeared inside her dreams.

Pem's eyebrows lifted into his hair, and then he grinned delightedly. "Ah," he said, looking towards the girls. "It just so happens that I received one earlier today in trade."

"How fortunate," Elaina said. Her eyes narrowed, a tad suspicious, but then Suppliers always did seem to have what you were looking for, and often things you were not but would ultimately need.

Pem opened the bag and reached inside, his arm disappearing to the shoulder, and then he pulled out, in rapid succession, two heavy gray cloaks, two pairs of softly glinting boots, a staff that nearly reached the top of Elaina's head, and a small cage.

Despite herself, Elaina was surprised and eyed the bag with a small measure of awe as Pem placed the items carefully atop her bed. The bag didn't seem big enough to hold much, certainly not a staff for a grown man.

"Are those Wanderer Boots?" Elaina asked, leaning closer. She could see activated runes glowing along the heel. They were magicked to keep the leather soft and supple and wick away exhaustion. Someone wearing these boots wouldn't complain of sore feet or ever develop a blister no matter how long they walked. If you had to wade through a river, you'd still find your feet dry on the other side.

Elaina wet her lips, thinking. A single pair of Wanderer Boots would empty her money pouch.

"Yes," Pem said. "The only boots you'll ever need! Lucky I have two." He reached into his bag again and pulled out four leather packs, four waterskins, a bronze kettle and several bundles wrapped in waxed paper. "Cheese, bread, apples, dried meat, a kettle, and salt for your stew pot," he said, as he laid them atop the cloaks. "Easiest thing to bring into the Veil."

Elaina nodded, pulling her attention away from the boots. The apples would have to be eaten quickly, or they would begin to spoil and turn purple. It was a peculiarity that Elaina had experienced on her first visit to the Veil. They were not safe to eat when that happened.

"Payment?" she asked. She narrowed her eyes in anticipation of a quick barter. She'd probably have to pass on the boots.

Instead, Pem cocked his head and returned his bag to his shoulder. "A favor," he said.

"A favor," Elaina repeated, fingers straying to her belt. What could a Supplier want of her?

"Nothing too dangerous, I assure you," Pem said, smiling. "I need something delivered." His fingers flashed inside his vest, and he withdrew a folded sheet of paper, sealed with black wax. "A letter."

Elaina raised her eyebrows. "Letters can be just as dangerous, if not more so, than a knife in the back," she said.

Pem shrugged and smiled, waggling the letter between his fingers. "You can say no."

"Would you accept anything else?"

"Ah, well the Soulworm is quite rare, you see. I'm not sure you're carrying enough coin for that."

Likely she was not. It had taken a lot of money to reach the girls quickly. Accepting Pem's letter was a bad idea, Elaina could feel it in her gut, but without the Soulworm, they might wander inside the Veil for weeks. She wracked her brain for another way to locate Runa's body, but all they had to rely on was luck and time. Time they might not have. Maybe Galgosha would find the Screamers, find Runa's body, but how long would that take? The girls could survive without the boots, but not the Soulworm.

"Deliver where?" Elaina asked.

Pem chuckled. "A woman, in Raendashar. Her name is Amana. She owns The Onyx Wing, a dress shop in the market district in Rathgar's Hold."

Elaina's lips pinched. Why did Pem presume she'd go to Raendashar? Or did he recognize her heritage by the color of her hair and think she'd return home upon leaving the Veil? "I can't promise when I will deliver it," she said.

"Before winter's end, will be fine," Pem said. He proffered the letter again, and Elaina took it in careful fingers. "It's spelled to turn the eye of all but its courier."

The paper was silky and felt more like a woman's dress than writing parchment. Elaina eyed the raised seal. It was a Valen moth, the familiar skull-shaped pattern exquisitely depicted upon its back. She'd never seen the insect used as a seal before.

"And thus our business is concluded," Pem said, his voice still bright and friendly.

Elaina tucked the letter into her belt and looked up at him, studying his face carefully. He seemed entirely sincere. Pem's innocence only heightened her suspicion, and she regretted accepting the trade, but what else could she do?

If Runa did not return to her body soon, real death would claim her. It was dangerous for a separated soul. It became comfortable on its own, shedding its ties to the organic shell that'd once carried it. The longer Runa stayed here in the Veil, the more it'd feel like home, and the more her soul would let go, move on. Elaina could lose her forever.

"Yes," Elaina said, ignoring the pain in her chest. "It is done."

Pem touched his fingers to his hat and opened the door, slipping back into the hall.

"Who was that?" a sleepy voice asked behind her.

Elaina turned and found Kell watching her. He wiped the side of his mouth and straightened in the chair, releasing a little groan.

"You should have taken my offer for sharing the bed," she said, looking him over.

"Yes, well," Kell said vaguely. He rolled his shoulders and glanced towards Lyric.

Abruptly Runa sat up, her eyes large in the dim room like a fox on high alert.

Lyric, perhaps sensing her sister's movement, groaned and opened her eyes.

It was unlikely anyone would sleep now. Elaina reached for the lamp and turned it on, tapping the rune on its base. Purple flame hissed to life beneath the glass shell, and Elaina squinted as her eyes adjusted.

"What is that?" Runa asked, her voice sharp, suspicious.

Elaina looked at the bed. "The Supplier came by," she said. She stepped up to the pile and examined what she'd traded the letter for.

The cloaks were dark gray and made from quality wool. She brushed her fingers along the heel of one of the boots and energy buzzed against her skin. As long as the girls didn't lose them, these boots would last forever. Reaching for the packs, Elaina separated the food into them. She looked sideways as motion caught her eye.

Runa and Lyric were sitting up, watching her.

"Is that a staff?" Lyric asked, her voice bright with wonder.

"What?" Kell asked.

Elaina felt him move behind her and she looked at him, smiling at the expression on his face. The first time she saw him, he'd been using one to knock an apple from a tree.

"Yes," Elaina said. "I thought you might feel incomplete without one. It's my fault yours was left back at the house."

Kell grinned at her, the excited smile rejuvenating him, and he reached for the staff. He lifted it reverently, cautiously stepping back, so he didn't hit the girls' legs.

It seemed to be an excellent, sturdy staff to Elaina's eye, crafted from pale brown wood. Whorls covered its surface, enhancing rather than suggesting flaws in the wood, and the head was carved into what might have been a dragon's head.

"It's beautiful," Lyric said. She beamed at Kell. "It suits you."

Elaina eyed her daughter, then glanced at Kell, catching the shine in his eyes. She should have expected this, sending a young man to her girls. Protectiveness and annoyance swelled in her chest, and she gave Kell a look.

His smile dipped uncertainly, and he cleared his throat, looking down at the staff in his hands.

She had to do something before Lyric grew attached. She couldn't let Kell become more entangled in their lives, not with the strings binding him to her father. Not with his mother a Daughter of Valen. What would happen when Kell remembered who he was? When they found his mother? What destruction would he leave in his wake?

Elaina handed two of the packs to her daughters, then passed them the cloaks and boots.

Lyric eyed her carefully, her brows furrowing over her green eyes. Maybe she'd caught the look she'd given Kell, and Elaina was taken aback by the maturity in her daughter's face. She saw glimpses of the innocent girls she'd left behind, but both Lyric and Runa looked older now, harder. Lyric's face was not as open as it used to be, not as trusting, and sadness stabbed through Elaina's heart. She deserved their mistrust, but it hurt.

Runa's unveiled suspicion was familiar, and Elaina drew strength from it, smiling at her red-haired daughter. They'd often butted heads while Runa was a child. Runa was all fire, just like Elaina had been. She'd known Runa would survive her disappearance and would protect Lyric.

"Why buy a cloak for me?" Runa asked, rubbing the heavy fabric between her hands. She stared at it skeptically.

"You'll need warm clothing when we leave the Veil," Elaina said. "You may not feel anything now, may not need to eat, but once you reunite with your body, all those things will return."

"I can touch things here," Runa said. She glanced up. "I could before sometimes, but I can *feel* them now."

Elaina nodded and tried to keep the alarm from her face. "It's the Veil, and you are a soul. Things work differently here for the disembodied." She nodded at the boots. "Put them in the pack; you should be able to carry it. If not, one of us can."

"I can," Runa said, her chin jutting out.

"Mama, have you ever dreamed of anyone while here?" Lyric asked, without looking up. She was changing her boots for the new ones.

"Dreamed?" Elaina asked. She raised an eyebrow. "Yes. Sleep works much the same here."

Runa glanced at Lyric, her eyes intense, and something passed between them.

Elaina waited to see if Lyric would ask anything further, but before she could prompt her, Kell pointed at the small wire cage.

"What is that?" he asked.

Elaina turned her head and reached for the cage, lifting it in her hand. Something black curled inside.

"It's a Soulworm," she said. "It will help us find your body, Runa." She grimaced apologetically. "I'm afraid you'll have to eat it."

Runa looked at her. "Eat it?" she asked. "Is that even possible?"

"Yes," Elaina said. "It's not like eating food, more like swallowing magic. Something incorporeal."

"It looks fairly real to me," Runa said.

"The Soulworm needs to become part of you to know what's missing. You should get a feeling inside your gut, tugging you in the direction you need to go. That's how we'll know where to start looking," Elaina said.

"It doesn't look too big," Lyric said, earning a glare from her sister.

"Any other suggestions?" Runa asked, addressing the room.

"Not unless you know a god," Kell said.

Runa huffed at him.

Lyric laughed and covered her mouth.

Sagging, Runa reached forward and snatched the cage from Elaina's hands. "Fine," she growled. Ripping off the lid, Runa reached inside with her thumb and index finger and pulled out the worm. She raised it, glaring and grimacing, as it hung limply from her fingers. It was not thick, but it was long, and Runa's face blanched.

The worm was thin and black, with an odd, rippling pattern on its slick back that glowed purple. It had no visible eyes, and its mouth was a tiny, flesh-covered hole that fluttered like delicate vellum.

"Oh," Lyric said. She coughed and looked at Runa's pale face.

Kell, eyes curious, leaned forward, and Runa flicked the worm at him, causing him to laugh and lean back.

"No one speaks of this," Runa said. "Ever." She uttered a curse that had Elaina's eyebrows lifting into her hair, and then she stuffed the entire worm into her mouth and swallowed. Coughing, Runa shook her head and forced it down, her throat working, and then she slapped the empty cage back into Elaina's hand.

"Odd," Runa said, sticking out her tongue. "I couldn't taste it. I could feel it though ..."

Lyric leaned forward, an impressed expression on her face.

"What happens after we find Runa's body?" she asked. "How do you get rid of the worm?"

Runa looked at her, alarmed.

"It disappears," Elaina said, gesturing absently. "When your soul reunites with flesh, it ... becomes something else." She shrugged.

"Well I'm glad you're so knowledgeable about the long worm I just put into my stomach," Runa said, her voice dark. She pressed a hand to her abdomen. "I don't feel anything but vaguely sick."

"It might not work until we leave Galgosha's," Elaina said, unconcerned. She grabbed her pack and handed the last one to Kell. "Her power blocks magic so it might be interfering with the Soulworm's ability. Let's go outside."

"Well I hope I didn't swallow it for nothing," Runa said, glowering.

"Should we change your dressing?" Lyric asked, gesturing at Elaina's arm.

Elaina shook her head. She'd already shoved the bandages into her pack. In truth, she'd forgotten about her burn. More pressing concerns occupied her mind. "It's fine," she said. "Let's get going." She waited as Kell, Lyric, and Runa slipped the bags on their shoulders and then opened the door. The hall was empty and quiet, and she led them back up the stairs.

It was much like when they'd arrived, the large room nearly empty, with only a handful of people scattered about the tables. The large, stone fireplace had been lit, and dark purple flames danced inside. A woman, with long, floor-length cerulean hair was tuning a gourd-shaped instrument beside it. As she manipulated the instrument's levers, it released a series of short, honking notes that punctured the low murmur of conversation inside the room.

Elaina turned, letting the girls slip past her, so she saw

when Kell staggered in horror and grabbed Lyric's shoulder. "What is that awful thing?" he gasped.

Lyric grinned and looked up at him, her eyes shining. "Aren't you supposed to love all instruments?" she asked as they walked past Elaina.

"Gods no," Kell said. "I'm not even sure what that is. It's like …"

"A dog mated with a goose?"

"A demon goose," Kell said. He surreptitiously tried to plug one ear.

"Stop being idiots," Runa said, rolling her eyes.

Elaina watched them banter, and a smile curved her lips. The companionship between them was light and happy, and for a moment, she felt hope that life might be kind to her daughters. That death and heartbreak would not be their future. Perhaps they could escape it all, and stay away from the war.

But they were women now, not little girls she could order to obey. Elaina doubted Runa would ever take her word again, ever trust her without argument. They wouldn't just forget the world she'd dragged them into and go back to their own lives.

Smile fading from her face, regret and weariness seeped back into Elaina's bones, and she followed them slowly to the bar.

Galgosha, writing in a dark leather ledger, looked up.

Kell, Lyric, and Runa paused by the exit, as Elaina reached into her money pouch and placed several coins atop the counter in front of Galgosha. "We're going to use a Soulworm," she said.

Galgosha nodded. "I'm sorry I couldn't locate them, Dandashara," she said.

"They're more careful than we expected," Elaina said. "I will find them. Until next time." She signed farewell, and Galgosha nodded at her, tapping the side of one hand against her upper chest.

"Until next time," Galgosha echoed.

Elaina walked between her daughters and opened the door, stepping out into the darkness of the Veil. The light and noise from the waystation disappeared, and she took a deep breath. The scent of decay was gone. Now the air smelled sharp like it'd been laced with peppermint. She breathed in again, drawing the chilled air into her lungs.

Tapping the stored light spell on her belt, Elaina summoned the glowing orb, which she split into four with a quick command uttered beneath her breath. She turned around and looked at her three companions. "Runa?" she asked, looking at her red-haired daughter expectantly.

Runa pressed a hand against her stomach, her face sour, and pointed. "That way," she said. "I feel a tug that way."

"How are you doing that?" Lyric asked, pointing at the light above Elaina's head.

"The light?" Elaina asked.

Lyric nodded.

"It's a spell, etched into my belt."

"It's permanent? Like Kell's tattoo?" Lyric asked.

Kell reached up and touched his throat, his face tightening.

Elaina cleared her throat. She didn't want to talk about magic, didn't want her daughters to become interested in it. She considered ignoring the question, but knew Lyric wouldn't let it go.

"In a way," Elaina said. "It's a stored spell, fed by my body's own energy. The drain is minimal, like feeling tired after a quick jog. I hardly notice it."

"It's reusable because of its connection to you?" Runa asked, drifting closer. She seemed happy to be thinking about something beside the worm.

"Yes," Elaina said.

"So you wrote the runes, activated it, and tied it to yourself?" Lyric asked.

It was a simplified explanation but more or less correct. Elaina nodded grudgingly.

"But you spoke again," Runa said. "First there was one light, and then four."

"I spoke a spell to split the light," Elaina said, "so it will follow you. At least, as long as you're within sight of me."

"I'd love to learn that," Lyric said. She bounced on the balls of her feet, reminding Elaina of her younger self. From the time she could walk, Lyric had been enthusiastic and inquisitive, approaching everything with an energy Elaina had envied. She was glad her daughter's spirit had not diminished in her absence.

"Is there a consequence for doing magic?" Runa asked. "Like your skin catching fire."

Elaina sighed, absently reaching for her arm. "Not usually in that way. Spells deplete the iron in your body, make you tired. If you don't rest or eat something to replenish it, like meat or vegetables, grown in Erith's soil, you will eventually drain your body of life." She looked at them, holding their gaze, praying they understood how dangerous it could be. "Mishandle magic and you can become a husk, a shell of a person, or you can die."

"But not from simple magic, surely?" Lyric asked. She looked pensive, not afraid. "You obviously have managed to survive."

"I've studied for most of my life," Elaina said. She gestured in the direction Runa had pointed. "We should get moving. We need to find your body, Runa."

"Why don't you want us to learn magic?" Runa asked.

"It's dangerous," Elaina said. She shifted, feeling uncomfortable, annoyed they were pushing.

"So was living on the border of the Umberwood alone,"

Lyric said. "So was some of our training, as wise women. Everything is dangerous in some way."

"Because," Elaina said, gritting her teeth. "This ties you more closely to my world."

"*Your* world," Runa said flatly. She set her hands on her hips and glared venomously. "The world you left us for. But we're part of it. Your blood is ours."

Were they going to do this again? Now? Elaina rubbed her temple, worry, frustration, and fear jostling to take over. "They will be more interested in you," she said finally, glaring at them. How could they not see it? "If the Sireni know your power, your potential, if they know you share the blood of all four dragons ... they will want to use you. And not just the Sireni. Your grandfather will want you. And that's if he doesn't decide to kill you because your blood is corrupted by his enemies."

Lyric sighed, the excitement dimming on her face. She chewed on her cheek, puzzling over something in her head.

Hand moving to her stomach, Runa looked off into the darkness distractedly. "What do I do once we find my body?" she asked.

Elaina breathed a sigh of relief. They were moving on. "Your body and soul want to be reunited," she said. "You should only need to touch your body and think about being whole again. Think of being flesh and blood and bone. Think of how it feels, to be living."

"No spell?" Runa asked, frowning. "You've witnessed this before? You know that will work?"

"I don't," Elaina said honestly.

Runa and Lyric glanced at her in concern, so Elaina smiled in what she hoped was a reassuring way. "It will work," she said. It had to. If it didn't, then she'd failed to save her daughter.

# 6

KELL

KELL FELT HAPPY, which seemed wrong somehow. He'd never expected to find himself here, traveling the Veil like it was something ordinary. He itched to weave his unexpected journey into a story, to describe the oddness of the place, the heaviness of the darkness, the lack of sound.

There was always sound around him in the living world in the rustle of leaves in the breeze, the shift of fabric as he walked, the sound of a bird trilling in the sky, even the thud of his pulse as blood moved beneath his skin. Here in the Veil, he couldn't hear anything except their voices when they spoke aloud. It was as if the Veil swallowed sound.

Kell couldn't hear his footsteps, his new staff against the ground or Lyric breathing beside him. It was disorienting and made his skin itch at the back of his neck.

Though Kell couldn't hear her movements, he was very aware of the woman walking beside him. He had been ever since he'd first laid eyes on her. Looking down, he caught Lyric's eyes and happiness flared inside his chest as she smiled. It felt like he'd walked into a beam of sunlight. Smiling back, Kell felt his body relax, and his steps lighten.

His reaction to Lyric was unexpected and unplanned. Kell thought it'd be a simple thing, checking on Marleena's daughters. No, *Elaina's* daughters. He'd had no idea who she really was. A part of him felt betrayed. He thought they'd been close, at least as close as they could be when she'd seen him at his worst.

Elaina had known how hard he'd tried to get the tattoo off his neck. She'd even gone with him when he'd tracked down a secretive practitioner of Velanian, begged for help in a dirty alley.

When she suggested getting him into King Rakarn's library, Kell had assumed she was either a member of the household or some minor relation. He'd never considered the Crown Princess of Raendashar had befriended him, or that her daughters, who he'd been sent to protect, were heirs to the Scorched Court.

Despairingly, Kell studied Lyric from the corner of his eye. Her heritage alone was a reason to abandon the idea that he could share something with her, have a future. Lyric had royal blood, she could rule Raendashar one day, and Kell, Kell was nobody. He was a songsmith without lands or family. And yet ... and yet he found himself drawn to her, drawn to her smiles and laughter and kindness. Lyric was like a balm on his soul, a reminder that there was light in the world. That maybe he wouldn't have to be alone.

Lyric was beautiful; her delicate face always open and curious. Her emotions flickered easily through her eyes and in the curve of her mouth, as though she were incapable of hiding them. She blushed easily too, and Kell found himself enchanted by it, and how her eyes shifted in color, darker when she was upset and lighter when she was happy.

*I need to walk away*, he thought, sneaking another glance at Lyric as they walked. *I need to leave before something happens.*

Smile fading, Kell reached for his throat, feeling as though the tattoo that bound him was tightening. It was not, he was not thinking of Thenda, he was not trying to recall those memories of whatever he'd witnessed, and yet it prickled his skin anyway.

*Everyone around me dies. Mother's dead, father's dead.* Kell's stomach hollowed, and he looked away from Lyric into the dark, hiding his face, not wanting her to see the pain in his eyes.

Tragedy had not first struck him in Thenda, on the day everyone died. No, he'd been unwanted long before that. His birth mother feared him for reasons he didn't know. Kell hadn't told Lyric that. He hadn't told her that the mother who'd died — that he'd lost — hadn't given birth to him.

He hadn't told her that the people who should have loved him had bound and discarded him. Thenda was not his only silencing. He thought about the tattoos on his back, about his scars. The emptiness that'd been his companion for the last thirteen years returned like a stone inside his stomach.

Something caught his eye in the darkness and Kell squinted after it. Was that a house? He blinked, trying to focus, and when his eyes opened again, it was gone. Had he imagined it?

"Kell?" Lyric asked, her voice sweet. Her hand brushed his, and heat returned once more beneath his skin, chasing away the miserable thoughts inside his head.

Kell looked at her, putting on his songsmith face, tucking away the sadness and hopelessness beneath a pleasant smile.

"You were far away just then," Lyric said.

"I was thinking about my mother," Kell answered. He hadn't intended to say anything, but he wanted to confide in her. His answer was partly true. He had been thinking of his mother.

Lyric's eyes filled with sympathy and she touched his hand more purposefully, flushing when he threaded her fingers through his and tugged her closer. He should let her go, but he couldn't.

Abruptly, Kell's boot sank into the earth. He stopped,

staring at his feet in confusion, and Lyric stopped in surprise beside him. The sand had vanished, replaced by thick, black mud.

Lifting his head, Kell looked to the side again, searching for the house he'd seen and instead found sickly gray trees, empty of leaves, thrusting up from the earth like skeletons.

"Those are new," he said, feeling a prickle of unease.

"This happens sometimes," Elaina said. She and Runa had both stopped and turned to face them.

Kell released Lyric's hand automatically, wondering if Elaina had noticed their closeness.

Elaina's eyes flickered over him and Lyric, but she merely curled back the sleeve on her un-bandaged arm and ran her fingers over a twisting line of mage runes tattooed across her forearm. The runes shimmered and seemed to shift beneath her skin, as if alive.

"Greetings, travelers." A woman's voice, low and husky, came from the darkness to Kell's left.

Kell's heart spasmed in his chest. Relieved he hadn't jumped or yelped like Lyric, he turned, back straight, staff tight in his hand.

Three women were standing about fifty paces away, illuminated by light that glowed over their heads like a tiny suspended moon. They were tall and muscular and wearing a mix of black leather and scale armor that covered everything except their arms. Tattooed runes glinted green from their wrists to shoulders, the symbols shifting in a way that made Kell feel vaguely sick to the stomach.

The woman in the center had long, black hair, braided in a crest across her skull, and left to fall loosely down her back in a mass of curls. Her face was scarred, but her pleasant smile softened the menacing way the old wound tugged at her skin.

The women bracketing her appeared to be identical twins, unlike Lyric and Runa, with startling blue eyes and short blond hair. They did not look as friendly as their companion, and the woman on the right repeatedly curled and uncurled a thin whip around her arm, the lash glinting green like her tattoos.

Kell's heart skipped again, and he eyed the strangers, unsure of their intent. There was something familiar about them that nudged the back of his mind. They seemed to belong to the Veil, not just traveling through like Kell and his companions.

"Good day," Elaina said. She'd taken a step closer to Runa, who'd noticed and was frowning.

The black-haired woman held up her hands, palms empty. "You need not fear anything from us. We felt a wandering soul and merely came to look." Her eyes shifted to Runa.

"A wandering soul?" Runa asked. She crossed her arms and eyed the women suspiciously.

Kell adjusted his grip on his staff. Who did they remind him of, and why did they make him nervous?

"We are Daughters of Valen," the woman said.

Panic and hope flared inside Kell's chest. Was one of these women his mother? Elaina had told him what she'd seen as a child, about the winged woman who'd brought him to King Rakarn. If the stories were true about the sons of the Daughters, then it was dangerous if they knew who he was. His birth mother, whether or not she'd truly loved or wanted him, had decided to hide him from the others.

Kell wanted to ask if they recognized him but was terrified of what might happen if they did. Swallowing, he prayed his emotions weren't visible on his face.

Lyric looked at him and moved closer, a wrinkle between her brows.

"Valen's Daughters?" Runa asked. "Wights who take the souls of warriors to Valenorn?"

"Warriors?" Lyric asked. She looked away from Kell, eyes bright with interest. "Does that still happen?"

The black-haired woman inclined her head. "Not as often as the days of the God and Demon Wars," she said, smiling. "I am Vara. These are my sisters Belain and Deshar." Her green eyes shifted between the four of them, lingering on Kell.

Kell forced himself to smile, repeating their names in his head. Did Vara recognize him? Did she know his mother? "I'm Kell Layreasha," he said, bowing slightly. "Songsmith of the Emerald Tones." His voice did not betray the maelstrom inside him.

Lyric touched his arm and Kell looked at her distractedly, not understanding the direct look she gave Vara.

"I'm Lyric," Lyric said, "and this is Runa and our—"

"I'm Dandashara," Elaina said.

Vara raised an eyebrow and shifted her eyes back to Lyric and Kell, dismissing Elaina. "There's a darkness around you," she said.

A chill settled across Kell's shoulders and he felt Lyric tighten her fingers on his arm. He worked to keep his face calm, his eyes unconcerned. Did Vara know? Would she tell the others? Were they going to kill him? Kill Lyric, Runa, and Elaina for being with him?

All three of the Daughters' eyes focused on Kell and Lyric, their bodies growing still. It was unnerving, like being stared at by three large birds of prey. Kell's pulse quickened, and he wet his lips.

"A darkness?" Lyric asked. Her voice was uncertain, and she glanced at Runa. "In me?"

*No, not you*, Kell wanted to say, but he didn't. He didn't say anything.

Vara's eyes burned with focus, looking through Kell, as though to the bones beneath his skin. "When that which is hidden becomes whole again, death will follow."

"Whose death?" Runa asked sharply.

"What is hidden?" Lyric asked.

Kell swallowed. His skin was clammy and cold. Was Vara talking about his silence or the spells on his back? Who was in danger? His own life? Lyric's life? What did it mean?

"What are you talking about?" Elaina asked. Her voice was jagged and dangerous.

Kell glanced at her and saw Elaina's eyes were wide, panicked. *It's about me; it has to be*, he wanted to say.

Vara blinked, and the other women shifted beside her, drawing in a deep, simultaneous breath as though they'd forgotten to breathe. The Daughters exchanged glances. "Be careful here," Vara said distractedly.

The sound of fluttering wings filled the air, and the women disappeared.

Kell turned, gripping his staff, watching the darkness. He saw nothing but spindly trees. Sweat chilled on his body, and he let his breath go, feeling the air hiss from his lungs. His arms trembled, and he curled his toes inside his boots, trying to calm himself.

"What was that about?" Runa asked. She'd crossed her arms over her chest and was glaring at no one.

"An omen," Kell said, his voice faint. He cleared his throat as Lyric looked up at him, eyes wide.

"No," Elaina said fiercely, stepping forward, drawing them together. "It meant nothing. They're playing with us." Her eyes were intense on Kell's face and she shook her head, a slight movement meant for him.

Not his mother then. Elaina must not have recognized any of the Daughters.

"For what reason?" Lyric asked. "To frighten us?" She looked between Kell and her mother. "Is this something they do? Give omens? Can they see the future?"

Could they? He didn't know. They'd been stories until today. He hadn't quite believed Elaina about his origins, not really. "I don't know," Kell said. "It just ... sounded like one." He looked at Elaina, who was staring at him pointedly.

"I'm sure it was nothing," Kell said. He smiled, swallowing his fear, burying it deep. "They sounded rather mysterious though, didn't they? Quite theatrical."

Though not entirely convinced, if he read her correctly, Lyric seemed relieved by the feigned lightness in his voice, and she smiled.

Kell, staring down at her, put his hand over hers. He had to leave her. If the omen had been for him and someone was going to die, he couldn't risk her life. She didn't deserve to be pulled into his misfortune. Kell moved out of Lyric's reach, turning away with the pretense of shifting his staff to his other hand.

Watching him, Lyric's smile faltered.

"Odd they'd say something cryptic for no reason," Runa said. "What, are you saying they're bored? Enjoy messing with the minds of mortals?"

Elaina shrugged, projecting unconcern. "They had to say something interesting after mistaking us for wandering warrior souls."

"You should write about this," Lyric said.

Kell turned, blinking at her uneasily. "What?"

"The Daughters of Valen," she said. "Have you ever seen one before?"

He shook his head.

"But you've told stories of them?"

"Oh, yes. Yes, of course." Kell smiled.

"Well, now you know what they look like," Lyric said.

"Yes, I suppose I do."

Lyric continued to stare at him expectantly, so Kell reached into the hidden pocket of his robe and withdrew his leather journal. He located his self-inking quill, a priceless gift from his old mentor, and opened the book, scribbling something on the stiff paper. He wasn't aware of what he wrote, feeling the heaviness of Lyric's eyes on him.

"You've had that this whole time?" Lyric asked, amused.

"Yes," Kell said, as he returned the quill and journal to his pocket. "Old habit." He grinned, noticing a scatter of gold freckles across Lyric's cheeks.

Lyric grinned back, her eyes sparkling. "I guess you didn't leave everything behind at our house."

"I've had a bag go missing a time or two," Kell explained. "Curious children have a habit of following me around. I might try to retrieve my bag from your house when this is over." He remembered the scarf tucked deep inside the pack he'd left outside on Lyric and Runa's porch. It was all he had left of Triska, his Thendian mother, the only physical reminder of the loving woman who'd raised him. Sadness formed a lump in his throat as he tried to remember her face, her eyes. She was fading.

The scarf was just a piece of fabric, nothing valuable, and yet the thought of never seeing it again filled him with desperation. He had to go back. Not now, but once Lyric was safe.

"It's probably still there," Lyric said. "I doubt anyone in Elae's Hollow would steal something off our porch. And the Sireni have probably realized we're here by now and assume we won't return, so I think we could stop by when this is done and—"

"No!" Elaina said sharply, cutting Lyric off.

Lyric jumped and looked at her mother. Her shoulders tensed, and Kell resisted the urge to reach out and brush his hand over the back of her neck.

*Death will follow*, he reminded himself. Was it arrogant to think the Daughter was referring to him? Vara couldn't have been talking to Lyric, could she? Lyric had no dark secrets. She hadn't even known about her family or magic until recently.

"You can't go back, Lyric," Elaina said. Her hand cut

through the air in a commanding gesture. "I'm sorry you've had to leave everything behind, but you can't risk going back."

"But the village," Lyric said. "They need me."

"No," Elaina said. "They'll survive without you. You don't owe them your life, Lyric."

Runa turned towards Elaina, her face cold. "Well, we all know how easy it is for you to abandon things," she said.

"Runa," Lyric said, chidingly. "We have lives, Mama. Responsibilities."

"You can't go back," Elaina said. Her eyes flashed, and her mouth tightened in a thin line. "Don't forget that I understand the dangers better than you."

"Don't forget," Runa echoed back, "that we aren't children. You lost the right to order us around the day you left us."

"It's not important," Kell said, "my bag." He could feel their emotions crowding around him, filling the air. *That's a lie*, he thought, thinking about his mother's scarf. It was important.

"This isn't about your bag, Kell," Runa snapped.

"Right," Kell said, nodding. "I just ... you're all she talked about." He looked at Elaina, saw how hard she was trying to keep it together.

Runa grunted, perhaps not believing him.

"We should continue," Lyric said, sighing. "Ru, can you still feel your body?"

Runa nodded, her eyes softening as she looked away from their mother. "It's that way," she said, pointing, "but I don't feel any closer."

"We need to hurry," Lyric said, touching her sister's arm. "We shouldn't be here. I keep wondering if ..." She shook her head.

Runa nodded, an unspoken thought passing between the sisters.

Feeling stupidly jealous about their bond, Kell looked at Elaina. She was watching Lyric, her brows furrowed. She was worried, growing increasingly restless the longer they walked. Did Elaina believe they were running out of time? If the Daughters had sensed Runa's presence, might Valen, the Lord of Souls? Would he try to take her to the Underworld? How dangerous was it for them to travel here? How dangerous for Kell?

"Let's go," Runa said. She glanced sideways at Elaina. "Focus on things we can fix."

Lyric nodded. Her shoulders were still tensed, and though Kell had promised himself that he'd stay away, that being near her was selfish, he reached out and rested a hand on her shoulder.

Runa started walking, followed by Elaina.

Staying beside Kell, Lyric smiled up at him. Her skin was luminous, her cheeks flushed. "I'm glad you're here," she said quietly, for his ears alone.

"Me too," Kell said. Regretfully, he dropped his hand from her shoulder and together they started after Runa and Elaina.

"What will you do after this?" Lyric asked, glancing at him. She twisted her hand in her hair, braiding it absently as they walked.

"After?" Kell asked.

Lyric's blush deepened, and she looked down at her hands as she threaded them through her hair. "After we get out of the Veil. My mother asked you to help us, but she's here now ..." Her voice trailed off.

Kell breathed in. He didn't want to think about that, about leaving. Honestly, he hadn't given it much thought, not since Lyric opened her front door and smiled at him. "I was going to go to Rathgar's Hold," he said. "In Raendashar."

"Oh, yes. Mama said she'd help you get into our grandfather's library."

"Yes," Kell said. He wasn't exactly sure how, considering Elaina didn't want to see her father.

Lyric looked at him, a quick flash of her eyes, and then began to unravel her hair. "Maybe that's where we'll go too," she said, her voice light.

Kell felt a thrill dance through his body.

"To Raendashar?" Kell asked. "Is that wise?" He winced, hoping she wasn't offended. He hadn't meant to imply she couldn't make her own decisions.

Lyric raised an eyebrow but didn't seem upset. "Well, Mama promised to help you, and I can't imagine her leaving us, not now, so what other choice is there?"

"Is that what you want? To go to Raendashar?" Kell looked at her curiously. Despite everything Lyric had heard about the war, about the Sireni, about her grandfather, she hadn't been scared away?

"Yes, I do," Lyric said. Her eyes grew distant, and she looked away as if seeing something beyond them. "I worry about our home, our village. There are people who depend on me, on my help. I know they'll be fine, of course they will, but I ... I wish I didn't have to abandon them. I wonder if they'll look for us."

"It wasn't exactly your choice," Kell said.

"No," Lyric said, lips turning up at the corners, "but I also can't stop thinking about the war. About people dying over land, over old grudges. If I can do something ... if I can maybe change our grandfather's mind ..."

"Trying to save the world?" Kell asked.

Lyric flushed. "Obviously I can't save everyone," she said. "And perhaps it's foolish to think I can do anything, but ... but we're from both sides." She looked at him, her eyes bright and hopeful. "We're proof that Raendasharans and Sireni don't have to hate each other. They can choose love."

Lyric was so earnest, so inspired, and as Kell watched her, he could imagine the possibility of a brighter future. Maybe she could change something. Maybe life didn't have to end in blood and death.

"What?" Lyric asked, flushing a bright red. "Why are you looking at me that way?"

Kell grinned. "You're inspiring," he said.

"Or delusional."

They grinned at each other. Lyric's shoulder brushed his as she shifted closer, and Kell found himself grabbing her hand. Touching her was starting to feel right, familiar.

*What are you doing, Kell?* He shoved the thought away. He could worry about it later, once they were back in the world of the living. Perhaps things would feel different there.

# 7

RUNA

RUNA STOPPED WALKING, earning a concerned look from their mother. She ignored the unspoken question and pressed her hand against her belly. She thought about the Soulworm, wiggling through her insides. Where was it now? What was it doing? The worm's odd directional pull throbbed as if noticing her awareness.

Looking up, Runa surveyed their surroundings. They'd walked into a small grove, the trees gnarled and gray like flesh-stripped bones. Large rocks lay scattered between them, a few lying in furrows as if they'd been dragged. Had someone been here before? Runa thought about her body lying somewhere in the darkness, guarded by strangers.

Something gurgled behind her.

Turning, Runa stared into Lyric's embarrassed face.

"Sorry," Lyric said, grinning. "My stomach."

"We can stop here," Runa suggested, pursing her lips. Her sister was always hungry.

Runa focused on her belly, searching for the once familiar sensations of hunger and thirst, but felt nothing beyond the unsettling pull of the Soulworm.

"It'd be good to eat," Elaina said.

Lyric beamed and flopped onto a low, flat rock, and Kell, following her like a shadow, sat nearby.

Runa eyed them, watching as they pulled bread and apples from their packs. When would Lyric learn to stop collecting broken things? She couldn't save everyone. Not even pretty boys with haunted eyes. Kell was trouble. Runa was sure of it. They shouldn't forget that their mother sent him. What else might Elaina have asked him to do?

"Do you feel any closer?" Lyric asked, looking at Runa.

Runa blinked. "What?"

"To your body."

Runa shook her head. "I'm starting to wonder if we'll walk forever without finding it. How can we be sure the worm is leading us to the right place?"

"Maybe your body is being moved?" Lyric asked.

Runa shrugged. If the Sireni intended to distract them, then it made sense to move her body. They might have been tasked not with kidnapping Elaina, but keeping her occupied, getting her to waste time wandering the Veil.

Or, maybe they hoped Elaina would find Runa's body and were prepared to grab both her and Lyric. Did the Sireni know Runa was here too? Did they think she was dead or did they know she had a Soulworm and was drawing closer? Was she drawing closer?

"Maybe we're going in circles," Runa said.

"Mama?" Lyric asked.

Elaina, biting into an apple, shook her head. "It seems unlikely," she said. "The Veil is a big, confusing place. It takes time to travel."

Growling, Runa wandered towards one of the trees and stared at it. She could probably eat, like the others, but she remembered how the worm felt sliding down her throat. It'd been worse somehow, being unable to taste it as it went down.

Runa focused on the tree's spindly branches, peering at the peeling bark. Disturbingly, it reminded her of papery skin, held together by dark, rust-colored sap.

"Something's coming," a voice said beside her.

"Gah!" Runa hissed, jumping sideways, hand raised to punch whoever had startled her. She blinked. Elenora's sharp face stared at her. "You're here!" Runa gasped. "What are you doing here?" She was fairly certain the scowling woman was not a demigod. A ghost then? Someone who knew their mother's family?

She looked back at Lyric and Kell, expecting to see their shocked faces, but their heads were bent towards each other. Lyric held her waterskin, and Kell reached out to brush something off her cheek.

Runa looked at their mother and found Elaina staring in the opposite direction, her hand bringing the apple to her mouth for another bite.

"They won't notice me," Elenora said, gesturing dismissively.

"You're not really here?" Runa asked. She looked back at Elenora and then glanced again towards Lyric and Kell.

"Not entirely," Elenora said. "Only you can see me. However, they will hear you speak, so unless you want to look mad, I'd be cautious. But enough about that, something is coming."

"Something?" Runa asked, looking around.

"There," Elenora said, pointing past Kell. "Don't trust it. It's a Flesh Eater."

"A what?"

"A creature, like a demon, that eats the living. It's not particularly fast, so it likes to wear the forms of humans to get close. Be careful."

Runa squinted, trying to see. Was it a woman? "It's an old lady," she said doubtfully, stepping closer towards the others.

"Don't trust it," Elenora said. She sighed. "I considered seeing how you dealt with it, without my help, but if it eats your sister, I assume you'll be inconsolable."

"What?" Runa gasped. She glared at Elenora, fury bubbling in her chest.

"Fire, it hates fire," Elenora said crisply, ignoring Runa's horrified anger. "Now listen closely." Elenora spoke a rune word, the sound harsh and guttural on her tongue.

"But how do I—"

Elenora disappeared.

Whirling, Runa stared at the figure ambling forward.

Lyric, seeing her staring past them, glanced over Kell's shoulder. "Someone's here," she said, surprised.

Elaina looked up and dropped her apple core onto the ground.

Kell swiveled atop his rock and followed their gaze. His staff was lying on the ground by his feet.

The old woman shuffled towards them, illuminated by their magic light as she drew close. She was hunched and small and wrapped in a black shawl, drawn up over her head. White curls frizzed out from beneath the shawl's moth-eaten fringe, and her rheumy eyes seemed only a shade darker than her hair.

Runa blinked, staring at the woman's gentle face with disbelief. She looked frail and ancient, hardly capable of hurting someone. Elenora was testing her, right? Subjecting her to a cruel joke, and waiting to see if she'd hurt an old woman?

Runa repeated the fire rune inside her head, testing the word. She couldn't attack this woman. What if she was wrong? What if Elenora couldn't be trusted?

"Oh my, I am so happy to have stumbled across you!" the old woman said. Her voice wavered as she spoke. "I've been wandering, quite lost I'm afraid, and I left my basket somewhere with all my food." She touched gnarled fingers to the side of her head and laughed. "Constantly leaving things and forgetting them, just like my dear Issac always said."

Lyric smiled warmly, unconcerned. "Issac? Is he your husband?"

"Oh yes, my partner of, oh my, fifty years? The time does slip by, doesn't it."

"Are you hungry? We have bread and cheese," Lyric said.

"Ly," Runa said warningly.

Lyric glanced at her, frowning at her tone. Then, assuming she'd chastised Runa sufficiently, she returned her gaze to the old woman and smiled a bright welcome.

Emboldened, the old woman hobbled towards Lyric, and Runa took a step forward, breath catching. Anticipation and fear knotted her muscles and sent her heart thudding against her ribs. Out of the corner of her eye, Runa thought she saw Elaina look at her. Had she noticed Runa's tension?

The old woman accepted a piece of bread from Lyric, but didn't sit down. She swayed back and forth on her feet, looking at Kell, Runa and finally Elaina, before returning her eyes to Lyric.

"Are you lost?" Elaina asked.

"Oh, I live not too far from here," the old woman said. "Not too far. I was taking a trip to town, er, the waystation nearby to sell my apples."

"You live here?" Lyric asked surprise showing on her face. "And you're able to grow apples?" She gestured at the gnarled trees. "I thought nothing grows here. Nothing you can eat anyway."

"Oh you just need to know how, that's all, sweet girl," the old woman said. Her teeth were large and white, and not a single tooth was missing from her mouth. It was strange, her teeth, quite unlike Old Granny Laen, who'd puttered around Elae's Hollow for as long as Runa could remember.

Narrowing her eyes, Runa took another step forward, repeating the word for fire again in her mind.

The old woman glanced at her, smile still plastered on her face.

"How did you end up living here, in the Veil?" Kell asked.

The old woman swayed, the motion taking her yet closer to Lyric. She waved the bread around, still untouched in her hand. "Funny story that. Long. Not interesting. Dear Issac says I prattle on so. I'd hate to bore you." Her eyes darted to Runa, then back to Lyric. She moved another step closer.

Dread buzzed along Runa's skin. Something was wrong. She spoke the rune word, hissing it under her breath, her tongue shaping it awkwardly.

Nothing happened.

Runa lifted her hand and repeated the word, believing fire would appear. She'd throw it; she'd protect her sister.

Something inside of her shifted as she called for it, rising to her awareness. The feeling hummed, overpowering the tug from the Soulworm, catching like a spark inside her chest. Runa reached for it, but it slipped away like a fish sliding from her hands. She grabbed for it again, panicked, trying to hold it, use it, but the more forceful she became, the faster it evaded her.

Runa spoke the word again, louder, more forceful, desperation clawing at her. The power slipped free, surging just out of reach.

Elaina stood, dumping her pack on the ground. She muttered something fast under her breath and fire flared inside her upraised palm.

Runa gasped as she felt the presence of heat in the air. She watched fire dance across their mother's skin, glowing threads coiling into a ball.

"Step away from my daughter!" Elaina snapped, her voice loud and commanding.

Runa tried speaking the rune word again, mimicking their mother's posture. Nothing happened.

Surprised by Elaina's shout, Lyric tumbled off her rock.

Kell scrambled upright, abandoning his staff to grab Lyric's arm and hauled her sideways, farther from the old woman.

The old woman growled, her face twisted angrily, all friendliness gone. Her eyes glowed a pulsing blood-red. Black saliva dripped from her mouth, as her lips drew back. She snarled and flung the bread into the dark, her fingers flashing into elongated claws.

Runa shouted the rune for fire, frantic, terrified. Why wouldn't it work?

"I'll strip the flesh from your bones!" the old woman growled, her voice fracturing into a multitude of ear-grating tones. She lunged for Lyric.

Gasping, Kell twisted, shielding Lyric with his body.

Elaina reacted, throwing the ball of fire. It smashed into the old woman's shoulder, igniting her shawl and driving her back.

The old woman flared like a lit candle, fire exploding across her chest and arms. She flailed, arms thrashing and screamed a horrible, multi-toned scream. Whirling, unbalanced, the woman ran off impossibly fast into the darkness. The red glow of the flames grew smaller the farther she fled until it was no more than a tiny smudge.

Kell stood up and helped Lyric to her feet.

"What just happened?" Lyric asked, eyes wide and horrified. Her head jerked between the red smudge and Elaina's fierce expression. "You ... you burned ..."

"She wasn't human," Elaina said. She sounded tired and drained. Shoving a hand through her hair, their mother bent over and picked up her pack.

"A Flesh Eater," Runa said, as she watched the tiny glow until it disappeared. Her voice sounded hollow. She could still hear the woman's, no, the *thing's* screams, echoing inside her skull.

"A what?" Lyric asked.

Kell, his face white, put an arm around Lyric's shoulders, and she leaned into him.

"A demon," Runa said. She looked down at her hand, flexing her fingers. Why hadn't it worked? Had Elenora lied to her? Had she told her the wrong rune on purpose? Runa had felt something though. She hadn't completely failed.

"How do you know that?" Elaina asked her voice sharp.

Runa dropped her hand and looked up, giving her mother a blank look. "Someone told me," she said.

"Someone ... told you?" Lyric echoed.

Runa looked at Lyric who'd pushed away from Kell. Her sister walked up to her and reached for her hand, gripping it tightly. Lyric's skin was cold and clammy.

*I shouldn't feel that*, Runa thought.

"Have you seen someone?" her sister asked softly.

"Seen?" Elaina asked. She sounded horrified.

Ignoring her, Runa stared into Lyric's searching eyes. "Someone talked to me when we first came to the Veil. She said her name was Elenora. I wasn't sure who she was at first, but now I think she's our ancestor."

"Is she Sireni?" Lyric asked.

Their mother swore.

"No," Runa said. "Raendasharan."

"Oh." Lyric chewed on her lip. "I saw someone too while I was dreaming in the waystation. Gandara, that's her name. She wants to teach me magic."

"Elenora claims the same thing," Runa said.

"Ancestors," Elaina said flatly.

Runa and Lyric looked at her.

Their mother's fingers were pressed against her temples, digging into the skin. "They must have sensed you when we came to the Veil. I don't know why," she said, answering their unspoken question. "It seems no matter what I do, we are all pulled back into this war, cycling again and again. Perhaps I was arrogant to think I could protect you from this; that I could keep you from them. We all return, one way or another.

"It seems if I don't teach you magic, it will be whispered into your ears. Please, daughters," Elaina begged. "When we leave here, let me take you somewhere safe. Somewhere away from the war. Somewhere no one will find you."

Lyric moved away from Runa and took their mother's hand. "I want to go to Raendashar, Mama," she said, her voice soft and reassuring.

Elaina groaned and gripped Lyric's hand tightly in both of hers. "No, Lyric. No. If you go there, you might be unable to leave."

"You have to go to Raendashar anyway, Mama," Lyric said. "You promised Kell you'd help him. I understand why you want to protect us ..."

Runa grunted.

"But you're in danger too," Lyric said, ignoring her. "The Sireni won't stop chasing us. Not now. And I don't think Grandfather will let us disappear, not if he knows we're alive. I want to meet him, Mama. I want to understand where you came from and what we are.

"You taught us to help people and to save lives. Is it truly a surprise that we want to stop the war and help you? You haven't told us what you've been doing since you left, but I think you've been fighting. We won't let you do this alone." Lyric looked back at Runa. Her eyes were bright and determined.

Sighing, Runa nodded. "Where you go, I go," she said to her sister. "Someone has to keep you from killing yourself while you try to save everyone."

Lyric smiled, eyes affectionate. "To the end and beyond," she said.

"To the end," Runa echoed.

Elaina gave Runa a tortured look, but Runa merely stared back, her jaw set.

"We should move on," Elaina said finally. She released Lyric's hand and pulled her pack over her shoulders. "The Flesh Eater may come back, or another."

"Yes," Lyric agreed. Her enthusiasm seemed to dim, and she looked nervously into the darkness. "Are there many demons here?"

Their mother paused, mouth twisting. "There shouldn't be," she said.

Runa watched as the others gathered their things. She hadn't removed her pack when they'd stopped, so she had no preparations to make. She focused again on the pull from the Soulworm, ignoring the echo of the failed magic. "This way," she said.

Back straight and mind filled with frustration, Runa led them away from the grove back into the endless dark.

# 8

LYRIC

A STATUE ROSE from the darkness, drawing Lyric's eye. "Look!" she said, pointing.

Ahead of her, Elaina and Runa had already spotted it, but she noticed Kell's attention shift beside her, drawing him from his thoughts.

The statue was remarkably visible despite the distance and darkness, and as they approached it, Lyric saw it'd been chiseled from pale stone. It was a woman, robed and crowned, with arms outstretched as if in welcome. Her hair was long, reaching her ankles, and her face was beautiful but cold, a hint of displeasure in the downturn of her mouth and her unpainted eyes. Perhaps her posture was not entirely welcoming.

The woman stood atop a dais, the stone weathered by time. There were words beneath her feet, but they were illegible, nearly worn away. Sitting on the base and ringed by deep purple petals from a flower Lyric didn't recognize, were candle nubs, melted down and unlit. Silver necklaces curled around them, each strung with small charms and onyx beads.

Walking around the statue's base, Lyric studied the stone. She bent down, peering at a relief carved into the side. "I think this is a statue of Hel," she said, eyeing the twisting forms carved into the stone. The old stories said Hel was the mother of the Underworld, the goddess who had created Valen, its caretaker, and his sister Velaine, the fallen god who'd caused the Demon War.

"Didn't she also create the Daughters of Valen?" Lyric asked aloud, thinking back to the beautiful and intimidating women they'd met earlier.

"Yes, that's what we believe," Kell said, looking away from the front of the statue.

"What's it doing here?" Runa asked. She turned in a circle, looking around them. "There's nothing but this."

Their mother, sipping from her waterskin, shook her head. "I don't know," she said. "I've only been to the Veil a few times. Things change, move around. Maybe there was once more here? Or maybe this is a reflection of something in the living world."

Lyric tentatively touched the stone. "Feels solid to me," she said.

"I also feel solid here," Runa said. Her lips quirked as Lyric looked at her, then her face changed, contorting, and she pressed a hand to her stomach. "Something's different," she said.

Their mother shoved her waterskin back into her pack and stepped up beside Runa. "What is it?" she asked, concerned. "What do you feel? Is it your body? Are we close?"

"Yes, but ..." Runa paused, cocking her head to the side. "It's almost like it's ... behind something. Like it's on the other side of ..." She made a reaching gesture, her fingers flaring.

Lyric blinked, and when she opened her eyes, they were somewhere else. She staggered, reaching out, her hand finding Kell's who'd moved towards her at the same moment. They grabbed onto each other, eyes meeting. Relief rushed through her.

It was strange to think that only a few days ago she hadn't known Kell existed. She hadn't expected to feel this way about someone, especially a man she didn't really know.

Abruptly Kell leaned away from her, looking uncomfortable, and dropped her hand. He turned, his attention purposefully shifting to their surroundings.

Lyric knew she didn't imagine Kell's interest or their connection. Why then, did he pull away from her? Why did he look afraid? *Focus*, Lyric told herself. She pulled her eyes off him.

They were standing in a long, dark hallway that seemed to stretch endlessly in both directions. It was wide enough that two of them could stand shoulder to shoulder without being pressed against the walls, which meant Kell, despite moving away, was still close enough to touch.

"That was disconcerting," Runa said.

For a moment Lyric thought her sister meant her and Kell. She blushed, her face growing hot before she realized Runa was looking at the walls and not at her.

*Of course she didn't mean me and Kell, stupid.*

"No wonder it felt like we were getting nowhere," their mother said. "The Sireni left your body in a reflection, like an image caught in a mirror. It follows you, but you never actually reach it."

Lyric studied the hallway, trying to understand what their mother was talking about. There were doors on either side, each a different color and material, and the handles varied as well. Some doors were stone, some wood, and some didn't even seem solid.

"Where do they all go?" she asked gesturing at a random door. "Do we open one? All of them?"

"That one," Runa said immediately. She pointed down the hall to a worn, wooden door.

Lyric shifted to stare past her sister. Green paint peeled off the wood, and the door was scoured in places as if once subjected to a harsh, sand-filled wind.

"They'll be waiting for us, won't they?" Lyric asked. "The Sireni? We can't just walk in."

Their mother nodded, her hand toying with her belt. "They know we're coming. They'll have someone guarding her."

"Can they feel us out here?" Kell asked. "In the hall?"

"I don't know," Elaina said. "Maybe, but I don't think so. This place is ... in-between."

Lyric flexed her hand, wishing she'd thought to break off one of the spindly branches from the trees she'd seen. Maybe she'd feel better if she had a club to hold on to. How would they protect themselves? Would the guards have knives? Would they use magic?

"They don't know me," Kell said. "I can go through the door first and try to distract them until you come in with Runa."

Elaina looked thoughtful. "Yes, that might work," she said. "You can act disoriented. Rush in like something is chasing you. Sometimes people dream themselves here, to the Veil."

"So after Kell goes in, we run in and I ... just touch my body?" Runa asked. "Will myself back together? It seems too simple."

"Your soul will want to return," their mother said.

"And this?" Runa asked, touching her chest where the runes were. "Will it prevent me from ... reuniting?"

"No," Elaina said.

Runa narrowed her eyes. "You know what these are, don't you?" she asked. "You started asking if I'd learned how to do something. Did I do this to myself?"

Their mother swallowed. She seemed resigned. "You must have unconsciously cast a spell when the Sireni tried to take you," she said. "You tried to flee, to go home or someplace safe, but you ended up shifting your soul away instead. I think you tried to go to Lyric." Her smile was proud but sad. "She's home to you."

"Are you saying we've been bound together?" Lyric asked.

"Yes. Runa's soul fled to you. I don't know how she did it," Elaina said. "Without training, without knowing the words …"

Runa frowned, her lips thin. "If it's a spell that did this to me then don't I need to know how to unravel it? Reverse it?"

"I'm not sure," Elaina said. "I don't think it'll be a barrier. Like I said, your soul wants to reunite with your body." Their mother scratched the back of her head. "However in case it's not that simple, I'll teach you the word for unraveling." Elaina spoke a rune word. It was a throaty sound, rough but also resonant, as though there was a sweeter tone caught within her voice as she spoke.

Lyric thought she could hear something echo, just on the edge of hearing, and she tilted her head to the side.

Runa repeated the word, a touch rougher than their mother had. She repeated it again, sounding clearer, more confident.

Elaina nodded, lips pressed together.

"What do we do after we follow Kell inside?" Lyric asked. She glanced at him, eyeing the staff in his hand. Could he defend himself? He didn't seem like a fighter, not like some of the men in Elae's Hollow.

Kell looked at her, maybe sensing her concern. His easy smile returned and Lyric, despite her frustration, smiled back. Why couldn't he make up his mind about her?

Lyric looked away, not wanting him to see her annoyance and confusion.

"Can you move us? Like before?" Runa asked. "If we jump in and then jump back out when we're done …"

"Ru!" Lyric said. "The last time Mama tried that, her arm caught fire!"

"To jump to us, yes," Runa said, "but it didn't seem as difficult when we came to the Veil."

"I can't," their mother said. "It's complicated to move like that, and using it consumed my prepared spell. I would have traveled on foot if I hadn't feared for your lives. I'd do anything for you, Runa, and Lyric. You're my world, the reason I'm fighting."

Runa gave their mother a flat look. "How did you bring us here then?"

"Sheer luck," Elaina said. "Our house is in an in-between place, like the Veil, existing on the edge of the prairie and the forest. Our realm, the living plane, is thinner there, allowing a person to slip across if they know what to look for."

Lyric wanted to ask their mother more about living in an in-between place, if Elaina had purposefully chosen their house, but she knew now was not the best time to indulge her curiosity. *Later, when we're safe*, she thought.

"What will we do after Runa gets her body back?" Lyric asked instead. Would they flee back into this strange hallway? Was there a thin spot somewhere where they could step out of the Veil?

Their mother rubbed the bridge of her nose. "It's easier to leave than it is to get inside the Veil," she said. "We have to open a window. Not a real one, more like a hole. It's not a difficult spell to return. I just need time to cast."

"Where will the window open?" Lyric asked. "Back in Kaliz?"

"No," Elaina said, shaking her head. "I can't control where we step out. We have to be ready. We may trade one fight for another."

Their mother glanced at Kell, who nodded.

"I'll be ready," Kell said.

"You know how to fight?" Lyric asked, looking at him.

Kell nodded, lips curving up at one corner. "My old master was a bit of a brawler. He insisted I make myself useful should a bar fight break out."

Lyric smiled, trying to imagine Kell scuffling with drunken men, then looked at Elaina. "And me?" she asked. "What should I do?" She had no weapon, and even if she did, she'd only ever used a knife for hunting and healing, never to kill a person. Lyric swallowed, worry souring her stomach.

Their mother looked at her consideringly, then smiled. "Lyric, remember how you elbowed Ilana Greenwich out of the way while playing hogsball at the Fall Harvest?"

Kell glanced at her, teeth flashing as he grinned wide, and Lyric flushed. "I was eight!" she said.

"If anyone gets close, use your elbows and feet," Elaina said. Despite her serious expression, her eyes twinkled with the memory. "But if they're using blades, don't fight. Run if you can, let them chase you. If they catch us, we can always escape, but I can't bring you back from the dead." Her hazel eyes flicked to Runa. "Not usually, anyway."

Lyric nodded and looked at her sister. Runa looked fierce, determined. Lyric doubted she'd let anything get in her way, and unlike the rest of them, Runa didn't have to fear injury.

"What if there's a lot of them?" Lyric asked. "What if that door opens onto the deck of a ship?"

"I think I can see what's inside without opening it," Elaina said. She walked up to the door and put her hand on the scoured wood. Closing her eyes, she raised her other hand, palm up, and began to softly speak in runes. A ghostly image appeared, growing stronger as their mother chanted until Lyric could see all four walls of a room. Appearing within the filmy, blue lines, were two pinpricks of light, one stationery beside the door, and another, moving around the opposite edge.

Elaina, sweat beading on her brow, stopped speaking and opened her eyes, studying the hovering image. The room's outline lingered for several breaths, then faded entirely from view. Their mother stepped back, putting distance between her and the door.

"That's incredible," Runa said. Her eyes had lightened, curiosity softening her face.

"Two people are in the room?" Lyric asked, hazarding a guess about the pinpricks of light. "Could you tell where Runa's body is? Was it the dot beside the door?"

"No," Elaina said, "that's likely a Sireni guarding the entrance. I'd guess they've placed her somewhere away from the door, against the far wall."

"Do you think there's another entrance or exit?" Runa asked. "It makes sense to have an escape route if someone comes through the front door."

"Maybe they don't want to flee," Lyric said.

"I think they'll try to trap us as quickly as possible," Elaina said. She looked down at her belt, examining the round bottles. "They're unlikely to attack Kell until they know who he is. That gives us time to surprise them."

"What are those?" Runa asked, pointing at their mother's belt.

Elaina glanced up, her fingers stilling atop one pale green orb. "Captured spells," she said. Her reticence returned, humming through her voice.

"Like the light spell?" Runa asked. "Something you can prepare and use later?"

"Yes, though these are one use. Held spells don't require energy to keep them alive. The glass is spelled to hold them in stasis. Now if we—"

"What do you have?" Runa asked.

Their mother pursed her lips. "Wind, a powerful flash of light, and a web spell ... it makes the floor sticky, trapping you in place."

"You don't always have to prepare spells though," Lyric said thoughtfully. "Like with that old woman. You chanted and created fire."

"Yes," Elaina said, "but that's slower."

"What happens if you break one while it's on your belt?" Runa asked.

"Nothing good," their mother said. "Now, our plan. The longer we stay out here—"

"Right," Runa said. "Kell will go in and then?"

"Kell, try to draw them away from the door," Elaina said. "Do whatever you have to."

Kell nodded, his eyes considering.

"Try to yell where Runa's body is in the room. Maybe you can keep the door from latching?"

"I'll try," Kell said. "I can't be too careful with the door if I want them to believe I'm being chased."

Elaina nodded. "I'll use my web spell, hopefully trapping them." She tapped her belt. "Runa, go straight to your body. We'll try to buy you time. Once it's done, we'll escape through the window. I'll have to open it shortly after we go in, so we don't have to wait around for it."

"Kell and I will protect you," Lyric said, "while you cast." She licked her lips. She wasn't entirely sure how she'd do that. She didn't have a weapon like Kell. No, that wasn't true. She knew the rune word for wind. Lyric narrowed her eyes, recalling the pronunciation of the word Gandara had given her. Would it work?

Elaina glanced at her, her mouth opening. Her eyes darkened, and she looked down at her hands, not saying whatever it was that'd been on her tongue.

"All right," Kell said. He leaned his staff against his chest and rolled his shoulders and shook his arms, as though preparing to step out onto a stage.

Worried, Lyric caught his eye, and Kell smiled reassuringly, just for her.

Shifting his staff back into his left hand, Kell contorted his face into an expression of panic and wrenched open the door. He rushed inside, his scream echoing out to them in the hall as the door swung closed. It thumped against something, maybe his heel, and didn't latch.

Elaina, Lyric, and Runa crowded close around the edge of the door, listening to the muffled sounds filtering out.

Lyric's heart thumped inside her chest and she swallowed anxiously. Sweat damped her dress. What if this failed? What if they captured Kell, captured all of them? What if they killed Kell? What if—

"Oh thank the gods!" she heard Kell say. "No, no, no, don't open the door! It's out there, some kind of monster. I ran, oh gods, it was horrible. I thought it would — but here you are!"

Kell's voice trailed off, and Lyric heard a man reply, but she couldn't make out his words.

"Look at this room!" Kell shouted. "No windows, that's good. Who's that in the corner? Is she ok? Oh gods, did the monster get her?"

"Good," Elaina said, looking at Runa. "Your body's in a corner. Run there right away, as soon as we go in."

Runa nodded curtly, her body tensed, ready. "He's a terrible actor," she said, half joking.

Lyric laughed breathlessly.

"Oh gods, you're one of them! You're—" Kell's voice cut off, and they heard a loud thump, then the muffled sounds of feet scuffling across the floor.

"Now!" their mother hissed. She wrenched open the door, and Runa ran past her.

Elaina charged into the room, Lyric on her heels. Heart in her throat, Lyric scanned the room. It was the size of a large bedroom, mostly empty of furniture, with a chaise in the corner. Someone was lying on it.

Kell was fighting two men, his staff knocking one in the stomach. The man stumbled back and growled angrily.

The second man grabbed the end of Kell's staff and yanked, slamming his fist into Kell's face.

Lyric gasped and her hand flew out reflexively.

Elaina moved in front of her, tossing the green orb from her belt at the man who Kell had knocked away. The man had seen them and was approaching fast.

The bottle shattered and something splattered at the man's feet, tangling his legs. White strands shot up from the ground and spread across his body like a quickly growing spiderweb.

Lyric's eyes bounced from the trapped man to Kell. He staggered back, the tall man he'd been fighting with coming at him again, fists raised, voice roaring from his throat. He was speaking a spell.

Joining him, the trapped man began to cast. His mouth opened, eyes small and angry and a shriek ripped from his throat, building in the air.

Lyric staggered against their mother, the bones vibrating inside her skull. The ground shuddered beneath her feet, the start of an earthquake.

Elaina hissed something beside her, rune words tumbling from her lips too quick to follow.

Bracing herself against their mother's back, Lyric looked again for Kell. He was bent forward, holding his head, his staff dropped from his fingers. The Sireni man approached him, his hand reaching out, and his voice rising with purpose.

*No!* Lyric thought. She whispered the word for wind and felt nothing. She whispered it again, urgently, prayerfully. *Help me!* she thought, calling for Gandara and not finding her.

She whispered again and again until something shifted inside. It was tentative, quiet, as if asking permission to move through her. It was like the wind, like water, a flow of something incomprehensible, something beautiful. Lyric opened herself to it, letting it flood her body.

Power flared in her stomach, warm and incredible. Lyric gasped as it unspooled. It felt like sunlight on the prairie back home as it rose up through her chest, her throat, and out her fingers. She could touch it. She could *use* it.

Lyric fell silent and her hair lifted as if caught in a breeze. The air gathered around her, slipping from her lungs, thickening and pressing against her like a solid thing. She couldn't breathe. Panic clawed its way up her throat. She was going to suffocate. She was going to—

She breathed out.

The wind rushed away from her, splitting into two currents as it raced towards both of the Sireni.

The man approaching Kell was thrown sideways, his body smacking against the wall.

The trapped man bent backward, unable to fall, as the wind filled his mouth and cut off his casting. Something snapped in his leg and his face went white.

The bone-rattling shrieks stopped. The shaking cut off.

Elaina yelled, and a window appeared at the back of the room, hovering above the floor — a hole in the Veil.

Lyric's eyes snapped towards it and she gasped, something shimmered beyond the opening as it rippled like a wind-touched pool. Was that a beach on the other side?

She looked sideways to the chaise. Runa was sitting up and swinging her legs off onto the ground. Her sister blinked, looking up, meeting Lyric's wide eyes, then she gasped and vomited onto the floor.

"Move!" Elaina hissed, shoving Lyric forward.

Lyric stumbled, looking to her right at Kell, past the disoriented Sireni man bent backward. Kell was standing again, moving unsteadily, staring at the man Lyric had thrown against the wall.

*I did that*, Lyric thought with shock, her legs slowing.

"Lyric!" Elaina yelled, desperation coloring her voice.

Lyric blinked. She had to get Kell's attention. He hadn't seen the window. "Kell!" she yelled.

Kell looked at her, and the man between them, turning his head as Lyric pointed at the window. Nodding, Kell shuffled forward, holding his right arm and leaving his staff on the floor.

Lyric ran towards the window.

Breaking free from Elaina's trap, the Sireni man watched Lyric as she ran past. He clutched at his leg, dragging it forward.

Elaina reached Runa and grabbed her arm. She scooped Runa's pack off the floor and hauled her towards the window. Her eyes met Lyric's and she nodded, then tumbled backward through the opening, carrying Runa with her.

Lyric stopped at the window and hesitated, looking sideways for Kell.

"Here!" he gasped, reaching for her.

The Sireni man lurched forward, trying to catch Kell's ankle, and Kell kicked his hand away.

Grabbing Lyric's waist, Kell stared into her face, breathing hard. His eye was starting to blacken and blood trickled from his nose.

"Stop!" one of the men yelled. The second man, the one Lyric had thrown into the wall was standing, staggering towards them.

The man with the injured leg started chanting.

Lyric grabbed a handful of Kell's shirt and jumped through the hole in the air. It was like being submerged in a deep pool of ice-cold water. She was falling, floating, drowning. She tightened her hand on Kell, felt the fabric twist between her fingers, and then her shoulder slammed down into sand.

# 9

RUNA

PAIN EXPLODED through Runa's head, and she closed her eyes, throwing an arm over her face to shield herself from the light. She cracked open an eyelid, tears leaking down her face into her hair, and tried to focus on the brilliance above her. There was something against her back, soft but firm, shifting as she moved. Eyes finally focusing, Runa realized she was looking into the sun. She gaped; the sky was an unbelievable shade of dazzling blue.

Someone moved next to her, and Runa tilted her head to the side, still shading her eyes. It was their mother, shoving herself upright, her hand pushing against the sand.

Runa watched as she stood, swaying unsteadily. Elaina raised her hand, facing the opening in the air. *The Veil!* Runa thought. *I was falling and—*

Lyric and Kell tumbled through the rippling hole and slammed against the sand.

Gasping, Runa pulled her legs away, scrambling up. She swayed, waves of nausea bringing tears to her eyes. Her body felt unfamiliar, sluggish. She could see inside the window and the room beyond. The faces of the Sireni men were angry and coming closer. The unsettling weight of their magic flared out, the scream trying to break inside Runa's head.

Grabbing something off her belt, Elaina lobbed it through the opening. Light exploded, blinding Runa, and she cried out, shielding her eyes as black spots danced across her vision.

Elaina shouted the mage rune for unraveling, the same one she'd taught Runa before they'd rushed into the room.

There was an audible crack, loud and final, and the pressure vanished. The Sireni's shouts cut off, and silence fell, heavy as a blanket. Sound slowly returned to Runa's ears, her own tired gasps and a groan from someone nearby.

Runa lowered her hand and cautiously opened her eyes, letting awareness flare out around her. Their breathing was not the only sound here; she could hear the rush of water. Squinting past their mother, now bent forward, hands on her knees, Runa saw a massive expanse of water stretching away from them. Was it a lake? Where was the opposite shore? She watched white-foamed water surge onto black sand, the sand beneath her feet.

No, this was an ocean, wasn't it? She'd never seen one before, but she'd heard about the Sea of Screams on Erith's eastern edge and Hebaria's Heart in the west. Which one was this?

A gull cried somewhere high overhead, and Runa looked into the sky, wincing as light stabbed down into her skull. Everything was too intense, too vivid. It felt like she'd never been inside her own body before, never used her eyes.

Runa wiped her mouth with the back of her hand, the sour taste of bile in her mouth. She spat onto the sand and wished for water. She couldn't drink the sea, could she?

Lyric, lying on her side a short distance from Runa, sat up with a groan and reached out to Kell who was lying beside her. They helped each other stand.

"It's gone," Lyric said, looking down the beach.

Elaina waved a hand. "I closed it." She sounded exhausted and sat down as Runa watched, her legs crumpling beneath her. "I just need a minute," their mother said, breathing in and out.

"I thought they were going to follow us through," Lyric said. Her voice was shaky, uncertain. "My eyeballs were vibrating in my skull."

"We're safe, for now," Elaina said. "They won't know which beach we're on." She didn't sound certain.

Runa straightened, eyes still narrowed, her lids attempting to block out the light. She looked around. Black sand stretched out of sight in both directions, and mounded into dunes to her right, speckled with silvery clumps of long, thin grass. Beyond the dunes spread watery marshland that rolled to the far, dark edge of a forest. At least that's what Runa thought the green smudge was in the distance.

She was staring west, wasn't she? If so, then this was the Sea of Screams.

"Where are we?" Lyric asked. She had an arm around Kell's waist.

Runa eyed Kell's face. There was a bruise on his jaw, and one eye was turning black. He must have fought the men in the room. She hadn't seen it herself; she'd barely seen anything at all but the shape of her body lying on the chaise.

Kell was staring past her up the coast. He seemed disquieted, his face drained of color.

"We're in Thenda," Kell said, his voice thin. He held onto Lyric, as though afraid she'd drift away, and reached up to the tattoo around his throat. It shifted in color and he swallowed, pain crossing his face.

Runa blinked. Had she seen Kell's tattoo move?

"The Tainted Shore?" Lyric asked, breathing the words.

Runa looked away from Kell's throat to the north. She didn't see anything foreboding, just black sand stretching away from them.

"We have to cross it to get to Raendashar?" Lyric asked.

Elaina stood up, her movements slow, tired. "We can head south," she said, "to Oleporea. We'll regroup. Decide what to do."

Kell looked at her, a frown creasing the skin between his brows.

"We need to go to Rathgar's Hold," Lyric said. "You promised Kell."

"The books will still be there if we take time to rest," Elaina said.

Lyric narrowed her eyes and straightened, looking determined. "We already discussed this, Mama," she said.

Runa's chin lifted proudly as Lyric faced their mother. *Yes,* she thought. *You won't control us. You won't tell us what to do.*

Elaina sighed, her eyes moving between Lyric and Runa. "Your grandfather is not going to welcome you with open arms. There will be no cozy reunion, no celebration in your honor, no loving meeting of family. Going there, to *him*, means giving up your lives, your freedom."

"You don't know that, Mama," Lyric said. She put her hand on Kell's chest, possessively. "We're going to help Kell, and we're going to talk to Grandfather."

Their mother's eyes shifted to Runa, hopeful and pleading.

"I don't care if I meet your father or not. Sorry, Lyric," Runa said, "but I don't want this war hanging over our heads, controlling what we do, shaping our lives. I want to be free of it, and that means getting involved."

Elaina swore and turned away, scrubbing a hand through her hair. She stared at the ocean for a long moment. Back straightening, their mother faced them, her hair blazing like fire in the sun. She didn't look defeated.

"Let me first take you to a friend, your uncle Eleden," Elaina said. "He's Sireni, but he'll help us. He can get us to Rathgar's Hold safely."

Runa exchanged glances with Lyric. She didn't like feeling hunted. Maybe their uncle could offer protection against the Sireni chasing them. Going south couldn't hurt. "All right," she said, seeing agreement in her sister's eyes. "Where is he?"

"We can contact him from Yanessa," their mother said. "It's a port town south of us, on Oleporea's border." She looked at Kell. "I will still honor our agreement, but I won't put my daughters in undue danger. You can continue, if you wish, and we'll meet you there. You don't have to stay with us." Her eyes flickered coldly. Was she mad at Kell? "I don't need you to watch over them anymore."

Kell looked repentant, shoulders slumping. "I'll stay with you," he said.

Lyric flushed, a pleased glow in her eyes.

Looking at Lyric, Elaina's mouth tightened, but she said nothing. Did she disapprove of their interest in each other? Why?

Their mother bent and picked up Runa's pack, holding it out. Runa took it reflexively, momentarily overwhelmed by sensation as she felt the rough strap slid against her skin. She looked up as she slipped the pack onto her shoulder and found their mother staring at her.

"How do you feel?" Elaina asked.

"Fine," Runa said.

Their mother raised an eyebrow. "Fine?"

Runa flushed, feeling petulant. Annoyed with her own emotion, she held their mother's gaze despite the heat in her face. "Everything feels new and overwhelming."

Elaina nodded. "Did you unravel your spell before joining your body?"

"No," Runa said. She thought back to how it'd felt, the faint but persistent pull towards herself, the strangeness of staring at her own face, devoid of life, of expression. She'd wanted to abandon her body and drift away, though she was unsure to where or why. Runa didn't know where the desire had come from. She *wanted* to be alive, didn't she?

Runa shoved aside the question. Of course, she did. She was young, had barely experienced anything at all. Her life could not be over yet, not before she did something important, something meaningful. Not before she was powerful, strong. Besides, Runa couldn't leave Lyric now, not while she was vulnerable.

And what about the Daughters and their mysterious omen? Had they meant Lyric or Kell? Runa had always believed there was truth in the old stories, in the gods and creatures who'd shaped their world. She'd offered prayers like everyone else, shown respect in case the Trinity was still watching and meddling unseen.

However, unlike Lyric, she'd always thought the gods weren't interested in Erith anymore. That they'd abandoned them, had walked away, just like Elaina. But their mother had come back.

Runa chewed on her lip, considering. What if the gods weren't as far away as everyone thought? What if they lurked out of sight, like the Daughters in the Veil?

"Do we follow the beach?" Lyric asked, drawing Runa back to the present.

"Yes," Elaina said. "There's a well-traveled road west of us, on the other side of the marshlands, but unfortunately we can't reach it." She gestured at the bog, visible through a gap in the dunes. It looked like a maze of reed-spiked mounds, treacherous islands surrounded by black water. As Runa watched, the water rippled near a rise nearby, something long and scaled sliding into the inky slough.

"We'll have to keep to the sand," their mother said. "Sleep

under the stars. Yanessa can't be more than a day or two." She glanced at Kell, who nodded.

"I don't recognize exactly where we are," he said, "but the water and beach are clean, free of the Taint, so we must be close to Thenda's southern border."

"What does it look like?" Lyric asked. "The Taint?"

"Green," Elaina said. "It glows, pulsing like stars are trapped inside. There's nothing natural about it. You'll know it when you see it."

The Daughters of Valen came to Runa's mind, and she recalled how their runes glinted green on their arms. Were they poisoned in some way? Like the Shore? Was that even possible? For an immortal being to be infected?

"If you see it," Kell said, "don't touch it." His eyes were serious, haunted. "Don't touch the water or anything that's come in contact with it."

"Thankfully we don't have to worry about that," Elaina said. "Once in Yanessa, we can join the Northern Road or sail north on Eleden's ship."

She set down her pack and rummaged inside. Examining her water, their mother unwrapped the cheese and dried meat and removed a single apple from her bag. She dumped all three on the ground. "Everything is spoiled," Elaina said. "Check your bags and dump any food you have left."

Curiously, Runa pulled her bag off her shoulder and opened it, looking at her untouched food. Everything was tinted purple. Her stomach flipped, the skin prickling on the back of her neck. Turning her bag out, she dropped it all without touching it. "Mine too," she said.

"We're out of food?" Lyric asked. "We're also low on water." She went silent, and Runa glanced at her. Lyric had stepped away from Kell and was staring west. Her lips moved, and she mumbled inaudibly, then nodded.

Runa raised an eyebrow.

"I think I can help," Lyric said, smiling. "Gandara just told me a spell to strip salt from seawater." Her brow furrowed as she looked at the ocean. "Are we sure the water's safe here? Free from the Taint, I mean?"

"Yes," Kell said, following Lyric's gaze. "If the Taint were here you'd see and smell it. We should fish and try to catch crabs before we head south. We won't be able to buy food until Yanessa."

"I agree," Elaina said grudgingly.

"Elenora?" Runa asked softly, looking around. If Lyric was being spoken to by their ancestor outside the Veil, then Elenora might be nearby too. She disliked the hawk-eyed woman's apparent ability to appear unannounced and unwanted, but Runa wanted to ask her, no *demand*, what had happened with the fire rune. Had it been a test? A cruel trick? Had Elenora expected her to fail?

"Elenora?" Runa repeated.

Elenora didn't answer or appear, and Runa, having nothing to direct her anger at, glared at the ocean.

Kell set down his pack beside Elaina. They began debating the best way to fish in the shallow water off the beach.

Lyric gathered up their waterskins and carried them to the ocean. She stopped just shy of the rolling sea and dropping them onto the sand, pulled off her boots and stockings, then tied up her dress to keep it from getting wet. Her ankles were pale in contrast to the black sand, and she stepped into the surf, gasping and giggling as the water rushed across her feet.

"Ru! You've got to feel this!" Lyric called over her shoulder.

Despite her mood, Runa had to admit her curiosity. She stripped off her boots, tying her dress up like her sister, then walked to the edge of the water. Hesitating for only a moment, she walked onto the wet sand, toward the approaching waves.

Water rushed her, foaming and tumbling. Runa gasped as it hit her skin, insistent as it swirled around her feet and calves.

The cold was exhilarating, refreshing. Arms lifting by her sides, she lifted her chin and let the sunlight warm her face. It felt wonderful.

"Hold this?" Lyric asked.

Runa opened her eyes, looking down, as Lyric shoved two waterskins into her hands. Her sister bent over, filling her own with water, then traded it for the others. Once she'd refilled them all, Lyric smiled at Runa and carried the waterskins back to the beach.

Twisting at the waist, Runa watched her sister kneel on the sand, away from the tide's reach. She didn't want to leave the water. Not yet. She listened, feet sinking into the wet sand beneath her, as Lyric spoke several runes over the waterskins. Following her sister's words, a sensation brushed across Runa's skin, like the tickle from an unseen feather.

Lyric held a waterskin to her mouth and sipped. "It's fresh!" she exclaimed, holding it up triumphantly. "We have water!"

Kell cheered, and Elaina smiled, clapping her hands.

Runa, feeling cold, turned back to the ocean. Why did magic work for Lyric, but not her? Was she doing something wrong? Jealousy soured her stomach, and Runa crossed her arms. She tried to ignore it and be happy for her sister's success. It was good what Lyric had done. It was amazing. And yet ...

Scowling, Runa stepped out of the water. Maybe the magic didn't work because she'd been close to real death. What if returning her soul to her body had broken the connection, and it'd never work for her now.

Trying to distract herself and hide her face from Lyric, Runa wandered towards Kell. He'd collected driftwood with their mother and fashioned several spears, sharpening them with a knife he'd procured from somewhere. He'd also woven a fishing pouch to tie to his waist, and started on a large basket.

"Here," Kell said, catching Runa's eye as she drew close. He gave her a handful of rockweed ropes. "I was about to show Elaina how to weave crab baskets. Do you want to help?"

Nodding curtly, Runa took the offered strips of rockweed and watched Kell as he demonstrated how to make the baskets. She was familiar with weaving, and Kell's method was quite similar to hers. The rockweed was slicker than the dried reeds she'd used, but her fingers found the rhythm quickly.

"Normally I'd bait the baskets with pieces of meat," Kell said. He glanced at their discarded food. "Maybe we'll be lucky, and something will wander into one."

He showed them how to attach floats, for marking the baskets' locations, using the leathery, orb-shaped bladders from large fronds of seaweed washed up on the beach.

Lyric came over, having set their waterskins down near their packs, and she helped them carry the baskets into the water. They waded out as far as they could and buried the baskets along a chain of submerged rocks.

Kell waded back to the shore and tied a rockweed pouch to his belt then retrieved the spears. He offered one to Runa, who took it.

She rubbed her fingers over the coarse wood. She'd never used a spear before, though she supposed it was like a pitchfork. She hefted it in one hand. There was no heavy end to unbalance it; the wooden spear was light and mobile. Runa expected that if she threw it, it'd sail far before hitting the ground.

Runa watched Kell as he fished, studying how his body stilled as he stared into the water. He looked poised yet loose, like a cat waiting to pounce.

Kell thrust suddenly with his spear, pulling it from the water with a silvery fish impaled on its end. Grinning, he held it up and looked at Lyric, who smiled. Jubilant, Kell tucked the fish into his waist pouch. He stabbed his spear back into the water and caught another fish and another, quickly outpacing them all.

Runa glanced at Lyric and Elaina. Compared to Kell, their movements were inelegant and clumsy. Kell was fluid and relaxed as though a childhood memory had returned, guiding him. Fascinated but also annoyed at his success, Runa looked at her feet. She could see her toes pale beneath the water, grains of dark sand pushing up between them. She looked for a flash of silver, a sign that a fish was nearby, but nothing swam close.

"You must have fished this way hundreds of times as a child!" Lyric called out to Kell.

Runa kept her eyes down, watching for fish, glaring at the empty water as it swirled cold and hungry around her knees. When one finally came, she was so surprised that she almost stabbed her foot. She cursed, splashing, and the fish darted away. Runa tried several more times without success. Luck, it seemed wouldn't favor her today.

"Ru! Let's go in," Lyric called.

Looking up, Runa saw the sun had sunk halfway into the ocean, delineating the horizon with a glowing line of orange. She hadn't noticed the light slipping away.

Lifting the spear onto her shoulder, Runa ground her teeth and followed Lyric and Kell back to the beach. Elaina must have given up a while ago since she was sitting next to a fire.

Lyric bounded towards their mother, excitedly holding up a fish she'd caught. She turned to Kell, proud of his success and together they showed Elaina his filled pouch.

"Look at this!" Lyric said as Runa walked up to the firelight. Lyric gestured as Kell emptied the fish into a basket beside Elaina. "Look how many Kell caught! It was like magic."

"No magic," Kell said, laughing. "Just luck."

"No," Lyric said, shaking her head. "You have your own magic." She grinned at him, bright and foolish.

Annoyed for some unclear reason, Runa stabbed her spear

into the sand and sat down beside the fire. Her irritation grew as their mother gave her a thoughtful look. *You don't know what I'm thinking*, Runa thought childishly.

"Well done, Kell," Elaina said. Her smile didn't quite reach her eyes. "We have food for our journey now." She grabbed a piece of dried seaweed and chewed it, reaching for a stick to poke at the fire. "We can cook the fish on the spits," she said, spreading out the hot coals and gesturing at several thin pieces of sharpened driftwood.

"You've been busy!" Lyric said.

"Yes, I admit fishing isn't something I particularly enjoy," Elaina said, smiling. "I'm quite good at carving though!" She held up a sharp stick. "Kell, maybe if you could—"

"Sure," Kell said. He held out his hand, and Elaina passed him her knife.

Kneeling, Kell grabbed a fish and swiftly killed it with the butt of the knife. He gutted it, then passed the prepared fish to Lyric, who slid it onto a skewer.

Runa, shoving aside her dark mood, held out a hand for another fish and mirrored Lyric's movements. She glanced at Elaina, still chewing seaweed. Had their mother suddenly become squeamish about cooking meat? Runa remembered her killing and dressing rabbits, though Elaina had taught her and Lyric to do it themselves when they were quite small. Maybe her aversion had always been there, and Runa had never been aware of it.

Was Runa too hard on their mother for leaving? She'd raised them to be strong and self-reliant and encouraged their independence. That was good, wasn't it? Or had she sought to prepare them for eventual abandonment? Maybe Elaina never wanted children and resented being trapped in their little valley.

Runa's mood soured again, and she stabbed the fish-laden spit into the sand. She leaned forward, forearms across her knees, and drew in a heated breath from the fire.

"Why are you chewing sea lettuce, Mama?" Lyric asked suddenly.

"The seaweed will replenish my blood," Elaina said. "Magic drains you, remember?" She sighed. "If you're going to practice magic, I suggest drying some yourself and carrying it with you. Seaweed's easier to get than red meat, especially here by the ocean. The stalk is tough; you'll need to strip the leaves."

Runa glanced at Elaina. *Something to remember,* she thought. Despite her troubles with magic, she wasn't ready to give up.

Eventually, all the fish were gutted and cooking over the fire. Lyric passed around the waterskins, and everyone took a tentative sip of the purified water, marveling at the taste. Runa had tasted the sea when a wave splashed into her face, and she was relieved that Lyric's water was fresh and not brackish.

"An invaluable spell," Elaina said. "You can't drink the sea. Too much salt."

"Have you used this spell before?" Lyric asked.

Elaina shook her head. "I've never had need before. If I had to, I could cobble something together with the runes I know, but that's always risky." She paled as if she regretted what she'd said. Throat clearing, Elaina shifted one of the spits over the fire.

Runa studied their mother curiously, thinking about her words. You could create your own spells? What else was possible? Irritation still crackled along her jaw like a toothache that wouldn't go away, so despite her desire to know more, Runa kept her thoughts to herself.

After a while, everyone lapsed into a comfortable silence, listening to the crackle of the fire and inhaling the scent of cooking meat. Elaina and Kell turned the spits, making sure both sides of the fish browned equally until finally, Kell declared them done and removed them from the coals.

Together they separated the fish they'd prep for travel, then each took one fish for their evening meal.

The sun had disappeared into the sea by the time they started eating and night unfurled, deep and dark overhead. Elaina added more driftwood to the fire, bringing it back to life and sending sparks up into the sky, drawing Runa's eyes up to the tiny stars appearing above.

Runa, biting into her fish, stared upward. She'd always loved the night and how the world hushed as if in collective reverence for the evening's beauty. Finding a familiar constellation, she followed the outline of a great bear with her eyes, smiling as she remembered the stories their mother had told her and Lyric as children.

"You should sing for us!" Lyric said, pulling Runa from her memories.

Regretfully Runa looked at Kell. He'd finished his fish and was leaning back on his elbows. His face glowed in the firelight and specks of light reflected in his eyes. "You wish a song?" he asked, beaming as if Lyric had just told him he was extraordinary.

"I heard you humming songs while we were in the Veil," Lyric said, smiling. She leaned next to him in a familiar way, skirted legs tucked to the side. "Come on. We have to know if you're good or not. If you truly earned that emerald pin of yours."

Kell laughed and looked up, considering the stars.

Finishing her fish, Runa wiped her hands, then wrapped her arms around her knees. She couldn't remember the last time she'd listened to someone sing, apart from Lyric.

"Hmm what should I tell you?" Kell asked. "A story of the stars? A story of a sea nymph who dreamed of land?"

"Dragons," Runa said. She clenched her teeth as everyone looked at her in surprise. She hadn't planned on speaking, but the idea had popped into her head unbidden.

"Dragons," Kell said. "Perhaps a song about the Three?"

Clearing his throat, Kell started singing a scale, each tone clear and beautiful.

Runa straightened, leaning towards him, drawn forward by his voice. Scenes arose in her mind with each entrancing note. She could see endless fields, castles of glass, towering mountains and birds soaring free in sun-lit skies. Runa's skin prickled, and she resisted the urge to run her hand down her arm.

Lyric, eyes rapturous, leaned towards Kell, her hand mere inches from his leg in the sand. It was like she was caught in a tide like Runa.

Kell's voice trailed off, and Runa blinked, rocking back again as if a tether had been gently let go.

Crossing his legs, Kell passed his eyes over each of them in turn. He seemed unaware of his effect on them. Drawing breath into his lungs, Kell began to sing:

> *"Lords of sky, earth, and fire,*
> *Lords of wing and claw.*
> *Arbiters of Erith, holders of peace,*
> *The last of Mother's blood.*
> *Pale as snow, black as night's stone,*
> *Red like the fire that'll cleanse all.*
> *Bloodied, challenged, scarred from battle,*
> *They hold back the poisoned tide.*
> *Binding and slaying our demon invaders*
> *Setting the world alight.*
> *Weary and fading, They pass us the mantle*
> *Trusting we'll keep towards the light.*
> *Old grudges flare as They pass into slumber,*
> *War once more rolls across the land.*
> *No longer guarded by divine creators,*
> *We're now free to inspire or fall.*
> *Eyes turned away; the Lords wait in shadow,*

*Dreaming until called forth again.*
*Though distant and sleeping,*
*They'll return to preserve us,*
*Ever the guardians of Man.*
*Lords of sky, earth, and fire,*
*Lords of wing and claw.*
*Eyes turned away; the Lords wait in shadow,*
*Waiting to return to Erith's light."*

Runa took a deep, shuddering breath as Kell's voice echoed and faded in the darkness. She hadn't realized she'd stopped breathing. She stared at Kell, trying to reconcile the youthfulness of his face with the power and magic of his voice. There'd been a presence while he sang, as though something big and unknowable, something celestial, had turned its eye upon them to listen.

The heavy awareness slipped away as Runa sucked another breath into her lungs, and she glanced over her shoulder, half expecting to see something there. All she saw were the dark waves, glinting with moonlight and lapping against the sand.

"That was beautiful," Lyric cooed. "Your voice ... honestly, you could have sung about folding laundry, and I still would have been mesmerized." She grinned, hair falling over one cheek.

"I suppose that's good?" Kell asked, laughing.

Runa was surprised that she didn't feel compelled to roll her eyes or make a snide remark. She agreed with Lyric; Kell's voice was something rare. She studied him appraisingly. He was pretty, that was true, but she hadn't expected such a powerful singing voice could exist in someone so young. There was something old about how he sang as if he'd had centuries of study. Obviously, he'd been instructed well in the Radiant Hall, but his voice was not pure training alone. Kell had been born with this understanding of music.

"It was beautiful," Runa said, drawing Kell's eyes.

"Thank you," Kell said, looking surprised.

"I wonder what would make the Old Ones return," Lyric said. "They didn't come when Thenda disappeared. What are they waiting for? Are they waiting? Or was their promise to our ancestors a departing kindness and nothing more, like a parent on their deathbed telling a child they'll see them again, will always be with them."

Runa glanced at Elaina before she could stop herself. Their mother was staring at her, her eyes hurt, regretful, and before Runa could unravel what she saw, Elaina turned her head away and reached for something besides her knee. Her hair swooped over her face, and she took a slow, controlled breath.

"It was a beautiful song, Kell," Elaina said.

Was there a slight tremor in her voice?

"Thank you, Mar— Elaina," he said.

"Serith wasn't mentioned at all," Lyric said. "Is it a Raendasharan song?"

Kell nodded. "Bethsin Amera composed it a hundred years ago. She was a favored songsmith of the Scorched Court, and likely sought to avoid ruffling any royal feathers."

"We should sleep," Elaina said. "Rest for tomorrow. If we're lucky, tomorrow night we'll be in an inn in Yanessa."

"Should we keep watch tonight?" Lyric asked. "In case the Sireni come?"

Runa opened her mouth to volunteer, but their mother beat her to it.

"I'll do it," Elaina said. "I need to wrap the fish for our journey."

Deciding not to argue, Runa shifted the sand around to form a comfortable hollow for her body, and laid down.

"All right, wake me next," Lyric said. She joined Runa on her side of the fire and laid down, head lolling against Runa's shoulder just like she did back home.

Wrapped in her cloak, head pillowed on the sand, Runa stared up at the sky and thought about dragons. Her mind churned as she wondered where they'd gone and why. She wondered if they'd really come back, and what would happen if they did. No one living had seen a dragon, and she couldn't imagine the kings and queens being happy about relinquishing their authority again.

When Runa finally fell asleep, it was to the sound of Lyric's even breathing as dragons soared and bellowed fire inside her mind.

RUNA WOKE FEELING UNEASY. There'd been no surprises during the night, no attack from the Sireni Screamers, nothing alarming at all, and yet Runa's stomach felt sour and uncertain. She'd dreamed of creatures, big like dragons, flying over them in the dark. She'd dreamed of claws and blood and screams. She'd dreamed of Lyric dead, and their mother missing.

*Dark thoughts for a beautiful morning,* Runa thought, eyeing the cloudless sky.

Kell, having woke first, had found clams and a green plant he called sea grapes that looked like tiny spheres. He'd checked the crab baskets and said something destroyed them in the night, shredding them to pieces. "Probably just an angry Sawmouth fish," Kell said, shrugging one shoulder. Runa wasn't sure she believed him but didn't challenge him, as she certainly wasn't an expert on marine life.

Breakfast was simple and salty — roasted fish, raw pieces of clam meat, sea grapes and dried seaweed, washed down with purified water. The sea grapes popped as Runa chewed. She liked their peppery flavor.

After eating and attending to their individual needs, Elaina and Kell poured water on the coals of the fire, and everyone gathered up their packs.

Kell and Lyric hung back, letting Runa and Elaina take the lead.

Runa found herself side by side with their mother, but thankfully she wasn't talkative, her head turning back towards Lyric and Kell as they followed the coastline south.

Behind them, Kell and Lyric carried on a rambling conversation as the sun climbed higher and higher into the sky. The clouds were relatively thin, the blue sky peeking through, and Runa soon grew warm enough to remove her cloak.

Glancing towards the ocean on her left, Runa glimpsed a sleek, gray animal bobbing in the waves. She thought she saw a whiskered snout before it slipped beneath the water, flipping a large spotted tail into the air as it dove. An ocean bird sang to her overhead, and Runa watched it, wishing she knew its name. She was grateful for the distraction.

"Why didn't anyone move down here after the Thendian cities were destroyed?" Runa asked aloud.

"I'm not sure," Elaina answered.

Kell, who might have known, didn't seem to have heard her. He was laughing at something Lyric said.

"Perhaps," Elaina said distractedly, looking back, "it's because of the dunes here, to the west." She gestured at the mounds of sand. "Farther north, the Thendians carved their cities into the cliffs. They wouldn't be able to do that down here."

"But if they were fleeing for their lives, why not camp here?" Runa asked. "Or build a hut? There's fish in the water and relative safety. It seems like a place they could have resettled."

"Not many survived the destruction," Elaina said. "Maybe the survivors didn't want to stay near the Shore." She shook her head. "I don't know. Maybe there's another reason. You can ask Kell."

"Yes," Runa said absently.

"Has she spoken to you again?" Elaina asked.

"What?" Runa blinked and looked at their mother, not understanding.

"The ancestor who speaks to you."

"Oh ... no," Runa said. Her face pinched and she looked ahead, not wanting Elaina to see her expression.

"You tried to do something with fire, when the Flesh Eater came," Elaina said. "It didn't work?"

"No, was I saying it wrong?"

Elaina hesitated. "No, not that I heard, but I was distracted."

Runa gritted her teeth. It was uncomfortable discussing this with their mother, and she kept waiting for an argument to begin, the warnings.

She thought about Elenora and her hand clenched, nails biting into her palm. If the ancestor truly wanted her to fail, then perhaps Elaina was her best hope for honest answers. Despite what Runa felt about their mother, all the anger and pain, she didn't believe she'd purposefully hurt her. Elaina would never knowingly risk her life.

"Could it have failed because I was outside my body?" Runa asked.

Elaina considered, her head tilting as they walked. "Possible. You are the first ghost I've encountered." She smiled, and Runa smiled back automatically. Elaina caught the movement, and her face relaxed, her eyes turning bright and welcoming. She looked much like she had when Runa was a child — patient, supportive, loving.

Runa's chest ached and she looked away. They'd lost so much time that they could never get back.

"Perhaps ..." Elaina said tentatively, "it's how you tried to use the magic. What did it feel like to you?"

"Like a river," Runa said, "rushing beside me, dangerous, tumultuous. I tried to reach for it, grab it, but it kept slipping away. The harder I tried, the more it evaded me. It was like trying to chase an animal ..."

"Hmm," Elaina said. "Would you say you tried to force it to do what you wanted?"

"I suppose."

"That might have been the problem," Elaina said.

"What problem?" Lyric asked.

Runa stopped, turning around.

Her sister was staring at her, face flushed and happy. Kell, beside her, pulled his waterskin from his pack and took a long drink. He wiped an arm across his forehead, shoving back his hair.

"When I tried to use magic," Runa said.

"You did?" Lyric asked with surprise.

Runa nodded. "When the Flesh Eater attacked us."

"Oh." Lyric's face paled.

"You did magic, didn't you?" Runa asked, furrowing her brows. "In the room with the Sireni. I was distracted but ...you did something with the wind. Or was that Mother?"

"That was me," Lyric said, nodding. Excitement flickered in her eyes.

"Was it difficult for you?" Runa asked.

A look of consideration crossed Lyric's face. "No," she said slowly. "It was strange and wonderful, and a little scary." Lyric grinned. "It was like I opened myself to it. Let it rush through me. I thought I'd drown, but I didn't."

Elaina nodded. "Lyric let it move through her. She relaxed. Forcing and controlling it doesn't work. It wants to work with you. It's alive, in a way. Like a shy animal," she said, nodding at Runa.

"You should try again," Lyric said.

Runa chewed the inside of her cheek. Could it be that easy? She didn't like the idea of giving control to something she didn't understand. How could she relax and let it do what it wanted? What did it want? What *was* it?

Grimacing, Runa wrenched back her spiraling thoughts. It wasn't like magic could do anything on its own. It had to create what she wanted. Runa had to name the runes first for anything to happen.

Taking a breath, and trying to ignore everyone staring at her, Runa raised her palm. She stared at her hand, at the space above her skin, and spoke the word for fire. An awareness of power came over her and it shifted inside her chest like an animal in the dark. The magic had heard her call but was hesitant to come.

*It's safe,* Runa thought, trying to be calm, to relax and let it flow naturally. For a moment the notion that the magic felt alive seemed utterly ridiculous, but she shoved that reflection away and focused on remaining serene and non-threatening.

The power flared, growing brighter, humming excitedly. Runa took a deep breath and held it, then let the air rush out of her lungs. She ignored everything but the awareness of her body softening, her muscles relaxing, as she let herself trust the magic. Imagining a tiny flame above her palm, Runa spoke the word for fire. Excitement filled her as orange-red fire sparked into life in the air above her skin. It was small and guttered in the wind, but it was *hers.*

A huge smile spread across Runa's face. She wasn't broken; she could summon magic.

# 10

ELAINA

ELAINA WATCHED HER DAUGHTER, a coldness spreading through her heart, even as her skin tingled pleasurably as magic sang out to her. The fire dancing above Runa's palm reflected in her large eyes. Elaina wanted to grab her daughter's hands, smother the fire.

Swallowing, Elaina forced her hands to remain at her side. "Let's keep on," she said.

Runa looked up, regret showing on her face, but she let the magic go and dropped her hand. Fierce pride burned in her eyes as hot as any fire.

As they started walking again, Lyric joined Elaina. Kell followed, a step behind her as if he'd tied himself to her wrist.

Elaina clenched her jaw in annoyance. *What are you doing, Kell*, she thought, shooting him a threatening look.

His sea-blue eyes flicked to her, then away. He did not fall back with Runa.

*I'll have to do something about this*, Elaina thought. She liked Kell, and trusted him, at least this version of him, unaware of his dormant power and past life inside the Veil. Sometime soon they'd find his mother or the Daughters of Valen would realize who he was.

One way or another, the Kell Elaina knew would change or die, and when that happened, she didn't want Lyric anywhere nearby.

Lyric glanced at Kell with a look of pure adoration, and her pale skin flushed. She'd fallen, as quick and hard as Elaina had when their father had shadowed her doorstep, arm bleeding from the wolf that'd caught him in her woods. She couldn't change how Lyric felt, couldn't spare her pain, but she could save her from heartbreak and desolation. She *would* save her.

"How did my mother help you?" Lyric asked suddenly as if Elaina's thoughts had entered her mind.

Kell cleared his throat, embarrassed.

Elaina smiled, unable to keep the satisfaction from her face. Might the story give Lyric pause? Make her look at Kell a little differently? Elaina looked at him, waiting for him to respond.

"I ... someone died," Kell said finally, looking down at the sand.

Lyric's head snapped towards him, breath puffing out with surprise. "Died?" she asked. Her eyes flicked back to Elaina.

Elaina swallowed her smile and nodded solemnly.

"Someone was blackmailing me," Kell said. "I got angry, refused to pay any more. He threatened me; we both started yelling. He hit me, then pulled a knife and I ... we were on a balcony, and I shoved him and then he tripped and ... he fell. I tried to catch him, but he slipped out of my hands. I tried to save him, Lyric, but I couldn't hold him." Kell's face was earnest, his eyes pleading as if Lyric held his absolution.

Guilt wriggled inside Elaina's throat and she looked away, down the beach.

"It looked bad, they wouldn't have believed it wasn't my fault and ... your mother helped me. Said I was with her, somewhere else. I can never repay her."

Elaina looked sideways, catching Kell's eyes and the guilt became a rock inside her stomach. "You didn't deserve to hang for it," she said, giving him a nod. "He tried to kill you first."

"Kell, I'm so sorry," Lyric said. Her voice was soft, sorrowful.

Elaina waited for her to ask about the blackmail, but her daughter put her hand on Kell's arm.

"I'm glad she was there to help you," Lyric said.

Elaina bit the inside of her cheek and stared straight ahead. *I'm sorry, Kell,* she thought. *But you're no good for her.* She'd have to find a way to keep them apart after they arrived in Rathgar's Hold, and send Kell away.

SEVERAL HOURS LATER, Elaina still hadn't figured out how to convince Kell to leave without Lyric chasing after him.

They stopped for a quick lunch, resting on large pieces of driftwood, then continued on their way. The dunes had mostly disappeared, the marshland coming to the beach's edge. Though the sand beneath their feet had started lightening to a pale gray, peppered with charcoal, the bog remained the same murky black, the islands of grass growing smaller and farther apart as if someone had poured a giant bottle of ink onto the ground, covering them up.

Elaina wished they had a boat to go across it, reach the Northern Road, but she knew their oars would stick in the dark muck and they'd be trapped. They had to stay on the beach. Surely Yanessa couldn't be much farther?

She was dreaming about a hot bath for her tired muscles when Elaina saw a faint ribbon of smoke rising in the air. Was someone on the beach? Had they reached the town? Instincts gave her pause, and she rested her hand on her belt.

"I see smoke!" Lyric said suddenly, pointing ahead of them. "Are we there?"

"I don't know," Elaina said.

The smoke disappeared, dispersing in the air. It'd come from behind a large dune that hid whatever was beyond it. To the dune's right was a massive pile of driftwood, half-submerged in the inky marsh.

"Let me check it out," Elaina said. "Wait here."

"I'll go with you," Runa said sharply.

Elaina looked back at her red-haired daughter and saw the set of her jaw. "Fine," she said. "Lyric? Kell?"

"We'll wait," Lyric said, exchanging a look with Kell.

Not wanting to leave them alone, Elaina hesitated. Lyric gave her a curious look, so Elaina grit her teeth and nodded, then began walking towards the dune.

Runa, tugging on the straps of her pack, followed after her.

They walked in silence, their quickened breaths and the whisper of sand shifting under their feet ushering them forward. Reaching the dune, they climbed up, using their hands. Elaina stopped Runa just shy of the top with an outstretched arm.

"Stay low," she whispered.

Lying down, they wiggled forward until they could see over the top of the dune.

Elaina's pulse quickened, her heart throwing itself against her ribs like a startled rabbit. A squad of Sireni waited on the beach below, arguing over the remnants of a fire. She recognized one of the men from the Veil. He had a bandaged leg, and he was gesturing angrily at a white-clad woman standing opposite him. Bracketed by two men, the woman held something in her hand.

South of them, another man lounged against a pile of bleached wood. He raised his hand, staring at a trio of rocks stacked atop each other, and Elaina felt magic brush across her skin. The ground vibrated beneath them, the stones toppling over, and Runa's hissed in surprise.

The woman turned away from the man Elaina recognized, and said something to the casting Screamer, her hand cutting through the air.

The magic cut off, and the lounging man gave a bored shrug.

Elaina touched Runa's elbow, then began to wiggle backward, as silently as she could. Her daughter followed, and they climbed down the dune. Brushing sand off their clothes, they hurried back to Lyric and Kell.

"What is it?" Lyric asked when they reached them.

"Sireni," Runa said. Her voice was tight, and she worried the strap of her pack with one hand. "One of the Screamers from the Veil is with them."

"What?" Kell said, eyes flaring.

Elaina gave a tight nod. "There are four of them, waiting on the other side of the dune. They must have realized where we are."

Lyric moved closer to Kell, her hip bumping his. "Can we get around them?" she asked.

"No. They'll see us if we go in the water."

Elaina swore inside her head. How could she reach Eleden if they couldn't get to Yanessa? They couldn't wait for the Sireni to leave. What if they started up the beach? She could fight two, but not an entire squad.

"We have to go back north," Runa said, staring up the beach.

Kell paled.

"Thenda?" Lyric asked.

Elaina swore again, this time out loud. "Yes," she said. "We don't have a choice. We can't stay here and wait for them to leave. I won't risk fighting them. We'll go back to where we camped, get as much food as we can, and go north."

"Is it safe? Walking up the Shore?" Lyric asked. She looked at Kell, who blinked and looked down at her.

"It will be dangerous," he said. "The Taint has poisoned the water. There are no cities or places to get supplies. We might find shelter and food, some people stayed, but I don't know."

"Are there other dangers?" Runa asked. "Besides the Taint itself?"

"I've never seen one, but I've heard of creatures in the dark," Kell said, eyes catching on Elaina.

Her face paled. She'd forgotten.

"I don't know what they are," Kell continued. "Maybe animals twisted by the Taint? They are dangerous."

Elaina nodded. They'd have to chance running into one. Better odds than the visible threat south. "We need to be vigilant." She glanced back at the dune. "We should go before they come this way. We need to get as far north as we can, camp before we reach the Taint. I don't want to come across it in the dark." *Or the creatures*, she thought.

She'd have to think about Kell and Lyric another time. Right now, Elaina had to focus her full attention on keeping them all alive.

# 11

KELL

DREAD FILLED Kell's stomach like rot, growing stronger with every step north, every step home. It was odd how he still thought of Thenda as home after all these years, after leaving it all behind. Despite what'd been taken, what he'd lost, walking the Shore's black sand filled his mind with sentimental memories.

As a child, he'd worked hard alongside his mother and father, fishing the Sea of Screams that thundered harshly against their eastern border, but even with their struggles, he remembered light and laughter. He couldn't recall a single day when he'd wished he was somewhere else. He hadn't learned to sing in the Radiant Hall as his professors claimed, but around evening bonfires on the beach as he made up stories with his mother, Triska.

Raised by Triska and Jiri, Kell hadn't dwelled on his origin or worried about the parents who'd marked him and gave him up. His new family loved him, and with the foolishness of a child, he'd assumed they'd be together forever.

Storm clouds gathered overhead, shifting across the graying sky as though drawn by Kell's mood, by his fear. The waves, whipped into a frenzy by a ferocious wind, crashed against the beach as though seeking to destroy it.

Walking beside him, Lyric bumped against his body as the wind shoved her sideways. Kell shifted her to his other side, away from the sea, trying to offer her some protection from it.

Lyric smiled, squinting as hair lashed across her face, and held her hood close. Pulled from his dark thoughts by the look in her eyes, Kell smiled back and put an arm around her shoulders. Together they struggled against the wind.

*Go back*, he wanted to say. *Go south. Slip past the Sireni. You can return home.* The people needed her there, in Elae's Hollow; she could have a good life, a safe life. He looked away, feeling selfish as he kept his plea to himself.

As the day passed, Kell watched for the Taint to appear, his eyes straining as they walked, but the Shore continued barren and unblemished. The western dunes were slowly replaced by craggy, sandstone cliffs, creeping higher and higher as they followed alongside them, the tops dotted with scraggly bushes and twisted trees. The cliffs were steep, and the soft dirt easily gave way, preventing attempts to climb them.

"Where is the Taint?" Lyric asked.

*Yes,* Kell thought. *Where—*

His thought evaporated as he stared at the ocean, tripping over his own feet. Lungs tight, refusing to draw breath, Kell gave a strangled cry. They'd found it. Floating atop the rolling, dark blue waves were scummy patches of green algae, poisoned by the Taint.

"It's there," Kell said. His voice sounded unfamiliar. "Don't touch anything."

"What happens if you do?" Runa asked.

Kell looked at her, catching her eyes. "It seeps beneath your skin, melting, and burning. Your blood turns black. There's no coming back once the Taint has touched you. I don't know how the night creatures survive it."

Lyric grabbed Kell's hand. Her fingers were tight around his, her skin clammy.

*Go back*, Kell thought. He looked at her, eyes imploring, but he couldn't bring himself to voice the words. Despite the risk to her, to her family, he wanted her with him. *I'm selfish and horrible. I'll never deserve you.*

"Walk carefully," Elaina cautioned, unaware of Kell's inner conflict.

Kell squeezed Lyric's hand, and they moved closer behind Elaina and Runa. He watched the water as they walked. Carried onto the beach by the waves, numerous clumps of green algae stained the sand, smelly and clotted like day-old porridge. It became impossible to walk in a straight line as they carefully stepped around algae, dead fish and crabs, their bodies covered in wet black sludge.

When they came across the bloated corpse of a seal, Lyric pressed a hand over her mouth and turned away. The smell of rot filled the air, making it uncomfortable to breathe.

"It hasn't gotten better," Kell said. His voice was hollow and bleaker than he'd intended.

"Has it spread? Gotten worse?" Lyric asked.

"I don't know," Kell said. "I'd thought it might die out or sink beneath the waves."

"It's drifted farther into the sea," Elaina said, looking out at the ocean. "I saw it on Eleden's ship."

"Why hasn't it spread to Raendashar or south where we camped?" Runa asked. "Why does it stay here?"

"I don't know," Elaina said, her face grim. "It doesn't make sense."

Dread returned to Kell's stomach, and he tugged Lyric closer, drawing strength from her presence. He glanced left, over the top of her head and saw that the cliffs had changed, the sandstone shifting to a darker, harder stone. The rock towered over them, casting shadows on the beach that seemed to worsen the stench of decay. Kell could see green veining running through it, oozing as if the rock had melted like sun-warmed butter.

Memories of pain, confusion, and horror tickled his mind, and Kell shoved it down, trying not to think of anything; trying not to open the door inside his head.

"What do we do when night falls?" Runa asked. Her red hair glinted as she glanced back at them, tracking Lyric's progress with her hawk-like eyes.

"Maybe there's an abandoned building ahead," Kell said. "A fisherman's shed that hasn't yet been destroyed by the Taint."

"I pray we find something soon," Lyric murmured beside him.

It was early evening when Kell saw the first abandoned city. Cut into the cliffs the houses were stacked atop each other, rising towers into the darkening sky. Jagged and broken as they were, the buildings reminded him of the points of a damaged crown.

Staircases that'd once led up from the sand into the bottom balconies had crumbled away. Whole terraces had melted into each other, the rock dripping from one house to the next like candle wax. Windows, set into the green-veined stone, gaped empty and black. The green rot was everywhere, winding through the chiseled stone like a network of vines.

"Kratho," Kell breathed. "This was Kratho." Though hours south of Salta, where the devastating event that'd released the Taint had occurred, Kratho hadn't escaped the horror. Kell had heard stories of stone cracking, erupting, people screaming and dying. "It was like the wind carried it down the length of the Shore. It was in the sand—"

Pain lanced across his throat, and Kell reached for it,

instantly clearing his mind. The tattoo squeezed like a fist around his neck.

Lyric, sensing his distress, helped steer him around chunks of melted stone in the sand. "Are you all right?" she asked quietly. Her hand was warm on his arm.

Kell saw the face of his mother. She was screaming, reaching— "No," Kell said.

Lyric slipped her arm around his waist and pressed her head against his arm.

"There!" Runa yelled ahead of them. "A light!"

Kell looked up, relief flooding through him. He could see a fishing cottage lit by a single orb lantern. Encircled by a balcony, the house was raised high above the waves on reinforced stilts of metal and wood.

"Someone's there," Kell said as he stared at the light. He was surprised someone was still living here, especially after what they'd seen. How were they surviving?

The door opened as they drew close, and a woman stepped out onto the platform. She leaned against the railing, watching them.

"By Ethethera's Name, safety and food to you on this dark night," she called. Her voice rasped unpleasantly like a knife against stone. "It's not safe to be out in the dark. Please, come share my firelight." She shifted back and lowered a ladder, gesturing at them to join her.

"Can we trust her?" Lyric asked hesitantly; her voice pitched low. "She's not a ... a *creature* is she, in disguise? Like the Flesh Eater?"

"No," Kell said, with more confidence than he felt. That'd be impossible, wouldn't it? Flesh Eaters didn't exist outside the Veil, and the creatures that terrorized the Shore were incapable of changing themselves. "No, the creatures here don't pretend to be human," Kell said. "I'm sure we're safer with her than out on the beach. Thendians are always kind to travelers, at least that was our way."

"I sense no danger," Elaina said cryptically. She stepped onto the ladder first, climbing gracefully to the platform above.

Kell, following behind Lyric, tried to let Runa go ahead of him, but she waved him away with a snort. He stepped up to the ladder and put his foot on the bottom rung, steadying it as Lyric climbed. He could see poisoned algae floating in the water nearby and scattered across the sand, but there was nothing directly beneath the woman's house. The water and sand were clear, as though it'd been swept clean.

Kell studied the pillars, holding up the woman's home, and was relieved to see they were undamaged by the Taint. How did she do it? How did she prevent it from crumbling like Kratho?

Lyric called down to him, and Kell climbed up the ladder, his eyes moving across the beach. He looked for movement in the darkness but saw nothing. At the top of the ladder, Kell stepped onto the wide balcony and moved to the side where Lyric was waiting. He smiled at her, brushing a strand of hair off her cheek, and then turned to look at the woman.

Tall and thin, she wore worn, gray trousers and a simple blouse with long sleeves. She was old, maybe eighty cycles, but her spine was straight, and her pale blue eyes clear as she studied each of them in turn.

Once Runa joined them on the platform, the old woman quickly pulled up the ladder with surprising speed and strength. She waved away Kell's offer of help and folding it up, tied the ladder to the railing.

"I'm Meara," the woman said, straightening. Crossing to the door, she wrenched it open and gestured for them to enter. "A storm's on its way. Please, come inside."

The fishing cottage was warm, heated by an old, black stove in one corner and lit by two lanterns hanging on the wall. Besides the door they entered through, there was another closed door facing the cliffs, that presumably lead to a bedroom.

A rocking chair sat next to the stove with a shabby gray blanket draped across one arm. Bracketed by two plank benches, a battered wood table sat in the center of the room. A handful of bird bones lay scattered across its surface and Kell drifted closer to look.

*Was Meara casting bones?* Kell wondered, glancing at her from the corner of his eye. He watched her clear the bones from the table and walk past a tall cabinet. Kell's eyes dropped to an old chest sitting beside it on the floor. Scratched glass orbs, a familiar dark green, balanced atop the closed lid. A coiled fishing net rested on the plank floor beside it. The items were familiar and reminded him of his life before, of his father.

Swallowing, Kell spun away, nearly hitting Lyric with his arm as he looked for something else to focus on. His eyes found the windows, and he stared at the waxed gray paper tacked across the openings. The shutters were closed, but he could still hear the wind howling outside and the rush of water rolling beneath his feet, far below.

"Sit," Meara said, somewhere behind him.

Kell felt Lyric gently touch his back, and he turned around. She'd set her pack on the floor against the wall, along with Elaina and Runa, so Kell did the same before sitting down beside her at the table.

Elaina introduced them, first names only, as Meara pulled cups from a shelf near the stove. She took the cups when the old woman handed them to her, along with a plate of freshly-baked hand pies, and set both on the table.

Meara grabbed a kettle from the stove and raised it with a questioning look. "Tea?" she asked, her eyes moving between them.

Kell nodded, and Lyric, Runa, and Elaina murmured their grateful assent.

Once she'd served them, Meara seated herself in the rocking chair with a long sigh. "My bones are old," she said, smiling. She reached for a cup of tea she'd poured for herself and left on the edge of the stove. "I feel the storms more strongly now than in years past," Meara said. She caught a glance between Lyric and Runa, who were considering the hand pies, and laughed, her eyes crinkling.

"Don't worry," Meara said. "The pies are filled with bird flesh from the gulls that fly the skies. It's not the softest of meats, but it's clean, free of the Taint, and it fills your belly."

"My mother made gull pie a few times," Kell said, "when fishing was bad." He reached for a hand pie and took a bite, chewing slowly, thinking about the taste and not his mother.

"Ah," Meara said, "I thought you had the look of a brine-born boy." Something dark and lost filled her eyes and Kell's pain surged in response. Meara understood. She'd lost someone here too.

Lyric picked up a hand pie and took a tentative bite. "It's spicy!" she declared with surprise.

"Yes." Meara's eyes twinkled. "Helps hide the taste of the gulls. Good for digestion too. So." She glanced between them, her eyes settling on Elaina. "What brings you to Thenda? Hunting for treasure?"

Kell thought Meara gave him a quick look of disapproval. Did she think he was helping them loot their dead?

"If scavenging is your game," Meara continued, "I should warn you, no one who's entered our lost cities has come back out again." She eyed their packs, piled against the wall. "Though, it doesn't look like you're prepared for much of an expedition."

"No, we're just passing through," Elaina said. "We're on our way to Raendashar."

"Ah," Meara said. "Visiting family? I'd wager you're not merchants, as you're traveling quite light."

"Yes," Elaina said. Her face was relaxed, unthreatening. "Family."

Meara nodded, eyeing her. "You came from the south? It would have been easier and safer to travel inland along the Northern Road, or buy passage on a Sireni ship ... though I suppose they don't stop in Raendasharan ports anymore."

"Did they ever?" Lyric asked, curiously.

"Occasionally," Meara said. "Trade agreements have been attempted before despite the war. Did you know, they once ruled together on the Council of Men? I'd speculate that the tension between them is what caused the Council's dissolution in the first place." She studied Elaina as if expecting an impassioned rebuttal.

"We had no choice but to head north on this route," Elaina said.

Meara seemed a tad disappointed by Elaina's response and raised her cup beneath her nose. "Oh?" she said.

Elaina smiled placidly and sipped her tea. "We were surprised and relieved to come upon your light," she said. "Are there others who still live along the Shore like you?"

"A handful," Meara said, "but we've had bad storms lately. I wouldn't be surprised if they've all moved on by now."

"How do you keep the Taint away from your pillars?" Kell asked. "I noticed there's no trace of algae beneath your house."

"Ah," Meara said, eyes crinkling. "I've learned a few spells over the years. I have to regularly clear the sand and strip the algae from the water beneath the house. It's ceaseless work, but if I were to stop, I'd soon lose my home. If the algae touches the pillars, it will rot through in a matter of days."

"And the night creatures?" Lyric asked. "They don't bother you?"

Meara pursed her lips. "They sometimes come, scratching and moaning, like ghosts outside my walls, but they've yet to tear through the wood." She glanced at Elaina. "They eat magic, you know."

"Spells?" Lyric asked, eyes wide.

Meara nodded. "They enjoy flesh too. Best to avoid them."

Lyric set down her half-eaten pie.

"Why stay?" Runa asked. Though her brows furrowed in an unnerving way, her eyes gleamed with curiosity.

"I lost my family here," Meara said. The wrinkles in her face seemed fathomless as her smile slipped away. "They're gone, but I can't leave them." She shrugged, her eyes finding Kell. "I'm old, and I've lived a full life; witnessed many sunrises and sunsets. Slept through some storms here that'd blow you across the continent if you weren't tied down." Meara chuckled and looked down at her hands.

"Do you ever travel to Raendashar?" Elaina asked. "For supplies?"

Meara nodded. "Yes, once or twice a season to supplement the food I get from the sky. But I only go to Ivernn on the border." Meara grimaced. "The land is too hot, too sharp. The Sea is different there. The wind screams at the land as though carrying the Sireni's voices, amplifying their displeasure.

"It's a shame you didn't see Thenda before the Taint," Meara said. "It was beautiful here." Her face warmed, and she nodded at Kell. "You remember. The air was always fresh, the fish fat and savory."

It had been beautiful. Kell looked away from Meara's joy-filled eyes and looked down at his lap. He laced his fingers together, squeezing until distracting pain rippled across the bones beneath his skin.

Lyric, sitting beside him, tentatively laid her hand on his knee and squeezed softly.

Kell looked at her, surprised and moved by the gesture. He unlaced his hands and covered hers with one of his own.

*I'm getting too used to this,* he thought. *Being cared for by someone.*

Runa's voice drew his head back up to the conversation around the table.

"Are we far from the border?" Runa asked.

Kell looked at Meara. Considering where they were, he'd estimate the border was only a few days away unless the storms or the Taint had drastically changed the land.

Meara eyed him, perhaps seeing if he'd speak up, but when he didn't, she looked at Runa and answered. "I'd say a day and a half, perhaps two depending on your pace and the weather. After bad storms, it becomes nearly impossible to walk the beach without stepping on Tainted kelp and dead animals torn from the ocean. The storm tonight might stir things up, but it doesn't sound bad yet. Do you agree, brine-born boy?" Meara asked suddenly.

Kell blinked, his heart skipping. "Yes," he said. "But it's been a long time since I've walked the Shore."

Meara nodded. "Most everyone who survived left. I don't blame you. It would have been hard here on a young lad like you."

Kell felt a flash of annoyance. He wasn't a child, not anymore. He'd likely traveled farther than she ever had; seen things she could only dream about. Kell probably knew more of the world and yet ... Meara had stayed. She hadn't abandoned their home, hadn't fled with the others.

Anger slipping away, guilt rushed in, sharp and bitter. He deserved her disgust.

"When was the last time you traveled to Ivernn?" Runa asked.

Meara cracked her bony knuckles, looking thoughtful. "Right after the winter chill," she said. "I missed my usual trip after hurting my leg. I'm fine now, but I'll likely have to head north again in several weeks. There's only so much gull meat you can eat before you crave something else." She chuckled.

"Is there anyone we can stay with along the way?" Lyric asked.

"Beyn is about a day's walk," Meara said. "He lives close to the cliffs, out of the reach of the sea. I don't know if he's still there, but if he isn't, you can take shelter in his house. Safer than risking the beach at night. I can send dried gull meat with you, and you're welcome to as much water as you need." Meara gestured at a barrel in the corner. "Gathered from the sky and purified with an old Oleporean method. I'm afraid I don't have more to offer."

"That'd be wonderful, thank you," Lyric said. "I know a way to purify seawater, but I've been afraid to try since we came across the algae."

Kell squeezed her hand, and Lyric glanced at him, smiling in a distracting way.

Meara nodded. "Best to get water from the sky. No matter what spells you have, it's not safe to take water from the sea. Not here." She looked between Elaina, Lyric, and Runa.

"Traveling here would be safer if you weren't mages," she said.

Kell narrowed his eyes. What was Meara implying?

Runa raised an eyebrow. "You're a mage."

Meara smiled, an unreadable look in her pale eyes. "Not exactly."

"What does that mean?" Runa demanded.

Chuckling, Meara sipped from her cup. "Nothing sinister, dear girl. Knowing one or two spells doesn't make you a mage. There's skill involved — the ability to quickly pick up the language, and to understand how to create and not just repeat others' spells. It took me quite a while to learn what I know." She shrugged. "Maybe that's what's kept me safe from the creatures. They can't sense the power in me since it's just a trickle."

Meara glanced at Elaina. "You though, should be careful."

Kell thought about Elaina moving the four of them into the Veil and studied her face. She had to be strong to do something like that. Stronger than he'd realized. What might that mean for Lyric and Runa's abilities, their potential? He'd been so sure the Daughters' omen was for him, but what if it was Lyric who was in danger? She didn't know her power yet.

Lyric pulled her hand away to drink her tea, and Kell shifted his hands back into his lap, heart racing.

"We'll be careful and find shelter before nightfall," Elaina said. "If we find Beyn's home, we'll stay there."

Meara nodded. "Good," she said. She eyed Elaina over the rim of her cup. "How did you end up south of the Shore, on the other side of the marshes?"

Kell's heart skipped, and he looked at Elaina.

"We were traveling with some merchants who, regrettably, were less than honorable," Elaina said. She shared a grim look with Runa, who looked appropriately outraged. "The plan was to take the Northern Road, but as you can see ... we had to adapt. My girls are safe though, that is all that matters." She eyed Meara, a challenging look in her eyes.

Lyric cleared her throat. "Can we stay with you tonight?" she asked.

Kell knew Meara wouldn't refuse, not after feeding them, and indeed, the old woman nodded.

"Of course, my dear. I'm sorry for your misfortune and pray that the remainder of your journey will be swift. I don't have spare beds, but you're welcome to sleep here, wherever you like." Meara gestured about the room. "It's warm, and nothing comes in that I don't allow."

Kell thought back to her statement about magic and wondered what, if anything, she'd be able to do if one of the creatures did break through.

A window shutter rattled, and Kell glanced at it feeling

unsettled. *Just the wind*, he told himself. He looked at the curve of Lyric's cheek. How would he protect her without his staff? He'd lost two in such a short time. If their situation weren't so worrying, he'd have laughed out loud.

"My bones are telling me to sleep," Meara said. She groaned as she pushed herself up out of the rocking chair.

Elaina, Runa, and Lyric stood and began to clear their dishes.

Standing, Kell curled his fingers around the table's edge. "Maybe we can move the table, make room on the floor to sleep?" he suggested.

Meara nodded her assent.

Returning to help, Elaina, Runa, and Lyric helped Kell shift the table towards the door, blocking it. They moved the benches out of the way beneath it, clearing a space in the center of the room.

When Kell turned back around, he saw that Meara was adding wood to the stove. She closed the heavy door and turned the wire-wrapped handle, then took a lantern from a hook on the wall.

"May your dreams be light," Meara said. She opened the door beside the cabinet and stepped into a small room. Kell briefly glimpsed a narrow bed before she closed the door behind her.

Elaina and Runa began to prepare themselves for bed, and Kell looked for a place to sleep. He picked a spot on the floor farthest from the stove, leaving the warmest areas for the women, and sat.

Lyric moved towards him, watching with bright eyes as he shifted his cloak around his shoulders. Kell looked up at her, unsure if he should wait to lay down.

"I noticed that Meara isn't silenced like you," Lyric said softly, squatting beside him.

A chill skittered across Kell's back, and he nodded, trying to keep his mind clear of Salta's destruction. "Yes," he said.

"Why you, and not others?" Lyric asked. Her brow furrowed as she studied Kell's face. "Might others have also witnessed what you did?"

"I don't know," Kell said. "I ... I left right after it happened."

"Why did you?" Lyric asked. She made a face and put a hand on his arm. "I mean, I think I understand but—"

"Why did I leave when others chose to stay?" Kell asked. His chest tightened, and he looked at his hands, clenching and unfurling his long fingers. "I was scared," he said, after a moment. He didn't like how small his voice sounded or how helpless he felt. "I had no one; everything was in chaos, I ... I stumbled upon a merchant several hours north of the city. He'd seen the aftermath, a big flash of something far away. He took me with him to Corsicayna. I knew my mother had studied at the Radiant Hall before she met my father, so I sought shelter there."

Lyric nodded, a lock of hair slipping across her face.

Distracted, Kell reached out and brushed her cheek, smoothing her hair between his fingers. "You're beautiful," he said softly. If he focused on her, on her eyes and her smile, he didn't have to think about the past.

Lyric flushed and ducked her head but didn't pull away.

Someone cleared their throat, and Kell jerked back, looking away from Lyric with a startled expression.

Elaina was staring at them, her face displeased, her hands on her hips. "Maybe you should sleep next to Runa by the fire," she said to Lyric.

"Mama ..." Lyric said. She stood, back straightening, the flush in her cheeks darkening in color. "I'm not—"

"I'll sleep here," Elaina said. Shuffling Lyric to the side, Elaina spread out her cloak on the floor next to Kell and laid down, turning her back to him.

Lyric bristled, and her eyes narrowed.

"It's not worth it," Runa called from beside the stove.

Lyric glanced at her sister, then at Kell and gave him an embarrassed smile. "Goodnight, Kell," she said.

"Goodnight," Kell said, smiling back. He watched her as she stepped over Elaina, and spread her cloak next to Runa.

Glancing at Elaina's back, Kell laid down facing the door. He stared at the table and benches that blocked it and wondered how much resistance they'd provide against anything intent on coming inside.

*We're safe*, he told himself. *Lyric is safe.*

## 12

LYRIC

LYRIC WOKE to the familiar sounds of someone preparing for the day. Was she back home? "Mama?" she asked, blinking groggily at the woman standing in front of the stove. No, that wasn't right, their mother had left her and Runa alone.

An old woman looked back at her, her wrinkled face stretching into a smile. She was not Elaina. "Just me," she said. "Meara. I'm heating water. I trust you slept well?"

Lyric blinked. "Yes," she said, remembering the evening before. She'd laid down beside her sister, said goodnight to Kell and then—

Runa groaned and sat bolt upright, her eyes snapping open. Her red hair was tangled from sleep, and as she swiftly eyed the room, she tugged at it with an irritated look. "Thenda," she pronounced. "The house."

Meara chuckled and turned back to the pot of water.

"Here," Lyric said, smiling. She turned Runa with a touch to her shoulder and began untangling her sister's hair with gentle fingers.

Glancing backward as she combed the knots from Runa's hair, Lyric saw both Kell and their mother were awake and gathering up their cloaks. Neither looked rested. Lyric smiled at Kell when he looked at her, earning a beautiful, sleep-edged smile in response. His hair was rumpled and stuck out on one side, and she grinned as he attempted to smooth it back down.

"Ow," Runa complained.

"Oh, sorry," Lyric said, looking back at her hands in Runa's hair.

"It's fine," Runa said, pulling away. "Now you, unless you're hoping to attract a family of birds."

Lyric stuck out her tongue and turned around. She winced as Runa plaited her hair. Her sister wasn't very gentle, but it only took her a few minutes to weave Lyric's hair into two fishtail braids.

Flipping the ends over Lyric's shoulders, Runa stood and grabbed her cloak off the floor.

Lyric followed her, and together, with Kell and Elaina, they moved the table and benches back to the center of the room, then refilled their waterskins at Meara's barrel.

"I have tea, biscuits, and gull meat," Meara said, setting the table. "I'm sorry it's simple. I'm nearly out of flour, and I ate the rest of my tubers the day before you arrived."

"We don't want to clear you out," Lyric said, feeling guilty. "We have some dried fish that we caught farther south where the water is clean."

"Oh, don't worry about me," Meara said, smiling. "Your company means a lot to this lonely old woman. Keep the meat for your travels. Unless you catch a gull, it's the only food you'll have. You'll be on your own until Ivernn if Beyn has left his home."

Lyric nodded and sat down at the table opposite Meara and their mother. Kell, briefly touching her shoulder, sat down on her left, and Runa on her right.

"How do you catch the gulls?" Runa asked, immediately reaching for tea.

"Nets mostly," Meara said. "They sometimes land on my balcony to rest." She grimaced. "I feel bad for them, but I have to eat."

"Have you had any other visitors?" Elaina asked.

"Just Beyn," Meara said, "but that was last winter."

*Half a year without seeing another person's face?* Lyric thought. *How had she survived the loneliness?*

"Don't feel sorry for me," Meara said, eyes twinkling. "I like my solitude."

"I wish we could bring supplies back to you," Lyric said. She thought about the old woman traveling the Shore alone. Meara seemed strong and resourceful, but if anything bad happened there'd be no one to help her.

Meara laughed and flapped a hand in the air. "Oh, no, no," Meara said. "Thank you for the kind proposal, but if you manage to reach Raendashar, I heartily encourage you never to travel this way again." She glanced at Elaina. "Be more mindful of the caravans you travel with and stick to the Northern Road on the other side of the Waste, or hire a boat."

"What is the Waste?" Runa asked.

Lyric glanced at Meara, her curiosity piqued. She'd seen a few maps of Erith back home, but they'd been old and tattered, the information of the lands outside Kaliz limited and likely no longer accurate.

Meara glanced sharply at their mother, and Lyric remembered the story Elaina had told the night before about the caravan. They'd supposedly meant to travel the Road. Should they be familiar with the Waste? Did Meara now suspect that Elaina lied?

"It's a barren strip of land on the other side of the cliffs," Kell said, his voice distracted. "Closer to Oleporea, it turns to forest on the other side of the marshlands, but up here it's just empty land. No one's certain why nothing grows there, at least that's what my father told me."

"Yes," Meara said, eyes narrowed on Elaina. "It follows the cliff-line up to where Thenda ends and Raendashar begins. I'm guessing it was one reason our ancestors built our cities in the cliffs along the beach, and not further inland. Well that, and that the Sea was always plentiful here before the Taint."

"We traveled by boat," Elaina said to Meara. "The girls haven't seen the Road." Her eyes were cautious as she looked at Lyric and Runa. "The Road separates Thenda and Jaina. It's quite desolate. Before the Taint, travelers preferred the coast-line to following the Waste. You would have seen it if we hadn't had troubles with the merchant."

"Yes," Meara said, nodding.

"This is nothing like back home," Lyric said absently, thinking of the forests and snow-capped mountains surrounding Elae's Hollow.

"Home?" Meara asked.

Lyric's heart jumped into her throat, and she looked up, her eyes flicking to Elaina.

"Oleporea," Elaina said. "This is the first time the girls have traveled farther than Seave." She smiled indulgently.

Lyric glanced down at her tea, hoping Meara took the discomfort on her face for embarrassment. She'd never been the best liar.

Elaina pushed aside her plate and stood up, indicating it was time to leave. "Thank you, Meara, for letting us stay the night," she said, "and for feeding us."

Lyric stood automatically and began to clear the table. "Thank you for taking us in, Meara," she said. She smiled at Meara gratefully.

Meara nodded. "My pleasure. I hope your journey will be safe and swift."

"Yes, thank you, Meara," Runa echoed, walking to the door to retrieve her pack.

Kell gave a Thendian farewell, something about the wind and fat fish, but Lyric was too distracted to pay attention.

Following after her sister, Lyric stopped by the door and adjusted her cloak, glancing sideways at Runa. Her sister was frowning, her lips soundlessly moving as if she were having a conversation with the wall. Was Runa talking to Elenora? About what? Lyric recalled Gandara's tattoos and long white hair. Did Elenora look similar, or more like Elaina and Runa with red hair? Was she old, like Gandara, or had she died young? How did she dress?

Gandara's warning about Runa came to Lyric's mind, and she shifted uneasily. Was it possible that Elenora was telling her sister the same thing; warning her that Lyric could become dangerous? Had she encouraged Runa to distance herself? Were their ancestors, Raendasharan and Sireni as they were, trying to drive a wedge between them?

Runa turned, her face irritated, and caught Lyric staring at her. Something dark flashed inside her eyes.

Lyric smiled uncertainly, unsure of how to act. Was her sister irritated or angry? She couldn't sense Runa's emotions. A gulf lay open between them, and for one terrifying moment, Lyric thought she'd lost her sister. Terror and grief crashed over her. She was alone, she was—

Runa shook her head and scraped her fingers through her hair, tousling the long red strands, then stomped over to Lyric.

"Are you well?" Lyric asked, her heart skipping. She resisted the urge to grab Runa's arm.

"Yes," Runa said. "I'm fine." She smiled, a tight press of the lips that Lyric didn't quite believe, but when she looked into Lyric's eyes, her own softened in a familiar way. Reaching out, Runa squeezed Lyric's shoulder. "We'll be fine," Runa said. "We'll make it to Raendashar; I'm certain of it."

Lyric blinked. Runa thought the worry in her face was about the Shore?

"Yes," Lyric said slowly. She wanted to ask about Elenora, and if the awareness of each other's feelings had deserted Runa too. Had their bond changed when Runa reunited with her body or was it because of something else?

*Don't let me lose her,* Lyric thought, beseeching Ethethera. The goddess never answered her, but she'd always felt akin to the One who formed the trees and land.

Runa squeezed Lyric's shoulder again and turned away, seemingly unaware of the roiling thoughts inside Lyric's head as she opened the door. Muted light streamed inside, illuminating Runa's face as she stepped through.

Stomach shifting uneasily, Lyric followed her sister outside. The morning was calm, the sky a soft shade of gray. Green-tinged waves lapped lazily against the dark sand. There was debris on the beach, but no more than before.

Joining Runa at the railing facing the open sea, Lyric looked north up the beach, following the cliffs with her eyes. She still couldn't see their end.

Kell, Elaina, and Meara walked out onto the balcony.

"Not a bad night," Meara declared, staring at the beach. "If you stick to the packed sand you should make good time as you head north."

"If our luck holds," Elaina said. She seemed ill at ease, and guilt tightened Lyric's shoulders. She hadn't given much thought to how their mother might feel about returning to Raendashar. Elaina had cut her father from her life, painted him as a monster. She'd tried to warn Lyric and Runa away, but here they were, forcing her back to her old life.

Meara moved towards her, interrupting Lyric's thoughts, and reached for her hand, pressing it gently between hers. "May you walk in Ethethera's light and find safe haven on your journey," Meara said, smiling.

"Thank you," Lyric said. "And may Ethethera's light shine on you, as well." She wasn't sure of the proper response to

Meara's farewell, but her answer seemed to suffice, for the woman nodded and turned to Runa.

Meara repeated the same statement to everyone, including Kell, then untied the rope ladder and lowered it down.

Elaina descended first, followed by Runa, Lyric, and finally Kell. Walking out from beneath the shadow of Meara's house, they stepped quickly across the damp sand until they were out of reach of the lapping waves. Turning back, they waved farewell to Meara.

She'd already pulled up her ladder and held up a hand high above her head. Then, with a look into the sky, Meara turned and walked around the side of her house, disappearing.

"Let's walk as quickly as we can," Elaina said. "I'd like to reach Beyn's house before nightfall." She set off, leading, and Lyric and Kell followed after her. Runa, drifting several steps behind them, brought up the rear.

KELL'S UNEASE seemed to grow the farther they walked from Meara's house, and Lyric held tight to his hand and tried to distract him. She asked him about the different birds she saw winging through the gray sky and was pleased when Kell latched onto the topic, talking about their light bones, the colors of their wings and the different calls they made.

As she listened, eyes on the sky, Lyric's mind wandered. Why did the Taint affect the beach and water, but not the air? Kell said he'd thought it was airborne when they'd seen the destruction of Kratho, but if so, why were the birds above them untouched? Why were they even here? What could they eat if there was no food? Did Meara call them somehow with magic? Would the skies be empty without her? Not wanting to return the Taint to Kell's mind, Lyric kept her thoughts to herself.

By the time they reached the Cliffs of Salta around noon,

Lyric had coaxed several smiles from Kell. But when his eyes drifted to his old home, his face shuttered closed. His eyes went hollow, and the chords in his throat protruded like hard reeds beneath his skin.

Lyric gripped Kell's arm, holding on to him as they walked beneath the city's shadow. The abandoned capital had been grand once, the decaying houses rising into pale, conical towers that spiraled into the sky like the tightly-wound whorls of seashells. The green rot was worse here, covering the city's pearlescent stone in a thick web of unnatural lines. Salta was breathtaking, despite the destruction, and Lyric barely breathed as they passed beneath it.

"It's incredible," Runa said, her voice reverent. She spun as she walked, her head tilted back to stare up at the spiraling towers.

Elaina didn't seem to look at much of anything, and her hands never strayed far from her belt.

Uneasy and worried about Kell, Lyric led him past the city as fast as she dared. His left hand spasmed up to his throat, as though to loosen a collar that'd grown too tight. "I can't ..." he whispered

"I'm here," Lyric said. She didn't know what else to say.

When they finally reached the outskirts of Salta, and the cliffs transitioned back to natural walls of dirt and stone, Lyric loosened her grip on Kell's arm. Her fingers cramped painfully, and she worried she'd left bruises on his skin.

With Salta at his back, Kell's breath became less labored, his eyes turning a calmer shade of blue. He wiped sweat off his brow with his sleeve, then glancing sideways at Lyric, bent his head and brushed a kiss across the top of her forehead.

Lyric nearly tripped over her own feet as heat raced through her. She smiled at Kell, feeling foolish and giddy and so relieved she thought she might cry.

"Thank you," Kell said.

Lyric nodded.

"Is it weird that I'm hungry?" he asked, grinning.

"No!" Lyric laughed. "I was thinking the same thing. We've been walking for hours. Maybe we should stop and—"

"What's that?" Runa asked.

Lyric stopped and turned her head. Runa stood beside her, staring up the beach.

Following Runa's gaze past Elaina, ahead of them, Lyric saw something large and black on the sand. "What is it?" Lyric asked, squinting.

"A seal?" Runa asked. "Or driftwood?"

"No, it's ... cloth," their mother said. "We should go around it."

"We should see what it is," Runa said. She strode forward past Elaina.

Lyric, curious despite their mother's expression, trailed after her sister.

The smell hit her when they were within a hundred paces; a foul, sharp smell that burrowed into her nose. Gagging, Lyric covered her nose and mouth with a fold of her cloak.

Kell made a disgusted noise and quickly covered his face. "Maybe we should stay away from it?" he asked, his voice muffled.

Runa looked at him, face pinched but eyes fierce and determined. "Where's your sense of adventure, choir-boy?" she asked.

Elaina, looking green, but breathing through her mouth like Runa, gestured again away from the black lump. "It's nothing good," she said.

"I have to know what it is," Runa said, stubbornly. She strode directly towards it.

Everyone followed.

Now almost atop the thing, Lyric thought it looked like a bundle of black rags with something long and bony jutting out from one side. Perhaps it'd been dumped off a ship and affected by the Taint in the water. She leaned closer, peering around Runa.

"That's a hand!" Lyric gasped.

Runa, finally covering her mouth as she bent forward, studied the hand. The fingers were abnormally long and sharpened into claws.

"Whatever it is, it's not human," Runa said.

Elaina, acquiring a stick from somewhere, lifted the tattered rags and uncovered a hairless head, turned to the side. The abnormally large eyes, caught in wrinkled folds of skin, were filmy with death. Its features were delicate but twisted, and ridges covered the creature's face. Some of the seams were sharp and bony, and the rest appeared to be hardened flaps of skin like the opening of gills.

"Female perhaps," Elaina said. It was her teaching voice, analytical and unruffled, one Lyric remembered well from childhood.

Lyric felt her unease shift, soothed by their mother's tone, and she leaned over Runa's shoulder to look more closely at the creature. Its mouth, slack and hanging open, was filled with needle-sharp teeth. "I think it was human," Lyric said, frowning. She looked at their mother. "How is that possible?"

"I think you're right," Elaina said. Her eyes filled with sympathy, and she looked at Kell. "This may have once been a resident of Salta."

Gasping, Lyric straightened and turned to Kell. His face looked strained, and tears glinted in his eyes. He swallowed and pressed a fist to the side of his head, then turned away from them, looking out at the ocean.

Lyric hurried towards him and slid her arms around his waist, pressing her cheek against his chest. "I'm so sorry, Kell," she said.

His heartbeat was loud and quick beneath her ear.

"Did you know?" Lyric asked.

"No," Kell said. His arms moved around her back, holding her tightly. "I ... I knew about the creatures, but I thought they were animals, *had been* animals."

"How did this happen?" Runa asked. "You said the Taint kills things, destroys, it doesn't transform. Not like this."

"I don't know," Elaina said. "I wish I did. My father must know about this."

Lyric shifted in Kell's arms so she could look at their mother. "You think he did this?" she asked, incredulously.

"I don't know," Elaina growled. Her face darkened with a mix of frustration and fury. "We'll get answers; I promise you that," she said. Her fierce, gold-green eyes shifted to Kell's back, still turned away. "We'll hold him accountable, Kell, I swear it."

Lyric stared at their mother, unsure of what to say, what to feel. Could King Rakarn truly be responsible for this tragedy? Had what happened been an accident or something planned, expected? Was her grandfather a monster?

"We need to keep moving," Kell said, his voice tight. "We can't be out in the dark."

"Yes," Elaina agreed. She stood, gripping the stick in her hand like a sword, then dropped it onto the sand. Her face smoothed, the anger tucked back deep inside her. "Come, Runa," she said. "We've wasted enough time here already."

# 13

LYRIC

NIGHT FELL FASTER than Lyric expected, the sun disappearing into a dark mass of angry clouds. The wind lashed at her face and cloak, simultaneously trying to rip it away from her fingers and send her lurching across the sand. Her braids had all but unraveled, her hair flailing around her face and getting into her eyes and mouth.

The waves crashed large and angry against the beach, drowning out any attempts of conversation. Lyric worried that the wind was blowing Tainted water into their faces. Could that kill them? Could the drops of water turn them into the twisted creature they'd found on the sand? Memories of its teeth and claws filled her mind. Maybe she was already transforming.

Nervously, Lyric squinted into the gathering darkness. They needed shelter. Where was Beyn's house?

They'd found nothing since leaving Salta, the beach stretching empty ahead of them save for scattered detritus, foul and green, that they could barely see to avoid. The wall of cliffs to the west offered no protection and somehow intensified the wind whenever they drifted towards them to get away from the waves.

As the night deepened around them, they fell closer together, walking no more than a handspan from each other. Elaina, scavenging through a clump of driftwood untouched by the Taint, fashioned torches and passed them around, using flint and steel from her pack to light them.

They held their torches high, but the spitting flames were too weak to chase away the shadows. Sounds became amplified and full of menace. Lyric shrieked when a piece of wood cracked loudly beneath someone's foot.

Heart still thudding in her chest, Lyric felt the hair rise on the back of her neck. "Did you hear that?" she asked, raising her torch and staring at the waves. She grabbed Kell, pulling him against her, finding comfort in the solidness of him against her side.

Something moaned in the darkness.

"There!" Runa hissed, pointing up the beach.

Dark shapes were flying towards them, nearly invisible in the night.

Runa held up a hand, and a tiny flame flickered above her palm.

"No!" Lyric yelled, but Runa had already thrown the ball of flame.

It soared through the air, arcing up and then exploding as it hit the ground. A gust of heated wind rushed into Lyric's face ripping back her hair and illuminating what was coming. In the momentary light, she saw six creatures racing towards them. They resembled huge disfigured bats; wings tucked as they dashed forward. The creatures shrieked as the remnants of Runa's magic washed over them, their skin rippling and glowing. Instead of slowing down, the displaced magic infused them with energy.

"Remember what Meara said!" Lyric yelled as darkness reclaimed them. "They eat magic!"

Runa glanced back, her hair blowing across her face, teeth

gritted in frustration. Crouching, she clawed at the ground and scooped up several stones into her hand. She turned and holding her torch high, began to sling the rocks, one after the other.

Lyric dropped Kell's arm and raised her torch like a club, ready to hit anything that got close.

"Run!" Elaina yelled, brandishing her torch. "Hoods up! Stay together!"

The creatures descended.

Lyric raised her arm, trying to shield her head as the monsters twisted overhead. Terrified, she could feel the weight of them as they darted above her, their shrieking hurting her ears. A claw struck her arm and cut through the hood of her cloak. She screamed, waving her torch.

*Keep moving!* Lyric told herself. *Don't stop!*

Her foot sank into the sand and Lyric stumbled, nearly falling onto her face. She scrambled forward, around a mess of algae, her eyes finding Elaina and Runa's feet. They were still ahead of her running. She couldn't lose sight of them.

Lyric heard her torch sputter as she blindly flailed it around her head. She prayed the thud of torch against flesh was a creature and not Kell beside her. Blood dripped into Lyric's eyes, and down her arms, more splattering across the sand ahead of her.

"Kell!" Lyric gasped, worried she'd receive no answer. All she could hear were her own terrified pants and the creatures' shrieking.

"I'm here!" Kell called. His voice was breathless and pained, but he was still alive.

He gasped suddenly, an agonized sound, and Lyric snapped her head up, staring sideways. She saw Kell pause, his back arching, his face exposed to the sky, then he crumpled forward, shielding himself, stumbling on.

"Kell—" Lyric gasped, reaching for him.

"Keep going!" Kell yelled. He grabbed her hand and pulled her forward.

Lyric stumbled, holding tight to his hand. A creature dove towards her, needled mouth opening, and she swung her torch up hard. Heat seared down her arm. She was bleeding again.

"They'll kill us!" Lyric yelled. Her hood flew back onto her shoulders, exposing her head.

Elaina glanced back, eyes huge in the sputtering torchlight. Blood dripped down her face from a gash on her scalp. She looked at Lyric, meeting her terror-filled eyes, then at Runa.

Runa was spinning, teeth bared like a cornered animal, her torch knocking one of the creatures away with a powerful back-handed hit. Sparks flew, and she whirled it back up.

Elaina met Lyric's eyes one more time then threw up her hands, screaming out a spell. Her words ignited every torch they held, sending the flames up and out. Fire exploded around them in a shell of flame.

Lyric gasped as heat washed over her, scorching her skin. The beach was bright, illuminated by the sudden red-orange light.

Caught by the eruption of fire, the creatures ignited. They shrieked, spinning and flapping like burning cloth in the wind. One by one they dropped to the ground, their death screams cutting off as the fire claimed them.

Flames still falling, Lyric saw a large shape swoop down beneath the spreading fire.

"Mama!" she screamed.

The creature's claws ripped open the side of Elaina's throat, and it drove her toward the ground. It gnawed at her neck, blood spurting over its jaw, as its hands gripped her shoulders.

Elaina screamed, but the sound was quickly cut off, reduced to a horrible gurgle.

Lyric ran forward, raising her arms.

Runa got there first. Sprinting from the side, she slammed her torch into the creature knocking it away.

It reared, eyes bulging; its mouth wet with their mother's blood.

Released from its claws, Elaina hit the sand. Her torch rolled from her fingers, and she clutched at her neck.

Lyric screamed the word for wind, releasing a gust that sent the creature tumbling back into the falling flames. She felt a peculiar tug in her chest, pulling her towards it, then the monster hit the fire.

The burning creature screamed and died.

Shoving her torch at Kell, Lyric dropped to her knees beside Elaina. She tore through her pack, searching for something to bandage their mother's throat but there was nothing. Thinking quickly, Lyric ripped a strip of cloth from her skirt's hem and wrapped it around Elaina's neck. She had to stop the bleeding. The cloth darkened beneath her fingers and she pressed her hand against her mother's throat.

"Are they dead?" Lyric asked, looking at Runa who'd kneeled beside her.

Runa nodded, her face white. "I think so, but there might be more. We need to hide."

Lyric stared around them. The fallen creatures were burning on the ground like campfires, sputtering and dying on the sand.

"We have to get Mama to a healer," Lyric said. "I don't have supplies, and this ... this may be beyond my skills." She tried to shove aside her fear. She couldn't think about that or the mess of flesh and muscle on their mother's neck.

Elaina was still conscious, her eyes staring at the sky, but they were unfocused, confused. She tried to speak, her words lost in a gurgle of blood as it bubbled from the corner of her mouth.

"Meara's friend should be somewhere close," Runa said. "We'll find it."

"Kell?" Lyric asked, turning to look at him. "Can you carry her?"

Kell nodded, stepping close, but Lyric saw him wince and remembered his earlier cry of pain.

"Are you hurt?" she asked.

"I'm all right," Kell said. "I can carry Elaina."

"If you're injured—"

"I'm fine!" Kell snapped.

Lyric blinked at him. "All right," she said slowly. "But if you want me to look at it I will."

"Later. We need to move." He stabbed both torches into the sand and kneeled beside her and Elaina. Lyric moved out of the way, and Kell carefully lifted their mother into his arms. She was still wearing her pack.

A muscle flexed in Kell's cheek, and he struggled a little to stand, but when he found his footing, he adjusted his grip and nodded, holding Elaina close against his chest.

Lyric adjusted the bandage at their mother's throat and picked up one of the torches.

"Let's go," Runa said, picking up a second torch. She looked like a bloodied warrior, her red hair unbound, her torches raised like swords in both fists. Fury boiled in her eyes and across her sharp face as she clenched her teeth, taut muscles trembling beneath her skin.

Staring at her, Lyric was equally proud and terrified. She wouldn't want to be the cause of such fury. Bolstered by Runa's fierceness, Lyric nodded. "The house can't be much farther," she said.

Runa turned, her shoulders tight, her head swiveling, and began to walk.

Kell followed after Runa, holding Elaina, and Lyric came last. She watched for more creatures to appear in the dark, adrenaline thrumming through her. Had they summoned more with their magic and fire? If they were attacked again, injured as they were with Kell holding Elaina, Lyric doubted they'd survive. They'd die, slowly, screaming and—

No. No, they'd find shelter.

Lyric shoved down her fears and concentrated on Kell's shoulders, the algae on the beach, the feel of the dying torch in her hand, and the burning in her legs as she pressed on despite her exhaustion. She fell into a stupor as she walked and looked for danger. She was so deep into the mindlessness of her movement that she nearly didn't hear Runa speak aloud.

"What?" Lyric asked dully. She stepped up beside Kell and examined Elaina's neck. The makeshift bandage was soaked with blood.

Glancing forward, Lyric saw a shed on the sand. It was broken, having fallen off short, notched stilts that laid beside it. Remarkably, the damage from the shed's fall was contained to its floor, now half-buried in the sand. The roof and walls seemed sound and the door, hanging in its frame, creaked in the wind.

Runa pushed her torches into the sand beside the shed and whirled back to face them. "Get inside!" she said, rushing towards them. "We'll stay here until morning. Hurry! Elenora said more are coming."

"Elenora—" Lyric said.

"Yes, Ly, help me!" Runa said, reaching for Kell.

Lyric's torch snuffed out, trailing smoke. Dropping the burned stump, Lyric turned and put her arm around Kell's waist. She gasped as he hissed under his breath and pulled back her arm.

"Just ... higher," he said.

Carefully, Lyric put her arm around Kell again, higher on his back.

Runa grabbed Kell's other arm and together, they helped

him carry Elaina up to the house and through the gaping doorway.

It was pitch black inside, despite an un-shuttered window in the back wall.

Runa brought one of the dying torches inside and held it up, revealing the inside of the shed. The wooden floor was shattered on one side and black sand mounded against the wall. Remnants of furniture, battered and toppled, piled in the far corner, presumably left where they'd fallen when the shed fell over.

Lyric couldn't see any sign of the Taint and breathed a sigh of relief. "There, away from the door," she said, steering Kell towards the sand.

Kell staggered forward, collapsing to his knees and nearly dropping Elaina.

Lyric and Runa steadied him and helped ease their mother to the ground.

Elaina groaned, her eyelids fluttering, and Lyric quickly pillowed her head on her knees.

Something shrieked outside.

"They're coming!" Runa said, scrambling towards the door.

Unable to move with Elaina on her lap, Lyric rechecked their mother's bandage and smoothed her bloodied hair off her face.

Kell scrambled up with a pained hiss and followed Runa to the door. They pulled on it together. It took several hard tugs before they could get it closed, the bent door frame resisting their efforts.

The bar that kept the door closed was missing, and Runa raced back to the mound of furniture. She kicked against a table leg, again and again until it finally splintered free, and she carried it back to the door, barring it shut.

Kell, meanwhile, had stumbled over to the window and pulled the shutter closed, latching it firmly. Moving back to

Lyric's side, he collapsed next to her, his head flopping back onto the sand.

Runa backed away from the door, the torch in her hand. The flame was small, barely a flicker in the dark. She raised her hand over it, hesitating, the fire touching her skin, and then she dropped her hand and sighed.

The torch blew out.

Lyric blinked, unable to see, trying to make out the shape of Runa by the door. She could hear their breathing, ragged, exhausted, and their mother's faint wheezing in her lap.

The howls grew louder, and Lyric held her breath. Her heart thundered in her ears, and she wondered if the others could hear the hot pulse of her blood.

Something scrabbled against the door. It shrieked, high pitched and frantic, and there was a thud as it slammed against the wood.

The house creaked, and sand fell on Lyric's head.

Another howl, another thud against the door.

Had they survived only to die here, trapped inside this broken house?

*They won't get in*, a voice said inside her head.

Lyric gasped, her fingers tightening in their mother's hair. "Gandara?" she whispered. She willed her heart back into her chest.

She felt the ancestor's presence shift inside her head and somehow knew she nodded.

Lyric winced as the scratching sound came closer on the wall beside her.

How did the monsters know they were here? Could they smell them? Were they tracking them like hounds?

"What do we do?" Lyric whispered.

"Lyric?" Kell asked softly from the dark.

Lyric ignored him, listening for Gandara's words.

*Wait*, Gandara said. *You can't use magic. They'll leave when morning comes.*

"Will my mother survive?" Lyric tightened her grip on Elaina's head and shoulders, pulling her against her stomach like she was holding a child. "I just got her back. I can't lose her again."

*Perhaps,* Gandara said. *She's strong.* The old woman seemed displeased when thinking about Elaina, and Lyric frowned, trying to separate the vague unease from her own worry.

"How can I help her?" Lyric asked.

Her ancestor's presence wavered, slipping away. "Gandara? How can I help her? Gandara?"

"Lyric?" Runa asked, squatting down somewhere in front of her. "Gandara came to you?"

"She said to wait," Lyric said dully.

"Nothing else we can do," Runa said. "Try to sleep. Rest while we can. Kell's passed out."

"Is he breathing?" Lyric asked with alarm, thinking of his injury. What if he'd lied and bled to death beside her?

"Yes," Runa said. "I think he's just exhausted."

"But Mama ..."

"You can't do anything for her now." Runa rested her hand on Lyric's, making her jump. "We'll leave as soon as it's light. We can't be more than half a day from Ivernn. There'll be a healer there. Mother won't die, Lyric. She won't."

A creature wailed outside.

"How can you sleep with them screaming like that?" Lyric asked, looking fearfully in the direction of the door.

"They won't get in," Runa said stubbornly. "And if they do, there's not much we can do anyway." She sat on Lyric's left and leaned against the sand, resting the dun torch on her knee. "Rest as much as you can," Runa said. "We can't carry Mother if we're too exhausted to move. We'll be fine, Ly."

Lyric closed her eyes, feeling Runa's presence, strong and familiar beside her.

# 14

RUNA

RUNA WOKE to the distant sound of waves washing onto the beach. Her lips were cracked and dry, and when she moistened them with her tongue, she tasted dried blood. A dull pain throbbed behind her eyes; it felt like someone had stuffed her head with wool and slammed a hammer against her temple while she slept. Feeling groggy, Runa swallowed a groan and forced herself to stand, stretching her stiff muscles.

The abandoned shed was murky with the door and window closed, but light leaked beneath the warped door and through cracks in the walls. Runa cocked her head, listening for the monsters. All she heard was the waves.

Runa pushed back her cloak and ran her hand over her arm. Her sleeves were stiff with blood and salt from the storm. She hissed as her fingers brushed across torn skin. Aware now of her injuries, pain burned down her arm, but she shoved it away and looked down at Lyric, who was starting to wake.

Groaning, her sister shifted her feet, unable to move much with their mother still lying in her lap.

Kell, stretched out on his side next to Lyric, groaned and

shoved himself upright. He reached a hand behind his back and looked up at Runa.

Runa knelt in front of Elaina and Lyric and studied their mother's pale face. "How is she?" Runa asked.

Head bowed, Lyric peeled back the edge of the bandage, and pressed her fingers against Elaina's wrist, taking her pulse. "Her pulse is weak," Lyric said. "We need help soon. She's lost a lot of blood." Her eyes, wide and exhausted from lack of sleep, shifted to the door. "Are they gone?"

"Yes," Runa said. "It's daylight."

She looked over at Kell. He looked terrible with blood on his face and clothes. His cloak was torn, and there were rents in the thick fabric of his pack. What might have happened to their backs and arms if they hadn't worn their cloaks and bags?

"We should eat," Kell said, looking at Lyric. "Try to restore our strength."

Runa nodded and reached for her pack. She'd dumped it on the floor during the night. Her bag bore multiple slashes, but nothing seemed to have fallen out. Not that there'd been a lot inside.

Raising her waterskin to her lips, Runa nearly drained the whole thing. She hadn't realized she was so thirsty. She popped a piece of dried gull meat into her mouth, then helped Lyric free her legs from beneath Elaina so she could stand.

"Can you carry her again?" Lyric asked Kell. She winced and bent over, rubbing her thighs.

"I'll manage," Kell said. He smiled, which made him look even ghastlier, bloodied as he was.

"Let me check your back," Lyric said.

"I'm fine," Kell said, waving her away with his waterskin.

Runa narrowed her eyes. Why didn't he want Lyric to look at his back?

Lyric shook her head. "No, I need to check it." She shoved open the window, letting in a beam of light.

"It's nothing," Kell insisted. "What about you? There's blood on your arms."

"You won't be able to carry Elaina if you're bleeding out as we walk," Lyric said. "Stop arguing." Her jaw set stubbornly, and she knelt behind him, peeling up his shirt to look at his lower back.

Kell stopped her hand with his, preventing her from pushing it up all the way. "How is it?" he asked.

Lyric stared at Kell's back with a curious expression, brows knotted over her eyes. She blinked and looked up at him. "Nothing too serious," she said. "It's not deep, and the bleeding has stopped. You'll end up with a scar." Her head cocked to one side. "What does it mean, your tattoo?"

Runa raised an eyebrow. A tattoo? Like the one around his throat or different? She shifted on her knees in a furtive attempt to see but settled back before either Kell or Lyric noticed.

"A story for another time," Kell said. He turned his head, giving her an imploring look Runa didn't understand.

Lyric blinked and looked back down at Kell's back, pulling down his shirt. "It needs to be cleaned and bandaged," she said, "but I think you'll be fine until we reach Ivernn. Normally I'd advise against lifting anything heavy." Lyric glanced at Elaina, lying on the floor. "Be as careful as you can," she said.

Turning towards her, Kell lifted his hand and brushed his fingers along Lyric's jaw. "I will," he said. Standing, Kell rolled his shoulders with a pained expression and walked to the door.

Runa stood to follow.

Not waiting for her help, Kell pushed up the bar and wrenched the door open, sticking his head out into the light. "Give me a minute to walk around," he said, looking back at Lyric. "Then, I'll be ready to leave."

Runa stepped into the doorway and watched as Kell walked around the corner of the shed, then she examined their surroundings. The beach looked different in the morning light. She didn't trust how calm it was; as if their ordeal the night before hadn't happened.

She'd been so focused on staying alive, on moving and fighting, that she hadn't considered how close they'd come to dying. That she was still here, battered and bloodied, left her with an incredible, heady feeling. Runa breathed in one deep breath after another, feeling the remnants of fear wash over her until she felt her usual determination take root.

Crossing her arms, Runa looked back into the house at Lyric, who was sitting by their mother and staring at her hands. Lyric's fingertips were stained as if she'd dipped them in red paint. She tried to scrub them off on her cloak as Runa watched, then gave up and pressed the heels of her palms against her eyes. Her hair, a tangled cloud around her shoulders, shifted forward as she bowed her head.

"Ly, are you ok?" Runa asked softly.

Lyric jerked and looked up; her green eyes glistened wetly, and bruises darkened the skin beneath them. "As much as I can be," she said.

Runa opened her mouth to say something; she wasn't sure what, but before she could, Kell returned. She shifted to the side so he could enter the doorway. His movements were stiff as he brushed past as if pain had replaced his flesh with wood, rigid and unbending.

"Should I pick Elaina up?" Kell asked, walking to Lyric and Elaina.

"Yes, but help me get her pack off first," Lyric said. "I'll carry it."

Kell slowly kneeled and braced a hand on the floor.

Runa walked over to them. She helped Kell and Lyric lift Elaina's shoulders off the ground so they could slip off their mother's bag. Like Runa's, the heavy cloth was damaged.

"Maybe you should transfer her belongings to yours?" Runa suggested as Lyric examined the straps on Elaina's pack.

"She'll still need it," Lyric said. Her jaw set as though prepared for Runa to argue.

Runa shrugged. "All right, if you have the strength to carry both together."

"Mine is practically empty anyway," Lyric said, reaching for her own. "I'll just roll mine up and stuff it into hers." She did so then pushed up onto her knees and slipped Elaina's bag onto her back.

Kell, holding Elaina's upper body, glanced at her.

"Ready," Lyric said.

Runa moved out of the way, ready to offer assistance if Kell required it, and watched as he lifted Elaina into his arms and pushed himself to his feet. Confident he wasn't about to collapse and dump their mother on the floor, Runa walked back to the door.

She paused in the doorway, brushing her fingertips across the weathered wood. They'd almost died last night. How had they survived? The shed didn't look like it could survive much of an assault. Had the gods been watching out for them?

*Thank you*, Runa thought, sending it to anyone listening. She promised herself that she'd find a shrine as soon as possible and light incense. With how things were going, it couldn't hurt seeking the Trinity's favor.

THE SUN BURNED high in the sky when they reached Raendashar's border. Kell had almost collapsed twice since leaving the abandoned house, and for the past two hours, Runa and Lyric had stood on either side of him, keeping him upright and sharing the weight of Elaina in his arms. They'd left all traces of the Taint behind, and Runa was relieved as she stared at the clean sand. The sea had washed everything away, including driftwood.

Breathing hard, Kell stopped and went down on one knee, cradling Elaina against his chest. He took a long, shuddering breath and stared at the sand as if not quite seeing it.

Runa released Kell's arm and straightened, studying the land with fascination. It was apparent they'd left Thenda behind. Rough black stone rose like a mountain in front of them, altering the coastline from flat, ocean-washed sand to an obsidian wall of flat-topped cliffs that jutted over the sea.

The beach narrowed, becoming no more than a thin line of sand between the water and the rising land. Following it with her eye, Runa saw that it disappeared entirely into the water.

Foamy and dark, the ocean seemed more violent here, crashing against the cliffs as if to break them apart. The wind bit against her face and yanked on her hair. There was no question in Runa's mind that this seething surf was indeed the Sea of Screams, and if they wanted to continue north, they'd have to climb the cliff.

Searching the black stone with narrowed eyes, Runa spotted a thin trail winding snake-like to the top. "There," she said, pointing. "There are buildings up there. This must be Ivernn."

Lyric kneeled next to Kell and put a hand on his shoulder then checked Elaina's breathing. She leaned her cheek over their mother's mouth, listening for a long moment before looking up at Runa.

"She's weaker," Lyric said. Her voice was distant.

"Just a little farther, Kell," Runa said, trying to sound encouraging. She hadn't thought him strong enough to carry Elaina as long as he had, and yet here he was, struggling once more to his feet, teeth gritted, the tendons in his neck taut beneath the skin.

Together, arms around each other, they climbed the trail,

each step agonizingly slow. Once they reached the top, Kell shuffled to a large flat stone and collapsed onto it.

Lyric scrambled next to him and caught Elaina's shoulders, steadying her limp body across Kell's lap. "You can set her down," Lyric said.

"No," Kell gasped. "I'll be unable to pick her up again."

Runa looked around. The trail opened up into a long street, bracketed by small houses of dark gray wood. She could see more buildings beyond it, the small town stretching in a long line.

"I'll find help," Runa said, looking at Lyric and Kell.

Lyric looked up, her eyes moving over Runa's face and body. "You look frightful," she said.

"Good." Runa bared her teeth in a grim smile. "They'll know I'm serious." She shoved her hair behind her ears and was about to take a step forward but paused, looking back at her sister. Healing was never free, and she had no money or anything with which to barter. "Give me mother's bag," she said, crouching beside Lyric.

Lyric, raising an eyebrow, slipped the pack from her shoulders and handed it to Runa. She watched as Runa opened it and shifted around the contents.

"Are you looking for money?" Lyric asked. "It'd be in her belt, wouldn't it?"

Runa, fingers passing over a small leather journal, nodded without looking up. "Check there too." Besides Lyric's empty pack and the journal, Runa found several pieces of dried fish, a small figurine carved from black stone, a bundle of tightly rolled clothes, a silky letter sealed with black wax, flint and steel, a waterskin, and soap. "Nothing useful," Runa said, shoving everything back inside.

"Here," Lyric said.

Runa set down Elaina's pack and looked up, accepting a

small leather pouch from Lyric. She shifted it in her hand and heard the clink of metal.

"There's some gold in there," Lyric said, eyes wide. "We should be able to pay for healing."

Runa nodded.

"And she had this," Lyric said. She lifted a fabric-covered bundle from her lap and peeled back a corner of the wrapping. A pendant glinted in the sunlight, a gorgeous stone of red and orange. Finely-spun gold cradled the large gem and twisted across its surface in the intricate shape of a dragon's head.

"A Dragon Eye stone," Kell breathed, staring at it with wide eyes. "Do you know what that's worth?"

Runa felt her mouth go dry as she stared at the necklace. A strange hunger rose in her chest, stirring like a thing waking. "Cover that up," she said quickly. Runa looked around them suspiciously, worried someone had seen it.

Rewrapping the pendant, Lyric returned it to one of the pockets on Elaina's belt. "We can't sell this, obviously," she said. "This must be important to mama."

Runa nodded and tried to clear her head. She would never have imagined their mother owning such a treasure, but Elaina was the daughter of a king, wasn't she? The necklace might be but a bauble to the royalty of Raendashar, one that could feed an entire village over the winter.

"The money should be enough," Runa said, tightening the pouch's drawstrings. "I'll get help. Stay here."

Lyric and Kell both nodded.

Runa strode into town. She passed the first house without stopping. It felt neglected, the closed door warped and covered by an old fishing net.

In the doorway of the second house, just past, an old man stood framed in the door. Runa veered towards him, raising her hand. "I need help!" she called. "My mother is injured and—"

Mumbling something she couldn't hear, the old man

backed into the house, shaking his head. He pulled the door shut as she stepped onto the front step.

Blinking in surprise, Runa moved to the next house. She caught sight of a face in the window and strode towards it, scowling as a pale hand yanked the curtain closed.

"Help!" Runa yelled, pounding on the door. "I need a healer! Please, my mother — help me! Do you have one here? Tell me where to go!" She pounded again, the wood scraping her fist, but whoever was inside didn't answer.

Hissing in frustration, Runa kicked the door with her foot and spun away, continuing up the street. She knocked on the closed doors of two more houses, receiving no answer, and was passing another when she saw the ruined foundation of a house that seemed to have recently burned to the ground. She hesitated in the street, staring at it with confusion. What had happened here?

Unimpeded by the blackened ruins, the wind rushed at her from the sea beyond. It yanked her cloak over her shoulder and filled her nose with the smell of old smoke and brine. Slapping at the fluttering fabric, Runa continued, passing a blacksmith's shop. Like the houses, the smithy was closed, the forge cold; an old sign creaked in the wind, making her wince.

"Where is everyone?" Runa growled. "Help!" she yelled, turning slowly. A bird crying overhead was the only response she received.

At the end of the street, Runa caught sight of what could only be an inn and stable, sitting between a line of half-dead, wind-stripped trees and a large, bleached skull of some mammal. An old wooden sign, nailed above the door, named the building as The Seabird.

Setting her jaw, Runa strode towards the weathered building and wrenched open the door. The room was dim, and it took a moment for her eyes to adjust to the low light.

Narrow, but clean, the inn's common room overflowed with

benches and tables, some occupied with the missing residents of Ivernn. In one corner sat a squat fireplace, inlaid with seashells. Large windows in the back let in the feeble light, the wooden frames filled with diamond-shaped panes of glass that overlooked the angry sea below.

Looking to the left of the door, Runa observed a man and woman laughing and sorting linens at a long bar. The man, bearded and broad-shouldered, ducked away as the woman slapped him with a napkin.

The woman snorted and shook her head, her brown eyes twinkling. She was plump with a kindly, heart-shaped face; her brown hair combed back into a bun. Eyes slipping to Runa framed in the doorway, the mirth slipped off the woman's face as she took in her bloodied appearance. Her eyes widened, her flushed cheeks paling.

Beside her, the man abruptly stood up. His eyes narrowed, and he reached beneath the bar.

Hefting the money pouch in one hand, Runa strode towards them. "I need a healer!" she said, her voice carrying louder than she'd intended in the small room.

"What happened to you?" the man asked. His eyes were suspicious, and Runa narrowed her own in response. Did he think she was dangerous?

"We don't want any trouble here," the woman said, coldly.

"Trouble?" Runa asked. "We'll hardly be trouble to you. Please, a healer. I can pay."

The man shifted, his chest swelling as he lifted a cudgel in his hand. "We?" he asked. He held the club low, but there was a threat in the way he studied her. "Who is with you?"

"We're wasting time!" Runa snapped impatiently. "Do you have a healer or not?"

Forehead wrinkling, the woman laid aside the napkins and brushed her hands on her skirts. She stared at Runa's red hair. "Who's injured?" the woman asked.

"My mother," Runa said.

Sympathy softened the woman's frown, and she walked around the side of the bar. The man hissed something at her, but she ignored him. "Was it the Sireni?" she asked.

"What?" Runa frowned. "No, we came up the Shore."

"Up the Shore ..." The woman glanced back at the bearded man. He seemed to lose some of his wariness and slipped the cudgel back beneath the bar before coming around to join them.

"We were attacked by some kind of ... animal," Runa said. She wasn't sure what to call the nightmarish creatures. Had anyone here seen one? If she started talking about monsters, would they think her mad?

"The creatures," the woman said uneasily. The look on her face mirrored that of Runa's neighbors back home whenever they discussed magic.

"We have a healer," the woman said, "Granny Gertrude. Elias!" She pitched her voice over the room, drawing the attention of a small boy, who scurried up. "Go fetch Granny Gertrude, at once," the woman ordered. "Be quick about it!"

The boy looked at Runa, his eyes wide.

"Now, Elias!" the woman said, shooing him with her hand.

"Yes, Ma!" He spun on his heel and ran off through the door Runa had entered. It slammed behind him.

"Did you and your mother travel alone?" the man asked. "Where is she?"

Runa shook her head. "No, with my sister and a friend. They're with my mother at the entrance of town. Should I bring them here? Where does Mistress Gertrude live?"

"Oh, my dear, don't worry about that," the woman said. "You look about to fall over. My husband, Jim, will fetch them. Here, please sit down." She gestured towards a table. "I'm Maggie. We own The Seabird."

"No, I can go," Runa said.

"No, no," Maggie said. "I insist. Please, sit."

Eyeing her, Runa nodded reluctantly.

"I'll bring them here, Miss," Jim said. "What are their names?"

"My sister is Lyric," Runa said, "and our companion is Kell. I'm Runa."

Jim nodded. "I'll get them right away. Elias will bring Granny here." He headed out the door.

Questioning her decision not to follow Jim, Runa let Maggie lead her to a table. She sagged onto the bench and felt exhaustion settle over her like a water-soaked cloak. She rested her hands in her lap; they felt impossibly heavy.

The room was quiet, too quiet, and when Runa lifted her head, she saw some of the people staring at her. They eyed her suspiciously, more hostile than she'd expected. There was an undercurrent in the room she didn't understand.

"What happened here?" she asked, looking at Maggie. "I saw a burned house."

Maggie looked at her; the anxious look back in her eyes. "By your hair, I'd guess you to be Raendasharan," she said. "You haven't heard?"

Runa raised an eyebrow. She'd never ascribed any significance to the color of her hair. "Heard what?" she asked.

"There was a great battle three weeks ago. Our entire royal fleet, gone to the bottom of the sea. Ten windracers and ten dragonlancers. We know about ships here, you see." Maggie smiled, though it didn't touch her eyes. "Well, not all were destroyed by the Sireni. Some survived but were badly crippled, and King Rakarn ordered them burned before they fell into Sireni hands.

"Since then, the Sireni have grown bolder, coming ashore, and burning homes." Maggie's lips tightened. "They haven't tried to burn us out completely, thank the Trinity, but perhaps they don't think it's worth the effort."

"The entire fleet?" Runa asked.

"Aye," Maggie said.

"You thought they attacked us," Runa said with realization. "That we might have led some here?"

"The thought crossed my mind," Maggie said. She gestured at the subdued room. "And likely theirs as well. You look dreadful, dear; quite fearsome. Maybe Granny should look you over as well."

"It's not as bad as it looks," Runa said. "I have cuts and scrapes, nothing serious." Exhaustion pressed again behind her eyes, dragging her towards sleep. "How much for a room?"

"Two silvers per night," Maggie said, "and four coppers for a hot meal."

Runa nodded, thinking about the gold in Elaina's purse.

"Unfortunately I only have one room available," Maggie continued. "Lukas Weldan's house, the one you saw, was burned by the Sireni last week. He's been living here since. I do have a cot in the stable for your friend. Hopefully, he's not afraid of horses?"

"That'll be fine," Runa said. Kell had surely spent many nights in barns and beneath the open sky, traveler that he was.

The inn's front door opened, and Lyric stepped through. She held it open for Jim, who strode in carrying Elaina. Kell followed on his heels, head bent wearily. As Jim passed, Lyric looked around and saw Runa. Her face softened with relief, and she walked towards her.

"Let's get you to a room," Maggie said, glancing at the locals. "Follow me, please."

Runa stood, and Lyric clasped her arm, squeezing gently. "Jim said they've sent for a healer?" Lyric asked as they walked towards the stairs.

Runa nodded. "She's coming here."

They climbed to the second floor, following behind Jim and Kell, and stepped out onto a landing that was barely wider than the stairs themselves. The hall was dim, but someone had hung paintings on the dark wood paneling. Runa craned her head, trying to examine them as they passed.

Maggie stopped at the last room on the left and opened the door, shifting back so her husband could carry Elaina inside and lay her on the bed.

Giving his wife a quick look, Jim squeezed past them and headed back down to the bar.

The room was too small for everyone, so Kell stayed in the hall. He sagged against the door frame opposite Maggie, his arms hanging limp.

Touching Kell's shoulder as she passed, Lyric immediately went to the bed. She dropped her pack and leaned over their mother, listening to her breathe. "Do you have any comfrey?" Lyric asked, looking back at Maggie, who still stood in the door with Kell. "For a poultice?"

"Comfrey? No, I'm afraid not," Maggie said. "You know herbs?"

"Yes," Lyric said. She gestured at Runa. "My sister and I are wise women, but we left behind our supplies."

"Granny might have what you're looking for," Maggie said. "Or something similar. I'm not sure that herb grows here." She eyed them. "Where are you from?"

"Oleporea," Runa said, remembering Elaina's response to Meara.

"Oh," Maggie said. She seemed confused.

Runa remembered her earlier assumption that she was from Raendashar. "But our mother's family is here, in Raendashar," Runa said. "It's our first visit."

Maggie nodded, seeming soothed. She turned to Kell. "This is our only available room, but I have a cot in the stable you can use. It's clean and warm."

Kell smiled tiredly. "That's fine, thank you," he said.

"Good," Maggie said. "Granny will be here soon. I'll get

hot water and towels. I'm sure she'll ask for them. I can show you to the stable." She studied Kell shrewdly. "It looks like you're injured too. There's blood on the back of your shirt. Jim can take a look at your back if you like. He's sewn up more than one sailor who cut himself on the rocks 'round here."

"No," Kell said, a touch too quickly. He smoothed his face into a smile as Maggie frowned. "No, it's ok. Lyric looked at it already. I'll be fine once I get cleaned up."

"All right," Maggie said, "but don't go bleeding on my floor because you're trying to impress the girls."

Kell flushed, eyes darting to Lyric. "Honestly, I just need to bathe."

Maggie relented and rested a hand on her hip. "I can take you to the stable now if you wish? I'll have Jim bring you water. Afterward, if you're hungry, you can eat dinner in the common room. My Jim makes a delicious stew."

Kell looked at Lyric.

"It's ok," Lyric said, smiling. "Go ahead. There's nothing you can do now. We'll be fine."

"Here," Runa said, fishing in the money pouch. Avoiding the gold coins, she handed a mix of silver and copper to Maggie. "For our room and evening meal. How much for Kell's cot?"

"No charge," Maggie said. She smiled and took the handful of coins, slipping it into an apron pocket. "There's a bathing chamber downstairs if you'd like to use it after Granny arrives. Don't forget to see to your own injuries." She gave them a stern, motherly look, and then turned back to Kell.

"This way, Mr. Kell," she said.

Kell glanced at Lyric again, then flicked his eyes to Runa, who nodded.

Runa closed the door as Maggie and Kell left and turned back around. Lyric was examining their mother's neck again.

"How bad is it?" Runa asked. "As bad as you thought?" She walked to the bed and looked over her sister's head.

"Yes," Lyric said. Her eyes were large and worried. "We can't lose her, Ru. Not after we got her back."

Bone-numbing fear tingled through their bond and filled Runa's chest. She gasped, surprised by the return of their connection. Sitting on the edge of the bed, Runa reached for her sister's hand.

"I don't know what to do, Ru," Lyric said. "She's still unconscious, though perhaps that's a mercy. Her breathing is so faint, and her wound ... I'm not sure how to even sew the ... There's muscle and bone and ..." Her fingers tightened on Runa's.

"She's strong," Runa said. No matter what she thought about their mother's choices and their abandonment, Runa knew Elaina was as fierce and relentless as a mother wolf. She wouldn't die on her back in bed. It was impossible.

A brisk knock on the door cleared Runa's head. "Come in," Runa called.

The door opened, revealing an elderly woman holding a large canvas bag. She was shorter than both Runa and Lyric, which was rare considering their height, and had thick, white hair gathered in a braid that brushed the floor. Wide and sturdy, the old woman's shoulders were strong and her back straight, a rare thing to see in a person her age. Her bright blue eyes were alert and set in a brown face wrinkled by the sun.

"I'm Gertrude," the woman said, looking them over. She didn't smile, but her eyes were not unkind. She shifted her gaze to Elaina and walked forward, closing the door.

Runa stood and shifted awkwardly out of the way, her tired legs protesting as she did so. She crossed her arms, tucking them against her waist, and watched as Lyric moved to the wall so Gertrude could stand by Elaina's side.

Setting her bag on the ground, Gertrude bent over their mother and unraveled the bandage. "Good field dressing," she said. "You likely saved her life. Maggie said you came from Thenda?"

"Yes," Lyric said. She hovered, hands clasped against her chest, a step behind Gertrude's left elbow, watching the woman closely.

"A creature did this, then?" Gertrude asked. Her tone was surprisingly matter-of-fact.

"Yes. You've seen this before?" Runa asked. "An injury like this?"

"Once," Gertrude said.

Someone knocked on the door and Maggie's voice called through the wood. Hearing their permission to enter, the innkeeper carried inside clean towels and a large bucket of water that steamed as she placed it on the floor beside Gertrude.

Lyric was forced to move again, her back hitting the wall beneath the high window letting light into the room.

"There's a basin beneath the bed," Maggie said. She eyed Runa and Lyric. "Find me when you'd like to bathe." Giving Gertrude a respectful nod, she left and closed the door.

"Maggie said this is your mother?" Gertrude asked. She reached beneath the bed for the basin and placed it next to the bucket.

"Yes," Lyric said. "Her name is Elaina."

"I'll clean her wound," Gertrude said, "and sew together what I can. I'm not sure she'll be able to speak once she heals. The muscles in her neck are badly torn. There's also the mage sickness on her."

"Mage sickness?" Runa asked. She studied her mother's pale, sweat-beaded face.

"Yes, I've seen this before," Gertrude said. "The creature fed on her magic and poisoned it, and then it got back in. I can't fix that. I'm not a mage. I can stabilize her, focus on the physical injury, but you'll need a Dragon Blessed to heal this wound fully."

"A what?" Runa asked.

Gertrude glanced at her shrewdly. "A mage healer."

"And if we can't find one?" Runa asked.

"Then she'll die. Perhaps in a week, maybe less."

Lyric gasped and moved to Runa's side, grabbing her arm. "Where can we find a Dragon Blessed?" she asked, her voice shaking.

"Rathgar's Hold, I'd say. You may find one elsewhere, but I expect they've all gone to the capital for the Feast of Souls."

"Can we send for one?" Runa asked. "A raven, perhaps?"

"We have no messengers here," Gertrude said. "You can ask Maggie if she knows someone who might volunteer to go on your behalf." She eyed them. "You should get cleaned up; wash all that blood off."

"We want to stay," Lyric said, holding Runa's arm.

"There's nothing you can do now," Gertrude said. She soaked a cloth in the warm water and started cleaning Elaina's throat. "I'll bathe your mother and tend to her wound."

"You may need us to move her," Runa said, eyeing the small woman.

Gertrude's lips quirked. "No need. I have done this many times. You won't be any help to your mother if you both collapse from exhaustion," she said. "I'll stay right here. Your mother is safe with me." She glanced at their arms. "You don't want to get blood sickness if you leave your cuts untreated."

Runa looked at Lyric. "She's right," she said softly. "There's nothing we can do now." She glanced at Gertrude. "You'll send for us if anything changes?"

"Of course," Gertrude said.

"We'll come back as soon as we've cleaned ourselves up," Lyric said. She squeezed past Runa and reached for Elaina's hand, holding her limp fingers. "Mama?" Lyric said. "Runa and

I will be right back. You're safe. Gertrude is taking care of you." She released Elaina's hand reluctantly and turned back to Runa.

Runa opened the door, letting Lyric step out into the hall ahead of her. She looked back at Gertrude. The woman hardly seemed the sort to harm anyone, and what would she do to Elaina anyway?

"We'll be back soon," Runa promised.

Together, Runa and Lyric walked down the hall and descended the stairs.

The sound of music enveloped them, drifting from the fireplace where a man played a fiddle. The room was crowded with more unfamiliar faces. Where had they been hiding? The town had seemed empty when she'd walked its length, trying to find help. She looked for Kell but didn't see him.

Looking to the side, Runa saw Maggie approaching.

"I'm glad you came down," she said, coming up to them. She was carrying a tray with several empty mugs on it. "Your mother is in excellent hands with Granny," she said. "Your companion is cleaning himself up. I wouldn't be surprised if he falls asleep without eating."

Lyric smiled tiredly. "Sleep does sound good about now."

"Can we take a meal in our room after we've bathed?" Runa asked.

Maggie nodded. "Of course. Here, let me set this down." She took the tray to the bar, then led them to a small room behind the stairs. "Here's the bathing room," she said. "No one will disturb you. I only let our female guests use it and Jim, when he's been particularly sweet to me." Maggie chuckled fondly.

"There's a latch there," Maggie said, pointing to the side of the door. "I filled the tub with hot water, and there's soap, bandages, and towels on the table. If you give me your clothes when you're done, I can wash them for you."

Lyric looked down at her dress, examining the torn sleeve on one arm. "I'm afraid this is all we have."

"We lost our belongings on the Shore," Runa said, thinking quickly. "Do you have anything we can buy? Something simple would suffice."

"Ah," Maggie said. "You poor dears. Hmm." She tapped her chin with a finger. "We don't have a clothier here but Fredrik's daughter, Peni, is about your size. She may have something to spare."

"Thank you," Lyric said with a relieved smile.

Maggie nodded.

"Mistress Gertrude said we need to find a Dragon Blessed," Runa said. "Is there someone we can send to bring one here? A messenger?"

"We don't have runners here," Maggie said. "Someone may take the task, but I warn you, given the Sireni attack recently I'm not sure anyone will be willing to make the journey. We're mostly fishermen here. I can ask ..."

"Jim pointed out the burned house," Lyric said. "I'm so sorry."

"One of us will have to go then," Runa said, nodding. She'd assumed as much. She'd been dreading sitting idle, waiting for someone else to track down a mage healer. It'd be better if she went herself.

"You might not have to travel to the capital," Maggie said. "A Dragon Blessed could have stayed behind in Heldon's Rock, despite the festival. The city is less than two days away."

Runa nodded. "Thank you. I'll check there."

"Find me when you're done," Maggie said, "and I'll have food brought to you."

"Thank you, Mistress," Lyric said.

"Just Maggie," Maggie said, with a warm smile. She left, closing the door, and Runa latched it.

Lyric shoved her hair behind her shoulder and started

unbuttoning her dress. "One tub," she grinned. "Want to share like when we were kids? I'm not getting into the dirty water after you."

The corner of Runa's mouth lifted as she remembered epic battles in the wash-bin back home. "Fine," she said, "but no hogging the water."

Climbing into the large tub, they sat in opposite ends, giggling as their knees knocked into each other. Lyric hissed as the water touched the lacerations on her arms, but after a moment of tentatively dipping into the water, she sighed and sunk deeper to wash her hair.

The warm water felt wonderful on Runa's sore muscles. Scrubbing dirt and blood from her skin, she breathed deeply, trying to relax, but the knowledge of their mother slowly dying upstairs crouched at the back of her mind stealing away her momentary pleasure.

*This is her fault,* Runa thought, then immediately felt ashamed. Their mother couldn't have predicted their ordeal on the Shore, and she certainly didn't deserve to die for it.

Stepping out of the bath, Runa wrapped herself in a towel and combed her fingers through her hair, braiding it slowly.

Lyric joined her, examining Runa's injuries then tending to her own. Most of their cuts were superficial and could be left alone. Only a deeper cut on Lyric's upper arm and one on Runa's forearm needed to be covered.

Cleaned and soothed by the warm bath, Runa and Lyric were slow to respond when Maggie returned and called softly through the door. She gave them a small stack of underclothes and stockings, and two modest dresses in blue and green with square necklines and long sleeves. The dresses were faded but tidy. Taking their soiled clothing, Maggie left them to dress.

The dresses fit well, though a touch snug beneath the arms and Runa was pleased with how it draped over her legs, loose enough that it wouldn't hinder her movement. Her Wanderer boots had survived unscathed, and after a quick clean, she slipped them over her new stockings.

"We look presentable again," Lyric said. "Maybe one of the locals will be more willing now to help us fetch a Dragon Blessed."

"Maybe," Runa said distractedly. Considering how the townspeople had looked at her when she'd first walked into the inn, Runa was reasonably sure she'd have to fetch a Dragon Blessed herself. Lyric certainly shouldn't travel on her own, someone would take advantage of her, and though Kell had shown bravery and steadfastness during their journey thus far, there was no guarantee he'd return once he was in the capital. Rathgar's Hold was where he wanted to go, after all, though he did need Elaina to get into the king's library.

*No, he'd come back for Lyric,* Runa thought. She considered Elaina's claim that their grandfather had destroyed Thenda and bound Kell. If that was true, then it'd be dangerous for Kell to go alone. *It has to be me*, she thought. She'd manage ok by herself; she had no doubts about that.

Walking to the door, Runa opened it and looked back over her shoulder at Lyric. "I'll pay Maggie for the dresses and let her know we're ready to eat. You can go up to Mother if you wish."

"Yes," Lyric said. "I want to see how she's doing." She stepped into the shadow of the staircase and scanned the room. "If you see Kell, can you ask him if he wants to join us for our meal upstairs?"

Runa nodded. "I'll tell him if I can."

"Good." Lyric looked for Kell again, then headed up the stairs to their room.

Runa found Maggie at the bar. The innkeeper was cutting a loaf of dark brown bread into thick slices; her head tilted as she listened to the fiddler play.

"Thank you for the dresses," Runa said. "They fit well. How much does the girl want for them?"

"Oh good, I'm glad," Maggie said, looking up. "Just a copper each. She was going to repurpose them anyway."

Runa nodded and took two coppers from the money pouch, setting them on the bar. "Do you need help draining the tub?"

"No," Maggie said, smiling. "Jim will take care of that." She set down the bread knife and looked Runa over. "You look much better. I was worried there wasn't much left of you beneath all that blood." She gestured at Runa's hair. "Your hair is such a pretty shade of red."

"Thank you," Runa said awkwardly, her lips pressing into a thin smile. "We were lucky." She eyed the bread. "Can you send up our meal, when you're free?"

"Of course."

"I'm going to ask our companion if he wishes to join us or take his meal here in the common room."

Maggie raised an eyebrow but didn't voice whatever thought went through her head.

"Thank you for fetching Mistress Gertrude," Runa said. "We appreciate your assistance."

Maggie inclined her head, and Runa turned around. She spotted the back of Kell's head in the middle of the crowd. He must have slipped inside while she talked to Maggie. Sighing, she started walking around the side of the room in an attempt to catch his eye.

# 15

LYRIC

GERTRUDE LOOKED UP, eyes taking in Lyric's cleaned face as she entered the room. The healer sat on a chair beside the bed, her hands folded and her bag packed beside her feet.

"How is she?" Lyric asked. She approached the bed and reached for her mother's hand lying on the coverlet, checking her pulse.

Elaina was bathed and redressed in a clean shift, and covered with a thick blanket. Her eyes were closed, her lashes copper against her pale skin, and though she still breathed, her chest barely moved.

Dark green salve covered a gash across Elaina's forehead, the torn skin sewn together with delicate thread. She seemed thinner as if the flesh had sunk into her skull, sharpening the planes of her face. Lying there, their mother looked like Runa. She seemed smaller, sharper, younger.

"She won't wake," Gertrude said. "Not until a Dragon Blessed removes the corruption inside her. She's stable, so you should have time to bring one here."

Lyric nodded. "What do we owe you?" she asked, sitting on the bed, still holding Elaina's hand.

"A silver," Gertrude said.

It was a high price, half the cost of their room for the night. Lyric glanced at the small table opposite the bed and saw their mother's bag and belt neatly stacked atop it. Had Gertrude found the pendant while searching for Elaina's shift?

"Runa will pay you," Lyric said, looking back at the healer. "Thank you, Mistress Gertrude."

Gertrude nodded and stood, her joints cracking as she bent to pick up her bag. "I'll return in the morning to change the dressing. I believe you have skill with that yourself if you'd like me to leave supplies?"

"Yes, thank you," Lyric said.

Gertrude removed a roll of cloth from her bag and placed it on the table. "I'll return in the morning anyway," she said, "to see how she's doing." She looked at Lyric, her blue eyes direct. "I applied salve to the burn on her arm," Gertrude said. "It's healing."

"Thank you," Lyric said. She watched the woman, wondering what thoughts drifted behind her penetrating gaze, but Gertrude just nodded and opened the door to leave.

Once she'd gone, Lyric looked around for their mother's soiled clothes and the towels Gertrude used to clean away the blood. She couldn't see them anywhere. Maggie must have collected them to wash with their dresses. She'd have to thank the innkeeper for her kindness.

The feeling of being watched prickled the skin on Lyric's neck, and she turned her head to stare at the wall behind her, finding nothing.

*She'll live, I think*, Gandara said inside her head.

Lyric jumped and looked down at Elaina's face. It was unsettling how easily Gandara slipped in and out of her thoughts like she'd carved out a place for herself inside Lyric's head. For a moment, she felt as if someone else stared through her eyes, sharing her sight.

"Yes," Lyric said softly. She knew she could respond to Gandara by thinking, but it felt less peculiar using her voice. "I'm tempted to check the stitching, but Mistress Gertrude's hands were steady."

*Will you head north? To find a Dragon Blessed?*

Lyric frowned. How did Gandara know about that? Was she listening inside Lyric's head even when she wasn't aware of her? Could she hear her private thoughts or only what Lyric heard outside her head? An image of Kell filled her mind, and Lyric flushed. Did Gandara know her thoughts about Kell?

"Yes, north," Lyric said, trying to ignore her embarrassment. "One of us will go, I think. Maggie said there are no runners here to send." A thought occurred to her. "Do you know any runes, any spells that could help my mother? Or perhaps you know what the Dragon Blessed will do. Can you teach me?"

*No,* Gandara said. *I was never skilled in healing.*

Disappointed, Lyric stroked Elaina's hand.

*Don't let Runa go by herself.*

"What? Why not?" Lyric asked. She hadn't begun considering who should go, but knowing her sister, Runa would volunteer. She'd wanted to travel ever since they were little, always making up stories about the lands outside their secluded valley.

*Can you trust she'll come back?* Gandara asked. *She's wanted to be free for a long time.*

"Of course she'll come back," Lyric said irritably. "Runa wouldn't abandon us, abandon me."

*The fire's growing stronger inside her blood. She's being changed by it.*

"I trust my sister, Gandara," Lyric said. Irritated, she let go of her mother's hand.

*Of course. That isn't the only reason I caution sending her alone.*

"We haven't even decided who will go," Lyric said.

*You must stay together.*

There was weight to Gandara's words that cooled Lyric's temper.

"Why?"

*Bad things happen when you're apart.*

"We've been apart many times on errands and trips to town," Lyric said.

*Not for long. Were you together when Runa slipped free of her body?*

"No, of course not."

*Were you together when your mother left?*

"I ..." Lyric paused, thinking back all those years ago. They'd been together, hadn't they? They usually were. Runa wanted to play in the field, and Lyric was ... no, she was searching the forest for goldenseal. Their mother had asked her to fetch some.

*You must stay together,* Gandara said.

"We can't all leave," Lyric said. "Someone has to stay with Mama."

*Stay together. Your mother will be fine.*

Was that admiration Lyric felt from Gandara? She'd seemed lukewarm about their mother before. What had changed?

A knock startled Lyric from their conversation, and she jumped, putting a hand over her thundering heart. "Yes?" she called.

"It's Maggie. I have dinner."

"Oh. Yes," Lyric said. She smoothed her hand over her waist and stood up, opening the door.

Maggie stepped inside, holding a tray with linen napkins, three bowls of broth, thick slices of bread and cheese, and two mugs of dark, foamy beer.

Lyric cleared their mother's things from the table so Maggie could set the food down. "Is Runa coming?" she asked.

"Yes, I believe so," Maggie said, smiling brightly. "She was settling up with Granny."

"And Kell?"

"I believe your companion is taking his meal downstairs."

"Thank you, Maggie. Everything smells wonderful."

Maggie beamed. "I brought a bowl for your mother in case you're able to get her to eat. Granny suggested trying to feed her something."

Lyric nodded. "Thank you for your kindness, Maggie. I don't know what we'd have done without you."

"I'm pleased I could help," Maggie said. She gave Lyric an apologetic look and rested a hand on her hip. "I couldn't convince anyone to go north to fetch a Dragon Blessed. I did ask."

"That's all right," Lyric said. She paused, thinking of her earlier conversation with Gandara. "If both my sister and I go, can my mother stay here until we return? We can pay for her care. Maybe your son, Elias, could sit with her occasionally for a copper or two?"

Maggie pursed her lips, considering. "Yes, I don't see why not. Jim shouldn't complain as you are paying customers. And I'm sure Granny will look in on your mother."

Lyric nodded.

"Your companion, Kell, should go with you of course," Maggie said. "It's not safe for two young women to travel alone."

"Thank you, Maggie," Lyric said. "I'll speak with my sister and let you know our plans in the morning."

Maggie nodded. "Leave your dishes outside the door, and I'll return them to the kitchen. Breakfast will be at first light, and I can prepare food for you to take." She reached for Lyric's hand, squeezing softly. "I'm happy to help however I can," she said. "My mother endured a long illness before she passed. I know how difficult it can be." She squeezed Lyric's hand again, then released it. "If you need anything, please let me know."

Runa and Kell appeared as Maggie was leaving, and exchanged greetings before slipping inside the room.

"How is she?" Kell asked.

Runa looked Elaina over, then prowled to the tray of food on the table.

"The same," Lyric said, as Kell stepped up to her. She leaned into him, breathing in his crisp, mountain scent. "She's getting weaker, I think, but the change is slow." She looked up at him, studying the features that'd become familiar and comforting. "Did you eat?" she asked.

He looked fatigued. Bathed and wearing another man's clothes, the only other hints of the horror he'd survived were scabbing cuts on his temples and his blackened eye.

"Just about to," Kell said. "I wanted to check on you first and Elaina."

"You could eat here," Lyric suggested. She wasn't entirely sure how they'd all fit, the three of them together, but she found herself offering regardless.

"I'll be fine downstairs," Kell said. "Unless you want me to stay?"

Runa snorted and picked up a slice of bread.

"No, that's fine," Lyric said, ignoring her sister. "I mean, of course, I'd like your company but, that's fine." She flushed, earning a crooked smile.

"What are you planning to do?" Kell asked. "Now that we're here?"

"Mistress Gertrude, the healer, thinks we need a Dragon Blessed to heal Mama," Lyric said.

"Oh," Kell said, brows knotting over his eyes. "Because of the creatures?"

"Something happened with her magic," Runa said. "It poisoned her somehow."

Alarm rolled across Kell's face. "The Taint?"

"No, I don't think so. Something else, something a traditional healer can't fix. I asked Gandara if she knows a spell that can help, but she doesn't."

"I hadn't thought to ask Elenora," Runa said, narrowing her eyes. "Though I think she won't know either. She seems more inclined to destroy something than put it back together."

"One of us will have to find a mage healer and convince them to come to Ivernn. Maybe the gold will be enough to pay for their journey back." She looked up, her eyes on Lyric. "I think I should go."

Gandara's warning echoed in Lyric's head, and she studied her sister's face without answering.

"I could go," Kell offered. "I've traveled through Raendashar before. There might be a Dragon Blessed in Heldon's Rock, a city north of here."

"Mistress Gertrude thinks they've all gone to the capital," Lyric said.

Kell frowned. "The festival," he said. "Their yearly pilgrimage. I can check along the way; see if one stayed behind."

"No, I'll go," Runa said. "If the closest Dragon Blessed is in Rathgar's Hold, then I'll speak with our grandfather and tell him what happened to Mother. I'm not sure we can trust him, but we are family. I might need more money to return with the healer swiftly, and he can hire a carriage for me or loan me a horse. A king should have fast horses."

"A horse?" Lyric asked. "You've only ridden one once!"

"I can manage," Runa said, sticking out her jaw.

"No." Lyric shook her head. "I'm not letting you run off on your own. What if something happens? You've never traveled alone before, and you're not familiar with the land or the customs here."

"Taking up Mother's mantle, are you?" Runa asked.

Lyric sighed and raised an eyebrow. "You know what I'm saying is true," she said. "I know you can take care of yourself, but if the Sireni are attacking, the road could be dangerous. What if someone tries to kidnap you or you get hurt?

"I talked to Maggie, and she said she'll care for Mama when we leave." Lyric gestured at the chair beside the bed. "She'll even let Elias sit with her, and Mistress Gertrude will keep Mama as comfortable as possible. We can't do any more than she can anyway, not knowing the flora here."

Runa pursed her lips.

"Don't give me that look," Lyric said. "I don't like the idea of leaving Mama any more than you do, especially with strangers, but we don't have a choice. We can trust Maggie. I'm certain of it."

"You're willing to leave Mother in the care of a woman you just met today?" Runa asked, arching an eyebrow.

Lyric hesitated, her stomach flipping. Honestly? She didn't like the idea of leaving their mother alone. What if Elaina died while they were gone, surrounded by strangers? But if Runa went to Rathgar's Hold alone and didn't come back ...

Guilt pressed like a fist against her chest. Runa had never abandoned her; why would she now? But after Gandara's warning, Lyric couldn't let her sister go off alone, even if that meant leaving their mother behind.

"We have to stick together," Lyric said lamely.

Frowning, Runa twisted the bread in her hands. "It's true we'll be safer together," Runa said, "but you forget, neither of us are exactly helpless." She wiggled her fingers as though summoning fire.

"I'd offer to stay with Elaina," Kell said slowly, tightening his arm around Lyric's shoulders, "but I worry about you traveling alone. As you pointed out, Lyric, neither you or Runa have visited Raendashar before. Elaina will be safe here. Maggie and

Jim seem honest and capable." He looked at Lyric, then shifted his gaze to Runa. "I don't want to alarm you, but the Sireni seem to have the upper hand. They recently destroyed the entire Raendasharan navy."

"Yes," Runa said.

Lyric glanced at her in surprise, her eyebrows raised. "The navy?"

"Maggie told me when I arrived," Runa said. She smiled grimly. "I forgot to tell you. They almost didn't help us. They thought the Sireni attacked me and I would bring trouble down on their heads. She mentioned the ships then."

"One of the men downstairs said they burned a house here," Kell said. "The Sireni seem to have backed off now, but they're patrolling up and down the coast, sinking or boarding every Raendasharan ship they encounter. Trade by sea is cut off, and all merchants now travel north of the Katrin Mountains from Chianseia."

Kell looked down at Lyric. "Despite the Sireni attack here, in Ivernn, I think your mother will be safer here than we will heading up the coast. They only burned one house. The capital would be their true prize."

Lyric nodded. She'd thought the same thing, and it wasn't safe to move their mother anyway. "We should keep our connection to our grandfather quiet," Lyric said. "I don't think Maggie or Jim would voluntarily give Mama to the Sireni, but we don't want anyone to find out who she is." Lyric thought about the pendant in their mother's belt. Had Mistress Gertrude seen it? If she had, what might she do?

"Fine," Runa said. "The three of us will travel together." She reached for a bowl of broth. "We may need to prove our connection to Mother when we seek an audience with our grandfather. He's a king after all. I doubt they'll let us into the castle on our word alone."

"Mama's pendant," Lyric said. "It looks like something special. Perhaps he'll recognize it?"

"Or they'll think we're thieves," Runa said.

"You look Raendasharan," Kell said, looking at Runa. "I can see Elaina in you. Perhaps King Rakarn will, as well." He smiled at Lyric. "You, however, look like you could be at home on the deck of a ship with the wind in your hair."

Lyric smiled, her cheeks heating. For some reason, she found Kell's comment intimate. "I look Sireni, you mean?"

"Enough to give pause," Kell said.

"That explains the suspicious looks downstairs," Lyric said.

Kell's lips curved and he brushed his fingers across her cheek. Despite his smile, his eyes were worried. "You look like your mother too," he said. "I don't think anyone will chase you away for fear you're Sireni, but I agree, we should keep your heritage secret."

"We'll leave tomorrow," Runa said. "We can make arrangements with Maggie in the morning."

Lyric nodded. "The sooner we leave, the better. We don't know how much time Mama has."

"I'll let you eat," Kell said. "I'll likely stumble to my bed after grabbing a quick bite downstairs. I'll find you in the morning?"

Lyric nodded, and Kell embraced her, resting his chin on the top of her head.

After he left, Lyric took a bowl of broth and sat down on the edge of the bed. "We should try to feed Mama," she said, "or give her water. We can soak a napkin, drip some broth in her mouth."

Runa nodded. "Eat first, Ly, then we'll try. We have a long walk ahead of us and need to sleep."

"Do you think he'll help us?" Lyric asked, taking a bite of bread.

"Kell?"

"No, our grandfather. What if ... what if he won't?"

Runa raised her eyebrows. "I thought you were the optimistic one."

"What if he won't let us leave?"

"Well, then we'll escape," Runa said, "and we'll come back here and heal Mother ourselves. He has secret libraries, doesn't he? Magic tomes? We'll bribe a maid. Even secret libraries need dusting, don't they? We'll figure it out like we always do. We won't let her die, Ly."

"You won't leave me, will you Ru?"

"Leave you?" Runa arched an eyebrow. "What are you talking about?"

"Nothing, I'm just tired." Lyric smiled. "To the end?"

Runa reached for a mug of beer and held it up. "To the end."

It was cold and foggy the morning Lyric, Runa, and Kell left Ivernn. Elaina was still unconscious and being watched by Maggie's son Elias. Though she hadn't worsened in the night, Lyric thought their mother felt colder when she'd kissed her cheek goodbye and promised they'd return.

They paid for a full week of Elaina's care with the promise of settling the account if something delayed their return. The Dragon Eye pendant and the rest of their mother's money, including the gold, they'd taken with them.

Maggie packed food for their trip — freshly baked bread, thick slices of cheese, dried fish, a bottle of wine, and crab and oat cakes, carefully wrapped in waxed paper. She'd also returned their clothes and cloaks, washed and repaired.

Fingers passing over her mended cloak, the neat stitches

reminded Lyric of the creatures' claws, and she shivered, lost in memories until Kell's touch returned her to the inn.

Looking towards the stairs, Lyric saw Runa standing in front of a middle-aged man with angry blue eyes and a thin mustache. He said something, gesturing towards the ceiling, and Lyric watched her sister lean forward and raise her hand. Fire sparked atop the tips of her fingers, and the man drew back, eyes widening and face draining of color. Mumbling something, he moved away and stumbled into Jim who was passing with an armload of wood.

Lyric raised her eyebrow as Runa stomped past, but her scowling sister didn't seem to notice. Giving Maggie a distracted farewell, Lyric followed Runa out of the inn. She wanted to ask her what had happened, but her sister took off while she waited for Kell.

The road leading away from Ivernn was not one of the smoother, well-traveled routes of the west, but a pitted and winding path that wandered along the steep, black cliffs. Kell fell into step beside Lyric, his face lightening as he took in the expanse of blue water to the east. Lyric was grateful for his height as a cutting ocean wind had diffused the fog, forcing it to lift, and it seemed quite intent on blowing both her and Runa over.

Stepping over a large hole, Lyric glanced sideways at her sister. "Did you threaten someone when we left?" she asked.

"He thinks we've brought them trouble," Runa said. "That the Sireni know us."

Lyric frowned, trying to recall the unfriendly faces watching them leave. "Who was he?"

"I don't know, a local, but he looked at the stairs and said it'd be better if we *all* moved on."

Lyric pursed her lips. "Maggie and Jim won't let anyone hurt Mama."

"You hope they won't," Runa said, face flinty.

"You danced flame across your fingers," Lyric said. "That was risky, Ru. The Sireni burned a home there."

Runa touched her red hair. "A Sireni, not a Raendasharan mage."

Frowning, Lyric stared at her sister's unrepentant profile. Did Runa truly not see the potential trouble she'd left in their wake?

"Sometimes people need an incentive to make the right choice," Runa said.

"Did Elenora tell you to do it?" Lyric asked.

Runa looked at her, eyes flashing. "Elenora doesn't make me do anything, Ly."

"It just ... it just seems impulsive."

"You trust Maggie and Jim?" Runa asked, raising an eyebrow. "Without question? That they'll choose our mother over their neighbors, their town?"

Lyric glanced up at Kell, who was listening thoughtfully and met her sister's eyes again. "I trust they'll care for Mama," she said. "They'll protect her." She ignored the guilt curdling her stomach. "We had no choice, anyway," she said. "We have to trust someone."

"And now that man will reconsider doing anything that might hurt Mother," Runa said.

"Or did you create an enemy where there was none?"

"Focus your worries on what lies ahead, Ly, not behind us."

Runa marched ahead, fists clenched at her sides.

Disquieted, Lyric resisted the urge to look back, though Ivernn was no longer visible. What drove Runa to display her magic so impulsively? It hadn't been necessary to threaten anyone.

"Perhaps it will have the desired effect," Kell said, tucking Lyric's hand over his arm.

"Or one we didn't anticipate," Lyric said softly.

"I believe they're honorable people. I'm sure they'll keep Elaina safe while we're gone."

"I hope so."

Falling quiet, Lyric let her thoughts drift and turned her eyes to the land around them. It was a barren landscape along the road, the black stone sharp and unforgiving. She was grateful more than once for the sturdy boots covering her feet. Occasionally straggly tufts of grass poked up from the uneven ground, having found a foothold in pockets of dark soil. Trees were few and far between.

Looking west, Lyric saw that the obsidian-like ground stretched away from her in an uneven expanse, rising and falling as though shaped by earthquakes. Far in the distance, she could see the land rise into hills that reminded her of jagged teeth. They were nothing like the pastoral slopes and majestic mountains of Kaliz.

Lyric spied several scraggly goats standing like sentinels atop the jagged hills, their black coats making them nearly indistinguishable from the rocky ground. She tugged on Kell's arm, pointing them out, and together they debated what such an animal might eat in Raendashar's harsh environment.

Birds were their more constant companions, a collection of seabirds and raptors wheeling through the open sky as if reveling in the strong winds. When one bird dove unexpectedly towards the ground, Lyric was sure it'd kill itself on the sharp rock, but it lifted at the last moment with a triumphant shriek, a small rodent dangling from its claws.

Around noon, the three of them stopped at a rocky overlook that jutted over the ocean, sharing a simple lunch of Maggie's crab cakes and small, reddish apples Kell found growing beside the road. Unable to entice Runa into a conversation, Lyric leaned against Kell's shoulder and ate in silence. She scanned the unending stretch of sea for a Sireni ship but saw nothing on the water.

Lyric's thoughts drifted to their mother. *Stay alive, Mama. Please hold on.*

She tossed the apple core off the cliff into the roiling ocean below, feeling her lunch settle like a rock in her stomach. Should she have stayed? Should she have let Runa go on her own? She doubted a different decision would have made her feel any better.

# 16

RUNA

RUNA WAS in a sour mood when they arrived at Heldon's Rock. Her head had throbbed for the past hour, and every time she looked at Lyric, walking cozily with Kell, she was reminded of her sister's words.

*I'm not acting impulsively*, Runa thought stubbornly. *You didn't have to come, Lyric. You could have stayed and watched Mother yourself.*

Elenora's stern presence coalesced in the back of Runa's mind, spiking her headache. *You did the right thing, girl. That man had murder in his eyes.*

Gritting her teeth, Runa stared down at the city and tried to shake off her irritation as Lyric stepped up beside her. Heldon's Rock sat at the bottom of a basin as if it'd slid down the cliffs and caught at the water's edge. She could see a large, sleek ship, with bright blue sails, sitting just outside the mouth of the harbor.

"It's preventing the fishing ships from leaving," Lyric said, pointing towards the dock.

Indeed, a large cluster of boats floated inside the marina. At this time of day with clear weather, the fishermen should have been out dragging their nets in the water.

"It's Sireni," Kell said. "The ship."

"Is it safe to go down into the city?" Lyric asked.

"We don't have a choice," Runa said, turning towards the road.

They followed the well-worn track as it zigzagged down the slope. Approaching the city's gates, they found them open with two uniformed guards watching the road. More guards drifted across the walkway above, their attention directed at the sea and not Runa, Lyric, and Kell.

One of the gate guards, a tall woman with blue eyes, gave them a disinterested look as she shifted her pike in the dirt and yawned, looking past them at the road. The second guard frowned then waved them over. He was short and shaped like a barrel with brown skin and a stubbled chin, a scar marking the cleft at its center. "Business?" he asked. His eyes narrowed on Lyric's face.

"We're looking for a healer," Runa said.

The guard studied them again as if to ascertain who required one. "Where did you come from?" he asked.

"Ivernn," Lyric said. She shifted closer to Kell and smiled pleasantly, clearly unnerved by the man's stare.

"There's a curfew at midnight," the guard said. "Make sure you're not out past then."

"Of course, thank you," Runa said.

The guard nodded, giving them a satisfied grunt, then waved them through.

The gate led directly into the market, and Runa, Lyric, and Kell paused at its entrance, getting their bearings among the shops and canopied stalls that lined the main street.

Runa felt an uneasy awareness in the air, a weightiness that pressed on everyone's shoulders and filled each eye that glanced her way with suspicion. Hearing the crisp crunch of something beneath her heel, she looked down and saw that bits of sea-tumbled stone and crushed shells covered the ground. Runa drew a deep breath into her lungs; the air smelled of baking sausages, fresh fish, crispy fry bread, and the salty smell of the ocean, weaving throughout.

Someone pushed her, and Runa shot a pointed glare at a man striding past, but he didn't seem to notice.

"It's so large!" Lyric said, staring around with wide eyes.

"Stop gawking," Runa snapped. "You look like a hayseed."

Lyric stuck her tongue out, making a face. "It's the largest town you've seen too, Ru," she said. "Don't be a snob."

Disapproval simmered through her, and Runa frowned as she felt her mood shift darker. It wasn't her feeling, though, was it? Lyric wasn't being that annoying. Runa focused, chasing the emotion, and felt Elenora shift in the back of her head.

*Elenora?* Runa asked.

Her ancestor didn't respond, pulsing irritably before she drifted away like the airy seeds of a cat-head flower. Immediately Runa's mind was lighter, calmer. Was Elenora intentionally influencing her emotions, or was it merely an unforeseen effect of their connection, similar to what she shared with her sister?

"Runa?"

Runa blinked, seeing Lyric's face in front of her.

"Are you well?" Lyric asked, raising an eyebrow. "You went away. Is Elenora here? Is she talking to you?"

"Just thinking," Runa said. They had more pressing issues than Elenora's sour mood affecting her. "Where would the Dragon Blessed be, do you think?" Runa asked, looking around.

"At their temple, I'd expect," Kell said.

Runa nodded and marched to one of the stalls. A dark-haired woman, a few years older than her, glanced up as she approached, smiling hopefully. She raised a polished wood comb in one hand and turned it, so the pearlescent shell inlaid in the handle caught the light. "A comb for you, Miss?" she asked.

"No, thank you," Runa said. "We're looking for a Dragon Blessed temple."

The woman's smile slipped, and she set the comb back down, eyeing Runa as the gate guard had. "Keep going until the fountain, then head right," she said. "It's several streets over. You can't miss it." Her eyes shifted to Lyric, and she began to lift the comb again, but before she could say another word, Runa hooked her arm through her sister's and hauled her away.

"I'm not a fisher-bird," Lyric said, grinning at her. "I don't become moon-eyed over every shiny thing I see."

"I've seen you at the tinker's wagon," Runa said.

Lyric laughed and elbowed her playfully. "I'm glad you're not still mad at me."

"I wasn't mad," Runa said. She scanned the faces in the crowd as they wove their way down the street, and kept an eye out for the fountain.

"No?" Lyric asked.

Runa felt her stare at the side of her face. "If there's no Dragon Blessed here, we should find a wise woman or healer," Runa said, thinking ahead. "Maybe Mistress Gertrude is wrong, and there is a way to heal Mother without a mage healer. She could have a treatable infection unique to this area."

"It doesn't hurt to ask," Lyric agreed. "It's better for Mama if we're not forced to go all the way to the capital." Her mood darkened again, likely worrying about their mother alone in Ivernn.

"There's the fountain," Kell said. Taller than either of them, he could see over the crowd.

A moment later, Runa saw the fountain herself. It was a single basin with a dragon statue in the center. The dragon stretched towards the sky on clawed feet, its mouth open mid-roar. Water sprayed out between its teeth and cascaded back into the stone bowl beneath it.

"Beautiful," Lyric mused. "Look at the painted scales."

Turning right, they followed along another shell-lined street, the shops giving way to narrow houses of dark wood. In the alleys on either side, Runa saw lines of laundry.

"Look, do you see those wings?" Kell asked, pointing ahead of them. "Maybe that's the temple?"

The street abruptly opened up, and they found themselves in front of a weather-beaten building, proud despite its aged appearance. "This is it," Runa said with certainty. Built from wood that might have once been a warmer hue, the Dragon Blessed temple had turned the uneven gray shade that Runa was starting to recognize as typical of a sea-side structure subjected to salt-filled winds.

The curved roof and iron spikes adorning the door made the temple look like there was a dragon perched atop it readying for flight. Unlike the other buildings in town, close together and sharing walls, the temple sat inside a large, clean yard bordered by a low barrier of black stone. A black sand path ran from the street to the front steps. The rest of the lot was pale sand and raked into zigzagging patterns.

"This is it," Runa said. They didn't have temples or houses of worship back in Elae's Hollow, just an outdoor shrine to the Trinity in the center of town, but there was always a tangible feeling in sacred places, as though the air had changed by years of whispered supplications and performed rites.

Setting her jaw, Runa marched up the blackened path to the front steps. She reached out and gripped the iron handle, yanking hard. The door opened noiselessly, the hinges oiled and well-cared for, and Runa stepped into a large, dimly-lit room. In the center of the floor was a large, metal basin, with a fire burning inside it. The flames were a fulgent red, and as Runa approached, she didn't see any fuel to keep it going.

Runa turned and eyed the walls covered with old and very intricate tapestries. She watched as one of the hangings fluttered gently, blown by an unseen breeze.

"Dragons," Lyric whispered, walking past Runa to stare at one of the hangings. "Look, there is Zeldayna, Mother of Creatures." Lyric pointed at a tall woman woven from gold and silver threads at the top of the tapestry. The figure's hands were outstretched, and her hair flowed around her body in soft silver like the shine of the moon. Beneath her feet were four dragons — Aery, ruler of air and sky in white; Fyre, the embodiment of fire in red; Rath, the avatar of earth in black; and Serith in blue, the sea serpent and ruler of water, Mother of the Sireni.

"I'm surprised Serith is shown, considering the general opinion of her here," Lyric said.

Runa nodded absently, her eyes caught on the red dragon. Staring at Fyre's red and gold form, she felt something kindle deep in her chest as if the fire within her recognized its origin.

"Over here is a depiction of the Trinity," Kell called from across the room. "Ethethera, Hel and Zeldayna are all shown creating our world, as well as the summoning of Aya, the Mother Tree."

Runa turned her head, following his voice.

"And there, the birth of the Seven, the demigods," Kell said.

Runa knew their names — Orion, Hebaria, Temien, Florion, Aren, Valen, and Velaine, though they weren't often mentioned in Elae's Hollow. The demigods had abandoned Erith after the Demon War, disappearing to wherever gods go when they've become bored with their creations. Their desertion hadn't endeared them to many Kalizans.

Even the dragons, who'd stayed for hundreds of years serving and settling disputes between the kingdoms after the demigods left, were hardly mentioned by the magic-fearing people of Runa's home. It was odd seeing them here venerated and displayed for all to see.

"They're beautiful," Lyric said, brushing the tips of her fingers against the fabric. "I've never seen anything like this." Lyric walked along the wall and stared up at another tapestry, this one depicting the Demon War where demigods and dragons fought side by side against the fallen god, Velaine.

Runa eyed Velaine's black shape with curiosity. The weaver had surrounded the demigod with a multitude of twisting green shapes, as though she stood inside a poisoned cloud. Its color reminded Runa of the algae poisoning the land and water along the Tainted Shore.

Opposite Velaine and her demon horde, in the bottom corner of the tapestry, Serith was depicted fleeing from battle. Small human-shaped shadows, dressed in white, clung to the sea serpent's back and ran behind her.

"I don't think they'd know what to do with this back home," Runa said. "Hang it in the inn?"

Lyric chuckled.

"Have you come for Brother Ende?" someone asked.

Jumping, Runa spun around, her hand rising and the word for fire buzzing on the tip of her tongue.

A teenage boy stood in the doorway, holding a broom and wearing an easygoing smile.

"We're looking for a Dragon Blessed," Lyric said, stepping up beside Runa.

Runa dropped her hand, irritated with herself that she'd been surprised.

"Yes, that'd be Brother Ende," the boy said, walking towards them. His eyes were curious as he looked them over, and he spent extra time staring at Lyric. "He's gone to the Feast of Souls. Won't be back until the end of the week, if not later."

"Who are you?" Runa asked, raising an eyebrow. The boy seemed too young to be a healer himself, but both Runa and Lyric had trained since childhood with Elaina. He could be an apprentice.

"I'm Colden," the boy said. "I keep the Dragon Fire burning." He pointed a finger at the basin. "I'm to ensure it doesn't go out."

"And if it does? Go out?" Lyric asked curiously.

"Well, then I'd tell Brother Ende."

"Who isn't here," Lyric said.

"Well, he usually is." Colden chewed on his lip thoughtfully. "I suppose I'd have to send a Skyrunner or raven after him, though I'm not sure Brother Ende would approve the cost of a Runner."

"A what?" Runa asked.

Colden looked at her, both eyebrows raising into his hair. "You don't know what a Skyrunner is?"

Kell, who'd moved up beside Runa when Colden arrived, leaned towards her left ear. "They're magic-enhanced birds," he whispered. "Faster and more biddable than ravens."

"Ravens don't always like to do what you tell them to," Colden said, grinning. "Too smart to be bossed around, I'd wager." He cocked his head. "Where are you from that you don't have a Skyrunner?"

"Are there no other Dragon Blessed in the city?" Runa asked, ignoring the question.

"Not that I'm aware of," Colden said.

"Might Brother Ende return earlier if we can reach him?"

Colden eyed Runa and leaned on the broom. "I doubt it. I don't think anything would draw a Blessed away from the Feast of Souls. It involves a rather demanding series of rituals, which typically take place behind closed doors at the Temple of Flame."

"Unless the fire went out?" Lyric asked. "Would he come back then?"

"Well ..." Colden looked at the fire burning in the basin. "That's never actually happened so who can say?" He looked them over again. "What do you need a Blessed for anyway?"

"Rather rude to ask, don't you think?" Runa asked. She tried not to glower, but the boy was getting on her nerves.

Colden grinned and tapped the side of his nose. "Ahhh, I understand. One of those problems." He looked between Kell, Runa, and Lyric, and chuckled.

"No," Runa snapped. "Not one of those problems."

Kell coughed, and Runa avoided looking at him.

"Mhm, well you'll have to wait until Brother Ende gets back, or you could go to the capital and try to find someone there," Colden said. "If you decide to do that though, I doubt you'll have much luck until the Festival is over. Maybe a wise woman can help you?"

"Where can we find her?" Lyric asked.

"Probably at the Lady and Crab," Colden said. "Down by the docks."

"Is that an inn?" Runa asked. It didn't sound like a place she'd have thought to look for the town's healer.

Colden mimed drinking. "Mistress Evie likes her beer. By this time of day, she's well into her cups. If she can't help you, then maybe one of the city guard's surgeons?"

"We'll try the inn," Runa said. "Thank you." She paused, remembering her oath. "Where can I offer devotions to the Trinity?" she asked. Despite being inside a temple, Runa didn't see any candles or incense for offering prayers.

"There are several shrines throughout town, but we have a supplication garden at the back of the temple," Colden said. "Should I lead you there?"

"Yes, thank you," Runa said.

Nodding, Colden gestured for them to follow. Walking to the back of the large room, he showed them a hidden hallway behind the wall. He led them through it to a door, covered by a curtain of black, wood beads, which exited to a small plot of land behind the temple.

Black sand covered the ground, raked into spirals. In the

center of the plot, three large black stone sculptures formed a triangle, with the point facing north. Their shapes were simple, but it was clear they'd been carved to represent the Three dragons, excluding Serith.

Inside the triangle were three additional figures, carved from white stone and standing on plain blocks.

Runa brushed past Colden and stepped into the center of the sand. Standing where she was, she could see the white figures were depictions of the Trinity. The sculptor had given shape to their faces and bodies, but hadn't carved their features or added any detail beyond the beautiful curving flow of their dresses.

Stepping up to one of the figures, Runa recognized her as Ethethera by a small etching of a tree at the base of her skirt. Several wooden bowls, filled with black sand and sticks of fragrant incense, surrounded the goddess' feet.

Lyric joined Runa on the sand, but Kell remained standing by the doorway.

Colden, having disappeared inside the temple while Runa examined the sculptures, returned with a small hammered metal bowl holding a burning candle. The candle's flame was the same vivid red as the Dragon Fire inside the temple.

Picking up one of the unlit sticks, Runa whispered a prayer and lit the incense with the candle in Colden's bowl. She waved it gently until smoke curled towards the sky in a thin, gray ribbon. Sticking the lit incense carefully in the black sand, Runa stepped back.

Lyric repeated Runa's movements, and for several breaths, the two of them quietly stood, heads bowed beneath the eyeless gaze of Ethethera.

"Thank you, Colden," Lyric said to the boy. She always did have a good memory for names.

"Of course, Mistress," Colden said. "If you decide to stay in town and wait for Brother Ende's return, I can send word when he's back."

"Thank you, but we don't have time to wait," Lyric said.

"Of course. May our Mother, the Great Wanderer, bless you and may the holy fire of the Three guide and protect you. By Sky, Earth and Fire, Wing and Claw. So it is."

"So it is," Runa murmured. She looked at Lyric and saw her sister's eyes were smudged with worry. "Let's go to the inn," Runa said.

Nodding, Lyric followed her to the temple's door.

Kell reached for Lyric's hand as they passed, and the two of them trailed behind Runa as she walked through the temple and returned to the street.

# 17

RUNA

Leaving the Dragon Blessed Temple behind, Runa, Lyric, and Kell started walking east, away from the towering cliffs above the city towards the docks. Kell spied The Lady and Crab wedged between a glassmaker's shop and a bookseller. He paused, and Runa caught a hungry look on his face as he stared at the bookseller's papered windows before opening the inn's door and ushering her and Lyric inside.

The Lady and Crab was crowded and dim, poorly lit by orb lanterns suspended from planks in the ceiling. The room seemed clean, but it was too dark for Runa to see much of the floor. Long tables stretched through the center of the room and booths hunched together against the walls.

A woman in a long, gray dress sat by the fire, her chair atop an elevated stage. She played a psaltery, cradled in her arms, and her haunting music hung in the air. The subdued attitude Runa witnessed in the streets outside was still present here indoors, and the ethereal sounds from the woman's instrument fit the crowd's heavy mood.

Kell elbowed a place for them at the bar and waved down a

harried-looking man with a broad, rosy face, reddish hair and pale brown eyes.

"What can I do for you?" the man asked, looking them over quickly as he tucked a dishrag into his belt.

"We're looking for someone," Runa said, leaning forward.

"Yes?" The man looked away impatiently.

"Mistress Evie, the wise woman?"

The man grunted and pointed a finger over her head. Looking back, Runa had to stand on her tiptoes to see over the crowd. A woman was sitting alone in a dark booth against the wall with several empty mugs in front of her.

"Thank you," Runa said. She edged around the tables and crossed the room to the booth.

Noticing Runa, the woman looked up and blinked owlishly. She was in her middle years with thick black hair and a diamond-shaped face. Her nose was long and sharp, and her eyes were a shade of brown so dark they looked black in her pale face. Adjusting her shawl, the woman glanced at Lyric and Kell, who'd stepped up beside Runa.

"What do you want?" the woman asked, a touch peevishly.

"Mistress Evie?" Runa asked.

"Who wants to know?"

"May we sit?" Runa slid onto the bench opposite the woman without waiting for permission and moved to the wall to make space for Lyric.

Kell perched awkwardly on the end of the bench, his long legs jutting out into the aisle beside the table.

"I'm busy," Evie said. She held up her beer mug and looked around for a serving girl.

"We need your advice," Runa said. She fished into the money pouch at her waist and palmed a silver coin, setting it on the table near the wise woman. "We'll pay for your time."

Eyes brightening, Evie snatched the coin so quickly she nearly grabbed Runa's fingers. She shook her mug more vigorously in the air, beaming as a pretty girl in an apron came over with a pitcher. "Keep the drinks flowing!" Evie said as she handed the girl the silver.

Glancing at Runa, Lyric, and Kell, the serving girl gave Evie an apologetic smile. "This only covers your previous tab, Mistress. Last refill, I'm afraid."

Evie sighed and watched as the girl refilled her cup. She thumped the mug on the table and leaned back, eyeing Runa with an unimpressed twist of her lips.

"Anything for you?" the girl asked the rest of them.

"A pot of tea, please?" Lyric asked.

"A cider for me," Kell said.

The girl nodded and hurried away.

"You've earned the time it takes me to drink this beer," Evie said, gulping the dark liquid.

"Our mother was injured on the Tainted Shore," Runa said.

Evie raised her eyebrows, a flicker of interest in her dark eyes. "That's not something you hear too often. She's still alive, is she?"

"Something bit her, and she won't wake," Runa said. "We were told that only a Dragon Blessed can save her now."

"A mage, is she?" Evie asked. "Used her magic?"

Runa nodded.

"She's gonna die then." Evie took an unconcerned sip from her mug and looked out over the crowd.

"You don't know anything that can help?" Lyric asked. She leaned forward and flattened her hands on the table. "An herb perhaps like wake-thistle?"

Evie raised an eyebrow. "You've studied herbs, have you? Nothing like that grows here; don't have the weather for it. Helthorian root works much the same, but it won't do you any good if there's corruption in her blood.

"Sorry if you don't want to hear it, but if anyone can help her, it'll be a Dragon Blessed." Evie sipped her beer. "But I wouldn't hold your breath. They like to wave their hands around, claim they're tapping into 'energies' leached from the Three, but they're more priests than true healers. Anyone can pray and take credit for a miracle or dumb luck."

Runa frowned and exchanged glances with Lyric. There had to be more to the Blessed than that. Maybe Evie didn't understand or care how their power worked or had a personal grudge against them. It wasn't unheard of for different healers to dislike each other and distrust alternative methods.

"What about the surgeons?" Kell asked. "Would they agree with you?"

Evie snorted and spat onto the floor, nearly missing Kell's foot. "Bloodletters," she said. "They'll hasten her to the Veil." She shrugged. "Perhaps that'd be a mercy."

Runa glanced at Lyric, who was staring at Evie with a shocked expression.

"How can you be so heartless?" Lyric asked. "You're speaking about our mother."

The serving girl returned and set down a pot of tea, three small cups, and a tall glass of cider for Kell, then bustled off again, unaware of the tense mood at the table.

"You should know better," Evie said, eyeing Lyric. "It's hard to see sense when dealing with family, I admit. I suggest you hurry home. She's probably not got much time left." Lifting her mug, Evie drained the remaining beer and slammed it down on the table. "Thanks for the drink," she said. Without another word, she slid off the bench, adjusted her shawl, and walked away, weaving somewhat as she worked her way to the door.

Kell stood up and shifted around to the opposite bench, scooting Evie's collection of empty mugs out of the way. He reached across the table and grabbed Lyric's hand. "She's wrong," he said, staring into Lyric's face in a way that made Runa uncomfortable. It was a look she'd given Dalen Pell once, a look of devotion.

Lyric nodded and tangled her fingers in the ends of her braid, twisting the brown strands in an absentminded way.

Kell poured tea and pushed the filled cups to both of them. "So," he said. "We continue to Rathgar's Hold then, right?"

Runa reached for the teacup and curled her fingers around it, appreciating the warmth. "Yes," she said. "If there was another Dragon Blessed in the city that boy should have heard of it. I can't imagine one visiting and not going to the temple. We can ask the innkeeper to confirm."

"Yes," Lyric said, lifting her head. She raised her tea to her lips, breathing deeply. "If what Colden said is true, and it's impossible to contact a Dragon Blessed during the Festival, we should go straight to Grandfather and seek an audience. Surely the Blessed wouldn't turn down a request from their King."

Runa nodded. "Sounds like a good plan," she said.

The serving girl returned, eyeing them with a cheerful smile. "Would you like anything to eat?" she asked. "We have a pot of fish stew and fresh pepper biscuits, just out of the oven."

"We should eat," Runa said, looking at Lyric.

Lyric nodded.

"Three bowls," Runa said. "How much?"

The girl told her and Runa handed her money. They were lucky Elaina had come for them with a full purse.

"How much for a room if we want to stay the night?" Lyric asked.

"Two silver per room," the girl said. "That includes your meal." She held out the coppers Runa had given her.

"Here, let me," Kell said, reaching into his robe and removing a handful of coins.

Runa took back the coppers and gave Kell a grudging nod. "Thank you," she said.

He nodded and looked back at the serving girl. "The ship outside the harbor," Kell asked before she turned away. "Is it Sireni?"

"Yes," the girl said, her smile slipping. "It's been sitting there for three days now. Won't let any boats out or in. I think we'll soon run out of fish in the harbor."

"Will the King send anyone down?" Kell asked. "Try to clear them out?"

The girl shrugged. "Did you hear about the navy? My da says that our cavalry and foot soldiers are stronger than the Sireni, so even without our fleet, if they move against the capital, we'll be ready."

"We heard they burned some houses recently," Lyric said. "Came onto the land."

The girl nodded. "They haven't tried that here yet." She glanced nervously at the wall, as though seeing the harbor beyond. "But the city guard's been on alert."

"How far is the capital?" Runa asked.

"A day and a half on foot, Miss," the girl said. "If you'll excuse me?"

Runa nodded, and the girl scurried off, responding to a call for more beer from a gruff-looking man several tables over.

"Curious why they'd burn a house in Ivernn, but not here," Runa mused.

"Maybe it's because Ivernn doesn't have any guards?" Lyric asked.

"But why burn down one house? Why not set the entire village on fire?"

Kell looked at Runa over the rim of his glass. "I don't know why they'd attack the coast at all," he said. "Usually they've only responded when provoked. They don't typically act like raiders."

"The people of Ivernn didn't seem like fighters," Lyric said. "I doubt they've attacked a Sireni ship or done anything that singled them out. As you said, Runa, Heldon's Rock seems like it'd be a bigger blow to the capital." Lyric looked at Kell and pursed her lips thoughtfully. "Who decides whether or not the Sireni go to war? Do you know?"

"Well, they don't have a king like Raendashar," Kell said. "They rule by council. They're divided into four clans, one for each direction that the wind blows, and the leaders of each clan sit on their council. It's called the Gale. Generally, I believe they stay on separate ships, gathering only when they convene the council. I imagine that the Gale decides what action to take for the Sireni clans."

"They live on their ships, don't they?" Lyric asked.

Kell nodded. "They anchor different places depending on the season."

"So if we wanted to stop the war, we'd have to speak with the Gale."

Runa choked on her tea and glanced sideways at Lyric, eyes watering. "You want to walk onto a Sireni ship? You realize they're trying to kidnap us, don't you?"

"Yes," Lyric said, "but if we hope to stop the war, we'll have to communicate with them. If we can convince our grandfather ..." She lowered her voice, looking around. "If we can convince him peace is in his best interest, for him and Raendashar, then at some point we'll have to attempt contact with the Sireni."

"I don't like the idea of people dying any more than you do," Runa said, "but I don't see how you can convince someone like *him* to give up. He seems quite intent on the war." Runa paused as the serving girl walked up with a tray of food and gave them three bowls and a basket of golden biscuits.

"Thank you," Lyric said, smiling at her.

The girl nodded and walked away with the tray.

"I think it's in his best interest," Lyric said, reaching for a biscuit. "The fleet's destroyed and trade's being disrupted. The Sireni are attacking cities. At some point, the people will have had enough and demand change, won't they? The war's why their fishing boats are stuck in the harbor. They're going to run out of food. What will they do then? What if the Sireni start killing people?" Lyric frowned. "Maybe they already have, and we just don't know about it?"

"The war has been ongoing for generations," Runa said. "This can't be the only time the Sireni have attempted to disrupt trade or burned a few houses." She reached for one of the bowls, examining the soup. Chunks of what she hoped was pale fish floated in the broth, and she saw green vegetables and pale orange roots as well. Taking a tentative bite, Runa was relieved it tasted good, albeit a touch spicy.

"I don't believe they've ever before destroyed the Raendasharan fleet," Kell said, gesturing with a biscuit.

Runa frowned. "I wonder how they managed that; burned the fleet. Sounds like something a Raendasharan Burner might do, not a Sireni mage."

Lyric eyed her thoughtfully and made a noncommittal noise in her throat.

"What?" Runa asked, narrowing her eyes.

"Mama's a Burner," Lyric said softly, "and she's been in contact with our uncle who's Sireni."

"Careful what you say aloud," Kell said quietly. "What you're suggesting is treason."

Runa swallowed another bite of soup and considered Lyric's theory. Had their mother left them to subvert her father, somehow destroying an entire fleet of ships? Surely that was impossible for one woman. You'd need a group of mages, wouldn't you? Were there other Raendasharans working against the King?

Thoughtfully, she twirled her spoon. If magic relied on the use of runes, then as long as you had the appropriate knowledge and skill to call fire, being Sireni or Raendasharan shouldn't matter. Anyone proficient enough, who knew the right words, should be able to replicate a Burner's power.

"I have more questions for Mother," Runa said absently.

"We can't be mad at her for leaving, Ru," Lyric said. "Our lives are insignificant compared to the hundreds who've died and will die because of this war."

"We certainly can be upset that our mother abandoned us," Runa said, feeling the old stirring of anger and hurt. "She didn't have to cut us out of her life as she did."

"Would you willingly take a child into danger?" Lyric asked.

"Would you willingly abandon your child?" Runa countered. "You seem to forget, Ly, that we nearly died more than once. Remember the winter you got sick?"

Lyric sighed and looked down at her soup, idly stirring with her spoon. "I wish you'd stop hating her."

"I don't *hate* her, Ly. I'm upset, and those feelings aren't just going to go away because she's hurt."

Looking at the wall, Lyric brushed a hand against her eye. She sucked in a shuddering breath and kept her face turned away.

Runa sighed and put her arm around Lyric's shoulders, tucking her sister's head against her neck. They sat in silence for a long moment, listening to the jumble of conversation inside the inn and the sad voice of the psaltery.

*I don't hate her*, Runa thought, though the words felt hollow.

# 18

LYRIC

LYRIC FELT DRAINED, her mind slow and disordered. She followed Runa and Kell as they purchased food and supplies for the road, working more on keeping her eyes open than contributing in any meaningful way. The bed in the inn had been reasonably comfortable, but Lyric slept poorly, wondering if she'd know if their mother died. Would she sense the loss? The disappearance of someone she loved from her life?

Unlike Runa, Lyric hadn't been convinced their mother was truly gone when she'd disappeared. Had her certainty meant something, and she'd known on some level that Elaina was alive? Was that wishful thinking? What if she reached Rathgar's Hold and returned to Ivernn with a Dragon Blessed, but their mother was already dead?

"Lyric?" Kell asked, pressing a bundle of dried fruit into her hands. "Are you well?"

"Yes," Lyric said, smiling automatically. "Just tired."

Despite her reassurance, Kell looked so concerned that she was tempted to put her arms around him right then in the market, and calm her thoughts by pressing her ear to his chest and listening to his heartbeat. He turned away, and Lyric regretted her hesitation.

Leaving the fruit seller, they stopped at a clothier at Runa's suggestion. "We can't arrive on the king's doorstep looking ragged," Runa said. "Not with Mother's pendant in our hands."

Kell stayed outside, filling their waterskins at a fountain, while Runa and Lyric surveyed the available dresses. Not wanting to spend too much of Elaina's money, they settled on one traveling dress each, the style fashionable enough for a lady of means but also suitable for walking along the road.

The shopkeeper, a woman with blond hair and calculating gray eyes, suggested a pale green dress for Runa and a creamy gold for Lyric. She attempted to talk them into replacing their cloaks, but Runa insisted they still performed their purpose.

Stepping back into the street, Lyric blushed as Kell's face lit up when he saw her.

"You look beautiful," Kell said, taking her hand and brushing his lips across the back of her knuckles.

"Hopefully they won't turn us away at the gate now," Lyric said, smiling.

Outfitted for the remainder of their journey, Lyric, Kell, and Runa left Heldon's Rock and climbed back to the top of the cliff that overlooked the city. Lyric looked out at the ocean, searching for the Sireni ship. It was still there, blocking the harbor.

The sun was bright and warm, and if it wasn't for the breeze coming off the Sea of Screams, Lyric was sure she'd have fallen asleep in the center of the road. A small wagon passed them, heading north, and Kell attempted to wave the driver down for a ride. Scowling suspiciously, the man nudged his skinny oxen faster, almost knocking Kell off the road.

Friendliness didn't seem to be a concern that day. The other travelers they encountered either met Lyric's greetings with hasty nods or by pretending they didn't see her.

"They're likely worried because of increased tensions with the Sireni," Runa said. "Don't take it personally, Ly."

"I'm not," Lyric said, though that wasn't entirely true.

TWO HOURS into their walk north, a glint of metal caught Lyric's eye. She squinted, unsure of what was poking up over the rise ahead. "Do you see that?" she asked.

"They look like spears," Runa said.

Kell cocked his head to the side. "I hear horses," he said.

Looking back at the hill, Lyric focused on the sounds around them. In the wind, she heard the unmistakable whinny of a horse. A vibration moved through the ground, rumbling against Lyric's feet and she grabbed Kell's arm.

A group of twenty men and women astride large black and gray horses crested the hill. They wore scaled armor and held pikes with obsidian blades, the long weapons braced in straps near their feet. Despite their number, they were inexplicably quiet. Lyric could see the soldiers' features before she heard the creak of shifting saddles and the thud of hooves striking the ground.

A woman, riding alone, lead the unit. She didn't hold a pike like the others.

"Soldiers," Runa said, quietly, as she moved to the side of the road with Lyric and Kell. "They must be responding to the ship at Heldon's Rock."

"Why didn't we hear them coming?" Lyric murmured, watching the leader.

"She's dampening sound," Kell said.

Lyric wanted to ask how he knew, but she fell silent as the woman drew even with them.

Loosely holding the reins of her horse, the soldier glanced at Lyric as she rode by, her blue eyes flicking back to the road dismissively. Her sleeves were green, like the soldiers behind her, but a deeper color that reminded Lyric of dark moss. Blond and short, the soldier's hair curled against the back of her neck and exposed her ears, making it easy to see the glinting orange runes tattooed down the length of her pale neck.

Lyric licked her lips, skin prickling. The woman was casting somehow, drawing magic, though her lips weren't moving.

The stimulating sensation disappeared as the woman rode farther down the road, and Lyric turned her eyes to the other soldiers, watching them with fascination. She saw no more visible tattoos or the thrilling return of more magic.

"Do you think they're going to fight the Sireni?" Lyric asked, stepping back into the road as the dust settled. Her stomach flipped, as she thought about the people of Heldon's Rock and her unknown uncle, somewhere out on the water, on opposite sides of the war. Would he get caught up in this fight?

"I don't know how they'll reach them," Runa said, "unless they take a fishing boat out to the Sireni ship."

"They're probably reinforcements for the city guard," Kell said, "though the calvary is more effective on the field than navigating the city's docks. I wonder why Rakarn didn't send foot soldiers instead."

"Maybe they're following behind," Runa said. "It's good we left when we did. A battle might have trapped us in the city."

"I hope it doesn't come to that," Lyric said. She thought about the Daughters' omen in the Veil. What did it mean? Who would die?

"How did you know the soldier was a mage?" Runa asked. Her eyes narrowed suspiciously on Kell. "I thought you couldn't do magic."

"I can't," Kell said, "but I can feel it, an odd chill on my skin."

Lyric blinked, thoughts shifting from the omen to Kell. Why could he feel magic when he wasn't a mage? She thought about the tattoo on his back, the twisting lines that were part of a larger design. It'd been hard to see it in the dark house, but his tattoo didn't look like the runes on the soldier's neck or their mother's arm.

What secrets was Kell hiding and why?

"I can't make up my mind about you," Runa said, staring at Kell.

Kell laughed, but there were shadows in his eyes.

WHEN EVENING CAME, Lyric was ready to collapse on the ground and sleep. She was eyeing a thick stonecrop patch of reddish-yellow buds when Runa, scouting ahead, shouted back that she'd found a secluded pool.

Holding Kell's arm, Lyric wearily stepped off the road and ascended a steep ridge of gray-veined stone. She found Runa waiting on the other side, facing away from her.

Lyric gasped, exhaustion fleeing, as she stared past her sister at a small turquoise lake at the base of a cliff. The crag beyond was monstrous, curving up from the ground like the spine of some forgotten beast. Eyes dropping back to the water, she saw it was clear and still, shielded from the biting ocean winds by the rocks they'd just climbed. Several trees grew nearby with rough, grayish-brown bark and scalelike leaves.

"There's a smaller pool down that way," Runa said, pointing towards the far edge. "It's tucked beneath an overhang. I think it's heated. I saw steam on its surface."

"That sounds wonderful, but I'm too tired," Lyric complained.

"Don't collapse just yet," Runa said, walking towards her. "Let's get a fire going. The air is cooling off. It might be cold tonight."

Gathering wood from beneath the trees, Runa and Kell

started a fire while Lyric prepared their meal. They ate quickly, not bothering to talk, and after Lyric swallowed her last bite and could no longer keep her eyes open, she mumbled permission to wake her for her turn to keep watch, then promptly rolled into her cloak and fell asleep.

LYRIC WOKE to Runa heating porridge in a small clay pot on the leftover coals from their fire. She looked for Kell, but he wasn't there. "You didn't wake me," she said, rubbing her eyes.

"We decided not to," Runa said, glancing at her.

"Where's Kell?" Lyric pulled off her cloak and shook it, knocking off dirt and small stones that'd caught in the heavy wool. Laying it across her knees, she felt across her scalp and began to re-braid her hair.

"He went down to the pool," Runa said.

"Oh." Lyric glanced towards the overhang. Was Kell naked down there? She flushed and stood up to help Runa with breakfast.

"You should be careful, Ly," Runa said, stirring little pieces of dried apple into the porridge.

"With what?" Lyric asked. She looked down at the ground for danger.

"With Kell."

"What do you mean?" Lyric blushed despite herself, her thoughts straying back to Kell bathing in the pool.

"You don't know much about him," Runa said. "Don't forget, Mother asked him to protect us. He's with us because he wants something."

"That's why he found us, yes," Lyric said, "but he's not staying now out of obligation."

"Maybe," Runa said. "He needs us now that Mother isn't here to take him to the capital. He's dangerous, Ly. He's involved in something he doesn't even remember or understand. What if our grandfather caused the Taint and tattooed Kell? What do you think happens if he recognizes him? Or what if Mother is wrong and our grandfather wasn't involved? What if Kell had a bigger role in Thenda's destruction and somehow caused the death of all those people?"

"You can't be serious," Lyric said, eyes wide. "You think Kell, as an eight-year-old boy, destroyed an entire city?"

"I don't think he did it alone," Runa said, "and it probably wasn't his idea, but maybe he has uncontrollable magic that was unleashed somehow; power he doesn't know he has. Why did he sense the mage, Ly?"

"Kell?" Anger flared in Lyric's chest, and she curled her fingers into fists, feeling her nails bite into her palms. "He's been nothing but nice to you, Runa, to both of us, and you're accusing him of — of killing people? If that were true, Mama would never have sent him to us."

"Mother's not infallible," Runa said. "I'm suggesting that you should be careful giving your heart to someone with secrets. And not just a little secret, Lyric, but something world-changing."

"You don't want me to be happy."

"What?" Runa's eyes flared, her spoon pausing mid-stir.

"You're afraid I'm going to leave you, that you'll be alone." Lyric couldn't stop herself. The words poured out of her mouth, fueled by something dark and angry inside her, something that wanted to lash out.

Mouth tightening, Runa glared at her. "Run along then, Lyric. Someday you'll realize you can't save everyone and that sometimes people don't deserve saving."

Lyric stood abruptly. She stared into her sister's eyes, glare meeting glare, and drew in a shuddering breath. "I'm going to get Kell," she said.

Turning, Lyric stalked towards the lake and down the

embankment beneath the overhang. As she rounded the corner, disappearing from Runa's sight, she saw Kell standing at the edge of the water. His back was to her, and he was wearing tan breeches and nothing else.

Anger forgotten, Lyric stopped short, breath catching in her throat. Tattoos covered Kell's back, a mass of looping, twisting lines in black and green that shimmered in the morning light. More startling than the intricate tattoos were two bony protrusions atop his shoulder blades. The nubs were rough as if cut by a saw.

A bird cawed overhead, drawing Kell's head up. He paused, tunic in his hands as he stared at the sky.

Lyric stared at his back, trying to comprehend what she saw. Had Kell had wings? Why and how? Who had done this? Did their mother know?

Runa's words rang in her mind, but Lyric didn't feel afraid as she stared at Kell. No, she longed to understand, to know who he was. *What are you?* she thought.

Kell resumed pulling his robe over his head and turned around before Lyric realized she was still standing in place, staring at him. He paused when he saw her, his tunic falling the rest of the way to cover his chest, skimming the tops of his thighs. His hair was wet and slicked back from his forehead, and his eyes were bright, almost crystalline like the cool water of the lake behind him. A smile broke over Kell's face, one of the lazy, skin-tingling smiles he had that surely made women go weak at the knees and innkeepers give him free meals.

"I'm sorry," Lyric said. "Breakfast is ready." Her words tumbled over each other as she hurried to explain why she'd been staring at him like an addled fool. She flushed, her face growing hot as Kell continued smiling without speaking. What was he thinking?

"I didn't see anything!" Lyric blurted. "I mean, I didn't ... I didn't see your ... I saw your back." She gestured loosely, searching for words and a way out of her humiliation. "Your tattoos, Kell. I didn't know. What are they?"

Smile slipping, Kell ran a hand over his hair. He didn't seem annoyed that she'd surprised him, but there was sadness in his face that she didn't understand.

"Did you get them in Thenda?" Lyric asked. She walked towards him, drawn closer by his eyes until she was an arms reach away.

"They're from before," Kell said.

"Before?" Lyric frowned. "I don't understand. Your parents did that to you?"

"Not Triska and Jiri, who raised me," Kell said. "They weren't my birth parents. They took me in when I was four or five years old. They didn't know where I came from or what my tattoos meant." He smiled sadly. "They loved me even though—"

"Even though?" Lyric asked.

"They're spells, Lyric," Kell said, taking her hand. "My tattoos."

Lyric looked down as Kell's fingers twined with hers. His palm was warm and dry, and she could feel the calluses on his fingers.

"What if I was bound because of something horrible inside me, something evil? What if my mother, my birth mother, tattooed me to prevent me from unleashing something? What if I'm dangerous?" Kell tried to pull away, but Lyric put a hand on his arm. "What if I caused the Taint?" Kell asked.

"No," Lyric said, shaking her head. "I don't believe it."

Kell smiled, his face sad and weary. "Sometimes, the monster in the room is an actual monster."

"No, whatever the reason this was done to you, you're not evil, Kell." Lyric shook her head again. She didn't believe it, and neither could her mother, not if she was helping Kell. Lyric thought back to the Daughters in the Veil and their omen.

They'd stared at her and Kell, addressing them alone. *When that which is hidden becomes whole again ...*

A chill settled inside Lyric's chest. Kell's nubs on his back. The Daughters had wings in the old stories. They hadn't in the Veil, but she'd heard the fluttering of feathers when they'd disappeared. Was Kell's mother a Daughter? What did that make him?

Lyric stared into his eyes, and all she saw was doubt and pain. She would not fear him.

"Maybe there's magic inside you that's powerful and unknowable, but you decide what it means," Lyric said. "You are not responsible if someone took advantage of you when you were a child."

Kell drew in a shuddering breath and closed his eyes. "You think I destroyed Salta. You think I killed all those people. My mother—"

"No," Lyric said. "I don't, Kell." She reached up and took his face in her hands. When he looked at her again, she held his gaze and stared deep into his blue eyes. They overflowed with grief and guilt that broke her heart. "There must be another reason you were there," she said. "Something you saw, not something you did. You're good, Kell, I can feel it in my soul."

Kell smiled at her, and she felt his hands settle on her waist. His fingers were warm through the fabric of her dress. "I don't deserve the way you look at me, Lyric," Kell said. "I don't understand how you can see my tattoos, my scars, and don't run away. The blackmail ..." His eyes dropped. "Another student saw my back at the Radiant Hall. Called me demon spawn, made up stories. If I hadn't paid—"

"People can be idiots," Lyric said fiercely. "I'm sorry." She dropped her hands to his shoulders.

"I should walk away from you," Kell whispered, his head bowing towards hers.

Lyric's breath caught, and she tightened her hands on his shoulders. "No."

Kell's eyes darkened to a deep blue, and Lyric's breath caught as he bent his head above her. Her heart thumped in her chest, and she shivered as his fingers shifted on her waist, drawing her closer. "Stay," she breathed.

He kissed her, and Lyric stopped breathing altogether.

It might have been hours or mere seconds, but when Kell's lips left hers, Lyric could do nothing but stare at him with a dazed expression, her lashes fluttering open. She smiled, a curve of the lips that grew wider and wider until they both grinned like addled fools, arms wrapped around each other.

"We should go," Lyric whispered, staring at Kell's face. A part of her was afraid if she looked away, he'd disappear. Nothing this wonderful would last. The giddy feeling sending sparks tumbling beneath her skin paled as thoughts of her mother resumed their place inside her mind.

"Yes," Kell said. He lifted a hand to Lyric's face and ran a thumb across her bottom lip. His eyes were still dark with desire. Stepping away from her, Kell reached for his pack and cloak, lying forgotten beside the pool, then held out his hand.

Blushing, Lyric slipped her hand into his, and together they walked back to Runa.

Returning to camp, they found Runa eating porridge. She eyed Lyric and Kell, then looked back down at her bowl and took another bite, saying nothing.

Lyric picked up the other two bowls and divided the remaining porridge between her and Kell, then settled herself on the ground to eat. Each caught in their own thoughts, they ate in silence, neither speaking of their shared moment by the pool.

What if Runa was right, Lyric wondered, and their grandfather used Kell to create the Taint despite his binding? Would King Rakarn recognize him when they arrived and prevent them from leaving? Were they all marching towards imprisonment?

*We could walk away*, Lyric thought. *Disappear.*

But no, that wasn't an option anymore. Not with their mother close to death. They needed their grandfather, his influence, and power.

Dread and need tangled together, as Lyric thought about the end of their journey. In a few hours, they'd reach Rathgar's Hold. One way or another, it would all soon be out of their hands.

## 19

### RUNA

RATHGAR'S HOLD WAS A NOISY, bustling city. It sprawled along the coast, a sun-beaten labyrinth of black stone buildings that punched into the sky, all vying for a view of the eastern harbor. Rising from the city's center was the hold itself, a massive stone castle built atop a vast plateau that lifted it high above the streets and buildings below.

Standing in the center of a broad, busy street that stretched into the city's heart, Runa could see their goal in the distance. The towering castle was impossible to miss.

"I need to sit down," Lyric said, staring at the distant plateau.

Runa eyed her sister, seeing sweat beading along her hairline. "What's wrong with you?" she asked.

"I just need a moment." Lyric wandered ahead, veering off the main street beneath a narrow archway.

Confused by her sister's unease, Runa followed her into what appeared to be a small public garden with a burbling fountain that misted the air. Arranged around it were three stone benches, shaped like half-moons. The garden felt private and quiet, the clamor from the market dampened by the high stone walls of the houses around them.

Lyric sat down on a bench and pressed her fingers against her temples. She looked at the ground, posture stiff, so Runa wandered along the garden's enclosing wall. Gray-green succulents trailed down the dark stone like long, braided tassels. Peering closely at the vibrant plant, Runa saw that small, pink pods peppered the fleshy leaves. They looked like tiny gems, and she scratched one with a fingernail.

Abandoning the plant, Runa resumed pacing around the garden, fingers tapping against her hips as she walked. She was impatient to keep moving. She could tell Lyric was nervous about presenting themselves at the castle, but unlike her sister, she wanted to get it over with as quickly as possible. Waiting wouldn't make it easier.

Runa stopped and stared at Lyric, crossing her arms. Her sister thought she didn't care and that she was too angry at their mother to be thinking of her, but every step away from Elaina felt momentous. She was still mad and doubted she'd ever get over it, but she wasn't ready for their mother to die.

"Drink something," Kell told Lyric, handing her a waterskin.

Lyric sipped the water, then passed it back and ran her hands over the front of her dress, smoothing the pleats at her waist.

"Lyric," Runa said, trying to keep her voice calm and even. "What's going on?"

"I feel anxious and unsettled. Sick." Lyric frowned. "More than I should be, I think. I'm afraid Grandfather won't see us or that he won't summon a Dragon Blessed for Mama. I'm worried he'll see—" Lyric paused, eyes flicking sideways to Kell. "That he'll imprison us. But I think ..." She frowned, her eyes focusing on the slate tiles covering the ground. "I think I'm feeling Gandara's emotions. She doesn't like being here in the city. She's scared, angry."

Kell reached for her hand and Lyric clung to him with a new familiarity Runa hadn't seen between them before. She frowned, eyeing them.

"I feel it too," Runa said, thinking of Elenora's presence in the back of her mind. "The bleed of emotions into my own. Elenora seems to enjoy when I'm angry, and it's hard not to feel overwhelmed with her emotions fueling mine, pushing them hotter. I can't always tell what's me and what's her."

Lyric nodded, and her eyes drifted to the path that led back to the main street. "Do you think we'll get past the guards at the gate?"

"I don't know," Runa said, accepting Lyric's change of subject. "If we can't, then we'll figure out where the Dragon Blessed temple is and pound on the doors until they let us in." She grinned, but Lyric didn't seem to notice.

Nodding, Lyric leaned her head against Kell's arm and stared at their tangled fingers. "Are you sure you want to come with us?" she asked softly. "What if ... what if our grandfather was at Salta and recognizes you?"

A muscle twitched in Kell's cheek, and he raised a hand to his throat. He swallowed, looking uncomfortable. "The plan was always to come here," he said. "Whatever happens, I'll finally have answers."

Kell swallowed again, and Runa saw the tattoo around his throat flicker, shifting in color before fading back to a calm blue.

Lyric looked at Runa, worry churning in her eyes. "I'm ready," she said.

IT TOOK NEARLY an hour to reach the castle's plateau, their

progress slow despite sticking to the main road. People crowded the wide promenade, wearing spiked masks and black and red clothing. Some of the women wore chain-shell tails tied to the back of their belts that swayed as they walked.

Halfway into the city Runa, Lyric, and Kell were forced to the side by an enormous paper dragon held aloft by young men and women wearing gray.

"Is this related to the Feast of Souls?" Runa asked Kell as they waited for the dragon to pass.

"Yes, the Dragon Blessing," Kell said. He smiled at a little girl waving vigorously at the dragon from atop her father's shoulders.

Cramped and impatient as the press of bodies surged around her, Runa found herself wishing, for the first time since leaving home, for the vast open fields of their mountain valley. The heat in Raendashar didn't bother her, but there were too many sounds and smells assaulting her senses.

Behind the dragon marched a squad of six men and women wearing red leather. Their expressions were fierce, their stride proud, as they escorted a brown-haired woman down the street. Rumpled and dirty, she wore a loose vest and white trousers. Blue tattoos capped her shoulders, the faded fish scale pattern curving down her warm beige skin. Though unmistakably a prisoner, the woman looked defiant, her green eyes moving over the crowd with disgust.

The lead soldier, a brown-skinned woman with black hair and a beaked nose, raised a hand and released a volley of fire into the air. The crowd screamed with excitement, and Runa flushed, basking in the Burner's magic as it washed over her.

"She's Sireni," Lyric whispered. She grabbed Kell's arm, her fingers white on his sleeve.

"She'll be executed by fire," Kell said, his voice low. "I've seen it before." He tried to angle Lyric away, but she stared after the Burners with horrified eyes.

A thrill curled down Runa's spine, and she shifted uncomfortably, confused. She wasn't happy the woman was going to die. She couldn't be. *This isn't me*, she thought.

Elenora pushed into her mind, wearing disgust like a shawl. *She's killed your sisters, your brothers. She deserves this.*

*No,* Runa thought, clenching her jaw.

*You're just like your mother. I know now what she did, her betrayal. I won't let you become her.*

*You'll do nothing,* Runa thought. She shoved the ancestor away and tried to close her mind.

Her sister still clung to Kell's arm, and she looked back at Runa with wet eyes. "We have to stop it," Lyric said.

Runa laughed incredulously, her voice harsh with the conflicting emotions burning inside her. "What do you think we can do?" she asked.

"This is barbaric," Lyric said, eyes turning angry. She stared at Runa until she looked away.

A vision of Lyric challenging the Burners filled Runa's mind. She could see the black-haired woman turn, and hear her sister scream as she burned. "We need to go," Runa said.

Elenora settled back; pleased Runa wouldn't interfere.

Rebelliously, Runa touched her sister on the shoulder. "You can appeal to the king," she said. "I doubt he'll listen, but you can try."

"Yes," Kell said. "There's nothing you can do here. There are too many soldiers."

Elenora pulsed with exasperated displeasure and disappeared, leaving Runa alone.

Relieved, she pulled on Lyric's shoulder. "We need to go, Ly. We might not be able to help the Sireni woman, but don't forget Mother needs us."

Lyric looked back at the squad of mages, but she let herself be led away through the crowd.

Feeling drained and on edge, Runa was relieved when they

finally reached the castle's outer gate. She stared at the large stone beneath the castle, impressed by its size. "It's like a giant sheared off the top of the mountain," she said.

She could see a narrow road winding around the base, leading from the bottom gate to the castle at the top. Along the ramp loomed two more gates, cut from the stone.

In front of them, the wall of the castle's outer gate was tall and sleek, topped with two watchtowers and rising from the ground as if it'd been grown from the earth itself. The massive gate was open; the banded iron doors swung wide. Two guards in black scaled armor stood on either side holding bladed pikes and watching a small crowd passing through the gate.

"I'm surprised there aren't more guards," Kell said. He adjusted his cloak, so his emerald pin was visible on his collar.

"Maybe they're patrolling the festival," Runa said, thinking about the Burners.

Ignoring them, Lyric nodded at the queue. "They're climbing to the second gate. We should follow them."

The guards watched but said nothing as Runa, Lyric, and Kell joined the back of the line. Walking through the first gate, they stepped onto the narrow path. It was just wide enough for the three of them to stand side by side, but Runa, on the road's edge, warily watched the drop as they started to climb. The rock was slick, but the path beneath their feet had been textured to provide footing.

"They don't need more guards," Runa said. "They could roll a stone down the ramp, and people would fall off."

Ten minutes of climbing brought them to the second gate where they reformed a line with the people who'd arrived ahead of them. As they waited for the other petitioners to speak to the guards, Runa considered the gate.

Unlike the one below, there were no visible guard towers, but she saw archer slits on either side of the closed door. The gate's stone, smooth and featureless like a frozen lake, looked impossible to climb.

In front of the closed gate were two tall pillars holding crouched stone wyverns carved from black Raendasharan stone. The creatures' wings tucked against their bodies, and their clawed feet curved over the pillars' edges as if they'd landed from a flight. Horned and fierce-eyed, the wyverns' long-snouted heads looked down on the petitioners as they waited to enter the gate.

Looking at the people ahead of them, Runa saw all but two turned away. Those allowed to enter gave the guards slips of paper before being let through a small door close to the rock wall. The full gate remained closed.

"There are still two more gates," a woman ahead of them grumbled. "We'll miss the assembly." She approached the guards, slip in hand, and after a few minutes was let inside along with the skinny white-haired man accompanying her.

"Our turn," Lyric said, letting go of Kell's arm.

Runa adjusted her cloak, revealing the front of her dress, then reached for the pendant in the pouch at her waist.

"Next!" the guard called, in a bored voice. "Present your writs of passage," he said, as Runa, Lyric, and Kell approached. Despite his tone, the guard's eyes were sharp beneath a fringe of black hair.

Lifting her chin, Runa smiled blandly, but let it slip off her face as the guard gave her a wary look. "We don't have a writ," Runa said, "but we seek an audience with King Rakarn." She hurried on as the second guard started to raise his hand to send them back down the road. "We're here on behalf of our mother, the Crown Princess Elaina'delaina Raendashara."

"We're his granddaughters," Lyric said.

The guards exchanged glances.

"Granddaughters to the King, are you?" the black-haired

guard asked, raising an eyebrow. He looked at Kell. "And you're what, their guardian?"

The second guard snickered, his brown eyes running down Kell's lean frame.

Kell introduced himself with an elegant bow.

"A bard!" the brown-eyed guard laughed. "Now that is a curious escort."

"We realize it's irregular traveling without a proper escort," Runa said, "but given the current political climate, we thought it best to arrive without much fanfare."

The black-haired guard glanced at the second. "Have you ever seen the Crown Princess?" he asked.

"Never, but isn't she a recluse?" the second guard said. He shifted his jaw, considering. "I've never seen her attend any event, including the Champion's Ball. I can't speak to their resemblance, but that one's got the right hair color ..."

"Red hair isn't limited to the royal family," the black-haired guard said. "You've met my sister."

"Definitely not a princess, that one," the second guard laughed.

"Excuse me," Runa interrupted, narrowing her eyes. "If you'd refrain from wasting our time it's imperative we speak with the King as soon as possible. If you can't take us to him directly, can we speak with an advisor? I have a keepsake from our mother." Runa pulled out the pendant and unwrapped the stone, holding it up to the light.

The guards leaned forward, humor slipping from their faces. "We should confer with Captain Pelaran," the black-haired guard said. He looked at Runa then eyed Lyric and Kell sharply. "Wait here."

"We have no intention of leaving," Runa said.

Turning around, the guard walked to the small door and rapped it with his knuckles. A foot-soldier with similar black armor and green sleeves stuck his head out, and they quietly conversed before he slipped back inside and closed the door.

Returning to his post with the second guard, the uniformed men stared at Runa, Lyric, and Kell with focused attention.

Waiting for the Captain, Runa glanced behind Lyric and Kell and saw a small group of hooded figures walking up the road. *More petitioners*, she thought, turning back to the guards. Impatient though she was, she resisted the urge to shift her weight from side to side and kept her posture straight and unmoving like the statues above her. She stared into the black-haired guard's eyes and was secretly thrilled when he eventually shifted and looked away.

The door scraped open, and an older man stepped through, striding towards them with purposeful steps. The young foot-soldier followed close on his heels.

Runa studied the new man curiously. He was armored like the guards but had red, metal bars pinned to the high collar around his throat. His sleeves were red instead of green, beneath a black gambeson. His strong jaw was scarred and grizzled, and a black mustache, carefully trimmed and peppered with gray, sat beneath a blunted nose as if he'd taken a shield to the face. His hair was short and silver. Despite his flattened nose, Runa thought he was rather handsome for an older man. He felt intelligent and dangerous.

The black-haired guard saluted crisply. "Captain Pelaran, these women claim they are the daughters of the Crown Princess and request an audience with King Rakarn. They have a pendant from the royal treasury and are accompanied by Kell Layreasha, a songsmith."

Runa kept the surprise from her face by sheer determination. Had King Rakarn reported the pendant as stolen? They'd intended it to help their cause, not land them in prison.

The Captain looked Runa over with hard, gray eyes, then shifted his gaze to Lyric and Kell. "I've heard rumors of heirs to the throne," he said, studying their faces, "but I've heard rumors of many things. This pendant you carry has been missing for over twenty years."

"It wasn't missing," Runa said, meeting the Captain's eyes without flinching. "It's been in our mother's possession, a reminder of home."

"Where's the Crown Princess now?" Captain Pelaran asked.

Runa saw the guards exchange glances behind him. Was it not common knowledge then, that their mother wasn't in the city?

"She waits for our return in Ivernn."

"Why did she send you alone?" Captain Pelaran asked.

Lyric brushed her fingers against the back of Runa's sleeve. "She was injured, Captain," Lyric said. "That's why we must speak to the King. We need a—"

"If the Crown Princess is in danger," the Captain said, cutting her off, "I'm bound to look into it. I can't, unfortunately, take your word alone that you are who you claim to be." He held out his hand for the pendant. "You need to come with me until we can verify who you are.

"Lieutenant Shefton," he said, looking over his shoulder at the foot-soldier. "Escort them to the Hold. We—" He cut off, seeing the Lieutenant's eyes shift beyond Runa's head and flare in alarm.

Captain Pelaran whirled and drew his sword. "Out of the way!" he yelled, as Runa's eyes widened.

Fumbling to put the pendant back in her pouch, Runa scurried sideways, bumping into Lyric as the Captain and guards rushed past.

Kell grabbed her shoulder and pulled her against the rock wall beside Lyric.

*What's going on?* Runa thought, eyes on the sprinting men. Looking past them, she saw the hooded people had reached the gate. They were drawing weapons and throwing off their cloaks, revealing loose, white breeches and bare chests. Knotted cords and blue sashes wrapped their waists, the ends dangling down to mid-thigh. One of them yelled something she didn't understand.

"Sireni!" Kell breathed.

One of the white-clothed men took a crossbow bolt in the shoulder, and Runa snapped her head back to the gate. Someone was firing a crossbow from behind the arrow slits. A bell started ringing, a loud, clanging sound.

"Hold!" Captain Pelaran roared, drawing back Runa's attention. He, along with the three soldiers, had closed with the attacking Sireni.

Lieutenant Shefton, fumbling with his sword, engaged a man with long, black hair. The Lieutenant was fast but frantic, barely able to parry the returning blows.

The Captain barreled into the knot of men, stabbing one in the thigh, then tossing another off the road with a solid hit from his shoulder. "Defend the gate!" he bellowed.

Runa darted another look at the gate. The small door several petitioners had been allowed to enter was hanging open. The bell fell silent.

Runa looked back and saw Captain Pelaran smash his fist into another man's face, knocking him back. Unaware or unable to turn, the Captain caught a powerful sword thrust in his side, the blade punching through the dense fabric of his gambeson and driving him down on one knee. He clutched his waist, swinging his blade wildly. Blood sprayed into the air as the Sireni pulled his sword free from the Captain.

Lyric gasped beside her and Runa felt Kell shift, moving in front of her and Lyric.

The Lieutenant, still battling with the long-haired man, tried to reach his fallen Captain. He pivoted and swung his sword, slicing deeply into the man's unprotected chest, and continued past him. Back turned, the Lieutenant didn't see the falling man's arm come up as he lurched, and the curved sword buried itself in the back of his head, knocking off his helmet. Both men fell.

Fighting with pikes, the guards feinted and stabbed. The Sireni seemed unable to flank them, restricted by the narrow width of the road. Runa wondered if the guards would succeed in driving the attackers back to the first gate when one of the men in white snapped his hand out, fast as an adder, and grabbed the black-haired guard's blade. Ignoring the blood dripping off his hand, the white-clothed man tugged, unbalancing the guard. Sliding underneath the long pole, the Sireni man slashed up with his dagger, catching the guard across the face.

"What do we do?" Lyric hissed, grabbing Runa's arm.

Runa thought quickly. Could she summon fire and toss it at the Sireni like a hogsball? Was she fast enough to get them before they reached her? Maybe Lyric could summon wind and if Kell still had his damned staff then—

The remaining guards fell. The Sireni, barely winded by the quick fight, turned their eyes and weapons on Runa, Lyric, and Kell. Three had fallen during their assault, but three remained. They were of various ages with tattooed, sun-bronzed skin, and eyes in different shades of blue and green. Two had long hair, both blond, braided back from their faces. The third man had brown curls that stuck out from his head in a sun-lightened cloud.

"Run to the gate," Runa whispered. If they could get through, they could run to the next gate, get help.

"Ru!" Lyric gasped again. "Look!"

Turning her head away from the men, Runa looked back at the gate. A woman stepped through the small door followed by a man with dark skin and shoulder-length black hair. The woman, dressed similarly to the others, was wearing white cloth crossing over her breasts and around her neck. Her hair was braided in a heavy plait and tied with jute, strung with small glass beads and bits of seashells.

Marching towards them, she pointed a long finger in Runa's direction. "Who are they!" she demanded. "Why did you attack? This was supposed to be a quiet infiltration!"

"We weren't going to make it through, Kaia," one of the men with braided hair said, "and I overheard that one say she's a Raendasharan princess." He pointed at Runa. "I reasoned a princess is better than being run off with empty hands."

Kaia's green eyes flicked between Runa, Lyric, and Kell. "That one looks Nilin," she said, looking at Kell. "And that one ..." She studied Lyric with a shrewd expression. "That one could be Rainaya's sister. They're a waste of time," she snapped, "and now we have to return to the ship. Soldiers are coming from the castle through the third gate; the guards rang the alarm bell. They know we're here."

The man shrugged, unconcerned by her anger. "Who'd pretend to be part of the Butcher's family who wasn't? You'd be putting your head in a noose."

"Let us go," Runa said, stepping forward. "We're not a threat to you."

Kaia whirled, the back of her ringed hand slapping Runa's face and driving her head sideways. "Quiet, girl!" she snapped.

Fury exploding inside her chest, Runa spat blood onto the ground and looked back at Kaia with a savage glare.

Lyric stepped forward, and the Sireni shifted, raising their weapons.

Kaia barked a laugh. "What, going to fight us all?" she asked challengingly.

The black-haired man leaned towards her, murmuring something that wiped the smirk off Kaia's face. Her eyes snapped back to Lyric and Runa, and then the ground started trembling beneath their feet.

Runa shifted to maintain balance, grabbing Lyric's hand. The sound of grinding stone grated in her ears.

"What—?" Lyric asked.

The wyvern statues were moving, coming to life. Their jaws opened, and their wings flexed. Bits of stone crumbled beneath their clawed feet as they scratched at the pillars, showering black dust onto the ground.

"Royal blood!" Kaia gasped. "She's Raendasharan royalty! Grab her! Back to the ship, now!" she roared.

"Leave my sister alone!" Lyric yelled, throwing herself forward.

Kell, gaping at the wakening wyverns, rushed after Lyric.

Runa threw out her arm, trying to knock back the short-haired man lunging for her. He ducked and punched her in the jaw, knocking her back into the wall. Stunned, Runa was unable to push him away as he spun her around and pressed her face into the smooth stone, tying her arms behind her.

"Grab them all!" Kaia yelled.

Runa bucked, trying to get away but her captor lifted her off the ground and tossed her over his shoulder. Hammering her tied fists against his back, she saw the man with Kaia grab her sister.

Kell was on the ground, hand covering his eye. One of the men with braided hair kicked him in the side, then hauled him back to his feet, tying Kell's hands tied together with the knotted rope from his waist.

Runa sucked in a breath to scream, but Kaia loomed up in front of her, staring hard into her eyes. "Do that, and I'll slit your sister's throat," she said, pointing at Lyric.

The air hissed out of her lungs, and Runa glared into the woman's face.

"Let's go!" Kaia ordered, moving around them. "Hurry!"

Arching up off the man's back, Runa looked at the wyverns. The shaking had subsided, but she could still hear the scratch of stone. Were the statues breaking free? As she watched, one wyvern lifted a foot off the pillar.

The short-haired man started running, ignoring Runa's curses as she bounced on his shoulder. She squeezed her eyes shut as she felt him slip on the stone.

A scream snapped her eyes back open, and Runa twisted to see Kaia sprinting through the first gate. Her sword swung as she passed one of the guards. Blood sprayed, and he toppled onto the ground.

The man with braided hair, the one not holding Kell, rammed his shoulder into the second guard and tackled him to the ground, slashing at his neck with a long knife.

Skidding to a stop beneath the gate, the short-haired man abruptly dropped Runa on her feet. She wobbled, almost falling on her face before he grabbed the rope around her wrists and yanked her upright. He shifted his grip to her upper arm and hauled her along beside him as they ran onto the cobbled street.

Screams rose into the air as well-dressed citizens, many still wearing masks, fled from the bloodied Sireni. Someone yelled for the city watch.

"This way!" Kaia called. She led them east past a row of trees then ducked into a shaded alley. They wove through a confusing maze of streets, their passage heralded by screams and shouts as panicked people ran away.

A group of pigeons scattered noisily high above and Runa looked up. Her mouth fell open. A stone wyvern was chasing them, its heavy wings flapping at the air, somehow keeping it aloft.

"They're following!" the short-haired yelled. He yanked on Runa's arm, and she tripped, unbalanced with her hands behind her back.

The Sireni ducked into another narrow alley, trying to maintain cover between them and the stone creatures above.

Runa saw a flash of black out of the corner of her eye. It was a squad of soldiers, yelling over a group of panicked people blocking their path.

Runa staggered as the Sireni man pulled her around a stack of crates and into an open street. Pain rippled along her waist, her muscles cramping. She panted, trying to ignore it. She could see the docks ahead and the masts and sails of ships on the water.

Kaia barreled into a uniformed dock guard gawking at the sky, a small crossbow halfway out of the holster on his back. She kicked him to the ground and whirled, cocking and raising the weapon, pointing it back towards Lyric and the man holding her arm.

Horrified, Runa yelled as Kaia fired, but the bolt flew over her sister's head. She watched it pass, resisting as the short-haired man yanked her sideways.

The bolt hit the diving wyvern square in the chest, knocking it away from Kell and the other Sireni. It tumbled sideways in the air, roaring soundlessly, and smashed into a cluster of wood barrels.

Lyric screamed as tiny shards of wood and black stone sprayed across their heads, drawing blood.

"Come on!" Runa's captor yelled. He dragged her across the nearest pier, the others scrambling behind him. They passed the bodies of four soldiers crumpled on the wooden dock and Runa stared at them in confusion. Unsure who'd killed them, she raised her head and saw four more white-clothed Sireni waving their arms by a small boat at the end of the platform.

"Hurry!" one shouted, jabbing a finger at the sky above their heads.

Tumbling into the boat, the Sireni shoved Runa, Lyric, and Kell into the center and piled around them. Once everyone was aboard, the four new sailors pushed away from the dock and began hauling on the oars.

Kaia, scrambling to the boat's prow, leaned over and stuck her hands in the water. She began chanting, her voice quick and lilting. Runa recognized her words as runes, but they sounded different on the Sireni woman's tongue.

Responding to Kaia's power, the water curled around the back of the boat and pushed, propelling them out of the bay into the open ocean. Unfazed by their sudden speed, the wyverns pursued them. The one Kaia hit with the crossbow had recovered and flew close behind the first.

Runa craned her head to see past Kaia. A boat waited ahead, a large, sleek ship with blue sails. She looked back at the wyverns and the rapidly receding docks of Rathgar's Hold. Whatever spell Kaia cast had increased the distance between them and the stone creatures. Looking at the city, Runa watched the black shape of the castle dwindle in size.

"He'll know now," Runa said softly.

Lyric, pressed against her, looked up. "What?" she hissed, shielding her eyes from the strands of hair the wind had pulled free from her braid.

"Our grandfather. My blood activated those creatures. They must be trying to help us. Grandfather will know we were there, or think Mother was."

"Will he come after us?" Lyric asked, looking back at the city.

"I don't think he can," Runa said. "What will he chase us in, a merchant's ship?"

Their boat bumped alongside the Sireni ship, and a rope ladder dropped down. Sailors lined the railing, firing at the wyverns with crossbows.

"Cut their ropes!" Kaia ordered. She grabbed Kell's hands, quickly slicing through his bonds.

The Sireni freed Runa and Lyric next and forced them to climb the rope ladder onto the deck. They were shoved towards the center mast and pushed onto their knees.

"Get underway!" Kaia yelled, running towards a tall, muscular man with gold-tinted skin and coarse, brown hair. "Blood trackers!" she said, pointing at the sky.

One of the wyverns shattered and fell into the sea, unable to withstand the barrage of crossbow bolts from the ship's sailors.

The other wyvern crashed into a sailor on the deck, ripping open his chest with stone claws. The man screamed. Runa smelled the tang of fresh blood. Crouched where she was, she was staring into the fallen man's eyes as his light faded.

Sailors fell atop the wyvern with curved swords, hacking at it until it came apart in large chunks. The sailor lay dead beneath it; his face turned towards Runa.

"Toss it into the ocean!" Kaia yelled, heading towards the prow.

The sailors began to haul the pieces of stone to the railing and throw them into the dark water. Others picked up the dead man and carried him away, leaving behind a trail of blood.

Runa grabbed Lyric's hand, and Kell put his arm around her sister's shoulder.

Kaia, hands raised skyward in the ship's prow, yelled into the air. The ship lurched into motion, wind rushing across the open deck.

Runa watched Rathgar's Hold disappear, as the Sireni ship carried them away into the open sea.

## 20

LYRIC

LYRIC CLUNG to Runa and Kell, watching the fast movements of the Sireni crew as they scrambled across the ship's deck, pulling on ropes and climbing the rigging. The sails snapped as they caught the wind, billowing out above their heads, and Lyric felt the ship speed up.

A woman came for them with blond hair and a square, sun-browned face. "Kaia wants them below decks," she said.

The man guarding them nodded and looked at Lyric. "Get up," he said.

Kell helped Lyric stand, and they followed the woman to a hatch in the center of the ship. She wrenched it open and pointed at Lyric to climb down. Doing so, Lyric found herself in a large room filled with hammocks strung between the posts and beams overhead; some occupied by sleeping Sireni sailors.

Once Runa, Kell, and the two Sireni climbed down into the chamber, the sailors propelled them past the hammocks to a storage room. It was filled with iron-wrapped barrels and stacks of bundles carefully wrapped in stiff, waxed fabric. At the back, secured to the sides of the ship and separating the room in two, was a tall iron cage. A large, flat plate was attached to the door where the lock should be, dark gold mage runes interlaced across its surface in a teardrop pattern.

The female sailor slapped her hand against the plate, and the door unlocked with a soft click. Wrenching it open with one muscled arm, she grabbed Lyric by the shoulder and stripped off her pack, tossing it in the corner. "Get in," the woman said.

Looking back at Runa and Kell, also being relieved of their packs, Lyric warily stepped into the cage. Runa and Kell were shoved in behind her, and the woman slammed the door shut. It clicked, the lock engaging.

"What do you intend to do with us?" Runa demanded, glaring at the sailors through the iron bars.

"That's up to the Captain," the woman said. Her eyes lingered on Lyric for a moment, and she shared an uncertain look with the second sailor. "Do you think that ..." she started, then trailed off, indicating something with a flick of her eyes.

The man shrugged and tapped the sword at his waist. "Where would they go?" he asked.

"True." She slapped the man on the chest. "Let's go."

Turning, the two Sireni walked back into the sleeping chamber and slammed the door.

Runa crossed her arms and started pacing back and forth like a cat, her face a mask of rumination.

A bone-chilling numbness sunk into Lyric's bones as she stared around their prison. It seemed like only minutes ago that they'd been speaking to Captain Pelaran at the gate. He'd been about to let them in. Whether or not he'd planned to detain them, assuming they'd stolen the pendant, they'd have been within the same building as their grandfather.

But now, kidnapped and sailing away from Raendashar, help for their mother was farther out of reach. How many leagues now stretched between them and Elaina? She was going to die, and they could do nothing.

Kell, shrugging off his cloak, pulled Lyric into his arms. She leaned into him, pressing her head against his chest and tried to rise above her despair.

It was unfamiliar being on a ship. The constant sway made Lyric's stomach flip. She'd been on a rowboat before, but only on a lake where the water was calm and free from waves.

"It'd be laughable if this weren't the worst thing that could have happened," Runa said.

Lyric blinked and lifted her head to watch her sister. "What?" she asked.

"The Sireni have been trying to kidnap us for who knows how long, and now they've done it," Runa said. "Only, the people who took us don't even realize who we are."

"Maybe not yet," Lyric said. "But they believe *you* are a princess. Maybe they think you're a daughter of one of Mama's siblings." She rubbed her forehead, trying to think. "They must be taking us to the Gale. Right, Kell?" Lyric asked, looking up at him.

The skin around Kell's eye had started to bruise, darkening to a wine-red.

Kell frowned and nodded. "I think it's likely. I assume kidnapping a member of the Scorched Court; specifically, someone from the Raendasharan royal family would require a meeting of clans. The Gale will be the ones to decide what to do with you."

"She'll interrogate us, won't she?" Lyric asked. "The woman, Kaia."

"I would if I were her," Runa said.

Lyric chewed on her lip, thinking back to Kaia's comment about her looks and the vague conversation between the two Sireni who'd locked them up. "They think I'm Sireni," Lyric said, "or that someone in my family is." She watched Runa pace. "But they don't think I'm a princess. They must not know our father is Sireni."

Runa nodded and worried her thumbnail with her teeth. "I wonder if it helps or hurts us when they realize we share their blood. Does it make us allies, or do we become more dangerous?"

"I suppose it depends on how much they hate us," Lyric said.

"Either way, you'll be valuable to them," Kell said. His arms tightened around Lyric.

"Should we tell them who we are?" Lyric asked. "Maybe we can negotiate. Agree to willingly meet with the Gale, if they let us send a message to help Mama."

"Send a message to who?" Runa asked. "King Rakarn?" She barked a laugh. "I'm sure they'd consider that treasonous."

"For one of them, maybe," Lyric said. "Not us. We have to do something, Ru. The longer we're captives, the longer Mama goes without healing. Grandfather might think it was Mama at the gate and assume she's hurt, but he won't know she's dying in Ivernn. He'll think she's here."

Runa nodded. "We try to negotiate then, and if that doesn't work, we'll escape." She glared around their cell with a fierce expression.

"Yes," Lyric said.

"If we can get to the smaller boat, maybe you can summon wind to blow us to shore," Kell said.

Lyric nodded, feeling hopeful. "Yes, we can't be that far from land."

UNFORTUNATELY FOR THEIR PLAN, no one came.

After pacing with Runa and Lyric, shouting for help, Kell had sat down with his back to the ship's hull, and Lyric joined him. It was rather intimate how they were sitting together, with Lyric leaning against his chest and framed by his legs, but she was too tired and thirsty to care what Runa might think. Also, it was decidedly more comfortable than having her back against the wood or iron.

Lyric's head lulled against Kell, as she watched Runa flex her hands on the iron bars. Her sister refused to sit, pacing like a caged animal intent on being free.

"The bastards could at least bring us water," Runa growled, her voice raspy. "Why hasn't anyone come down? Where's Kaia?"

"Maybe they forgot we're here," Lyric said, shifting her legs. She was beginning to worry that the sailors intended on ignoring them until they reached their destination. What if they had hours more to sail? What would she do if she had to relieve herself? She couldn't, *wouldn't* go in front of Kell. She blushed, happy he couldn't see her face.

"We're willing to talk, but no one is here to listen!" Runa said. She growled and stalked back towards Lyric and Kell, finally sitting across from them atop her cloak.

Lyric looked at the large metal plate on the door and chewed on her lip. She thought about how the sailor had opened it with her palm. The woman hadn't said anything, hadn't whispered a rune word. Why had it opened? Was the lock tied to the woman in some way? No, that wouldn't make sense; having a cage only one person could open. Could it be like the wyverns? Could the lock read your blood and respond in a specified way?

"The lock," Lyric said. Her words were barely audible, and she cleared her throat, repeating herself. She needed water. "It opened because the sailor was Sireni," she said.

Runa looked at her, raising her eyebrow. "Did Gandara tell you that?"

"No," Lyric said. "Just puzzling it out myself."

Runa nodded and looked at the door. "Makes sense."

"Which means, we can probably open it," Lyric said. "Being

half Sireni should be enough, right? If we can unlock the door, we can get water, find Kaia, and make her talk to us. Maybe we can't escape just yet, but getting out of here would be an improvement. I can't sit here and wait, Ru. Mama needs us."

Runa nodded. "Worth trying." She scratched at her scalp. "I've been trying to call Elenora, ask her how to replicate Mother's spell that took us to the Veil. If we could move like that, we could use the spell to escape." Runa sighed. "She's silent though, muttering in the back of my head like she's on the other side of a wall."

Lyric nodded. "Gandara's been distant since Ivernn," she said. She shifted, pushing against Kell's knee to help herself stand, and walked to the door.

Leaning against the cage, Lyric stuck her arm through the bars and reached up for the lock. She bent, contorting awkwardly, trying to reach higher and get her palm on the flat plate. Ignoring the pain in her shoulder, she twisted again, inching her fingers across the metal until she felt it beneath her entire hand. Lyric pressed her palm flat against it and willed the door to open.

Nothing happened.

Lyric shifted her hand again, pressing her skin against the cold metal. Was it growing warmer? She pushed harder. Something clicked.

"I think I did it!" Lyric said, sliding her arm back through the bars. Bracing her feet, she pulled on the door. It opened easily, and she rushed through it, diving for her pack. Ripping it open, she dug out her waterskin and gulped down water.

Lyric wiped water off her chin and looked up to find Kell and Runa behind her. They'd hunted for their water as well, and the three of them stared at each other, momentarily elated by their success.

"What now?" Lyric asked. "Walk up on deck?"

"We should disguise ourselves," Runa said. "There might be

clothes in there. Maybe we'll have an opportunity to steal the small boat and escape that way. We should be ready."

Lyric nodded. "Yes, I think you're—"

The ship lurched to the side, throwing them off their feet. Lyric's cheek slammed against the wall, and she groaned as a knee jabbed into her back. Something boomed, loud and close, and she heard wood splinter somewhere above.

Untangling themselves, the three of them staggered towards the storage room's door.

"Is it Grandfather?" Lyric asked.

Runa frowned. "He doesn't have a ship."

"Maybe he's allied with someone who has a fleet," Kell said.

"Whoever it is, this may be an opportunity to escape in the confusion," Lyric said. "I don't want to stay down here if the ship is being torn apart."

To free their movement, they stuffed their cloaks into their bags and slung them over their shoulders.

Runa pressed her ear to the door, listening, then opened it. The ship shuddered again, and they braced themselves in the doorway, staring into the dim room beyond. They could hear the clang of metal striking metal somewhere above.

"Someone's fighting," Runa whispered. "I don't see anyone here. I doubt anyone is sleeping through this."

They moved cautiously into the room, eyeing the empty hammocks. Some personal belongings had been knocked free and were rolling across the floor as the ship bucked.

Lyric winced as something smacked into her ankle. She staggered to a trunk, strapped to the floor, and opened it. Riffling through the clothes inside, Lyric pulled out a bundle of white breeches. "This isn't going to work," she hissed at Runa, "unless you want to bare our chests up there."

"Here, throw this on," Runa said, tossing a sheepskin at her. "Tie up the bottom of your dress, so it looks like trousers, like when we went fishing. Better than nothing, right?"

"Here," Lyric said, tossing the trousers to Kell. Turning her back to him, she draped the sheepskin around her shoulders and tucked the bottom of her dress up into her belt. She swayed as the ship shook again, staring down at her exposed stockings and boots. "This isn't going to fool anyone," Lyric said.

Runa shrugged. "Maybe it'll confuse them enough that they won't try to stop us right away." She pulled off her stockings and boots and stuffed them into her pack.

Copying her, Lyric straightened and saw Runa staring past her appraisingly.

"He might avoid their notice," Runa said.

Lyric looked behind her and felt her mouth go dry.

Kell had traded his clothes for the loose, white trousers she'd given him. His chest was bare, the lean muscles of his body pale in the dim room. He'd found a vest from somewhere and pulled it on, likely thinking to cover the tattoos and nubs on his back. He grinned as her eyes slid down his chest.

"Enough gawking, Ly," Runa said.

Lyric blushed and spun back around. She staggered to the ladder leading back to the deck above and put her foot on the bottom rung. "What if we walk out into a battle?" Lyric asked. She flexed the fingers of one hand, remembering how it'd felt to summon the wind.

"We're not defenseless," Runa said, "though I shouldn't create fire unless we know we can get off the boat."

"Let me go first," Kell said.

Lyric looked back at him and arched an eyebrow. "Not to diminish your offer, but you're the only one who doesn't know magic."

Kell smiled crookedly. "Fair enough," he said. "After you, then."

Feeling a thrill of excitement, Lyric climbed the ladder and put her hand against the hatch. She shoved it open and stepped out into chaos.

Fighting sailors filled the deck, wrestling and attacking each other with swords. They were all Sireni, though some wore green sashes while others wore blue.

Lyric scrambled out of the way as Runa and Kell joined her and scanned for the sailors she recognized. Didn't Kaia's crew wear blue? Who were the new Sireni?

Magic crawled across Lyric's skin, and she whipped her head sideways, seeing another ship drawn close. She knew with certainty that there was a mage aboard the new vessel churning the waves beneath them.

Someone shrieked and the air massed around her, bringing pain to her temples like it had when they'd fought the Screamers in the Veil. The ship bucked and Lyric fell into Kell.

Shaking her head as the pressure released, Lyric grabbed Kell and Runa, and together they scrambled away from the hatch. They tried to avoid notice by keeping away from the thickest of the fighting, but everywhere they turned someone blocked their way.

Watching the battle shift around them, Lyric thought the Sireni were avoiding killing blows, resorting to fists and cudgels instead of the knives and swords on their waists. The wounds the sailors received were crippling, but not severe.

"Hey!" one of Kaia's sailors yelled, pointing at them.

Lyric, Runa, and Kell hurried away, taking cover beside a stack of crates. The man who'd spotted them began to chase but was quickly distracted by an attack from a woman wearing green.

Lyric caught sight of Kaia in the melee. The woman was smashing her fist into a bald man's face. Shoving aside the bleeding man, Kaia turned, and her eyes focused on Lyric. She straightened in alarm, eyes wide and disbelieving. "Secure the prisoners!" Kaia yelled.

An older man, with thick brown hair, streaked with silver, spun at Kaia's shout. His green eyes met Lyric's as he shoved aside a sailor and drove him downward with a hard jab from his elbow.

Lyric watched him, caught by his stare. He was muscled and bronzed. His face was square with an angular nose and a series of rings in his left eyebrow. An old scar crossed through his left cheek and down the side of his neck.

Shoving a blue-belted Sireni out of the way, the man advanced on Lyric, Runa, and Kell with a purposeful stride.

Lyric put her arms out, shoving Runa and Kell back. Her eyes darted past the scarred man to Kaia.

The man held up his hands as he approached. He wasn't holding a weapon. "I'm here to help you," he said. His voice had a rough quality to it with an odd, lilting accent similar to Kaia's.

"Who are you?" Runa demanded, raising her hand.

The man's mouth lifted at one corner as he met Runa's fierce gaze. "Someone who doesn't want you to become a pawn for the Fire or the Sea. Please, we must go now." He gestured towards the other ship.

A trio of green-belted Sireni crowded behind him, fending off Kaia's sailors with seasoned efficiency. Blocked from reaching them, Kaia screamed furiously for her crew.

"Please, Lyric and Runa," the man said. "I'm a friend of your mother."

"How do you know our mother?" Runa asked. "How do you know who we are?"

"I'll explain everything, but we must go now." He looked at Runa. "You look like her," he said, "like Dandashara. Same untamed look in her eyes."

Lyric looked at Runa, thinking quickly. Could he be their uncle? The one they'd tried to reach? "We should go with him," she said.

Runa, eyes narrowed, stared at her then gave a sharp nod.

"Kell?" Lyric asked, looking at him.

Kell nodded. "Can't be any worse," he said.

The man laughed and clapped his hands. "Good," he said. "Follow me." He ushered them to the side of the ship, the other green-belted sailors clearing a path.

Kaia screamed furiously, unable to reach them, as the new Sireni helped Lyric, Runa, and Kell down into a smaller boat. She attempted to pull them back as they shoved away, but the other mage, unseen on the second ship, was stronger and blew apart her spell. The waves made an odd sucking sound, and their little boat broke free and shot across the water, making Lyric's eyes water.

Reaching the second ship, they were helped aboard by green-belted sailors, and then the little boat was hauled onto the deck and secured. The sails were adjusted, the lines pulled free, and the ship skimmed away across the water, heading north. If Kaia attempted anything else with her magic, Lyric didn't feel it.

The man who'd seemingly rescued them attempted to direct them to the ship's cabin, but Runa planted her feet and fixed him with a commanding stare. "Tell us who you are," she demanded.

"So like your mother," he said grinning, "all fire. We can talk in my cabin. It's quieter there. We won't have to shout." Indeed, the wind was picking up and tearing their words away, making it hard to hear.

Lyric put a hand to her face, trying to keep her hair out of her mouth and eyes. "Is this all your Screamer?" she asked, gesturing at the darkening sky. She glanced towards the prow and saw a woman with her hands on the railing, staring at the clouds.

"No, a storm's coming," the man said. "We'll have to ride through it. It's going to get rough. I'll tell you our plan once we're inside." Smiling encouragingly, he turned and walked to the cabin.

A large, bald man with a winged fish tattooed around his

neck, watched them but made no move to force them to follow. The other sailors had already returned to whatever duties they had on the large ship, leaving Lyric, Runa, and Kell unguarded.

Not knowing what else to do, and curious who the man was, Lyric shared a glance with her companions and followed the man into the cabin.

# 21

### KELL

KELL RESTED his hand on Lyric's shoulder and inspected the cabin. It looked much like the quarters of any sea captain with a large writing desk and chair, both secured to the floor, and a curving window of rippled, pale-green glass letting filtered light into the room. In front of the table, sat two wooden stools, easy to stow when the need arose.

To Kell's left were a heavy wood trunk and a bunk set into the wall. A narrow mirror hung beside the bed, framed in hammered copper. The room was clean and orderly, much like the man who'd seated himself behind the desk.

Kell studied the man's weathered face and watched as he moved a stack of maps and lit a small lantern with something from his pocket.

"I'm Captain Eleden," the man said, looking at Lyric and Runa, "and this is my ship, the Talan. Please sit. I know you're wondering why Sireni are fighting each other and what my interest is in the two of you." He gestured at the stools.

Kell glanced at Lyric, wondering if she recognized the Captain's name, but she merely touched his hand and sat down on the left stool. Keeping quiet, she removed her pack, setting it on the ground by her feet, and adjusted the sheepskin around her shoulders.

Runa sat on the other stool and braced her hands on her knees, fixing Captain Eleden with a hard-eyed stare.

*They must not want him to know yet that they've heard of him,* Kell thought.

"I apologize I've no seat to offer you," Eleden said, looking at Kell with sharp eyes. "Who do I have the honor of addressing?"

"I'm Kell," Kell said, not bothering with his full title. He moved closer behind Lyric and gave the Captain a direct look.

"He's our friend," Lyric said.

Eleden glanced between her and Kell and a knowing smile curved his lips.

Feeling the tips of his ears flush beneath the man's keen eyes, Kell was saved from further embarrassment by the sound of the door opening.

The bald man stepped inside, carrying tin cups and a dark green bottle with rope wrapped around the neck. He placed them on the desk and nodded at Captain Eleden.

"Thanks, Laerdi," Eleden said, nodding back. Uncorking the bottle, he poured pale wine into all four cups, then, selecting one for himself, leaned back in his chair. "Not all Sireni want to continue the war with Raendashar or approve of kidnapping or killing the heirs of the Scorched Court. When I learned the Gale intended to abduct you, we tried to prevent it."

"We?" Runa asked.

Eleden drained his cup and set it on the table. "Your mother and I. We were together when Dandashara received word you'd been kidnapped. Regrettably, I was unable to accompany her when she left to help you."

Kell frowned, recalling Lyric's theory at the inn in Heldon's Rock that Elaina was responsible for burning the Raendasharan fleet. Their discussion must have crossed Lyric's mind as well for her back straightened, and her hand twitched atop her knee.

"You destroyed Raendashar's fleet," Lyric said.

Eleden raised an eyebrow and smiled. Pride and satisfaction filled his green eyes.

Lyric looked at Runa. "I told you she did it," Lyric said. Her eyes shifted back to Eleden. "You're our uncle."

"Yes," Eleden said. "I was alerted that Kaia found the princesses in Rathgar's Hold and was taking you to the Gale. I sailed immediately to intercept. I promised your mother I'd protect you if you ended up in Sireni hands."

"She figured it out," Lyric said, surprised. "I thought she didn't recognize me." She cocked her head. "They didn't seem to know we're half Sireni. Is it a secret that our father had children?"

"Yes," Eleden said. His face grew grim, and he flexed his fingers on the arm of his chair. "Dandashara didn't want anyone to know. I didn't know until your mother and I met four years ago."

Kell thought about his birth mother, and how she'd given him up. "Does their father know they're alive?" he heard himself ask.

Lyric looked back at him, eyes filled with a longing he understood.

Eleden hesitated then gave a short nod. "Yes," he said. "When your mother found me she was looking for him. I sent him a message."

"A message?" Lyric asked. "He isn't with you or the other Sireni?"

"No."

"Where is he now?" Lyric asked.

"I don't know," Eleden said. "I haven't spoken with him for several years. He said he was unwell."

"And you didn't hunt him down?" Runa asked. "Make sure

he wasn't dying?" She made a disgusted sound. "You're his family."

"He disappears sometimes," Eleden said. He didn't seem upset by Runa's reproach, but there was something in his eyes that Kell couldn't decipher. "He's not ... he doesn't live like regular men."

Lyric straightened again, her head turning as though to look at Kell, but she shifted back without meeting his eyes. "Is he human?" Lyric asked.

Runa raised her eyebrows. "Is he human? What kind of question is that, Ly?"

Kell felt his mouth go dry and worked hard to keep his face blank.

"He's not just a man," Eleden said, looking at Lyric appraisingly. "Your father is my half-brother. We share our mother, Faeden. She was a powerful Windcaller and a formidable captain." He grinned ferociously, memories shifting through his eyes like wind-nudged clouds. "She once took down a fleet of six ships with a single Windracer."

"Not just a man? What is he?" Runa demanded. "What else is there?"

"There are creatures deep in the Sea of Screams, god-children of the great serpent Sae'shara, or Serith as you likely know Her. Your grandfather, your father's father, was one of those creatures. He could appear human, and Mother didn't know what he was when they met. He caught her eye and well ..." Eleden spread his hands. "Egan was born."

"Egan," Lyric said. "Our father."

Kell put his hand on Lyric's shoulder, feeling his heart flip as she reached up and covered his hand with hers. He was becoming accustomed to having her nearby, and it frightened him.

"Are we ... are we not fully human?" Lyric asked. Her fingers tightened on Kell's hand.

"I don't know," Eleden said. He stroked his chin thoughtfully. "Your mother would know better than I. When we were children Egan didn't seem much different than me most of the time. Except for..." Eleden paused, a memory lifting the corners of his mouth.

"Except for what?" Lyric asked.

"He can breathe underwater," Eleden said.

Runa leaned forward, eyes intent on the Captain's face. "Are god-children powerful?" she asked.

Eleden's brow furrowed. "Yes."

Kell looked at Runa, considering. If Elaina was a powerful Burner and their father was a god-child, how might that affect their magical ability? What would this revelation mean to King Rakarn? What might he do to them?

Worried, his thoughts returned to Raendashar. He'd been so close to finding the truth about his silencing. He'd been on Rakarn's doorstep. What would he have learned if he'd gotten inside?

Kell thought about his Thendian mother and father and felt the familiar ache deep inside his chest. Lyric shifted under his hand, and Kell blinked, returning his focus to the room. He relaxed his fingers, realizing he'd tightened his grip on her shoulder.

"I don't know what it'd mean to the Gale," Eleden said. "Being part Sireni should extend our laws and protection to you, but there's hatred in the hearts of many, passed down for generations."

"You want to stop the war," Runa asked. "Why?"

"I don't believe Sae'shara wants us to remain locked in this conflict," Eleden said. "We are more than this war. The land we're fighting over is just land. It's not the life-giving water beneath us that carries our ships, greets our young, and buries our dead. The Sea is our home, not Raendashar.

"We are proud, just like Raendasharans, and it's hard to let go of old grievances and choose a new path. To stop meeting blood with blood." Eleden spread his hands. "But when does it end, if every knife is met with another?"

"Have you tried to negotiate with King Rakarn?" Lyric asked. "Tell him you want peace?"

"He doesn't want to listen," Eleden said. "Your mother tried persuading him many times." His face darkened, and a muscle twitched in his cheek.

"How can you lay aside vengeance after what he did?" Runa asked. "Mother told us about the woman who came to Raendashar to discuss peace."

"Yes," Eleden said. His eyes glittered dangerously like shards of glass. "Iledasha, the daughter of Bethseida, one of the Gales and the head of my clan."

Kell studied the Captain's face. How could he be willing to work with a man who'd murdered someone from his clan? What kind of man must Eleden be to be able to set that aside?

"Your clan?" Runa asked. "And yet you still seek an end to the war?"

"It's what we've worked for," Eleden said. His eyes still blazed, but he seemed to have mastered his emotions. "Hating the man does not help our people. If we keep fighting, maybe we'll win, but at what cost? How many Sireni will be left at the end? Bethseida understands this, and despite her loss, she continues to speak for peace whenever the Gale gathers. She's a stronger woman than all of us, and I will see her vision carried out." Eleden steepled his fingers, eyeing them in turn.

"The survival of our people, our way of life, isn't the only thing we must consider," he said. "There's a greater danger to all of us; not just to the Sireni or to Raendashar, but all of Erith." Eleden looked at Kell, and Kell realized that with his shirt off, the man could see the tattoo ringing his throat. Did Eleden know what it meant?

"A greater danger?" Lyric asked.

"The Taint," Eleden said, looking at her. "The poison that edges farther out into the Sea of Screams that wiped out Thenda. The nations of Erith seem content to leave it be, to think it will remain where it is, but it's growing." He grimaced, irritation shifting through his eyes. "Even the Sireni clans don't see its magnitude. They think the war is more pressing, and so they ignore it. A problem for another time. They don't see the Sea Reaper drifting towards them."

"The what?" Runa asked.

Eleden blinked then laughed. "I'm sorry, you're not familiar with the Sea, are you. It's a fleshy, bell-shaped animal, transparent, quite beautiful actually but its sting can kill. It's slow, so if you pay attention, you can swim away from it. Avoid the danger."

He paused and stroked his chin, eyeing Lyric and Runa. "Dandashara would likely wish that I return you to her so you can hide from those who seek you, but that's not a solution. I hope she'll forgive me for suggesting this, but I believe you can help us end the war."

"Return us to her?" Lyric asked. "You'd let us go?"

"If you wish it," Eleden said, "but I urge you first to consider my proposal. You are from both sides with Sireni and Raendasharan blood. You belong to both the Sea and the land, and can be the bridge between us.

"Like your mother, it's unlikely Rakarn will listen to you on your own, but if you have strong allies at your back, he'll be forced to reconsider. He's drawn to power and will seek an alliance, but if he or the other Sireni clans capture you, you'll be powerless, a tool to use how they wish." Eleden leaned forward, his eyes fierce and passionate, ablaze with hope.

"With allies to protect you, you'll be free to make your own choices," Eleden said. "Free to demand change. You can broach peace with a mandate to work together to heal the Taint before it destroys us."

"What allies?" Runa asked. "Your crew?"

"No," Eleden said. "We are too few. I propose speaking to the Ayanarans."

"The Ayanarans?" Kell asked, surprised. The Ayanarans were a peaceful people who lived in a forest on the western coast of Erith, as far from Raendashar as you could get. They believed they were descended from Aya, the Mother Tree, and that their sacred duty was to cherish all life. As a result, they'd always sought to remain apart from conflicts. Kell had always wanted to visit their forested country but had never traveled farther west than Elesieayn.

"We share a border with Ayanar," Lyric said slowly. "They're peaceful, aren't they? They live in the forest?"

"Yes," Eleden said. "I hope you won't ask me to turn around. We're heading there now. I believe they're your best chance for maintaining autonomy. Kaia's chasing us, the woman who took you from Rathgar's Hold. She'll hound us until she can take you to the Gale as ordered. I don't think I can protect you if we don't go to Ayanar."

"But we can't," Lyric said, drawing Eleden's eyes. "Mama is dying. We have to go to her."

"She's what?" Eleden asked. He pushed up from his chair, his eyes wide.

"We were in Rathgar's Hold to find a healer, a Dragon Blessed," Runa said. "When Kaia took us, we were trying to gain an audience with our grandfather."

"What happened? Where is she?" Eleden asked.

"We traveled up the Tainted Shore," Runa said.

Shock crossed Eleden's face, and he sat back into his chair. "Up the Shore?"

"We ended up there when Mama came for us," Lyric said. "After we left the Veil—"

"The Veil!" Eleden swore and scrubbed his hand through his hair.

"A Tainted creature attacked us," Lyric said. "It bit Mama, and the wise woman in Ivernn said the only way to save her is for a Dragon Blessed to remove the corrupted magic. We have to go back."

"I can't take you back to Rathgar's Hold," Eleden said, frowning. "We'd sail straight into Kaia's arms. Maybe I can send someone to get your mother and take her to a Lifesinger."

"A what?" Lyric asked.

"A Sireni mage healer," Eleden said. "I can have her brought to us in Ayanar."

"You can do that?" Lyric asked. She looked at Runa, then at Kell behind her.

"Laerdi!" Eleden bellowed, his voice echoing in the room.

The door creaked open, and Laerdi stuck his head in, letting in a blast of rain-scented air.

"Laerdi, tell Elverna to send a gull to Hurlen," Eleden said. "Dandashara has the mage sickness and is at an inn in Ivernn. Tell him to get her on a ship and have them follow us. That is ..." He looked at Runa and Lyric. "If you'll let me take you to Ayanar? It'll be faster to send Hurlen than to go ourselves. If she's there, he'll help her."

Lyric and Runa exchanged glances.

"It sounds like the quickest way to help Mother, without a Dragon Blessed," Runa said.

"Yes," Lyric agreed. She swiveled on the stool, looking up at Kell.

He felt a thrill at the question in her eyes and nodded. She always sought to include him.

"Yes, please hurry," Lyric said, looking back at the Captain.

Laerdi, listening to the conversation, nodded. "At once, Captain," he said. He shut the door with a solid thunk, cutting off the howling wind.

"Can the bird fly in this storm?" Lyric asked. "What if it gets lost?" She glanced at the window, worry creasing her face.

"This is but a light breeze to Elverna's gulls," Eleden said, waving a hand. "They'll enjoy the challenge."

"You'll let us know as soon as you hear something?" Runa demanded.

"Of course," Eleden said.

"Thank you," Lyric said. "We just got her back."

"Of course, Dandashara is family," Eleden said. "Now. You should eat and rest, recover your strength after your ordeal. I'll have Laerdi bring you food. You're welcome to rest here in my cabin. We're on the edge of the storm so we should make good time to Ayanar."

"You're familiar, then, with the creatures?" Runa asked.

Eleden, adjusting something on his desk, looked up.

"You said she has mage sickness," Runa said. "You've heard of this before?"

Lyric, caught in the motion of stretching her back, reached out for Kell. He shifted closer, enfolding her hand in his.

"Yes," Eleden said gravely. "Shortly after Salta's destruction when survivors were deciding whether or not to rebuild. There were mages then who tried figuring out what happened. Whatever they did called the creatures."

"What are they?" Lyric asked. "They looked human, but they had gills and claws."

"I don't know," Eleden said. "I think they were Thendans. Perhaps they were inside the city when it happened."

Kell felt a buzzing in his head as he listened to Eleden. If he just tried to remember and— No. No, he had to keep his mind clear. He couldn't think back to that day.

Swallowing, he looked down at Lyric's hand and focused on her smooth skin. He sensed her looking at him as he moved his thumb back and forth across the back of her hand, trying to ground himself.

"Let's talk of something else," Lyric said, her eyes still on him.

"What?" Runa barked. "Why?"

Laerdi's arrival saved Lyric and Kell from responding. The wind brushed past the big man as he carried in a box and set it on the table. He uncovered four bowls filled to the brim with thin green noodles and shredded white meat in light brown broth. Reaching for a small woven basket, Laerdi lifted its lid, releasing a cloud of steam and revealing four pale dumplings.

"The gull's been sent," Laerdi said, then left the cabin.

"Hurlen will send word once he has your mother," Eleden said. "Now, please eat."

Lyric's belly rumbled, and she laughed, leaning over Eleden's desk with a hungry look.

Eleden chuckled and even Runa's lips twisted into a grudging smile. Faces a little brighter, everyone grabbed a bowl and began to eat. The food was warm and delicious, and Kell found himself wishing for an extra dumpling.

After eating, Captain Eleden repacked the dishes in the box Laerdi left, then stepped over to the bunk, stripping off the blanket and tossing it over his shoulder. He removed clean blankets from the trunk near his bed and handed them to Lyric and Runa. "You can share my cabin," he said, nodding at them. "I'll sleep with my crew."

"We don't want to force you out of your cabin," Lyric protested.

"No need to show us special treatment," Runa said. "There are women on the ship. We can sleep as they do."

Captain Eleden smiled. "I'm sure you can manage hammocks just fine, but you're my guests, and I insist. Kell, here, can join me with the crew." He smacked Kell good-naturedly on the shoulder, nearly knocking him over. "I'm sure my crew would love to test your knowledge of Sireni sea shanties," he said.

Kell grinned. It'd been a while since he'd hunted for new

songs. "I look forward to the challenge." He turned to Lyric. "You'll be fine?" he asked softly.

"Of course we will," Runa snapped.

Lyric rolled her eyes at her sister and stepped into Kell's arms, tucking her head beneath his chin.

Kell couldn't resist looking at Eleden to see if Lyric's uncle disapproved of their intimacy, but the older man merely smiled.

"I'll be close by if you need me," Kell murmured against Lyric's hair.

Lyric tightened her fingers on his back then stepped aside, smiling at him in a way that made him feel like they were alone. When she looked at Eleden, tucking a lock of hair behind her ear, Kell felt apprehension prickle his skin.

*What are you doing, Kell?* he asked himself. Ignoring his inner voice, Kell turned to Eleden. "Ready to go," he said.

As Kell followed Eleden from the cabin into the cold, rain-filled wind atop the deck, he glanced back and saw Runa say something to Lyric. He couldn't hear their words, but he saw Lyric shake her head and turn away from her sister with a blanket in her arms.

The door shut, hiding the sisters. Kell chewed his lip. Had Lyric told Runa yet about his back? No, if she had, Runa would have confronted him. He frowned, stomach twisting. Why did it bother him that Lyric had kept his secret? He didn't want her sister to know, did he? Runa was unpredictable and quick to judgment. But if Lyric hadn't told her twin, was it because she was afraid Runa would reject him, try to pull her away, or was it because she feared him herself?

"This way!" Eleden yelled over his shoulder.

Holding on to his cloak, Kell followed the Captain across the deck to the hatch below. As he climbed down to the crew's quarters, he tried to ignore his worries.

# 22

LYRIC

THE NEXT MORNING the storm had dissipated, and the sky stretched clear and blue in all directions. A strong wind drove them swiftly west. Runa was in a dark, brooding mood, so Lyric had left her staring at Captain Eleden's maps and retreated to the ship's open deck. She'd almost brought up Kell's back, curious what ruminations her sister might have about his origins and concerns.

*Should you risk it?* Gandara had asked, slipping into Lyric's head as easily as the near-constant breeze skipping over the waves. *She already doesn't trust him.*

Afraid of what Runa might say or do, Lyric had stayed silent.

"Be careful of the Captain," Runa had called as Lyric reached for the door. "We don't know if his loyalty is to family or his people first."

"He's our uncle," Lyric said, incredulous.

"And Rakarn is our grandfather," Runa countered back.

Out on the deck, Lyric watched the sailors as they scurried about the ship, tying ropes and adjusting the sails. Not wanting to get in the way, she leaned against the south-facing rail, studying the coastline as they sailed past. From what she understood when she'd asked Eleden over breakfast, they'd sailed north along Raendashar then followed Erith's landmass west on their path to Ayanar.

They'd left Raendashar behind hours ago and were currently sailing along the northern border of Elesieayn, a country that, according to Eleden, was very rocky and difficult to navigate unless you enjoyed scaling the sides of mountains. Elesieayn's primary and only export was very large, very mean, bearded mountain goats, who lived everywhere on the treacherous peaks. The goats had rich milk and thick, warm wool, but their tough, stringy meat kept them out of the meat market.

Lyric was watching several dalphinea swim alongside the Talan, sleek, bottle-nosed mammals with blowholes and shiny, black eyes when Kell slipped an arm around her waist. She knew it was him even before turning her head. He smelled like the fresh air that swooped down off the mountains back home, but there was a spiciness underneath it. "You smell like cinnabark," Lyric said, taking a deep breath as she leaned into him.

"What?" Kell asked, laughing. "Is that good or bad?"

"Definitely good."

"Well, then thank you," Kell said, his voice amused.

Lyric pulled free several strands of hair that'd blown into her mouth when she'd turned towards him, and looked back down into the water. "I've been watching the dalphineas," she said. She pointed at their silvery bodies as they cut through the water alongside the boat. Occasionally they'd flip into the air and land with a splash, sending droplets of water sprinkling across Lyric and the deck.

"One of the sailors told me their name," Lyric said watching them. "They look so untroubled, don't they? Like all that worries them is the feel of the sun on their backs and where the next fish is."

"Thinking of your mother?" Kell asked. His arm tightened around her waist, and Lyric leaned her head against his chest, listening to his heartbeat.

"Yes," Lyric said, softly. "I keep wondering if Eleden's man will reach her in time. I keep wondering if ..." She shook her head. She wouldn't go down that road — not today. "No, I'm sure he'll bring her to us. She'll be ok. Do you think we're doing the right thing, going to Ayanar?"

Kell absently ran his hand along her back, his eyes far away as he stared at the water. "I'm not sure there's a better choice," he said.

"That's what I think too," Lyric said. "We're caught between two sides now. Maybe we could try to go back and see my grandfather, but if Kaia captures us again, we'd be right back where we started, waiting for someone else to decide what to do. Going to Ayanar at least feels like we're doing something ourselves, taking control." She tilted her head back, looking up at Kell's profile. "Will you try to go back? To Rathgar's Hold? I'm sorry you didn't get what you wanted."

"I will when I can," Kell said. "I have to know if there are answers there."

Disappointment and sadness twisted Lyric's stomach, and she slipped her arm around his back, leaning her cheek again against his chest. "Perhaps you can buy passage on another boat once we reach Ayanar," she said. "Find a merchant to take you to Raendashar."

"Oh," Kell said. He cleared his throat, looking away into the wind. "I thought I might ... yes, maybe there is another ship."

"What did you think?" Lyric asked, pulling back.

Kell's eyes, like captured storms, stared down at her. "I thought I could stay and offer support if you wanted it. I don't want to leave you alone, not until Elaina is back with you."

Lyric's heart clenched, and she smiled hesitantly up at him. "You want to stay with me? Even if it means delaying your return to Raendashar? Though I suppose it'd be hard to get into my grandfather's library without us." She frowned. Was he staying with her because he had to?

"Yes," Kell said. "I'm not sure what I could accomplish in Raendashar without you or Elaina, but even if that wasn't the case, I want to be with you. I won't leave you, Lyric, unless you want me to."

Lyric smiled, her worries melting away. She felt light and giddy; a giggle caught in her throat. "And if I never want you to leave?" she asked boldly.

Kell's eyes darkened to a deep, fathomless blue. "Then I won't," he said.

Twisting in his arms, Lyric pushed up on her toes and kissed him. She twined her fingers in his hair, holding him fiercely as heat sizzled down her arms and through the soles of her feet, prickling her skin. She was caught in a storm's eye; teetering on the edge of a precipice.

*He's a dangerous one.*

Lyric broke the kiss falling back on her heels with a confused exhalation of air. Her heart thundered, beating to a loud tempo in her ears as Kell grinned down at her. His eyes were bright, reflecting the brilliant blues and greens of the water beneath their ship.

*What do you mean?* Lyric thought to Gandara. She was afraid of her ancestor's meaning, but also irritated and embarrassed at the interruption. Why was Gandara here *now*, of all moments?

*He's a silver-tongue,* Gandara said. Her voice brimmed with knowing laughter. *All songsmiths are. He'll be a dangerous lover.*

"What's wrong?" Kell asked, still smiling.

Lyric made a face. "Gandara," she said. "She has horrible timing."

Chuckling, Kell leaned his elbows on the railing as Lyric turned back to the ocean. The dalphineas were gone.

"What did the sailors think about your knowledge of Sireni sea shanties?" Lyric asked, casting about for a new topic.

"They said I have a better ear than most landborn," Kell said. "Luckily I have an ear for songs, so what I didn't know I learned as they sang it for me. They said if I sail with them for a couple of months, I can fill in the holes in my musical education."

Lyric laughed.

"What's Runa up to?" Kell asked.

"She's looking at Eleden's maps," Lyric said. "I think she's determined to memorize every major city across the continent. We didn't have good maps back home. We learned the kingdoms of course, but not much beyond that. I can't even tell you the name of Ayanar's capital."

"They don't have one, I believe," Kell said. "At least nothing permanent like Raendashar or Kaliz, your home. They move around."

"What about their Mother Tree?" Lyric asked. "The tree doesn't move, I assume. So they'd probably always stay close to it."

"That's a good point," Kell said, grinning. "Well, you'll see for yourself, soon enough."

Lyric turned around, leaning her back against the rail, and caught sight of Hali, the Sireni Screamer who'd helped them get away from Kaia's ship. She watched the tall woman stride across the deck.

Hali's thick, reddish-brown hair was loose around her shoulders, the curls floating wildly around her head. Despite the strong wind, the Screamer's hair somehow stayed out of her face.

*That's a neat trick,* Lyric thought. Her eyes moved down Hali's bare back, and Lyric flushed. Despite seeing Gandara without a shirt, it'd still shocked her when she'd realized the majority of the Sireni women walked around bare-chested like the men. No one seemed to pay much attention to it besides Lyric, and she wasn't entirely sure Runa had even noticed.

Lyric expected Kell to gawk, at least a little, but he hadn't seemed shocked or overly attentive. Perhaps he'd already known about their clothing and traveled with Sireni before. Jealousy brushed across her skin, and Lyric shoved it aside. She didn't want to think about Kell with other women, or even him admiring another.

"Have you talked to Hali, the Screamer?" Lyric asked, watching Kell's face.

Kell glanced over his shoulder. "A little," he said. "Her hammock's close to mine, but she's usually out here. They call her a Windcaller. She doesn't manipulate sound and create vibrations like the Screamers."

"A Windcaller?" Lyric felt the wind blow across her face. "I should talk to her," she said. She looked back at Kell, who smiled, then nodded at a knot of sailors working on netting on the other side of the deck. A tall man with golden hair and a broad, friendly face was leaning on a barrel beside them and holding a gray horn flute.

"You should," Kell agreed. "Braysa, there, has a gemshorn that he's promised to let me play."

"It's made from an ox's horn, isn't it?" Lyric asked, staring at the golden-haired man. "Seems more like a shepherd's instrument than a sailor."

Kell grinned. "Supposedly he got it from a farmer's daughter during a port visit in Oleporea. He's quite talented."

"I'd like to hear you play sometime," Lyric said, giving Kell a sly look. "You should join them. I'll introduce myself to Hali."

Kell smiled and brushed his fingers across Lyric's cheek.

"I'll find you after," he said, then walked over to the sailors.

Lyric watched him for a moment, admiring the shape of Kell's waist and shoulders. He'd kept the sailor's vest and the airy, white pants he'd found on Kaia's ship. It suited him, softening his movements, as though by wearing the Sireni garments he'd assumed their relaxed presence and manner of walking. Lyric liked that his body had lost some of its tightness. His sadness seemed to have diminished aboard the Talan, as though he'd allowed himself to breathe.

Flushing when she realized one of Eleden's sailors had noticed her staring after Kell, Lyric straightened and headed towards the front of the ship. She gripped the handrail and shifted her skirt out of the way, climbing up the ladder to the bow. The deck was clear except for Hali.

The older woman stood with a steadiness Lyric envied. Her feet were bare, her toes spread on the rough wood deck. Arms relaxed, her hands swirled as though she were strumming unseen strings. The wind tugged at Hali's loose, white pants, whipping them around her legs, and fluffed her hair around her head. When she turned to look at Lyric, her hair shifted out of her face like before.

She was somewhere in age between Lyric and her mother, though Lyric wasn't sure by how much. Tanned to a deep gold by the sun, Hali's skin bore a smattering of freckles across her cheekbones and pale blue fish scales tattooed down the sides of her neck.

"The wind knows you," Hali said, eyeing her.

"Knows me?" Lyric asked, stepping up beside the older woman.

"Power recognizes power."

*But I'm not doing anything, am I?* Lyric thought. She smiled uncertainly. "I'm Lyric. You're Hali the Captain's Windcaller?"

"I am," Hali said. "You're the granddaughter of the Butcher."

Lyric grimaced. "It seems so," she said. "I don't know the man, but I've yet to hear a story of his kindness. I'm sorry for whatever he's done to you and the Sireni."

"We can only be held accountable for our own actions," Hali said.

Relief unknotted Lyric's shoulders. After Hali's words, she hadn't known if she'd condemn her or ask her to leave. So far, out of the Sireni Lyric had met, only Kaia and her sailors had shown outright hostility.

"What does a ship's Windcaller do, if you don't mind me asking?" Lyric asked. "Do you break up storms?"

"No," Hali smiled. "I'm not a god, trying to dominate the sea. I don't try to control the weather, merely dance alongside it. I listen to the wind, the storm, find her cadence, then ease our movement through it. We move like the birds or the fish beneath the waves."

"Is that what you're doing now? Listening to the wind?" Lyric had felt a tingle across her skin when Kaia and Hali battled earlier, a resonance of what she thought was their magic. She didn't feel anything now.

"Just listening," Hali said. "There's a storm to the north. You can smell it."

Lyric inhaled curiously, and the tang of the salty ocean air filled her nose. She didn't detect anything out of the ordinary.

"Sometimes I can smell when other Windcallers are nearby," Hali said.

"When they use magic?"

"Yes. Whenever we use our power, any of us, it leaves a trace in the air. You simply have to know how to hear it, smell it, see it. In the beginning, Windcallers only cast when they intend to, but the longer you sail the sea, the more you move with the winds, whether you're above deck or below. You're always listening, always tasting the air." Hali gestured as though plucking a string from the wind. "You release a constant thread of power without realizing it."

"Does that drain you?" Lyric asked. She remembered how tired her mother looked after casting.

"There's iron in the water," Hali said, grinning. She wet her lips with the tip of her tongue. "In the wind."

Lyric tentatively licked her lips and tasted the salt of the ocean. "Do you sense someone now, nearby?"

"No," Hali said. "Just you and your sister." She cocked her head, eyes curious. "There's something different about you."

"Different?" Could Hali sense Gandara in her mind? Or was Lyric doing something unconsciously?

"I don't know," Hali said. "Maybe because of your father."

"You know him?" Lyric asked, hopefully.

Hali shook her head. "I know he's the Captain's brother and a god-child. His blood flows through you."

"Do you think that makes me different?" Lyric asked.

Hali smiled and shook her head. "I don't know. You know yourself better than I."

Sighing, Lyric looked at the distant horizon. "Will she catch us, do you think? Kaia?"

"The Blue Pearl lost us in the storm," Hali said, "but they know where we're headed. She'll chase us to Ayanar and try again to take you to the Gale. They'll wish to punish us."

"The Gale?" Lyric asked, studying the woman's face. "That doesn't seem to bother you."

"They're wrong."

"Captain Eleden said the head of your clan wants peace."

"Yes," Hali said. "Bethseida is wise."

"She's alone in seeking an end to the war?" Lyric asked. "Is she the only Gale who thinks as you do?"

"I do what my clan and my Captain request of me," Hali said cryptically.

Lyric eyed her. Did that mean Hali only sought peace because of Eleden? Would she move against him if she disagreed and give Lyric and Runa to Kaia? Hali didn't seem about to betray them, but Lyric didn't know her. She considered the Sireni woman. What might it be like to be forced to protect the granddaughter of someone who'd killed your friends, your family, your people? She couldn't begin to imagine.

Something bumped the boat, causing Lyric to wobble unsteadily. She glanced at Hali with alarm, but the older woman grinned broadly. Unlike Lyric's ungraceful stumble, Hali merely swayed as the boat shuddered.

"What was that?" Lyric asked, reaching for the railing.

"A shadow ray," Hali said. "If you look over the edge, you might see it."

Lyric leaned over as far as she dared, staring down into the water below. Something enormous and black glided beneath the surface.

"They're drawn to magic," Hali said. "They like to chase Windcallers."

The women watched the shadow ray slowly swim alongside them, its sleek, black back gleaming as it broke the surface. It rolled, gracefully moving the tip of its fin through the air. It was slower than the boat, and the Talan began to pull away from it, leaving the animal behind. As Lyric watched, the shadow ray sunk out of sight, perhaps losing interest or drawn by food deeper in the water.

## 23

LYRIC

HALI LEANED AGAINST THE RAILING; her face turned towards the sun. There was an ease to her movements, confidence that Lyric envied. Despite Lyric's small size, she often felt gangly and self-conscious, nothing like the boldness this woman exuded merely by breathing.

Aware of the older woman out of the corner of her eye, Lyric splayed her hands on the railing and raised her face to the sun. She closed her eyes, drawing the cool ocean wind into her lungs. She could feel a hum along her skin like the faint vibration of bees from somewhere far away. The Talan shifted, rolling atop the waves as the wind pushed them westward. She could feel ...

Eyes snapping open, Lyric turned her head and found Hali staring towards the back of the ship.

"Something's coming," Lyric said. "*Someone's* coming."

"Yes," Hali said. Her eyes glazed, as if she were staring at something Lyric couldn't see. Hali lifted her chin and scented the air like an animal, nostrils flaring.

"Is it Kaia?" Lyric asked. She felt a burst of energy rush through her veins.

"Laethreshi," Hali said. She looked at Lyric, eyes dark and wicked. "Want to have fun?"

"What are Laethreshi?" Lyric asked.

"Pirates," Hali said. "You can see the mast of their ship. They're coming fast, using magic."

Lyric squinted but couldn't see anything. "You see a ship?" she asked doubtfully.

"Yes. Sireni have very sharp eyes. Come!" Hali took off towards the ladder, dashing across the deck and up another flight of stairs to the stern.

Lyric scrambled after her, slipping in her haste to follow. Kell gave her a startled look as she rushed past him and the other sailors, but she ignored him, intent on Hali.

Scrambling up the stairs at the back of the ship, Lyric saw Hali rake her fingernails across the helmsman's collarbone in a familiar way as she passed. "Laethreshi," she told the man.

He nodded, his pierced lip stretching in a savage smile.

Lyric stopped at the back railing and squinted across the water. There! She could see the tiny outline of a ship, the shape of its sail black against the sky. "What are you going to do?" Lyric asked.

Hali's smile was all teeth. "Slow them down." She raised her hands and began to chant.

Lyric tried to follow along, recognizing some of the mage runes that Hali spoke. The tone and intonation sounded different than the words Gandara had taught her, but the longer she listened, the more she understood.

*It's her clan*, Gandara whispered in her ear. *She speaks with the lilt of the Sae'kan.*

*Are you not of Captain Eleden's clan?* Lyric asked.

Lyric could feel pressure build around her, and she worked her jaw to unstop her ears, watching Hali out of the corner of her eye.

*I am Sae'tal, The Heart*, Gandara said.

The wind gathered and began to spin, forming a funnel in the air in front of them.

Lyric's hair tore free from her braids. "A cyclone!" she gasped. The swelling power was making her giddy as if every mote inside her body and soul thrummed with energy. Goosebumps rushed down her arms and across her chest.

"Now it just needs a little push," Hali said. She wiggled her fingers, casting again, and the column of air shot away from the Talan. "I wish I could hear their yells," she said, tightly gripping the railing. Hali grinned fiercely, eyes blazing as she stared at the Laethreshi ship chasing them.

"Will it rip up their ship?" Lyric asked. She worried about the people pursuing them. Would they drown if Hali's cyclone ripped their ship apart? Were they close enough to shore to swim to safety?

"Maybe," Hali said, "but they have their own Windcaller. It'll probably slow not cripple them unless their mage is weak. Do you wish to try?"

Lyric thought again of the faceless sailors. Being pirates didn't inherently make them bad people, did it? What if she killed someone? Would she even know if she did?

"Maybe I can slow them another way," Lyric said slowly.

Hali raised an eyebrow. "Don't feel bad for them, Lyric. The Laethreshi steal and burn ships."

"Do they kill?" Lyric asked.

"Sometimes."

Lyric stared at the pirates' ship. It was drawing closer. She couldn't tell what damage Hali's cyclone had wrought, but it'd blown apart, the sky clearing over the Laethreshi ship. Could Lyric knock them off course? Slow them down?

*Gandara? What's the rune for water?* Lyric asked. *What do I say if I want to create a wave and shove them back?* Lyric tried to picture what she wanted to do in her mind.

Her ancestor hummed distractedly then spoke several

runes. *You don't wish to summon wind? To be a Windcaller?* Gandara asked.

Lyric started chanting. She imagined the water gathering, thickening. She thought back to how Kaia had shoved their boat away from the docks at Rathgar's Hold. She thought about the water flowing, moving, pushing.

Power flooded through her, prickling the skin on her arms; Lyric felt caught in a flood, pushed towards the edge of something unseen. She sagged against the railing, the runes rushing out of her. The Talan surged forward, picking up speed, and Lyric felt the ocean beneath them reverse its direction. The water rolled up, a massive wave rising back towards the Laethreshi ship.

"How did you do that?" Hali asked, awe in her voice.

Lyric watched the huge wave swell as it moved, the following ship disappearing behind it.

"You've pushed them back," Hali said. "Impressive. Here, eat this." She pushed something into Lyric's hand.

Lyric looked down and saw a bundle of dried seaweed.

"What's going on?" Runa demanded.

Lyric looked behind them and found her sister staring at her with a quizzical expression. Elation, exhaustion, and hunger filled her, and she smiled sheepishly, then bit off a piece of the salty, dried plant instead of answering.

"I could feel whatever you're doing up here in the Captain's cabin," Runa said. She eyed Hali.

"I'm Hali," Hali said, smiling at her.

"Runa," Runa said. "What are you doing?"

"We're being chased," Lyric said, gesturing at the ship in the distance. It was far away and rapidly dwindling in size. She doubted the Laethreshi would catch up now after having lost all their speed.

"We *were* being chased," Hali said, clapping Lyric on the shoulder.

"Sireni?" Runa asked.

"No, pirates," Lyric said.

Narrowing her eyes, Runa stared at the small ship with a raptor's focus. Her lips moved silently, and her fingers twitched at her side.

Lyric felt a rush of heat across her skin, and she shivered.

Hali, narrowing her eyes, looked back at the Laethreshi ship, and Lyric followed her gaze. She saw a flare of red-orange flames; black smoke puffed up into the sky.

"Runa!" Lyric gasped. "You may have killed them!"

"They're predators," Runa said unapologetically.

"That doesn't mean you should set them on fire!"

"We're close enough to land; they can swim."

"She has a point," Hali said, nodding at Runa. "I wouldn't worry about it."

"Not worry! I was trying to avoid killing them!"

"And you didn't," Runa said. "Come, Ly. Laerdi brought lunch."

Lyric stared at her sister, eyes wide. How could Runa be so unconcerned about killing? They'd never killed anyone before. They were supposed to be healers, not executioners. They were supposed to save lives. Lyric watched Runa walk back down the stairs and disappear into the cabin below.

"I doubt she killed anyone if that's what you're worried about," Hali said. "She's not wrong, though."

"If we resort to killing, are we any better than they are?"

"Sometimes you have to end a life to save one," Hali said. "You may want to remember that. This war you want to stop, it's unlikely you'll see peace without more death first. Even the Ayanarans, peaceful though they are, kill to save lives."

Lyric blew out a breath of air and rubbed her fingertips across her temples. "I know it's naive to think I can save everyone, and I know I'll sometimes be forced to protect myself and the people I love and if it comes down to me or someone else, I can't say I'd choose them over me."

Lyric thought about what she'd do if someone threatened Runa, or Kell, or their mother. She'd kill to protect them, but only if she had to.

"Eat with your sister," Hali said. "The Laethreshi won't catch us now. Be content we weren't forced to kill today, to defend our ship. If they'd boarded us, it would have been bloody."

"Thank you, Hali," Lyric said. She smiled distractedly, then headed down the stairs and opened the door to the Captain's cabin.

Runa was sitting in front of Eleden's desk, a bowl of rice and dark red beans in her hands. She eyed Lyric as she entered.

"I hope you left your self-righteousness outside," Runa said blandly, scooping beans into her mouth.

Lyric glowered at her sister and walked to the second stool. She grabbed a bowl of hot food and sat with a thump. "Don't forget who we are, Ru," she said testily.

"And don't forget you're not Ethethera," Runa said.

"Ru! Not wanting to murder a bunch of sailors, who hadn't even boarded our ship, does not make me a sycophant!"

"I didn't murder anyone," Runa said. "I set fire to their ship. If you're trying to put things in perspective, then getting captured by pirates doesn't help Mother or stop the war."

"They weren't going to capture us," Lyric said. "I slowed them down."

"And now I've ensured they won't attempt to follow." Runa took another bite of rice and beans, looking as satisfied as a cream-drunk cat. "We already have one hound on our tail, or have you forgotten Kaia?"

"Just show a little more compassion for human life," Lyric said.

"I never hurt anyone who doesn't deserve it," Runa said.

Growling, Lyric shoved food into her mouth and chewed angrily. There was no point debating force or justification with her sister any longer.

Someone briskly rapped on the door and Lyric called garbled permission to enter.

The door opened, and Captain Eleden walked inside, followed by Kell. Both men were laughing.

Kell, eyes lighting on Lyric, seemed to sense the mood inside the room and he looked at Runa with a curious lift of an eyebrow.

Lyric rolled her eyes, shaking her head, and Kell reached for a bowl of food without comment.

"We'll reach Ayanar by tomorrow," Eleden said, settling himself behind the large table. "I believe you saw the Laethreshi ship?" he asked.

"Yes," Lyric said. She avoided looking at her sister.

"Well, thanks to you two we don't have to worry about them anymore," Eleden said. "They're a nasty crew with rather barbaric views about women."

Runa made a smug noise in her bowl, which Lyric promptly ignored.

"Any sign of Kaia?" Lyric asked. "Hali and I didn't see another ship."

"Not yet," Eleden said, "but I have suspicions she's changed ships."

"Changed ships?" Lyric asked, frowning.

"Are you familiar with the Nilin?" Eleden asked, giving Kell a sidelong look.

"Not particularly," Lyric said. "They're inventors, aren't they?"

"The airships!" Kell breathed, his eyes alight.

"The what?" Runa lowered her bowl, eyes filled with curiosity.

"The Nilin have been experimenting with ships that can

fly," Eleden said. "They use large air bladders to hold them aloft. Kaia got her hands on one of their ships. It's fast, faster than a water-bound ship if the wind is right. And if the captain is a Windcaller ..."

"Ships that can fly," Lyric said wonderingly. "I thought the sky belonged to birds and dragons, back when they lived in the world."

"And now to man it seems," Eleden said.

"Why don't you have one?" Runa asked.

Eleden laughed. "Too expensive."

"Then how did Kaia end up with one?"

"Ru!" Lyric said.

"It's a logical question," Runa said, rolling her eyes. "What, you think I'm going to offend Kaia, who isn't even here?"

"The Gale decided the Sireni should have one," Eleden said. "Kaia can be quite persuasive when she wishes to be."

"I got the impression she's more a blunt hammer than a deft blade," Runa said.

Eleden chuckled and raised his bowl to his mouth. "You're not wrong."

"Will she overtake us in her airship?" Lyric asked.

"I doubt it," Eleden said, "but she'll likely arrive not long after we do. She may try to interrupt our meeting with the Ayanarans."

Lyric nodded. "We'll speak to them. If they're as strong as you say, then they should be able to stop Kaia and maybe they'll have an idea about how to approach peace between our kingdoms."

Eleden, Kell, Lyric, and Runa spoke of idle things for the rest of their meal. Lyric wanted to ask Eleden if he'd heard back from the man he'd sent after their mother, but she knew not enough time had passed. Unsettled and worried, she lapsed into silence, listening with half an ear as Kell recounted a story he'd heard from the sailors.

Usually, Runa would have sensed Lyric's mood and offered a comforting word or touch on the shoulder, but her sister seemed caught in her own reflections. From time to time, Runa twitched as if someone whispered in her ear. Lyric wondered, like she always did, what Elenora was telling her. Gandara had hated being in Rathgar's Hold. It was likely that Elenora enjoyed the Sireni ship even less.

"I'm going for a walk," Runa declared abruptly, thumping her empty bowl onto the table.

Eleden and Kell glanced at her, startled.

"Would you like company?" Lyric asked, studying her sister's face.

"No," Runa said. She walked over to her cloak and grabbed it from a hook on the wall. As she opened the door, Lyric saw her other hand clench at her side, the knuckles whitening. Then the door slammed shut, and Runa was gone.

"You've been through a lot," Eleden said, perhaps in response to Runa's abrupt departure.

"Yes," Lyric said, turning back around. "She's not usually ..." She trailed off. She didn't have to give excuses for her sister.

"Wine?" Eleden asked. He'd pulled a bottle from somewhere and was waggling it over three cups atop his desk.

Kell sat down on the stool Runa vacated and reached for a glass. "Yes, thank you," he said.

"Yes," Lyric said distractedly. She studied Eleden's sun-darkened face and the scar that crossed his cheek and neck. "What was he like, my father?" Lyric asked.

Eleden smiled, his face softening with memory. "Bold and wild, shifting between calm and motion with the delicacy of a squall."

"A bit of a troublemaker?" Lyric asked, smiling. She tried to imagine her mother being charmed by a passionate man, but she couldn't. Elaina had always favored control and keeping a clear head. Lyric knew there was fire in her mother, like Runa, but unlike her sister, it didn't regularly flare out in fits of intensity.

In contrast, Lyric had always cried easily, quick to tears instead of temper. She'd never seen her mother cry when she was a child, but Lyric's emotions had ever lived beneath the surface of her skin. Was she like her father in that way?

"Oh yes," Eleden said, laughing. "Egan once filled our mother's boat with so many fish that it was impossible to cross the deck without slipping. They were piled thigh-high!" He gestured with his hand. "I still don't know how he did it. Egan could call to sea creatures sometimes, and they'd listen."

"He spoke to fish?" Kell asked, raising an eyebrow. "That'd make fishing easier."

Eleden chuckled and nodded. "If you seek to cheat while fishing with your brother, sure."

"What happened to them?" Lyric asked. "The fish?" An image filled her mind of fish flopping across the deck of a fishing boat, gasping for breath as the sun dried out their skin.

"They didn't die, if that's what you're thinking," Eleden said. "Egan summoned a wave right up over the ship's railing and swept them back into the sea, all with a sweep of his arm. He nearly sent old Alesha into the water with them. Mother was furious and made him swab the deck for a whole week!"

"Why didn't he become a captain, like you?" Lyric asked.

"He didn't want to be in charge of anyone," Eleden said. He lifted his glass and took a long drink, some of the light fading from his eyes. "Not everyone enjoys command."

Lyric sipped her wine and shifted the glass in her hands. "Do you know how my father ended up in Kaliz? It's far from the sea."

"I don't know," Eleden said. "Egan was traveling then. I'm not sure why he was there."

"He told you about meeting our mother?"

"Yes. He said he'd met the most beautiful woman he'd ever

seen." Eleden smiled into his wine. "I admit I was jealous. If I'd known the most beautiful people were inland, I'd have traveled there myself."

Lyric choked on her wine, blushing. "I hope I get to meet him," she said.

"I'm confident he'll turn up again," Eleden said. "I imagine he's heard of your presence with the Sireni; how could he not? He'll come. I'm sure of it."

Kell reached for her hand, and Lyric twined her fingers through his, letting their joined hands rest atop her knee. What would it be like to finally meet her father?

# 24

RUNA

RUNA STALKED along the ship's railing, avoiding the eyes of anyone who looked at her. Elenora's displeasure was like a sore in her gut, souring her stomach and filling her with a restlessness she couldn't shake.

*They're weak and cowardly,* Elenora railed inside her head. *They've corrupted your mother, turned her against your people. Slit their throats before they poison and betray you!*

"I'm not killing anyone," Runa hissed beneath her breath. She paused by the rigging that ran up along the mainsail's edge to the crow's nest above and wrapped her fist around one of the thick ropes. The coarse fibers grated against her palm, and Runa twisted her hand, fixating on the sensation. It helped her focus. She breathed in the salty air and held it in her lungs, feeling the pressure deep inside her chest. As she let her breath go, Runa tried to relax the tight muscles in her neck and back.

It was becoming harder to ignore Elenora's contempt. Runa's own emotions were raw and confused, tangling with Elenora's and riding the ancestor's focused anger until Runa wanted to set everything on fire and lash out at anything nearby.

*It's not me*, Runa thought, twisting her hand around the rope. *This isn't me.* She stared into the wind, feeling it brush across her skin.

"Why are you here?" Runa asked, her voice soft. No one was nearby to overhear, but she still kept her face turned away, not wanting the crew to think she was talking to herself.

A white seabird with a hooked beak and spots of orange on the tips of its wings, dove down into the water nearby, rising with a silvery fish in its mouth.

*Don't trust them*, Elenora said. *They'll become afraid of you when they realize your potential, your power. They'll try to drown you, feed you to the coward Serith's beasts.*

"The Captain is family," Runa said. "My uncle."

*He's not of the blood.*

"Go away," Runa hissed, glaring at the bird as it ripped the fish apart in midair. "I don't want you."

*Of course, you do, little Burner. Who else will tell you about magic? Who else will bring you power? I know what you want, stupid girl.*

"Why seek me out in the first place?" Runa asked. "You don't only wish to train me, which you haven't been doing much of by the way. You have another reason."

Elenora shifted in her head. *Raendashar has grown weak*, she said, her voice dripping with disdain. *Rakarn has yet to crush the Sireni. The war's end has been in his hands for years, and he's been unable to bring them to heel. The Sireni mock him, spit in his eye, burn our fleet. Never in our entire history have we lost all of our ships.* Elenora cursed Elaina again, her fury snapping across Runa's mind as she railed against her mother.

Runa laughed a harsh, bitter sound. "You think I'll do what my grandfather hasn't?"

*Your fire will rival the dragons! You are strong, though untrained. I could feel you when you first stepped inside the Veil, feel your power, your anger. You wanted vengeance! You wanted strength!*

"I don't want to kill the Sireni," Runa said. She tightened her hand on the rope, focusing on the pain. "I want to end the war. I want those in power to stop crushing the weak beneath their feet. Do you think it's the people who keep the war going? No, it's the nobles and the administrators who turn the wheel. They don't care who's crushed beneath it or how much blood is spilled. They want power and money. They're greedy!" Runa paused, realizing she'd grown louder.

She glanced over her shoulder and caught the passing gaze of a young man. The boy swallowed at her aggressive expression; his eyes nervously dancing away.

*I can help you,* Elenora said. She sounded eager, excited by Runa's loss of control. *I can shape you. I can make you a weapon.*

"I won't fight your war," Runa hissed. "Your revenge is not mine."

Elenora shifted in her mind, perhaps deciding if she wanted to push further. Instead, the ancestor drifted back, her presence weakening. *We'll speak again,* she said, then disappeared.

Runa sagged against the railing, feeling drained. She still felt angry, but it was old, familiar anger, the anger she couldn't seem to let go of since her mother had left her and Lyric. Even now, after Elaina had come back, there was something new for Runa to rail against — her mother's injury, her ancestor's manipulation, Lyric's distractions.

Surprised, Runa realized she was mad at Lyric, not enraged but disappointed. Lyric was drifting away from her, drifting to Kell. What would happen after they allied with the Ayanarans and sought an end to the war? Runa and Lyric wouldn't return to Elae's Hollow. They'd be important, caught in the heart of negotiations. Would they seek a place in Raendashar or sanctuary with the Sireni?

Lyric seemed to be enjoying their time on the Talan, but Runa couldn't imagine living at sea at the mercy for the water and weather. She didn't like the constant sway and the lack of solidness beneath her feet. She didn't like how far away the mountains were and how deep and wide the water stretched around them. What would happen if their ship drifted so far from land that she could no longer see it?

And Kell; Runa doubted he'd go back to whatever he'd been doing before Elaina scooped him up and sent him after them. Kell would follow Lyric, or she would follow him. Sometime in the future, they'd leave Runa behind. It was inevitable. Women married and created new families of their own. What place would be left for Runa then? She wouldn't trail after them like a shade. What did she want for herself?

Jealousy and loneliness wrapped their arms around her, ripping open the old wound Elaina had left in her wake all those years before. It could get worse. Runa hadn't thought that it could.

"Ru?"

Runa jumped, hand raising as she spun around. She flushed, embarrassment heating her skin, then anger chased it away. "What!" she snapped, glaring into her sister's face.

"I just wanted to see if you are well," Lyric said, eyes flaring. Her cheeks flushed an angry pink.

"I'm fine," Runa said.

"Fine," Lyric said. "I'll be with Hali if you need me." She stormed away, the hurt plain on her face.

"Ly, I'm—" Runa said. Her voice trailed off as Lyric climbed into the ship's bow.

Feeling miserable, angry, and frustrated, and wanting to scream, Runa turned back to the deep water. She tangled her fingers in the ends of her braid and pulled hard, feeling pain as her hair tugged on her scalp. *Let us get there soon*, Runa thought desperately, *before I set fire to this whole cursed boat.*

315

THE SKY WAS clear when Captain Eleden anchored the Talan in a large cove along the Ayanaran coastline. Their trip, which should have been a week, had taken mere days, Hali's skill with the storm propelling them faster than a mageless vessel. There was no hint of a city or village or even a dock for their ship. All Runa could see was an unbroken line of trees curving along the beach like a living wall.

The forest was massive, the trees lush and green and they rolled away from the beach as far as Runa could see. Mountains stood in the distance, jutting up from the sea of green like tiny spikes.

Captain Eleden's crew lowered a skiff lashed to the Talan's side, and Runa, Lyric, and Kell climbed down into it via a rope ladder. Eleden and three other crew members joined them — Laerdi, who Runa was familiar with, a woman named Sashala with tightly-coiled black hair and dark skin, and a bald man named Teaeth with pink coloring, bony shoulders and the widest grin she'd ever seen. Teaeth seemed unable to force his face into anything other than a broad smile, and Runa could see every single gold-capped tooth inside his mouth.

The Windcaller, Hali, was staying behind on the Talan. Eleden had given her command of the ship in his absence. Hali gestured something at Lyric, who smiled and raised a hand in return, then Runa felt a tingle of power dance across her skin. The boat surged away from the ship, propelled by an unseen hand, letting them flow right up onto the beach without once needing to lift an oar.

Before the boat had ceased moving, Sashala leaped out onto the sand, landing cat-like on her feet. She hauled the boat farther out of the water, away from the hungry tide that sought to drag them back out to sea.

Captain Eleden vaulted out of the boat with impressive vigor, followed by Teaeth, Laerdi, and Kell. Unlike Eleden's dramatic exit, Kell's landing on the pale sand was markedly less agile. Despite his awkwardness, Lyric beamed when he reached back to help her, and she lingered in his arms as he took an unnecessary amount of time to set her down.

Rolling her eyes, Runa avoided Teaeth and Laerdi's outstretched hands and climbed over the side without assistance. Her feet splashed into the shallow water, splattering wet sand across her skirt. Ignoring her dirtied hem, Runa stomped purposefully up the beach.

She realized they weren't alone as she approached the trees. Men and women stood within the shadow of the forest, as silent and unmoving as the trees themselves. They were tall, like Kalizans, though thinner and darker than the folk back home with warmer undertones to their skin. Some of the figures wore dark green trousers and shirts with longbows on their shoulders, and others wore pale robes of undyed cloth. One of the robed people, a tall woman with long, dark brown hair, raised her hand in acknowledgment as Captain Eleden called out a greeting.

"This way," Eleden said quietly, heading towards the woman in the trees.

Teaeth stayed behind with the boat, presumably guarding their exit, and Sashala and Laerdi fell into step behind Runa, Lyric, and Kell as they trailed after Eleden.

The Captain seemed relaxed when they stepped up in front of the tall woman and gave her a pleasant smile, which she returned with apparent familiarity.

Up close, Runa could see the woman was in her middle years and quite beautiful. Faint lines were etched around her eyes, but there was a youthfulness to her tawny face that made her seem younger. Runa, years her junior, felt envious of the woman's radiating energy. Though the woman's robe was unadorned, she wore a striking, woven belt knotted around her waist, spun from purple, green, and gold threads.

"Laenadara," Captain Eleden said. "It's good to see you again."

"Eleden," the woman said, voice husky. "My shade and water are yours." Her bright green eyes shifted to regard Sashala, Laerdi, and Kell, and she nodded at them before moving on to Lyric and Runa. "Welcome, Daughters of Fire and Sea," she said. "My shade and water are yours. I am Laenadara, High Priestess of the People of Greenhome. Your journey has been long. I will share refreshments with you if you wish it."

"With all of us, I hope?" Runa asked, eyeing Laenadara. There was something about the woman that immediately put her on edge, but she couldn't figure out what it was.

"Of course," Laenadara said, smiling. "I have refreshments for all of you."

Lyric elbowed Runa. "Thank you for the welcome," she said. "I'm Lyric Graymorn, and this is my sister Runa. Have you been expecting us?" She glanced at Eleden. "Did our uncle send word we were coming?"

It was a good question, Runa thought. Eleden had told them when he'd sent a gull to help Elaina, but he'd made no mention of contacting Laenadara ahead of their arrival.

"There wasn't time," Eleden said. "I apologize for the surprise. I knew we'd arrive ahead of any message."

Runa frowned and looked back at the High Priestess, sharpening her study of the woman's enigmatic face. "How did you know?" she asked, suspiciously.

"The Mother told me," Laenadara said.

"Aya, the Mother Tree?" Lyric asked.

Laenadara inclined her head, smiling serenely.

Runa raised an eyebrow. "It speaks to you?" she asked.

Lyric elbowed her more sharply, but Runa ignored her.

"Not aloud, like our conversation now," Laenadara said, "but She honors a few of us with a communion of minds."

"She puts images in your mind?" Lyric asked.

Runa thought of Elenora whispering in the back of her head. Maybe it was similar.

Laenadara inclined her head.

"I didn't know the Tree was sentient," Runa said. She shifted to the side to avoid another jab from Lyric's elbow.

"Of course She is," Laenadara said, smiling indulgently. She didn't seem upset by their questions. "Her roots stretch down into Erith's Heart, and her branches reach up into the realm of Sky and beyond. She bridges all things. She's the heart of everything."

"How would She know we were coming here?" Runa asked skeptically. "We only just decided that ourselves several days ago."

"We don't understand all Her mysteries," Laenadara said, "only that She is everywhere."

"Ah," Runa said. She wasn't sure she believed a tree could be omnipresent, but she knew there was much about magic and the old gods she didn't know. Perhaps Eleden's gullmaster, Elverna, had sent ahead a bird without him knowing. Or the priestess had somehow heard about their capture in Rathgar's Hold and assumed Eleden would rescue them and bring them to Ayanar.

She glanced sideways at Eleden. It was also possible the Captain had shared his intention with Laenadara, and for some reason wanted to keep this hidden from Runa and Lyric. Why, though? So they'd believe in the magic and power of the Ayanarans' tree? It didn't make sense.

"Let me take you somewhere to rest," Laenadara said. "Once I've shared our hospitality, I'm more than happy to answer any questions you have."

"Yes," Lyric said nodding. "Maybe we should get off the beach."

"We're being followed," Eleden said. "I rescued Lyric and Runa from another captain's boat, and she'll likely come here with the intent to take them back."

Laenadara nodded. "We'll be ready," she said, gesturing at several of the green-clad figures. "If you'll follow me?"

Led by the High Priestess, they entered the loamy forest. There was no defined path beneath Runa's feet, and she studied the ground curiously as they walked. It was covered by a leafy, green plant that crawled all over the forest floor, giving the appearance that someone had unfurled a lush blanket. Scattered across the thick, grass-like plant were tiny, blue flowers, catching Runa's eye like scattered jewels that'd fallen from someone's pouch.

It was verdant and wet beneath the forest canopy, and a diversity of plants bloomed and flourished across the ground, some growing off the sides of tree trunks. Out of habit, Runa studied the plants they passed; seeing some she recognized, but many she did not. Wetter than the Umberwood back home, there was more color and vitality here.

Something dripped onto her forehead and Runa jerked her head up, staring into the large leaves overhead. *It's too humid here*, she thought, wiping sweat from her face. It felt like standing over a hot pot of water on the stove.

Birds trilled from every direction, and the flash of a small, white-tailed deer caught her eye. Runa looked at Captain Eleden and his crew to see how they felt about the forest. They looked comfortable, despite being off their ship, moving easily through the damp undergrowth. Their lightweight clothing was breathable and airy, suitable for Ayanar's environment. Perhaps that's why they didn't seem to mind it as Runa did; they weren't sweating inside their clothes.

Kell and Lyric walked hand in hand, seemingly oblivious to the sweat dampening their faces and hair. Her sister's skirts were still tied up like she was Sireni, and Kell hadn't removed his loose, white trousers or the vest, showing off his bare chest.

Watching them, Runa narrowed her eyes as Kell's vest

shifted across his shoulders. What were those lumps beneath the blue fabric? Had he hidden a weapon on his upper back? *Maybe you're smarter than you look*, she thought.

"We're here," Laenadara announced. She'd stopped atop a small hill, moving aside so Runa and the others could see past her into the canopied hollow below.

Nearly indistinguishable from the lush foliage were a handful of large, basket-like structures woven from branches still attached to the trees. With no cleared paths between them, the buildings seemed more like a collection of nests than anything human-made. Men and women moved around the village on various tasks, their movements unhurried, almost reverent. A man with a basket full of dark purple berries cradled in his arms glanced up and caught Runa's eye, smiling like she were an old friend.

"This way," Laendara said. The priestess led them down to one of the structures and held aside a curtain of vines to reveal a doorway.

Passing her, Runa stepped beneath a flowering archway into a large, circular room. She turned in the center, curiously examining the room. Interwoven branches formed the walls, insulating them from the rest of the forest, and arched over-head in a dome. Softly illuminating the enclosed space were small, glowing lights that shifted lazily along the curve of the ceiling. Runa narrowed her eyes. Were they fireflies?

Pillows and blankets were arranged around the room, providing comfortable places to sit. Several low tables, crafted from polished pieces of driftwood, held fruit-filled baskets and small figurines woven from pale greenish-blue grass.

Turning again, Runa saw a man waiting beside one of the seating areas. She stared at him, distracted by his beauty. He was short, no taller than her or Lyric.

Lyric grabbed Runa's arm. "He has ... horns?" she murmured.

Runa raised a surprised eyebrow. She'd been so distracted by the man's features that she hadn't noticed the small, black horns curving out from his golden curls.

"Faun-born," Kell whispered behind her.

The man, perhaps overhearing, dipped his head with a bemused smile. Small tendrils of steam curled up from the earthen pot in his hands, as he poured bright green liquid into seven small cups.

"Sit, rest," Laenadara said, gesturing at the circle of pillows beside the horned man. The High Priestess seated herself first, lounging against several pale yellow cushions.

Eleden sat next, followed by Laerdi. Sashala remained standing with her arms crossed. Lyric and Kell sat down together, and Runa sat beside her sister, ending up right next to the horned man.

Setting down the pot, the man picked up a clay cup and leaned over her, holding it out in his hands.

Runa blinked and accepted the cup.

The man's fingers lingered on hers unnecessarily, but she was too distracted by his long, purple-tipped nails to object. "I'm Theo," the horned-man said as he drew his hand away. His voice was lower than she'd expected.

"Good day," she said, her voice flat.

Grinning as if they'd shared an intimate moment, the horned man moved on to Lyric and Kell, then the others. As Runa continued watching him, she saw him give everyone lingering glances and brush their hands with the same familiarity that he'd shown to her. She wasn't sure whether to be annoyed or amused.

Kell, predictably, seemed jealous when Lyric accepted her tea, but his irritation quickly shifted to confusion when he received the same close attention.

Eleden gave Theo a surprisingly friendly grin, the two men exchanging an inaudible greeting.

Returning her attention to her cup, Runa lifted it to her mouth and inhaled the fragrant steam. It was tea and smelled like the first day of spring, fresh and grassy.

Theo handed Laenadara the last cup then bowed to the room. He caught Runa's eye and winked at her, much to her annoyance, then walked out the door, passing through the curtain of vines and between two, green-clad Ayanarans who'd slipped inside unnoticed.

Eyeing the Ayanarans over her cup, Runa wondered if they were there to prevent them from leaving or if they were guards for the High Priestess. There was nothing overtly threatening about any of the Ayanarans so far, but the uneasy feeling Runa felt when first meeting Laenadara was still there, prickling her skin and drawing her eyes towards the exit.

"Thank you for your welcome, Laenadara," Lyric said. She tilted her head to the side, her brown braids slipping off her shoulders. "You know who we are, so I assume you know our mother?"

The High Priestess sipped from her cup. "Not directly," she said, "but I know who she is. King Rakarn has worked hard to keep it quiet, but we learned that the Crowned Princess of Raendashar has been absent from the Scorched Court for over twenty years. The Mother, Aya, told us when Lady Elaina left, thinking we could be of use to each other."

"So you know our mother is against Raendashar's war with the Sireni?" Lyric asked.

Laenadara inclined her head.

"You called us Daughters of Fire and Sea," Runa interrupted. "Why is that?"

"You are children of both bloodlines," Laenadara said. "You are of the Three and Serith, the sea serpent."

"Did you tell her?" Runa asked, staring at Captain Eleden.

Eleden seemed confused, brows knotted over his eyes. "I did not," he said.

"Your uncle didn't betray your secret," Laenadara said. "The Mother told me of your heritage."

Runa raised an eyebrow. How did the Mother Tree know about her family? The Tree, Aya, was said to bridge worlds. Theoretically, you could travel through it to the Veil and Underworld, and other worlds beyond, but she'd never heard a story about it speaking or communicating with anyone. How conscious was Aya? The Tree wasn't divine like the Trinity or demigods, nor a creature like the dragons. It was something else.

The old stories did say that Ethethera gave part of herself to facilitate Aya's creation. Maybe the Ayanarans were talking to an echo of the goddess Herself through the Tree?

Runa rubbed her temple and tried to bring her mind back to the conversation. She was frustrated by how little they knew. How could she and her sister make intelligent decisions about the war, about their lives, when they barely understood their place in the world?

"We did speak of allying against Raendashar and the Gale," Eleden said, nodding at Laenadara. "I discussed it with your mother before she returned for you, but she wanted to keep you hidden. She refused to involve you."

Lyric seemed distracted, and then she shifted her attention back to Laenadara with a curious expression. "You're willing to stand against both Raendashar and the Sireni," Lyric said. "Why? Your land is far from the war. What happens between them doesn't touch you here. Why risk allying with us and getting involved? King Rakarn will likely see your support as a sign you're siding with his enemies. He could turn his eyes on you. Even without his fleet, he has troops, mages; he could probably find a way to come here."

Laenadara rested her cup in her lap, fingers curled around it. "Erith is dying," she said.

Runa frowned. Dying? She'd seen no sign of disease in the land back home.

Eleden cocked his head to the side, his face clouded.

"Dying?" Lyric asked. "What do you mean?" She gripped Kell's arm.

Watching her sister reach for Kell and not her, Runa felt a pang of sadness.

"The Taint," Eleden said, his voice thoughtful. "It's drifted farther into the Sea of Screams away from the Tainted Shore. The bordering reefs no longer contain it. We've done what we can to shift it back, run it aground with the tide, but we've seen its effect on the fish and animals despite our efforts."

At the mention of the Shore, Kell grew still beside Lyric. There was a grinding sound beneath his hands as his palms crushed the cup braced between them.

Laenadara glanced at him curiously, a calculating look entering her eyes. "Yes," she said, after a moment. "The Taint is growing and spreading beneath the earth like rot along the root. In months or weeks, it will begin to surge to the surface, spreading pockets of death. We've ignored it at our peril, believing it contained to Thenda."

"How do you know?" Runa asked.

Laenadara raised an eyebrow. "Are you asking what evidence I have?"

Runa nodded curtly, exchanging a look with Lyric who'd begun to frown.

"The Mother shared visions with me," Laenadara said, a faraway look in her eyes. "I have seen what lies beneath the dirt, the death that pools around Her roots."

Runa studied her. Whatever the High Priestess had seen scared her.

"What is the Taint?" Lyric asked.

Laenadara blinked, her eyes clearing. She no longer looked visibly shaken, resuming her composure. "I cannot say for sure," Laenadara said. "What we know is that it was released by corrupted magic from a failed ritual that required massive amounts of power."

Laerdi made a pained sound and rubbed a hand across his jaw.

Sashala, standing behind him, touched his shoulder.

Gravely, Captain Eleden set aside his cup and rested a closed fist on his knee. "We weren't sure what it was when it happened," he said. "Our Screamers and Windcallers felt a surge of energy charging the air. Before we could move our ships in to observe, the power exploded outward. It knocked every one of our mages unconscious within a league of the Shore. Their noses bled, and they suffered vertigo for days afterward.

"All sea life within range was killed, pulverized. It was weeks before we began to see the Taint's effect showing itself as a green tide upon the Sea. By then, we realized Thenda was gone."

"Why didn't you go to them after you felt the surge of power?" Lyric asked, eyes wide.

"After what happened to our mages, the Gale decided we should stay away. They believed someone inside Thenda tried to use dark magic, something old and forbidden. The Gale thought it'd corrupt us and forbade anyone from helping or looking for survivors."

"You stayed away?" Lyric asked Eleden, her hand tight on Kell's arm.

Kell was pale, his face slick with sweat. One hand touched the skin of his throat, pressing against the tattoo. As Runa watched, the blue line writhed, and Kell took a shallow breath.

"No," Eleden said. "We went to the Shore. A handful of people survived, and we helped them best we could. Most chose to move on, to seek refuge in Oleporea or Raendashar.

They wanted to forget, try to start over. Some believed the Old Ones were displeased and unleashed something against them."

"Mother felt their pain and suffering," Laenadara said.

"Who performed the ritual?" Runa asked. "Was it someone in the Thendan government or a priest mishandling with old magic?"

Laenadara lifted an eyebrow. "No, it was King Rakarn of Raendashar."

Kell inhaled sharply and leaned forward, his hands surging to his throat.

"Kell?" Lyric asked, her voice panicked. She put her hand on his back and tried to look into his face.

Blood dripped from Kell's nose.

Laenadara set aside her cup and stood up, crossing to Kell. She kneeled in front of him. "He's bound," she said, voice soft with wonder. "I thought you were Nilin, but ..." The priestess touched Kell's hand, shifting aside his fingers to see the tattoo beneath. "You were there. You saw something."

"What's happening?" Lyric asked, torn between staring at Laenadara and Kell's anguished face.

Kell's eyes had lost focus; his hands curled into claws against his neck.

"His mind is trying very hard to keep his memories locked away," Laenadara said. "The spell around his throat prevents him from remembering what he saw; *who* he saw."

"Rakarn," Runa breathed. What had Kell seen? What would make the King tattoo an eight-year-old boy?

"Can you help him?" Lyric asked.

"We can't remove the spell," the High Priestess said, "but we can calm his mind." She stood, gesturing to the guards by the door.

One slipped outside. Several minutes passed and the man returned with two robed men.

"This is Haetha and Bren," Laenadara said, gesturing the robed men over. "They'll take your friend to rest nearby."

"Kell," Lyric said, standing as Haetha and Bren helped Kell to his feet. "His name is Kell. I should go with you," she said.

Runa, eyeing her sister and the unfamiliar healers, stood up. She wouldn't let Lyric leave her sight. Not here where they didn't yet know the Ayanarans' intentions.

"I'll go," Sashala said, pushing down on Eleden's shoulder, who'd started to rise. "You need to stay. Kaia will be here soon. You must make your plans."

Lyric looked to Runa, eyes large with worry.

Reaching for her sister, Runa felt a flicker of terror pass between them, a thread of Lyric's emotions reaching out as she grabbed Runa's hand.

"Please get me if he grows any worse," Lyric said.

Sashala nodded.

"We'll care for him," one of the healers said. Then, supporting Kell between them, they walked him from the room, Sashala trailing behind.

Runa tugged Lyric back down to the cushions. "Have you received word from our mother?" Runa asked, looking at Laenadara. "A message that she's on her way?"

Laenadara, sitting back, shook her head. "We've received no communication from her."

"Hurlen will send word," Eleden said.

Laerdi nodded. "I'd guess by tomorrow. They're likely on their way here."

Runa squeezed her sister's hand, feeling worry rise inside her throat for their mother, and Kell. Would Kell be taken from them too? Curiously, she found that the idea of losing him saddened her. He'd helped save their mother, carrying her for hours without complaint up the Shore to Ivernn.

She dragged her mind back to Laenadara's words before Kell's nose started bleeding.

"You said King Rakarn is responsible for destroying Thenda," Runa said, "and for creating the Taint. Why would he do that?" *And why there?* she thought. Why not in Raendashar? Had their grandfather known how destructive and lethal his attempt could be? Why had Thenda allowed him to perform such a dangerous ritual there? Had they known the risks? Had anyone?

"The war," Eleden said, his voice rough and brittle. His fierce eyes glittered dangerously.

Laerdi, a hulking shape beside him, crushed his cup in one hand, shards of pottery falling between his feet. He blinked at his hands, seeming surprised as green liquid dripped on the floor.

"Yes," Laenadara said. "King Rakarn sought a weapon in his battle with the Sireni. He chose Thenda because the Mother's roots run beneath the Cliffs of Salta."

"A weapon?" Runa asked. She thought about Elenora's insistence that she could turn Runa into a weapon. Did the ancestor know what Rakarn had done?

"He sought to wake the dragons," Laenadara said.

"The Old Ones?" Lyric asked, her head turning away from the door.

The High Priestess gave Lyric a measured look. "Yes. Rakarn wanted to control them to destroy the Sireni and extend his rule over all of Erith."

"How do you know that?" Runa asked, narrowing her eyes. "Were you there in Thenda? Have you spoken to Rakarn?"

"The Mother told us," Laenadara said.

Runa's frown deepened. If Rakarn had unleashed dangerous magic atop the Tree's roots, it seemed plausible it'd feel what happened, but how could it comprehend the King's desires? How could the Mother Tree know the thoughts inside Rakarn's head? Had he sought the Ayanarans' help in the past? Did they have a connection to Raendashar?

"But the dragons are gone," Lyric said.

"Yes," Laenadara said, "but they're not far away. They're sleeping within the Veil, just as Serith sleeps beneath the Sea wrapped around the Mother's roots."

"But how would Rakarn know how to summon them?" Lyric asked. "I can't begin to imagine the power required—"

"I don't know where he learned the spell," Laenadara said, "but there is old magic, lost to time, that's capable of bringing the Old Ones back to the living world. If Rakarn knew the words and had a god-child's blood, it's possible to call the dragons home."

Runa tightened her hand on Lyric's. "A god-child? Like—"

"Egan," Eleden said, face bleaching of color.

Runa's heart thundered in her ears. Their mother had not mentioned their father when she'd accused Rakarn of destroying Thenda. Did she know? Did she care?

Laenadara clasped her hands in her lap and gave Eleden a somber look. "It was Egan," she said. "Rakarn used him in the ritual, but Egan fought against it. It was his resistance that resulted in the ritual's failure."

Pride for the man she didn't know welled in Runa's chest. He was a fighter like her.

"How could you know Egan was involved?" Eleden asked. "Did the Mother Tree tell you or did Egan come to you?" Hope kindled in his eyes. "You've seen him? He was here?"

"Yes," Laenadara said. "He's here now."

Runa dropped her empty cup and felt it hit her skirt. Their father was here?

"What?" Eleden exploded to his feet, fury contorting his face.

Looking up, Runa saw Laerdi drop the remaining shards of his cup on the ground and shift his eyes towards the guards by the door.

"He's here with you, and you never told me?" Eleden raged.

Laenadara held up a calming hand, remaining seated on the ground. "He's been here with us for the last few months. He sought our help. He's not well."

Runa stared at the High Priestess, fury burning in her chest. Why would Laenadara wait to tell them about their father? What game was she playing?

"What do you mean?" Lyric asked. "What's wrong with him?"

"When Rakarn's failed spell poisoned the land on which it was cast, it also corrupted your father," Laenadara said. "Because of his god-blood, Egan didn't die or turn into one of the mindless creatures that roam the Shore at night, but it changed him. He hungers for power, for magic, and he's tried valiantly not to harm anyone, but his efforts have starved him and broken his mind. I'm afraid Egan is more creature than man now. We've done our best to protect him from others and himself, but we cannot reverse the damage."

Runa was returned to the Shore, her mind replaying the moment the creature ripped open their mother's neck. She could still see the shock in Elaina's eyes, and hear the sound her torch made when she'd knocked the monster free.

"I'll kill him!" Eleden growled, clenching his fists.

"Our father?" Lyric asked, eyes wide.

"Rakarn," Runa said, looking at Eleden's angry face. "Did Rakarn kidnap him? And why pick *our* father?" She didn't understand. She'd thought Rakarn hadn't known who their father was or that he was Sireni.

"I don't know," Laenadara said.

It didn't make sense. Their mother claimed she'd hid Runa and Lyric to protect them from their grandfather. She'd refused to tell them their father's name. Why? To protect him? If she'd been so careful, why was Rakarn so entangled in their lives? Why did he seem to know everything?

And Kell ...

"Why not kill Kell?" Runa asked. "If he witnessed Rakarn's ritual and Rakarn was afraid he'd tell someone, why bother with a spell?"

"Ru!" Lyric gasped, wrenching her hand away.

Runa gave her sister an annoyed look. "I don't think he should have, but it seems excessive to use a complicated spell to silence someone. And a child, no less. Why go through all that effort? Our grandfather hardly seems merciful."

"Maybe he was unable to kill him," Laenadara said.

Runa narrowed her eyes. "Unable?"

The High Priestess shrugged.

Lyric straightened beside her and Runa eyed her sister's profile. She seemed uncomfortable. Did she know something about Kell? Something Runa didn't?

Runa looked back at Laenadara. "So in Rakarn's quest for power, he's doomed us all."

"Does he know?" Lyric asked. "Our grandfather? Does he know what he's done?"

"He knows," Laenadara said, "which is why none of the kingdoms are aware of his involvement. No one who witnessed the ritual is still alive, besides your father and friend. I can't say, however, if Rakarn is aware the Taint has spread or its danger."

Runa frowned. Eleden said there'd been people who'd tried to figure out what happened. How had no one found the connection to Rakarn?

"I wouldn't be surprised if he knows," Eleden said darkly.

"Has anyone else tried to summon the Old Ones before?" Lyric asked.

Runa looked at her sister, raising both eyebrows. "What are you suggesting, Ly?"

Lyric looked at her. "No one living knows how to cleanse the Taint, right? If someone did, then they would have done it already."

"Sure," Runa said, narrowing her eyes.

"But what if the dragons can?" Lyric asked. "They know magic beyond our understanding. They themselves *are* magic and created the runes we use for spells. If anyone can stop the Taint from spreading across Erith, it would be them, wouldn't it?"

"All right, but they're gone, Ly," Runa said. Realization slid coldly down her back. "Are you suggesting we try Rakarn's ritual? Think of the risk. Even if we knew a god-child willing to attempt the summoning, remember what supposedly happened to our father." She studied Lyric's face, curious despite her concern. It was odd being the voice of caution. Runa was usually the one taking significant risks and leaping into the unknown.

"You can't be serious, Lyric," Eleden said, shaking his head.

"It is possible," Laenadara said, drawing everyone's eyes. "You may be able to summon the dragons."

# 25

LYRIC

LYRIC BLINKED, her heart skipping. She hadn't expected her wild suggestion to be met with acceptance.

"Possible?" Runa asked sharply. "You're not proposing we put our father through the ritual *again*."

"No," Laenadara said. "There's no need. You and your sister are Egan's children. His blood, Serith's blood, is in your veins, and if that wasn't enough, you're also descended from the Three. You are closer to their power, to *all* their power than anyone else alive."

"Would it kill us?" Lyric asked. "Corrupt us like our father?"

The High Priestess shook her head. "No, as you will be willing participants, it is unlikely another destructive result will occur."

"Unlikely but possible," Runa said.

"We cannot know the exact effect of a ritual thousands of years old," Laenadara said, "but I'm confident there's no danger in the summoning itself."

"This is madness," Eleden said, voice ragged with disbelief. He leaned forward, fixing Runa and Lyric with his eyes. "The last time the ritual was attempted Thenda was destroyed, and the Sea poisoned. Your father, my brother, was poisoned!"

Lyric shifted beneath her uncle's gaze. Was she being foolish?

"It's not without risk," Laenadara said.

"How do you know the ritual, anyway?" Runa asked.

Lyric frowned. How did the High Priestess know the ritual? If it was forgotten magic, how had both Laenadara and Lyric's grandfather learned the spell and its requirements?

"Mother shared it with us," Laenadara said.

"So, you already believe the ritual is necessary?" Lyric asked. "Has the Mother Tree told you it will work?"

"If the Three are awakened, their fire can burn away the Taint as it was created by corrupted magic."

"Would you have asked us to do the ritual if Lyric hadn't suggested it first?" Runa asked.

Laenadara inclined her head. "I would have asked, as we are running out of time. I know Eleden brought you to us because he thought it'd be safer here, away from both Raendashar and the Sireni. We do wish to be your allies. We cherish life, and their war only brings pain and death. We'd help you for that reason alone, to save the lives of our brothers and sisters, but there's a greater threat now, a threat to all of us. Not just to you and me, but to all people; all life on Erith. The Mother Herself is at risk if the Taint spreads unabated."

Fear loosed in Lyric's mind as she thought about everyone dying. She imagined the plants wilting and the trees back home twisting and melting as unnatural green lines ravished their trunks. She thought about birds dropping from the sky, and animals decaying on the ground, their melted corpses spreading the Tainted magic.

"What does the spell do if it works?" she asked. "What happens if we call the Old Ones and they answer?" Lyric laughed, a breathless, terrified sound. It seemed so ridiculous to be discussing this like it was something that could actually happen. Dragons lived in stories.

"We'll ask for their assistance," Laenadara said. "We'll call on their wisdom and love for Erith to save Her. The Old Ones are tied to this world. If they didn't care what happened to Her, then they would have followed the Trinity and the Seven to the Beyond. The Three would not have stayed in the Veil."

Lyric thought back to the song Kell sang all those days ago on the beach near Thenda. *Eyes turned away; the Lords wait in shadow, dreaming until called forth again. Though distant and sleeping, They'll return to preserve us.*

"I wonder what Rakarn would have told them if his ritual worked and he'd summoned the dragons," Runa said. "Oh, excuse me Great Ones, would you mind destroying my enemies, please?" She snorted, an incredulous look on her sharp face.

"He must have thought he could control them," Eleden said. He exchanged a glance with Laerdi, both men looking ill at ease.

Lyric thought about Laenadara's face when she'd recalled the visions she claimed the Mother Tree had shared. She'd looked scared as if she'd stared into Valen's face, seen her death and the death of everyone she loved.

She thought about a man who'd died in her village from a poison inside his body. By the time they knew what was wrong, saw its effects on his skin, the blood in his eyes, it was too late.

"I think we should try the ritual," Lyric said, looking at Runa. "If there's a chance we can stop the Taint we have to risk it. Laenadara's right, even if we're able to end the war and mediate peace, none of it will matter if the world rots beneath us."

"It seems somewhat blasphemous, doesn't it?" Runa asked quietly. "Compelling the Old Ones to attend us? Asking them to clean up something we created?"

"Not us," Lyric said.

"Will that matter?" Runa asked. She leaned her head close, her voice barely a whisper by Lyric's ear. "Why push so hard for this, Ly? We don't know anyone here, not really. How can we trust that the information we're being given is not a careful manipulation? Mother lied to us, and she loved us. We can't say the same for anyone here."

"I don't see another option," Lyric said. "We can choose to do nothing, but that feels wrong to me. I think she's right, that we're running out of time. Remember Mr. Ilion? Who died from blood rot?" She chewed on her lip. "Maybe we can wait for Mama, ask what she thinks before we decide."

"I want to see my brother," Eleden said abruptly.

Lyric looked up. Laenadara was staring at her, her face unreadable. "I want to see him too," Lyric said. "I want to see what happened."

"Of course." Laenadara inclined her head. "I must warn you that Egan is not the man he once was. It won't be easy to look upon him."

"We're discussing performing the same ritual that altered him," Runa said. "We will see him."

"Of course." Laenadara stood, with a smooth, graceful motion, and clasped her hands in front of her. She waited for the others to rise, then led them to the door.

"Kell?" Lyric asked as she followed behind the High Priestess. "Will you tell him where we are?"

"Yes. I'll have him brought to you after you see your father," Laenadara said.

Worry knotted Lyric's stomach as the memory of Kell's bleeding nose replayed inside her head. He would be fine, wouldn't he?

Returning to the forest outside the structure's door, the two guards at the entrance fell into step behind them. Laerdi shifted between walking by Eleden's side and at the back of the group to keep an eye on the guards.

As they walked away from the village, Lyric realized that she hadn't felt Gandara's presence since stepping on Ayanaran soil. Why hadn't she chimed in during their discussion with the High Priestess? Lyric would have asked her about the ritual or if she had any useful knowledge about the Ayanarans.

*Gandara?* Lyric asked.

She received no answer.

*This connection would be more useful if Gandara were available when I need her,* Lyric thought. "Has Elenora talked with you since we arrived?" she asked Runa in a low voice. She didn't want Laenadara to overhear and ask for an explanation.

"No," her sister said curtly.

Lyric frowned at her, but Runa stared straight ahead. Sighing, she returned her attention to their walk.

They climbed a short hill, then trailed down the other side into a valley. Lyric gasped, feeling a sense of awe as they walked between two large, moss-covered stones. The valley was long and deep, rock formations towering on either side, visible between the trees. It was quiet, the air warm, and Lyric was grateful she'd left her skirts tied up in mimic of the Sireni's trousers.

*I'll have to borrow some of Hali's clothes,* Lyric thought as sweat trickled down her back. Her dress stuck to her skin.

Someone screamed.

Lyric stopped short, snapping a hand around Runa's wrist. "What was that?" she asked, staring at the trees.

"Egan," Laenadara said softly.

Anxiety lodged like a rock inside Lyric's throat, and she didn't let go of her sister as they climbed another small rise. The path twisted and opened into a clearing. Tall trees grew around its edge, their branches arching over the sky and blocking Lyric's view of the clouds.

In the center of the clearing was a pit. Two green-clad women, their hair braided back from their faces, sat near its edge. One was holding a bow, loose but ready, and the other had a knife sheathed at her waist.

Another scream split the air; it's sound primal and raw, more animal than human. Lyric's skin prickled, and her heart shuddered inside her chest. Her stomach filled with dread as the scream weakened into a rasping whimper.

"You have Egan in a pit?" Eleden asked furiously. He strode past Laenadara to the pit's edge with Laerdi on his heels. Together they leaned over, looking down. Laerdi recoiled, and Eleden rocked back on his heels as if something had struck him. His hands clenched against his legs, his fists tight enough that Lyric heard his knuckles pop from the strain.

"It's him?" Lyric asked, taking a tentative step forward.

"No!" Eleden said, whirling around and holding up a hand. "No, Lyric. This shouldn't be the first glimpse you have of your father." His face was pale, his eyes wild and round.

"We don't need to be protected," Runa growled. She strode forward, unconsciously towing Lyric along.

Drawn to the edge by her sister, Lyric swallowed and looked down into the pit. It wasn't dark like she'd imagined but softly lit by glowing lights high on the earthen walls. There was a blanket, shredded and soiled in one corner, and an earthen pot tipped on its side that'd perhaps once held water. In the center of the pit stood a man head bowed and back hunched. He was naked from the waist up, and his linen trousers were stained and torn. His feet were bare; his toes curled in the gashed dirt.

As Lyric stared down at their father, her fingers clenched around Runa's arm, Egan's head snapped up. Matted, silver hair flew back from his eyes. They were green, like Eleden's and Lyric's own, but they were wild, unfocused, and shone with unnatural light. He was handsome or had been, the square face drawn, the cheeks sunken. A scraggly beard covered his cheeks, matted and thin in places as though he'd torn parts free with his fingers.

Long, bloody lines crossed his chest as if he'd tried to scratch away the skin on his abdomen. Egan's ribs stuck out visibly, his belly hollowed. Wrapping both his arms from elbow to armpit, were seven, tattooed rings of mage blue. There was no recognition in his eyes, and he inhaled, scenting the air like a dog. Fury darkened his eyes to a deep, unsettling green, almost black, and he howled, running towards the wall beneath their feet.

Lyric yelped, grabbing Runa, as their father's body slammed into the wall. Egan scrabbled vainly, trying to climb, to reach them, but he slid back to the pit's bottom with every attempt. Howling again, he stalked back and forth, watching them, and muttering something unintelligible.

Tears filled Lyric's eyes, and she looked back at Laenadara. "This is our father?" she asked, voice breaking. She could hear Runa breathing raggedly beside her, and she slipped her arm around her sister's waist.

"Can't you do anything for him?" Lyric asked.

"Nothing we've tried works," Laenadara said. "He's beyond our abilities. However ..."

"However?" Runa asked. Her voice was rough and angry. "Don't toy with us," she spat. "Say what you're thinking!"

The High Priestess folded her hands together. "If the Taint is burned from the world, it's possible the creatures poisoned by it will be cleansed. Your father's illness is from the Taint's corruption. I believe there's a chance he can be saved."

"You're manipulating them!" Eleden said accusingly. He glowered at Laenadara, causing one of the green-clad guards to step closer to the High Priestess.

"That's not my intent," Laenadara said. "I don't wish to force you to do anything. I only want you to make an informed decision."

"We have to do it," Lyric whispered to Runa. "We have to try. I can't walk away, not now."

Egan screamed, scrambling at the wall of the pit, and both Lyric and Runa jumped.

"What else can we do?" Lyric asked. She could not give up on him or leave him here. She would not walk away.

Runa gritted her teeth. Her eyes were dark with pain and worry. "I don't know, Ly," she whispered. "It's all falling apart around us."

"To the end and beyond?" Lyric asked. *Are you with me?* she thought.

Runa smiled, a sad, bitter twist of her lips. "To the end," she said, "but I think you're right, and we should wait for Mother. She'll be here soon. Maybe she knows something about the ritual."

Lyric nodded and together, they turned back to Laenadara. To the side, Eleden and Laerdi stared at them, their faces strained, caught between worry and anger.

"We want to help," Lyric said, "but we need to speak to our Mother first. She's on her way."

Annoyance flashed across Laenadara's face, the look gone so quickly Lyric wondered if she'd imagined it. "I understand, but you need to make your choice soon. The ritual must be performed within the next two days while the Veil is thin. The moons are aligned above us, ensuring a successful summoning. We cannot miss it, or we'll be forced to wait another year. By then ..." She gestured, her eyes sad. "The Taint will have consumed Erith."

Lyric gasped, feeling cold. She studied the High Priestess' face, her confidence faltering.

"Why didn't you mention this before?" Runa asked, frowning.

"I did not want to rush your decision," Laenadara said. "I hoped we would—"

"High Priestess!" A green-clad woman rushed towards them from the trees, her bow held over one shoulder.

Laenadara turned, lips tightening. "Yes, Elwin. What is it?"

"There's an airship approaching from the east with blue sails."

"Kaia!" Eleden swore, staring up into the sky.

Lyric followed his gaze but saw nothing but branches stretching overhead.

"I'll speak to her," Laenadara said, looking at Lyric and Runa. "I'll tell her you're under our protection. That is, if I may speak on your behalf?"

Lyric and Runa glanced at each other. "Yes, thank you," Lyric said. "You can tell Kaia we'll meet with her once she agrees to your terms of conduct." She eyed Runa, who nodded.

"We need to speak to the Gale anyway," Runa said, "to discuss the war's cessation."

The High Priestess opened her mouth, perhaps to press the deadline she'd given them.

"We understand the urgency," Lyric said, "and will make our decision, but given the gravity of this undertaking, we want to wait for our mother to arrive. We need her counsel. You said we have at least two days?"

Laenadara inclined her head, the skin tight around her eyes and mouth. "I'll take you somewhere to rest, where you can confer in private. I'll have Kell brought to you, and Kaia, if you wish, once we have officially greeted her."

"Thank you," Lyric said.

Runa gave a curt nod, glancing back at the pit.

"I'll come with you," Eleden said, his eyes on Laenadara. "Kaia can be damnably cunning when she wishes. I'll ensure her compliance."

# 26

## RUNA

RUNA PACED, her hand trailing sparks along the interlacing branches of the wall.

"Careful!" Lyric called from across the room. "What if you set fire to the tree?"

"I'm not going to set fire to it," Runa said. She murmured the rune for fire again beneath her breath and felt a surge of satisfaction as the wood scorched beneath her fingers.

They were back in the village in a small, pod-like structure that Laenadara's people had furnished with blankets and cushions. The Ayanarans had brought water and food then left them alone. Eleden and Laerdi had gone with Laenadara and had yet to return, and Kell was still with the healers.

*Don't be a child,* Elenora hissed inside her head. *You can't ignore me forever.*

Runa pivoted on her heel and walked the other way, glancing sideways at Lyric who was picking at a plate of fresh vegetables and dip made from mashed beans and spices. Her sister's eyes kept drifting to the doorway, as though expecting Kell to walk through at any moment.

*Your sister trusts too easily*, Elenora said. Her voice was sour with displeasure.

Runa gritted her teeth and tried to focus on the sensation of the branches beneath her fingers.

*She'll weaken you. She's holding you back. Did you see how quickly your sister sided with these outlanders over you? She chooses others over blood. Who do you think she'll side with when an agreement is made? Not Raendashar.*

Go away, Runa thought, rubbing her temples.

*What do you think the Sireni will do when we're no longer regulating their movements? Do you think they'll forget their supposed claim to our land? No, they are devious. They'll sneak into the Scorched Court through your sister's tainted blood.*

"Enough!" Runa hissed. "You forget we're the same!"

"Did you say something?" Lyric asked, looking up from the plate in her hands.

"Nothing," Runa said. She forced herself to walk over to her sister and sit down.

Lyric offered her a long yellow pepper spear and Runa took it, absently ripping off a chunk with her teeth.

"I still can't wrap my head around this," Lyric said. "Can the fate of the world, of life itself, truly hinge on our decision to participate in the ritual?"

"Laenadara could find someone else," Runa said recalling what the High Priestess had said. "I doubt our father's the only god-child in the world. She's likely exaggerating our importance so we'll agree to help because she doesn't have the time or desire to find someone else."

"Maybe," Lyric said. "But if it were a simple thing, then why wouldn't she have tried the ritual with someone else?"

"We didn't ask if she has," Runa said. She narrowed her eyes at the pepper. They should have thought to ask her. What if Laenadara had already tried it and failed? Even if the ritual could only be performed a specific time of the year, she'd had twelve years to try.

"But if she has performed the ritual," Lyric said, "and it failed like Grandfather's, we would know, wouldn't we?"

"If the effect was the same," Runa said. "Maybe she tried, and nothing bad occurred. Maybe nothing happened at all. If our consent determines whether the ritual works or not, then all Laenadara would need is someone to agree."

"Maybe ..." Lyric said, her voice trailing off. "I don't get the sense that Laenadara is hiding anything from us. If she performed the ritual before she'd have told us. I understand why she didn't mention the deadline right away."

*Foolish*, Elenora hissed.

"It should work, shouldn't it?" Lyric asked. "The only reason Grandfather's spell failed was because Father fought against it. As long as we don't fight ..."

"And if Laenadara is wrong?" Runa asked. "What if the ritual requires our death? What if that's what Father was fighting against? Do you still want to go through with it if the cost is our lives?"

Lyric's eyes were thoughtful. She was actually considering Runa's question.

"You'd die to summon the dragons?" Runa asked. Her cheeks heated. The truth was, she was afraid. But why? She'd almost died once already. She knew how it felt. What was one more brush with death? But this, this would be agreeing to it beforehand. No accidental spell pushing her out of her body. Was this better or worse?

"If this is the only way to save Erith," Lyric said, "to save everyone ... how can we not?" She was tormented, it was clear on her face, but she'd still do it. She'd sacrifice herself.

"It's not your job to save everyone," Runa said. Her voice came out fiercer than she intended, but Lyric just smiled sadly.

"We've fought so hard to save Mama," Lyric said. "We've

traveled across the world. How can we give up now? I'm surprised by you, Ru. You've always been the risk taker."

"And you've always been the cautious one," Runa said. She smiled suddenly, her lips moving as if they had a mind of their own. "What's happened to us, Ly?"

"Forced maturity?"

They grinned at each other, and for a moment it felt like they were home again. Runa clung to the feeling. In that moment, she wanted to go back. She wanted to go home and shut the door against the world until it was just her and Lyric again. Life hadn't been simple and uncomplicated in Elae's Hollow, it'd been hard and challenging, but Runa had understood it. She'd known who and what to trust.

"For what it's worth, I don't think we need to die for the ritual to succeed," Lyric said. "If the Old Ones stayed behind so they could return if we need them, why would they require someone's death to do so?"

"Unless they didn't create the ritual themselves," Runa said. "What if the spell's purpose is to force the dragons to obey the summoner? Who, if I'm not mistaken, will be Laenadara?"

Lyric shook her head, setting aside the half-eaten plate of food. "The Ayanarans' entire society is based on the sanctity of life. They seek to protect it."

"There's a problem in that," Runa said. "Protection is subjective. Mother, for instance, thought she was protecting us when she abandoned us as children. Obviously, we disagree with her choice. In our eyes, she wasn't protecting us."

Lyric sighed and rubbed her fingers over her face. "I feel like we could discuss this for hours and still have doubts. We have to choose whether to trust Laenadara or not, and if we trust Eleden's judgment in bringing us here." Lyric sighed again and dropped her chin into her hands. "He was angry with her, though. Accused her of manipulating us. Did he know about the ritual? I wish Mama would arrive so we can ask what she thinks about it."

"You heard Eleden," Runa said. "She didn't want us to come here at all."

"To keep us out of the war," Lyric said. "I don't think she knew about the ritual. If she knew the Taint was spreading and that we could eliminate it—"

"Lyric?" a man's voice called from outside. "Are you there?"

Lyric's head jerked towards the door, and she stood, hands flying up with anticipation. "Kell! Come in!" she called.

Kell pushed through the vines in the doorway, smiling tiredly. He looked haggard and pale. There were dark shadows under his eyes, but the blood was gone, as was the sightless stare from before.

Lyric rushed at him, her hands flying around his neck.

Kell caught her, staggering slightly, then pulled her into him. They clung to each other like they'd been parted for days and not hours. Kell's eyes closed, and he rested his cheek against Lyric's hair.

Runa shifted uncomfortably, feeling as if she was witnessing a private moment. She considered leaving, giving them privacy, and then was irritated by the thought. If they wanted to be alone, *they* could leave.

Runa reached for another vegetable from Lyric's plate and took a savage bite, barely registering its taste.

"I'm sorry," Kell said as Lyric pulled away to look at him.

"It's not your fault," Lyric said, shaking her head.

"You needed me and—"

"Kell, we're fine," Lyric said. "We were fine. I've been worrying about you. How are you?"

"I'm all right now, I think," Kell said. "I guess I lost consciousness for a while. The pain was excruciating. When the High Priestess mentioned King Rakarn ..." He paused, a muscle flexing in his cheek. "It was like there was a door in my mind. I could feel it, knew that the memories of what happened that day lay beyond it. I've always stepped away from it before, listened to the tightening of the spell around my neck but ... I wanted to understand."

"Will it break you again if we tell you what we learned?" Runa asked bluntly.

Lyric gave her an annoyed look over her shoulder.

"No, I don't think so," Kell said, his lips quirking. "I'll avoid opening any mental doors."

"We saw our father," Lyric said.

Kell looked at her, his eyes widening with surprise. "Your father?"

"Yes, he was—"

"Rabid, like an animal," Runa said. She raised an eyebrow at another irritated look from her sister. It sounded terrible, yes, but how else could you describe the state of him?

"Mama was right. Our Grandfather performed the ritual in Thenda," Lyric said carefully, "and he used our father to power it. When Egan fought against it, against Rakarn, the ritual collapsed, and the Taint was released or created, Laenadara doesn't know for sure. Our father is like one of those creatures now, on the Shore, but different; still human. Laenadara said he's been fighting the effects, and only now succumbed to it. He didn't recognize us."

Kell ran his hand across Lyric's back. "I'm sorry," he said.

Runa watched him and noticed a muscle twitching along his brow. She eyed the tattoo around his throat, but it didn't writhe like before.

"Lyric thinks we should perform the ritual again," Runa said.

Kell's eyes widened, and he pushed Lyric back to stare into her face. "You want to what?" he demanded.

"The Mother Tree told the Ayanarans that dragon fire will destroy the Taint," Lyric said.

"Aya, the Tree," Kell said, his voice flat.

"Yes."

"The Mother Tree doesn't speak," Kell said, looking between Lyric and Runa.

Runa pursed her lips. "Apparently, it does."

Lyric gave Kell a concerned look. "You knew that, Kell. Laendara said the Tree spoke to her while you were there."

He blinked, confusion crossing his face like a man just now realizing he was drowning. "I'm sorry, I ... it was hard to focus. I felt ..." He shook his head. "You're right, I remember, I just never heard ... well, I've personally never been here before." Kell moved his hands up onto Lyric's shoulders. "But even if the Tree does speak to them, the ritual destroyed my home, Lyric. It killed my parents and nearly killed your father! How can you even consider trying it?"

"We'd be willing participants," Lyric said. "We'd ask the Old Ones for help, guidance. It'd be like your story, Kell. The one you sang on the beach? Though distant and sleeping, They'll return to preserve us. Isn't that what you said?"

Kell gave Lyric a helpless look. "It's a story, Lyric. A legend. It could be someone's fantasy or interpretation of something that happened. We don't know if the dragons are waiting for us or if they'd want to help us." He shifted his hands to Lyric's shoulders, eyes imploring. "Don't forget, Lyric that the Old Ones were not always charitable and kind. They were fierce and dangerous. They warred with the Seven over who should rule Erith after the Trinity left us. They killed just as many humans as they saved."

"Yes, but after the Demon War, they stayed when the Seven left," Lyric said. She put her hand on Kell's wrist. "The Old Ones helped us recover and rebuild. They mediated disputes, and when they left Erith to us, they first created the Council. Whether or not they were sometimes terrible, they didn't want Erith to die. They'll want to help. I know it."

"She's nothing if not idealistic," Runa said when Kell looked at her. "You should have learned by now that Lyric will try to save everyone she meets."

"Lyric, please don't do this," Kell said, framing Lyric's face with his hands. "It could kill you or worse. I don't think I could survive if you ... if I lost you."

It was touching the way Kell pleaded with Lyric, heartbreaking and painfully sad. There was a desperateness in his eyes that even Runa could see.

"You're being selfish," Runa said. She wasn't entirely speaking to Kell when she said it.

"I don't care," Kell said. He didn't yell at Runa, just tightened his hands on Lyric's face. "Lyric, please! If you're wrong and it doesn't work; or if it does, but the Old Ones are displeased—"

"I understand your concerns," Lyric said, "but we're in a position to ensure no one else has to die from the Taint."

"We should do it," Runa said. She felt a shiver of excitement as her words hung in the air. Maybe they'd fail, but maybe taking this risk and returning the dragons would preserve the world. If they walked away, what good was stopping the war, earning their freedom, if death waited at the end? "I still think we should wait for Mother, but if she doesn't have a better solution ..."

Lyric pulled free from Kell's hands and looked at her, surprise crossing her face. "What changed your mind?"

"I hadn't decided against it," Runa said, "but I didn't want to rush to make a decision. We can't know for sure if we can trust Laenadara's word. We can't verify what she says, what she claims Aya has told her. But, Eleden trusts her, and Mother trusts him, and if the Taint has genuinely spread across the entire continent, then it might be weeks or even days before more cities are threatened. Thenda could be the beginning.

"Can you imagine what would happen if Elae's Hollow falls

to the Taint? Or somewhere bigger, like Rathgar's Hold or Corsicayna? Can you imagine the number of dead and infected? We barely survived a handful of the creatures on the Shore. What if hundreds descended on a village? Though it feels arrogant and ridiculous to think we can do something about it, us of all people, I'd regret not trying."

"Your ancestors," Kell said, his voice hoarse. "Have they shared no words of caution?"

"No," Runa said, thinking of Elenora's words about Lyric.

"Gandara has been ... distracted since we came here," Lyric said. "I'm not sure what's wrong with her, but it's as if her mind is constantly wandering. I haven't been able to make much sense of her. I thought she was gone, but she's been muttering in my mind since we spoke with Laenadara."

"Maybe that's a sign. A sign to—"

"I know you're worried, Kell," Lyric said, "I am too, but I feel like I can actually do something. With the war, I didn't see where I'd fit, I don't know anything about negotiating peace, but this ... if the Old Ones return, if they help us, we can save millions of people. We can save our father. I can save you, remove your silencing. We can stop the war!

"I know we shouldn't rush into this, decide too quickly, so we will wait to talk to our mother, but I feel this is right."

Kell groaned and buried his face in Lyric's hair.

Runa looked away, crossing her arms. There was a certainty in Lyric's face that she envied. A passion, she wished she could feel.

"Lyric? Runa?" Captain Eleden stepped inside, his face grave. His eyes flicked to Kell and Lyric, who'd pulled apart as he entered with Laerdi.

Sashala and Teaeth stopped in the entrance, watching something outside.

"I've heard from Hurlen," Eleden said without preamble. "Your mother's been taken."

"Taken?" Lyric gasped, fisting a hand in Kell's vest.

"By King Rakarn," Eleden said. "He was there when Hurlen went to retrieve her from the inn. Hurlen followed them to Rathgar's Hold."

"How is she?" Runa asked. Worry sucked the heat from her chest, and she crossed her arms, hands against her sides.

"She was unconscious when he saw her, but alive." Eleden's eyes deepened with sympathy. "I'm sorry we didn't reach her in time."

"He won't hurt her," Lyric said, looking at Runa. Her eyes were worried, but hopeful. "She's his daughter and heir."

Runa took a breath, considering. Lyric was right. Rakarn would want to save her, help her. Whether or not he loved Elaina didn't matter, and perhaps she was better off with him. If they went ahead with the ritual and it failed, then Ayanar might be the least safe place to be.

What could they do, anyway? Stage a rescue? Assault the castle? The Ayanarans had bows and were surely capable of protecting themselves, but would they attack Raendashar? Could they, even if they wanted to? They had no ships, no way to quickly travel long distances.

"Mother is probably safer away from us," Runa said slowly.

Lyric nodded reluctantly, her fingers leaving creases in Kell's vest. "Will Hurlen keep an eye on her?"

Eleden nodded. "I've asked him to stay nearby and send word if he catches a glimpse of her. She's in the castle. He'll keep us apprised of her condition and tell us when she wakes. Rakarn will probably try to show her off, quiet the whispers about her absence, which should allow Hurlen to approach her."

"Thank you," Lyric said. She leaned against Kell, her arms wrapping around his waist.

Kell held her tightly, his face a mask of misery and acceptance.

"Has Kaia agreed to leave us be for now?" Runa asked, remembering the airship.

Eleden nodded and braced his hands on his belt. "She's agreed to wait."

"Does she know what Laenadara has asked us to do?" Lyric asked. "Why we're here?"

Eleden shook his head. "She's been told you're communing with the Mother Tree at Laenadara's request. If she knew the delay was about the Taint, she'd interfere. She thinks my clan is exaggerating the urgency, to convince the Gale to abandon the war." He stroked his chin, his eyes conflicted.

"I know you hoped to speak to your mother about the ritual. Forgive me for bringing you here," Eleden said. "I didn't know Laenadara would ask you to do this."

"It was my suggestion," Lyric said.

"I only wanted to protect you and help my people. *Our* people."

"Do you think we should do it?" Runa asked, studying Eleden's face. She wasn't sure if they could trust him to be impartial, but he hadn't done anything to betray them yet.

Eleden scrubbed a hand across his jaw. "Dandashara will kill me for this."

"You'd have them risk their lives," Kell said, strain hollowing his face.

Eleden barked a harsh laugh. "If you could save your father, or Lyric, or someone you love, wouldn't you do anything? If you knew the world was ending ..."

"This is not their responsibility," Kell snapped. "They should not—"

Lyric put a hand on his chest and he cut off, looking down at her.

Anger at Kell's tone had begun to bubble beneath Runa's skin, and she clenched her fist. She wanted to burn something, set it on fire. Slowly, pushing down her annoyance, Runa relaxed her hand and looked at her sister's face.

"I think we should try the ritual," Lyric said, "but only if you agree."

Runa looked at Laerdi, standing like a silent mountain behind their uncle. He seemed to have drawn inward, his eyes masked. She looked at the others. Sashala shifted restlessly, toying with a knife in one hand, and Teaeth had lost his smile. They were worried.

What would happen if the dragons responded? Would Serith come with the Three? What would the Sireni do when faced with their god? *And me? Am I ready?*

"Yes," Runa said. She gave her sister a fierce nod. *I will not be afraid.*

# 27

---

### RUNA

RUNA SAT on a ledge of sun-drenched rock, legs dangling over the edge, and stared into the valley below. After they'd decided to go ahead with the ritual, the Sireni had lingered inside the room, unwilling to leave her and Lyric alone. Though they didn't say it aloud, Runa suspected they were worried Kaia wouldn't keep her agreement with the Ayanarans. Why else was everyone on edge? Surely it wasn't only because of the impending ritual. What did Runa and Lyric mean to Laerdi, Sashala, and Teaeth? She could understand Eleden's attachment but the others?

Unable to stand the palpable tension in the air or Kell's tormented eyes after a sleepless night and solemn morning, Runa had shoved her way outside and started walking. She'd picked a direction randomly, weaving between trees and climbing rocks, focusing on the feel of her muscles propelling her forward and the movement of air in and out of her lungs. She felt someone follow her but didn't look to see who and they stayed far enough back that Runa pushed them from her mind.

She'd only stopped, sweat trickling down her back, when the land abruptly opened up onto a large, rocky ledge, impassible where it jutted over a sea of trees below. She'd taken a deep gulp of air, unraveling as her emotions bubbled up through her chest until she was crying for no apparent reason at all.

In front of her, the forest stretched unbroken, the thick tree canopy lush and green. She could see a waterfall off to the side and hear the rush of water tumbling a great distance, but wherever it led was hidden by the trees. There was a river down there somewhere, carrying the water away, but she couldn't see it.

Runa wasn't sure what drove her to the edge, but she'd sat, precariously high, imagining what would happen if she fell off. Would she float like a leaf spiraling down? Would it feel like flying? Would she hit the trees, her body breaking as it fell, or would she tumble weightlessly until she hit the forest floor far below? What'd happen then? Would she go to the Veil? Would it feel like before?

*Are you thinking of ending it already?* Elenora asked, her voice sharp and caustic.

Runa wiped her cheeks and stared out across the trees.

*I shouldn't be surprised.*

"We're going to summon the Old Ones," Runa said, her tone flat, unaffected.

Elenora shifted. Despite being unable to see her, Runa knew she was curious, surprised.

"Haven't you been listening?" Runa asked. "We're going to do the ritual. The one Rakarn attempted."

*A rather bold gesture,* Elenora said. *The dragons may be allies, but you also risk becoming their attendants. It's better to fight your own battles, girl.*

"What?" Runa asked, frowning at the air. "I'm not calling them for Raendashar. We're going to ask them to cleanse the Taint."

Elenora's mood shifted to tense brooding.

"Don't you care?" Runa asked, "if Raendashar melts into the Sea of Screams?"

*We will never be diminished,* Elenora said.

Runa gritted her teeth. "Is there a reason I shouldn't trust Laenadara or the Ayanarans?" she asked. "Is there a reason I shouldn't do the ritual?"

*It'd be better if you had something to offer the Three,* Elenora said absently. *So you're not in their debt. You don't want to make alliances from a place of weakness.*

"I have nothing that would interest an Old One," Runa said.

*That's unfortunate.* Elenora seemed to shrug.

"What could I offer anyway?"

*Well, you could offer them the kingdom, though they'll probably simply take it. We're their brood, after all.*

"The what? Raendashar?" Runa asked.

*Yes, they've been gone from the world for a long time. You could renew your oaths.*

"I don't speak for Raendashar. King Rakarn does."

*You'd have to kill him, obviously, and your mother, unless she abdicates, but if the people knew of her treachery—*

Runa mouth dropped open, horrified by her ancestor's suggestion. "I'm not murdering anyone!"

*You asked for my advice. I hope you survive it, the summoning. I'd hate to have wasted all this time on you.*

"That's nice of you to say," Runa said darkly.

Elenora made a noncommittal sound and disappeared, leaving Runa to herself.

Runa sat for a time, irritated by the lack of help from her ancestor. The sun started to shift, the day droning on into late afternoon.

*I should get back,* she thought. Rising slowly, Runa stretched her back and arms then turned and walked into the trees. She was so familiar with walking unguided through forestland, that it was easy to retrace her steps.

As Runa walked, she listened to the Ayanaran forest and found it mostly silent save for the movement and calls of birds. She didn't hear or see another person, and if she hadn't known the village was ahead of her, she could have believed she was the first to walk here.

She caught no hint of the person who'd shadowed her to the cliff. Had it been one of the Sireni, Sashala or Teaeth, or had it been an Ayanaran?

Runa paused by a boulder to stare up at a tall tree, its trunk thick and skirted with white mushrooms like enormous, lacy frills. Studying the fungi, she heard the murmur of voices. She tilted her head, listening. Was that Laenadara's voice?

Moving closer to the rock, Runa shifted along its edge until she could peer around to the other side. Laenadara was there, standing with her back to Runa and talking to an older man. The man was similarly robed with long, brown hair and a neatly trimmed beard.

"You don't think they'll listen, do you," the man said. "Despite the old stories and their sacrifices during the Demon War."

"It's been thousands of years since they concerned themselves with our affairs," Laenadara said. "I think it's dangerous to assume they'll feel obliged to help. What if they come and decide to give in to their bestial nature? What would we do then? Appeal to their kindness? No, we must be ready."

The man shifted his weight, looking uncertain. "What guidance has Aya given?"

"She promised their submission."

"Are you sure it's worth the risk?" the man asked. "The words are Velanian. The cost could be—"

"I'll do what I must," Laenadara said, cutting him off.

The man looked like he might argue, and then he nodded, stroking his fingers over his beard. "It's fortunate we learned of the girls' existence," he said.

"Aya is all-knowing."

"If Egan had not come to us ..." Laenadara and the man began to walk away, their words too quiet to overhear.

Runa frowned as she watched them leave and moved back from the boulder. It sounded like the Ayanarans were not as confident in the Old Ones' willingness to help as Laenadara had implied. How exactly could their Mother Tree promise the dragons' submission? And what was Velanian? Runa had never heard of it before.

*It's powerful blood magic,* Elenora said inside her head. *An adaptation of Celestial, or bastardization of it depending on your sentiments.*

Runa blinked. "Blood magic? I would not have expected that from the Ayanarans," she said, thinking of what little she knew of their axioms.

*You're calling dragons,* Elenora said, her tone crisp and impatient. *That's not a simple thing.*

"And Celestial? What's that?"

Elenora sighed. *Your mother should be ashamed of your education. It's a language for magic. What, you thought everyone uses dragon runes? Even those who are not of the bloodline?*

Runa flushed; Elenora's scorn like thorns against her skin. She longed to ask more, but anger was rolling red-hot through her. Her nails scraped across her palms as she tightened her hands into fists. "I need to speak with Lyric," she said.

WHEN RUNA RETURNED to the room she shared with her sister, she found Teaeth and Sashala loitering outside. They nodded as she passed, apparently left on guard duty by Eleden.

Lyric and Kell were inside reclining on the cushions in each others' arms. Their heads were bent close, Lyric murmuring something as Kell shook his head.

Runa cleared her throat, smiling thinly when they glanced up at her, startled. "I overheard Laenadara talking with another priest," Runa said.

Lyric shifted against Kell's chest. "What did you hear?" she asked.

"She's not as confident in the Old Ones' help as she implied," Runa said. She picked a cushion and plopped down onto it, shoving her skirt out of the way.

"She thinks it'll fail?" Kell asked with alarm.

"No," Runa said, "she said the Mother Tree would ensure their submission."

"Their submission?" Lyric asked. She raised both eyebrows. "What does that mean?"

Runa shrugged. "The Mother Tree was created by Ethethera ... maybe it's more powerful than the Old Ones?"

Lyric tipped her head back to look into Kell's face.

He was frowning, his eyes dark and troubled. "In theory, I suppose," Kell said reluctantly. "There aren't many stories about the Mother Tree beyond what happened at the end of the Demon War."

"What happened?" Lyric asked.

"The Tree sacrificed a branch, not a physical one, but a connection to whatever realm Velaine conceived her demons. At least that's the story they taught at the Radiant Hall."

"To trap her there after the Demon War?" Runa asked. She frowned, thinking of the fallen god, Velaine.

Kell nodded.

"Then perhaps the Mother Tree is powerful enough," Lyric said.

"There's something else," Runa said. "The priest said the ritual is in Velanian."

"Velanian, as in ..." Lyric began.

Kell swore, nearly dumping Lyric over as he bolted upright.

"The demon language!" he said. He twisted, gripping Lyric's arms. "Don't do the ritual, Lyric!"

"Kell, I already told you—"

"They're going to do blood magic," Runa said, drawing Lyric's eyes. "That's what Velanian is."

Lyric opened her mouth then closed it. She chewed distractedly on her lip, pushing off Kell's chest to sit up.

Runa opened her mouth, but Lyric held up a hand. She tilted her head to the side, listening. After a moment, Lyric looked back at her, her green eyes refocusing.

"It's not inherently evil," Lyric said, "that's what Gandara says. It's dangerous, taxing on your body, but with Velaine gone from the world, the risk is different. The demigod can't possess you or exact a price beyond energy loss, exhaustion, and whatever blood is required for the spell. At least that's what Gandara has heard. She never used Velanian herself when she was alive."

Kell groaned and slammed his fist into the pillows. "Do you hear yourself, Ly?" he asked, growling out her name. "Whatever *blood* is required?"

Lyric's eyes narrowed in annoyance. "I didn't say it wasn't dangerous, but what part of this whole situation isn't? We're not the ones performing the ritual. We're not taking on the same danger as Laenadara is, but if the burden were mine and mine alone, I'd still willingly offer myself to save our family, to save you, to save Erith. This doesn't change anything!" Her jaw set stubbornly, and she shifted her heated stare to Runa. "Right?"

Runa shook her head, feeling uneasy. "It does, Ly. Laenadara is withholding information. What else isn't she telling us?"

Lyric scowled, then doubt crept into her eyes, and she nodded. "It is troubling, but if she's taking the danger on herself—"

"Is she?" Kell asked. "I've read about Velanian, Ly. It's unpredictable, chaotic. It was created by Velaine! I tried to find a practitioner once to remove my tattoo." He touched his throat.

"You did?" Lyric asked, eyes wide.

"He couldn't do it, he wasn't strong enough, but there was something wrong with him. He looked ... damaged."

"We should confront her," Runa said. "If Laenadara continues to lie, we'll know we can't trust her. She may be limiting what she tells us because she sees us as children, or—"

"Her reasons for the ritual are not what she claims," Lyric said.

Runa stood up and brushed off her skirt. Walking to the door, she stuck her head through the vines and found a young Ayanaran woman talking to Teaeth.

"Can you fetch the High Priestess?" Runa asked. "We'd like to speak with her."

The girl nodded, her cheeks flushing and dashed off into the trees.

"Finally," Sashala said. "She's been out here flirting with Teaeth. I don't think his head can get any bigger."

Teaeth rolled his eyes, grinning.

Lips quirking, Runa ducked back inside. Lyric and Kell were whispering to each other again, so she sat down by the door and looked at her hands, focusing on a scratch across her knuckles.

When Laenadara arrived, she looked relaxed and happy, her eyes untroubled. "Ashlain told me you'd like to speak with me," she said, voice bright. "We've been preparing for tonight."

"Yes," Runa said, "we have a few questions."

"Yes?"

"The ritual is in Velanian," Runa said. "Isn't that dangerous magic?"

Laenadara's brow twitched, and she laced her hands together. "It can be," she said, "but with Velaine bound and gone, unable to touch our world, the risk is just a physical one.

I'll shield you as much as I'm able. My fellow priests and I will perform the ritual on your behalf. The price will be mine."

"You're wondering how we found out," Runa said, watching Laenadara's face.

"I did not want to burden you with worrying about our safety."

Runa snorted, but by the look on Lyric's face, her sister seemed receptive to Laenadara's explanation.

"There's no need to shield us from the truth," Lyric said. "We want to know the risks."

"I overheard you," Runa said, watching the High Priestess' face.

"Oh?" Laenadara's eyebrow twitched, a tiny flicker of movement.

"You're not certain the Old Ones will listen."

"We do have our concerns," Laenadara said patiently. Her face looked serene; immune to Runa's attempt to get under her skin. "Though the ritual itself is on our shoulders, it is you and Lyric who will speak with the Old Ones. Regrettably, we don't have time to prepare you for such a meeting properly. The dragons may be cautious considering your youth. I didn't want to overwhelm you, so I thought it best if I kept our worries private. I apologize."

"You're concerned they won't listen because we're young?" Runa asked skeptically. That hadn't been what she'd thought Laenadara and the male priest were discussing.

"It's a possibility," Laenadara said. "The Old Ones may be confused about how you summoned them, given your age, but we'll be close by and offer our support. I hope you haven't changed your mind about participating in the ritual. We cannot do it without you, and we must do it tonight."

Runa glanced at her sister. The High Priestess actually seemed sincere. It wouldn't be the first time someone older had thought to shield them. Still, something felt wrong.

Lyric looked at Kell, who was scowling, his eyes focused on Laenadara's face.

"What if you speak to Aya," Laenadara said. "Perhaps She can put your mind at ease."

Surprise flashed across all their faces.

"I thought she only speaks to you?" Runa said.

"I think She'd wish to assure you. She can show you why the ritual is urgent. Share Her visions. Would that ease your minds?"

Lyric blinked, curiosity drawing the doubt from her face. "Yes, yes, that would help."

Curious, but still suspicious, Runa gave a sharp nod. Why hadn't Laenadara suggested this before? Though she had doubts about the High Priestess, surely they could trust the echo of a god?

Laenadara beamed. "Wonderful. If you permit it, I'll have dinner brought to you and baths prepared. You, of course, can give your final decision after you've communed with the Mother, but we will prepare everything, so we are ready to begin the ritual."

"All right," Lyric said. "Is there anything we need to learn? Something we need to do or say during the ritual?"

"If we do it," Runa said under her breath.

"You will not need to speak during the spell," Laenadara said. "Your challenge will be to remain open and to accept the power as it moves through you."

"Have you tried the ritual before?" Runa asked.

Laenadara's eyes snapped back to hers. "What?" the High Priestess asked. She blinked, seeming confused. "No, we have not."

Runa stared at her, uncertain if she was lying. She couldn't read Laenadara, but the priestess actually seemed confused by her question, as if it was something she'd never considered.

Laenadara looked at Kell and frowned. "I'm not sure you

should be present tonight," she said. "Considering what Rakarn did to you, it may be difficult to watch Lyric take part."

Kell looked at Lyric and grabbed her hand. "I won't let you do this alone," he said.

"Is that wise?" Runa asked, watching the tattoo on his neck.

"Is any of this?" Kell shot back.

Laenadara stood up. "I'll ask Ashlain to bring your food."

# 28

---

RUNA

A SIMPLE DINNER was brought to them after Laenadara left, flat-bread covered in green sauce, goat cheese, and fire-roasted vegetables. After sharing the meal in the seclusion of their room, several Ayanaran women came at dusk to take Runa and Lyric to soak in secluded hot springs, while Kell went in search of Eleden and the others.

Attended by the women while they soaked in the warm, blue-green pools, Runa was unnerved by the reverential shine in their eyes. It was like they were all holding their breath, waiting for her and Lyric to do something marvelous. Sharing uncomfortable smiles, Runa and Lyric bathed in silence.

After they'd soaked in the deep water for nearly half an hour, their attendees stepped forward with towels. Runa and Lyric were helped out of the warm pool and dried, then covered in oil that smelled of nuts and flowers. The Ayanarans gave them both gray robes and led them barefoot back to their room where they combed out their hair with wooden combs.

"Is this part of the ritual?" Lyric asked one of the women.

"You must be cleansed before we seek the Mother's blessing," one of them answered.

"Has the Tree ever spoke to you?" Runa asked, wincing as the comb scraped across her scalp.

"Never," the woman said, her voice hushed. "That is an honor for our High Priestess. And what a blessing for you, that you will hear Aya's voice. I wonder what She sounds like?" She flushed as if embarrassed by her words and stepped back, clutching the comb against her chest.

Runa stood and smoothed her hands across the soft robe enfolding her body. They'd left her hair loose around her shoulders, and it felt heavy against her back.

"It's time," a dark-haired woman said, gesturing at the door.

Glancing at Lyric, Runa pushed through the vines.

Laenadara was standing outside with the bearded priest beside her. She'd traded her robe for a black one with a deep hood that she'd pulled over her hair. Two others accompanied the priests — an elderly, white-haired man with unsettling gray eyes, and a middle-aged woman with short, gray curls, and a hooked nose.

To the Ayanarans' left waited Kell. He'd bathed and was wearing green trousers and a long shirt, unlaced at the throat. Beside him stood Eleden, Laerdi, Sashala, and Teaeth, all wearing their familiar Sireni clothes, and still looking ill at ease.

"You're ready?" Laenadara asked, meeting Runa's eyes.

Lyric grabbed Runa's hand, and she felt her sister's nervous pulse beneath her fingers.

"To speak to Aya, yes," Runa said.

Laenadara inclined her head.

Eleden stepped up beside the High Priestess, muscles flexing in his arms, and gave the Ayanarans a challenging look. "We're coming too," he said decisively.

Kell, Laerdi, Sashala, and Teaeth formed around him, looking dangerous despite holding no weapons.

"You may be present, but Aya will only speak to Lyric and

Runa." Laenadara's eyes flicked to Runa. "After, if we begin the ritual, you must not interfere. This is crucial. Once it begins, we cannot stop it. No matter what happens."

Eleden looked at Runa and Lyric. By the expression on his face, Kell had told him their concerns about Laenadara. "Agreed," he said, "but the girls will decide if the ritual begins."

"Of course," Laenadara said. "Now, if you'd follow me?"

Runa, Lyric, and the others followed the Ayanaran priests away from the village. They climbed a steep hill, passing beneath a dense cover of leaves that grew ever more tangled until shadows surrounded them.

Runa felt the skin on her neck prickle, sensing unseen eyes on her back. She tightened her grip on Lyric's hand and for several breaths, all Runa could hear was the thud of her heart in her ears and the ragged pull of air into her lungs.

The foliage lightened, and they stepped inside a large clearing. Bright green moss covered the ground, and pale purple flowers adorned every bush around its edge. In front of them was an enormous tree with large, looping branches that curved up into the leafy ceiling above. Thousands of diamond-shaped leaves covered the tree, the colors ranging from deep green to dark purple.

A woman, plump with a luminous, umber face and large green eyes, smiled beatifically from beside the tree. She was robed like Laenadara and held a staff in her hand. Beside her was Theo, the horned man, grinning as his eyes fell on Runa. He had a bowl in his hands, filled with pearlescent liquid that sloshed dangerously close to its edge as he winked.

Nodding at Theo and the woman, Laenadara knelt in front of the tree and pressed her palms against its dark gray trunk, her fingers splayed on whorls that covered every inch of the uneven wood. "Kneel beside me, please," she said, not looking over her shoulder.

Runa eyed Lyric, and together they knelt on Laenadara's left still holding hands.

The ground felt cool beneath Runa's knees, and she stared at the High Priestess as she closed her eyes. Was that the shape of a face above Laenadara's hands?

"The Mother is pleased by your presence," the High Priestess said, turning her head. "Place your hands on Her like this."

Anticipation fluttering inside her stomach, Runa pressed her hand against the tree. The bark felt rough and warm against her skin. Swallowing, she prepared to listen to the Ayanarans' god.

*Aya?* she thought.

Nothing happened.

Runa looked at Lyric who gave a small shrug, her brows knotted over her eyes.

"I don't hear anything," Runa said, looking at Laenadara.

The High Priestess seemed confused and looked at the tree, flattening her fingers against it. The consternation grew on her face. Swallowing, Laenadara glanced back at the other priests.

The woman with the staff frowned down at Theo, who returned her gaze with confusion. He shrugged, nearly spilling the liquid again.

Suspicion narrowed Runa's eyes. Had Laenadara lied? Why did she look so shaken? From the looks passing between the Ayanarans, they'd expected their Tree to speak.

Dropping her hands, Laenadara stood, her face smoothing out, unreadable. "I apologize, but it seems the Mother has been called away."

Runa stood up. She glanced at Eleden, who was frowning and watching the trees.

"The agreement was we'd speak with Aya," Runa said.

"I'm afraid that's not possible," Laenadara said. "I regret I cannot soothe all your worries, but we must continue. What

I've told you is true, the dragons are the only way to save Erith before the Taint destroys Her. We cannot wait another year."

"No," Runa said. "If you've lied about your Tree—"

"I have not lied," Laenadara snapped, her calm shattering. Anger filled her face, and her eyes blazed. "We will continue. I won't let arrogant *children* decide if our world dies. Take them!"

Whirling, Runa saw green-clad archers step out from the trees, bows drawn and pointed at her and Lyric.

She raised her hand, sparks sizzling between her fingers, but Lyric caught her wrist. "No!" her sister gasped.

Runa hissed, following Lyric's gaze. Kell, Eleden, and the other Sireni were on their knees with arrows pointed at their heads. Laerdi, eyes furious, had a hand to his forehead, blood dripping between his fingers.

"I thought you need our consent, freely given," Lyric said, voice shaking.

Laenadara looked composed again, confident, superior. "And you will give it," she said, "or your companions will die."

Lyric's eyes filled with panic and she looked at Kell.

His face was stricken, his body leaning towards her as if he wanted to grab Lyric and run.

"I don't know if—" Theo began.

Laenadara silenced him with a look, and Theo looked uncomfortably down at his hands.

"I regret force is required," Laenadara said. "We truly wished to be allies and thought you would see the importance of what we're doing. I know how this seems, but the ritual is too important. It's a harsh truth, but your lives mean nothing compared to the millions of souls the Taint will kill. It's time." She gestured at an opening in the trees.

Runa looked at the other priests. There was no hesitation in their eyes. They didn't care what Laenadara was doing or seem concerned about her murderous threat. Whatever surprise they'd felt when Aya had not spoken had been swallowed by utter devotion to their High Priestess.

"What do we do," Lyric whispered, clutching Runa's hand.

Runa was angry, angry enough to set the forest on fire, to burn that confident smile off Laenadara's face, but what then? Was she lying about the Taint?

"Do you think she's lying?" Runa hissed. "Do you think the Taint has spread?"

"I think it has," Lyric whispered. "She believes what she's told us. They all do."

Runa bared her teeth, glaring. As much as she hated the High Priestess, she couldn't see another way to save their father, their world, or even Lyric beside her.

"Then we continue," Runa said. "Better that than dying here."

Watched closely by the bow-holding Ayanarans, Runa and Lyric followed Laenadara and her priests back into the thick forest. They walked for several minutes, climbing up until another large clearing opened ahead of them, exposed to the darkening sky. Lit torches created a circle several steps in from the field's edge, and in the center, someone had raked a small circle of black sand. Around the sand sat four earthen bowls.

Eleden, Kell, Laerdi, Sashala, and Teaeth were forced to stand in a line outside the torches, each watched by a green-clad archer. The rest of the archers fanned out to encircle the clearing, their bows ready and their eyes on Runa and Lyric.

"Walk onto the circle of sand," Laenadara said. She was no longer asking nicely, merely giving commands she expected them to obey.

Runa's fingers itched, and she had to swallow the desire to call fire, to fight, to flee. Instead, she walked with Lyric towards the black sand.

Behind them, Laenadara and her priests stepped inside the ring of torches.

"Are you sure about this?" Runa asked, her voice low. "We could still run. Figure something else out."

Lyric eyed the archers then looked at Kell.

Runa followed her gaze and saw that Kell's face was a tormented mask. He stood at Eleden's side, as tension-filled as a taut bowstring, and for a moment she thought he might dash across the clearing, priests, and archers be damned.

"I don't think that's an option anymore," Lyric said quietly. "I pray this isn't a mistake. That I haven't misread her." She glowered at the High Priestess. "Not that we have another choice. We can't fight it. For Erith's sake, for Mother, for Father."

Gritting her teeth, Runa nodded. She eyed the bowls as they passed and saw that one held a collection of sticks and dried moss, another water, the third dirt, and in the fourth was a flute.

When they stepped onto the sand, Runa glanced down in surprise. It felt silky beneath her feet. Gripping each others' hands, Runa and Lyric faced each other as the priests formed a circle around them. The priests picked up the bowls, Laenadara choosing the one with sticks and moss.

"Aya, Great Mother, we call upon your guidance," Laenadara said, her voice loud and firm. "Walk with us this evening. Know our hearts are pure, our purpose true. I call upon fire." Fire flared in the bowl in her hands, the sticks and moss catching alight. "Let it illuminate that which is hidden."

Runa's skin tingled as she felt Laenadara's magic permeate the air. She frowned. She hadn't known she was a mage. How had Laenadara called fire without speaking a single rune word?

"I call upon water," the bearded priest said. The water hissed in his bowl, steam rising from its surface and flicking little drops of water into the air. "Let it cleanse that which is clouded."

The gray-haired woman raised her bowl of dirt. "I call upon earth," she said. "For it is to which we shall all return."

"Is this the ritual Grandfather did?" Lyric whispered. "What does this have to do with the Old Ones?"

"I call upon air," the gray-eyed man said. He lifted the flute and played four short, haunting notes that lingered in the air. "May it fill our ears and dispel lies."

"I don't know," Runa said, watching as the priests set down their bowls. "The dragons are tied to the elements."

A light breeze had picked up, and it tugged on her hair. The torches flickered and sputtered. Runa glanced at Kell and the Sireni, clumped together outside the torch line.

The priests raised their arms out to each side, fingers splayed and stretching towards each other. They began to speak in an unfamiliar language. It sounded similar to the dragon runes Elenora had taught her, but the dialect seemed smoother and oilier, less harsh and guttural and more seductive. Runa's skin tingled, simultaneously feeling too hot and cold. Sweat trickled down the small of her back.

The wind picked up speed, and Runa gasped as it became a solid, rushing thing that whipped around them in a circle, spinning and separating into visible threads of air. It distorted the faces of the chanting priests and Kell and the Sireni beyond.

"Ru," Lyric said, her voice shaky.

Runa locked her fingers around Lyric's, meeting her wide, scared eyes. "Something's wrong," she said, staring at her sister. Something terrible was going to happen. She could feel it.

Icy cold bit her fingers and Runa yelped as Lyric tore away from her, hand slipping from her grasp. She gaped as her sister was lifted off the ground, caught in a column of churning water. Lyric thrashed, her hair floating around her head, mouth gaping. Her eyes were boring into Runa's with unrestrained terror. She was going to drown.

Screaming, Runa dashed forward, intending to grab her sister and pull her free from the water. She reached out, then screamed as her arm caught fire. Pain exploded over her body, and Runa disappeared into a maelstrom of fire. She was burning, her body awash in searing flames. It crackled and roared. She couldn't see anything but red-gold fire. Runa screamed again or tried to, but there was no air in her lungs. *I'm going to die!* she thought.

Panicked, Runa flailed her arms, trying to run, but she couldn't move. Was she still standing on the ground or caught in the air like Lyric?

*You're not going to die, stupid girl!* Elenora's voice, spiteful, disapproving, thundered in her head, shoving aside the blinding pain. *Did you think this would be easy? What an arrogant, foolish child! You are fire! Raendasharan! You're descended from the Three! Take control of it now!*

*I don't know how!* Runa screamed. Her skin was burning, peeling away, exposing her bones. Her blood was boiling. Soon she'd be nothing! Soon she'd be—

*It is part of you, or it is not!* Elenora shifted, and it felt like she'd pressed her fingernails into Runa's brain, the uncomfortable sensation momentarily displacing the pain consuming her. *Maybe you will die,* Elenora sneered. *Maybe you're weak, like your grandfather. Like your mother.*

Elenora's presence pushed against her, her displeasure a solid, comforting thing, and Runa grabbed it, onto the feeling of her and her words. Runa would *not* die with Elenora watching her, waiting for her to fail. She would not give her that satisfaction!

*I am fire,* Runa thought, trying to shove aside the panic, the pain. *I am fire!* The fire could not hurt her. She *was* fire. She had the blood of dragons inside her. She was Runa. She could not be burned. She *would* not be burned or die at the hands of Ayanaran priests. She would not let them kill Lyric.

Lyric!

Rage seared away the panic, building, and rising with

familiar strength. Runa was furious with Laenadara, with herself for trusting her. She'd hurt them! She would—

Runa realized she no longer felt pain. She could see again. Blinking, she stared at the flames covering her arm. They were not burning her skin but dancing across it like light upon paper.

Runa willed the flames to go out, and they disappeared, winking from existence as if they'd never been. Her skin was smooth, unmarred, and she stared at her hand in wonder, flexing her fingers. She hadn't imagined the pain, the burning, yet she was unharmed.

Lyric.

Runa jerked her head up, frantically searching for her sister. Had she drowned? Was Lyric dead?

## 29

LYRIC

LYRIC GASPED air into her lungs as the water released her, and she fell on the ground. She pressed her fingers into the damp sand, shuddering, and breathed in again. Her throat felt raw, her chest tight. The water dried off her skin as if something were sucking it away. She felt her hair dry, impossibly fast, and it floated around her head before settling down her back and shoulders.

Shoving herself to her feet, Lyric swayed. Her sister, where was her sister? Looking straight ahead, she met Runa's raging eyes; they were glowing, actually glowing, with red-orange light. And there, hovering behind her sister's shoulder was a small, red dragon covered in scales and spikes.

Lyric yelped, pointing a finger at the apparition, just as Runa, eyes flaring, pointed past her shoulder. "What is that!" they said at once.

Lyric jerked her head to the side, looking back, and saw a small, blue dragon floating behind her. It was sleeker than the one by her sister, with leafy wings that looked like the seaweed from their first night on the beach. As it floated there, Lyric realized it wasn't solid. There was a ghostly quality to it, its body shimmering, allowing her to see the ground and trees behind it. Its gold eyes were staring at her with disconcerting familiarity.

*Hello*, a small, unfamiliar voice said in her head. Unlike Gandara, the voice was composed of images and sensations. When it spoke, she saw a massive wave rolling onto a shimmering, white sand beach, and another image of a large, scaled creature swimming through a pink cloud of hundreds of bell-shaped animals, their translucent bodies rippling like long sheets of fabric.

*Gandara?* Lyric called uncertainly. She listened, but Gandara didn't respond. Lyric didn't feel any connection to her at all. Her mind felt clear and unburdened.

*What are you?* she thought at the creature.

*I'm your guardian*, the dragon said. It shifted in the air, wings rippling as if underwater. *I'm a wyvern, or at least I'm taking the shape of one. You summoned me.* It shifted again, turning its head to stare through the spinning threads of wind that still trapped Lyric and Runa on the sand.

*I summoned you?* Lyric asked in confusion.

*Do you require protection?* the wyvern asked, staring in the direction of the priests. *Someone is casting.*

"Protection?" Lyric asked aloud. She thought back mere seconds ago to when she'd thought she was going to die and put a hand to her cheek. "No ... no, I'm part of the ritual." She looked at Runa, several paces away, who was staring at the red wyvern.

Lyric squinted, staring at her sister. Runa looked different like there was light trapped beneath her skin. What had happened to her while Lyric drowned? Had Runa been caught in water too?

Lowering her hand, Lyric stared at it and flexed her fingers. She felt stronger, more alive as if she'd been charged with energy. Had Laenadara known this would happen? Was this some effect of calling power through her and Runa to summon the Old Ones?

But why had she nearly drowned? Why had the water come at all? Because Lyric was Sireni? What would have happened if she hadn't accepted she could breathe water? That it couldn't hurt her? Gandara had been yelling something at her, telling her to breathe and ...

*Gandara?* Lyric asked again.

*Who?* the wyvern asked.

Pain rippled across Lyric's palm, as her skin split in a neat line, spilling blood onto the black sand. She yelped, pulling her hand against her chest.

The wyvern roared inside her head, whirling towards the priests. Something shot away from the creature and shattered against the spinning strands of air, bits of ice and water spraying upward.

An arrow of fire shot towards the same point from Runa's direction, exploding right behind whatever Lyric's wyvern had spat towards the priests.

Lyric looked at her sister and saw Runa crouched, hand raised, as if unsure who to attack. Blood dripped from her palm onto the sand. She was enraged, her eyes glowing red. Her lips started moving, flames flickering across her fingers.

"Ru!" Lyric screamed. "We can't fight it! The ritual!"

Runa's eyes snapped towards her, and she faltered, the fire dying on her hand. The wyvern beside her spun and spat, shaking its head as if confused.

"Stop," Lyric said, turning back to the blue wyvern. "Don't attack!"

*They hurt you!* the wyvern said, sounding confused.

Lyric could hear the priests now, the sound of their voices rising to a commanding yell. She couldn't understand their words. She cradled her hand against her chest and tried to see through the spinning wind. Was that Leanadara, with her hand upraised? Did she have a knife?

Pressure gathered in Lyric's chest, and she gasped as power rushed through her. It felt like a damned river had been unleashed, sending a torrent of energy ripping through her body. She staggered, and the wyvern wheeled towards her, flapping its wings uncertainly as it stared at her face.

Lyric's skin felt thin, too thin, and she wondered if her body would rip apart from the strain of holding the magic inside. Water beaded across the tops of her feet, and the air around her rippled, distorting.

She clutched her head, droplets of water spinning around her, growing larger, becoming ribbons. Wind ruffled the hem of her robe, pressing it against her ankles, then the air rushed up her body, lifting her hair around her head.

Everything exploded. The pressure, the energy inside Lyric's chest, blasted outward in a rush, filling the air with a thunderclap of sound. Water sprayed away from her, hissing as it dissipated and collided with intense heat from Runa's direction. The sand was blown away beneath Lyric's feet, and the spinning wind ripped apart, tossing the priests to the ground.

As one, the torches snuffed out, plunging the clearing into darkness. The first line of trees exploded, filling the air with fragments of wood and torn leaves.

Eyes wide, Lyric searched for Kell. Had he been hit? Where was he? Was that him, lying in the dirt?

A light broke the darkness to her left, and Lyric turned her head. Runa's wyvern was emitting a pale red glow as it hovered in the air over her sister's shoulder.

"Kell?" Lyric called, looking back towards where she'd last seen him with Eleden and the other Sireni.

"What was that?" Runa asked, coming towards her. Her hand was shaking as she reached towards her face.

"I don't know," Lyric said. She caught sight of Kell struggling to his feet. She took a step towards him, intending to rush into his arms.

The ground shook, bucking violently. Lyric gasped and fell onto her knees. Runa crawled towards her, reaching out, and Lyric grabbed her sister's hand. She could feel the tiny prick of claws as the blue wyvern grabbed her shoulder. The earth rumbled, and the ground split between them and the stunned priests, dirt cascading into the opened fissure.

"Ly! Look!" Runa gasped, neck craned upwards.

Lyric looked up. Color filled the night sky, rippling ribbons of purple, green, and red. The dazzling lights wavered, then the colors disappeared, and darkness returned. The sky looked wrong. Where were the stars? Something was blocking their light. Something huge. It was coming towards them.

"Get up!" Laenadara yelled. "Face them on your feet!"

Lyric whipped her head towards the priests and saw Laenadara standing and staring up into the sky. She was wounded, blood smeared across her cheek. She held a dagger.

"Get up, Ly!" Runa said, hauling on her hand.

Standing, Lyric stared upwards, her mouth falling open, as four massive dragons slowed above them. The dragons' wings stirred the air into little eddies that tugged on her hair and robes. Her wyvern buzzed around her, its chest puffing like it was a smaller bird valiantly trying to scare off one much larger.

Lyric felt impossibly small beneath the weighty presence of the dragons' eyes. It was an effort to remain standing with a straight back, and if Runa hadn't been beside her, defiantly staring up at the Old Ones, she would have cowered on the ground.

"We need your help!" Runa yelled. Her voice was fierce and determined. "Erith is dying!"

The eyes continued to watch them, and one of the dragons, its color unknown in the darkness, opened its mouth, releasing a burst of mesmerizing blue flame. In the blinding flash of light, everything disappeared.

Lyric squeezed Runa's fingers as blindness overtook her, clinging on for dear life.

"Ow, Ly!" Runa hissed, attempting to wrench her hand free.

Lyric loosened her grip but didn't let go, blinking furiously until her eyes refocused on her sister's pained face, and the hissing red wyvern.

They were standing in ... nothingness, the world replaced with pale gray mist. There was no visible floor beneath Lyric's feet, but it didn't feel like she was floating either. What was below them, holding them up? Were they back in the Veil? Inside a cloud? Or was this another in-between place, suspended between the living world and the Veil?

Lyric could still feel eyes on her. Looking up, she saw four dragons, gliding high above with wings outstretched. One dragon was pale white, like snow; another deep black, the color of obsidian; and the third dragon a brilliant scarlet. The fourth was blue and unbelievably long, with flowing tendrils curving back from its long head and fins like a gigantic water serpent. The others looked like she'd imagined, all scales and teeth, with horns and long, spiked tails.

The dragons circled, watching, the blue dragon hissing at the others, and then, just as suddenly as their arrival in this place, they were gone. Four figures appeared in front of Lyric and Runa, tall but not overly so. They seemed to be human, but she knew they were not. There was something feral in their eyes and the way they held themselves. Something ancient.

In the center stood a woman with long, white hair and impossibly blue eyes. She was beautiful, with a pale, narrow face and thin arms. A shimmering white dress, seemingly made from diamonds of ice, draped her slender frame.

To her left, was a man with dark red hair and dangerous, golden eyes. His face was strong, imperial, and his unamused stare made Runa's glare look petulant and childish. His skin was the color of heated copper.

On the woman's right, was another woman, taller and muscular, like a warrior, with dark, umber skin and short, black hair. Her eyes were gold, like the man's, but a darker, deeper color. Her dress was a mixture of white, brown and black, like a beautiful stone with gemstone veins running through it.

Slightly off to the side, standing well away from the other three, was a curvaceous woman with pale blue hair and wide-set eyes that, when they briefly crossed over Lyric's face, seemed to shift between green and blue like an ocean storm. The woman glared at the other Old Ones, an expression of pure venom contorting her heart-shaped face. "No," she said, and promptly disappeared.

The white-haired woman sighed, a weary sound that swept from her lungs like a winter wind through the mountains, and turned her piercing eyes on Lyric and Runa.

Lyric's wyvern shifted uneasily beside her, its eyes tracking the movements of the remaining three dragons.

*Are you in danger?* the wyvern asked inside her head.

Lyric didn't respond, staring at the legendary figures in front of her. The white-haired woman had to be Aery, and the muscular woman in black was likely Rath. That meant that the man with red hair and golden eyes was Fyre.

"Who summoned us?" Aery asked. She blinked, a slow, dispassionate movement like someone still waking from deep sleep.

"We did," Runa blurted, her fingers tight on Lyric's hand.

Lyric searched for her sister's emotions, the shared nervousness and awe Runa must also be feeling, but she felt nothing. Ever since Runa's separation from her body, their connection had been muted, unreliable. Lyric still wasn't used to it. And now that Gandara was gone, she felt unusually hollow.

*Are you well?* the wyvern asked inside her head.

Lyric blinked. Well, not entirely hollow. Warmth trickled through Lyric's chest outward, moving through her arms and legs. Her fingers tingled. Was the wyvern sending her energy?

*Focus,* Lyric reminded herself. Runa was introducing them.

"You are ours," Rath, the woman in black, said. Her eyes were unnerving and dangerous. "And ..." Her nostrils flared as if she was scenting the air. "You are also of Serith."

Fyre curled his lip in disgust. "She abandons us again," he said. "Did you notice?"

"Erith is dying," Lyric said. Her mouth dried as all three dragons stared at her, their eyes ancient and knowing. She felt completely naked, stripped bare of everything but the bones beneath her skin. Could they see her heart beating in her chest? Could they hear it?

"Dying?" Aery asked. She frowned, and her eyes lost focus as if she could see something beyond them in the mist.

Rath crouched down and pressed a hand against the nothingness beneath their feet. "The Taint," she said. Her voice was grim, concerned.

"It's back?" Fyre asked, eyes widening with alarm. "How? We trapped her!" He whirled, his hands clenching, and bared his teeth at Lyric and Runa. "Did you release her? Foolish children! Did she seduce you with promises of power? Of eternal youth? I should strip the flesh from your bones! I should—"

"Calm, Fyre," Aery said, putting a hand on his arm.

Lyric swallowed; her heart had stopped beating.

The white dragon shifted her gaze to Lyric, and the tense wyvern beside her. "Soothe your guardians," she said. "We won't harm you."

Lyric glanced sideways and saw blue light glowing along the wyvern's mouth. She looked at Runa and saw flickers of flame flaring up along the red wyvern's clenched jaw.

*Calm,* Lyric thought, hoping the wyvern couldn't feel the terror inside her. *Don't attack.*

It glanced at her, gold eyes uncertain, then settled atop her shoulder like a heavy bird. Lyric's anxiety retreated somewhat as its tail curled loosely around her throat.

"How did the Taint return to Erith?" Aery asked.

Lyric exchanged a look with Runa, both frowning in confusion. "Return? All we know is it was released when someone attempted to summon you before, thirteen years ago."

Rath, standing back up, exchanged a look with Fyre. "Someone attempted to summon us before?"

"King Rakarn of Raendashar," Runa said. "He wanted to control you, use you in his war against the Sireni."

Aery looked sad and regretful. "They fell to war then. The Council disbanded?"

"What other outcome could there be?" Fyre barked. "After what Serith did ..."

"Yes," Lyric said, looking between Aery and Fyre. "It disbanded centuries ago. We wish to stop the war too, but—"

"But that's not why we called you back," Runa interrupted. "When the ritual failed, it destroyed the cities of Thenda, poisoning the land and the Sea of Screams. We thought it contained, but the Mother Tree in Ayanar told them it's been spreading underground for years."

"Aya?" Fyre asked. He frowned and arched a thick brow.

"Whatever the Taint touches dies or becomes corrupted and twisted," Lyric said. "If left free—"

"Yes," Aery said. "We know the destruction it can cause. It is good you summoned us. Perhaps it is not too late."

"Your fire can destroy it, right?" Runa asked. "Stop it from spreading?"

Aery inclined her head.

Relief flooded through Lyric, and she squeezed her sister's hand. The Old Ones would save them; they'd save their father, save Mama. They could remove Kell's silence, give him back his memories. They could end the war!

"We need to examine where it was released," Aery contin-ued, "determine if—" She cut off, frowning. "Something's wrong," she said.

"What are they doing?" Fyre demanded, his fingers rising to brace his skull.

Rath spun, her fingers elongating into sharp claws. "Who is—"

Aery roared, throwing her head back, the sound dangerous and angry, ripping from her throat in tones no human could make. White flames shot from her mouth, rushing upwards impossibly high and burning a path through the mist.

Fyre and Rath roared with her, writhing as though some-thing crawled beneath their skin. Their eyes glowed wild, animalistic. There was nothing rational in their eyes, no enlightened understanding.

Gasping, Lyric grabbed Runa's arm as Rath screamed and scratched long furrows in her own cheeks.

The blue wyvern, roaring beside Lyric's ear, gripped her shoulder hard enough that its claws pierced her skin. Lyric could feel power building in its body, and corresponding pres-sure in her chest.

Runa pulled away from her.

The dragons leaped upwards, their bodies changing, growing impossibly large as they clawing up into the sky, their human shapes abandoned. Fire blasted from their mouths.

"What's going on?" Lyric yelled, turning towards her sister. She staggered; it felt like she was moving, shifting sideways.

The mist vanished, the clearing popping back into view. Trees burned to her left, lighting the night, and screams filled the air.

Lyric gasped as pain exploded in her head. She reeled, reaching shaking fingers to her skull. The pain fled, almost instantly, and she blinked tears from her eyes, focusing on Runa.

Her sister's wyvern shrieked, back arching, and then it focused its eyes on Lyric. Fire shot from its mouth.

"No!" Runa screamed, her hand flying out.

Lyric shrieked, falling backward as a burning bolt rushed straight towards her.

*Danger!* her wyvern screeched inside her head. It spun and something curved out in front of Lyric glittering as the fiery arrow exploded across it.

Lowering her arm, Lyric stared at the shield with wide eyes as it flickered and died, red spiderwebs of color crackling across its surface as both faded away. It'd absorbed the fire from Runa's wyvern.

"It tried to kill me!" Lyric yelled.

*She's compromised! I'll protect you*, the blue wyvern said.

"What?" Lyric turned and saw her wyvern erupt with blue light. "No!"

An arrow of water shot away from it, aimed at Runa.

Runa yelped and dove sideways, her wyvern throwing up a shield and deflecting the attack away from her.

"Lyric, stop!" Eleden yelled, his voice loud and commanding from somewhere to Lyric's right.

Sashala appeared beside her, running out of the darkness, her hand clamping onto Lyric's wrist and wrenching her hand sideways.

"It's not me!" Lyric gasped, twisting in her grip, trying to put herself between her wyvern and Runa.

*Danger!* the wyvern shrieked inside her mind.

"Stop it! Stop attacking!" Lyric yelled. She could feel a connection to the wyvern, a tether of power inside her chest, but when she tried to grab it, it slipped away from her.

She turned wild eyes to Sashala, who stared at her with grim confusion. "Get me out of here!" Lyric yelled, pulling the Sireni woman towards the trees. "I can't stop it!"

Without a word, Sashala yanked on Lyric's arm and sprinted into the forest.

Towed along, Lyric ran after her, ignoring the pain in her feet as she dashed across rocks and twigs. She looked behind her and saw the blue wyvern flying after her, its head moving between Runa in the clearing and Lyric.

Eleden and Laerdi moved in front of Runa, blocking her from Lyric's view.

Stumbling, Lyric nearly fell over a green-clad body on the ground, as Sashala yanked her around it. "What happened?" Lyric gasped, as they fled into the trees. "The dead!"

"The dragons," Sashala yelled over her shoulder.

"Where's Kell?" Lyric asked, sudden panic surging through her. "Where's—"

Kell ran at her from the left, intersecting with their path as he jumped around a fallen tree. He was breathing hard, his face and clothes dirty and covered in sweat and blood.

Lyric stopped abruptly and was almost yanked off her feet by Sashala who was still running.

The Sireni woman stopped, letting go of Lyric's arm as she saw what had caught her attention.

Tears sprang into Lyric's eyes, relief flooding into her, as Kell grabbed her. He wrapped his arms around her and pressed his face against the top of her head. Head against his chest, Lyric could hear his breath, fast and ragged, and the cadence of his heart beneath her ear.

"You're alive," Kell breathed.

"We're far enough away now, I think," Sashala said. "Your ... dragon isn't attacking anymore."

Lyric pulled back from Kell, remaining in his arms, and looked back at the blue wyvern.

It was no longer glowing and had landed on a stump nearby, staring at Kell, unblinking. Blessedly it only seemed curious, if that was the right emotion.

"A ... friend," Lyric told it.

Kell made a surprised noise. "Is that a dragon?" he asked.

"It's a wyvern," Lyric said.

"Where did it come from? Is it ... one of the Old Ones?" Kell asked. "Seems rather small ..."

An amused sensation filled Lyric's head, and she realized the wyvern had sent it.

"It's protecting her," Sashala said, "or thinks it is. Why is it attacking Runa and not us?"

Lyric frowned and studied the wyvern with a worried expression. "I don't know. Why did you attack my sister?"

*She's corrupted.*

"No, she's not!" Lyric said.

"Is it ... speaking to you?" Kell asked uncertainly.

"Yes," Lyric said.

"What did it say?" Sashala asked. She stepped closer, eyeing the wyvern warily.

"It said Runa's corrupted. I don't understand."

*She's dangerous.*

"Not to me," Lyric said.

"Did Laenadara do this?" Kell asked. "Some consequence of the ritual?"

"I don't know, but I intend to ask her." Lyric narrowed her eyes. What had happened with the ritual? The dragons had been ready to help, and then they'd changed. Was it something the priests had done? Or had someone else interfered?

"You can't," Sashala said.

Lyric blinked and looked at her, her anger faltering as confusion took over. "Why not?"

"The dragon, the red one, killed her," Sashala said.

"Oh." Numbly, Lyric glanced back towards the clearing, hidden by the trees. She could see smoke in the distance.

"What happened?" Kell asked. "You disappeared, and Laenadara and the other priests kept chanting. Then she sliced open her wrist, and there was blood everywhere. We tried to move forward, but the archers stopped us. I didn't know where you were, I was yelling, Laenadara was screaming at the sky, and then the dragons came back. They ripped into the priests, killed some of the archers, set fire to the forest. They were enraged, wild. We didn't know what to do, and then you just reappeared and—"

"Attacked each other," Sashala said.

"Not us," Lyric said, looking at the wyvern. "The wyverns. They must both think we're dangerous to each other. I don't understand."

*You may call me Azora*, the wyvern said in her mind.

Lyric blinked. Azora?

"What did you see?" Kell asked. "When you disappeared? Were you with the Old Ones?"

"Yes," Lyric said, looking back at him, "but they were human, became human. They talked to us."

"It must not have gone well," Sashala said.

"No, no it was," Lyric said. "They were going to help us and cleanse the Taint, but then something happened. They said something was wrong, and then they became beasts, turned back into their dragon forms."

"The priests," Sashala said, "whatever they did after you disappeared."

"But why?" Lyric asked. "Why would they want the ritual to fail? It doesn't make sense. The dragons turning savage, how does that help them? And the dragons attacked them and set fire to the forest."

"Maybe they didn't realize how dangerous the ritual was," Kell said, his voice tight.

"Perhaps they wanted to control them, like the Butcher," Sashala said, spitting on the ground.

"Did any of the priests survive?" Lyric asked. "We should question one who performed the ritual with Laenadara."

Sashala glanced back towards the clearing. "I can go and see who is left. The dragons flew off, heading east, so it should be safe enough." She eyed the wyvern and looked at Lyric. "You should wait here."

"The dragons ..." Lyric said. She glanced around them with a worried expression. "What do you think they'll do?"

Kell's arms tightened around her, and Lyric leaned against him. "Nothing good," he said grimly.

# 30

---

RUNA

RUNA SAT ON THE GROUND. Her wyvern, Raith, was sitting beside her and watching the tree line. She'd demanded to know why they'd attacked Lyric, but the damned creature kept repeating that her twin sister was compromised and dangerous. When pressed, they couldn't tell her why. When Runa insisted Lyric was safe, and Raith had to trust her, the wyvern maintained it had to protect her, even if that meant protecting her from herself.

Eleden, pacing in front of her, scrubbed his hand through his hair and gave Runa a worried look out of the corner of his eye. He'd sent Laerdi and Teaeth to get Egan from the pit, worried the Ayanarans had abandoned him when the dragons attacked.

Before the dragons had flown east, they'd set fire to a swath of trees leading away from the clearing. From the smoke in the sky, the forest was currently burning northward in the direction of Runa's father and the village. It should have been too wet for the dragon fire to advance, but it burned through the trees like they were nothing more than dried sticks.

Though worried for his brother, Eleden had insisted on

staying with Runa, presumably to guard her. The Ayanarans who'd survived had all fled, perhaps to check on the Mother Tree, and Runa and the Sireni were the only ones left in the bloodied clearing.

"I'm fine," Runa said, though she didn't feel it. She'd been reaching out to Elenora ever since Sashala dragged Lyric into the trees, but her ancestor hadn't responded. Runa couldn't feel her grating presence at all, as if their connection had been severed.

"Did you do something to her?" Runa asked, looking at Raith.

"What?" Eleden asked, pausing.

"Not you," Runa said.

*To who?* Raith asked.

*Elenora*, Runa said. It was probably better if she stopped speaking aloud when Eleden couldn't hear the other half of the conversation.

*I don't know that person*, Raith said.

*She was in my mind. She talked to me.*

*Your mind is safe*, Raith said. *I'm protecting you.*

Runa frowned. *Are you preventing her from speaking to me? You've severed our connection?*

*I've shielded your mind from psychic attacks*, Raith said. The wyvern looked back at the trees.

"Sashala," Eleden said.

Runa looked up and saw Sashala jogging towards them. She stood up, brushing off her skirt. Raith leaped off the ground and hovered near her shoulder, watching as the Sireni woman approached. Runa eyed the wyvern warily, but they didn't give any indication that they were about to attack.

"Lyric?" Eleden asked as Sashala ran up to them.

"Safe," Sashala said. Her dark eyes brushed over Runa's face. "Her wyvern only seems to respond to Runa now that the priests are gone."

"Laenadara," Runa growled. "She did this." She looked over at Laenadara's body. Eleden told her Fyre had nearly bitten the High Priestess in half when she'd yelled at him, waving her dagger and screaming Velanian. Whatever she'd been trying to do hadn't worked, unless she'd wanted to die.

Why had Laenadara summoned the wyverns, the guardians, for Runa and Lyric? Had she hoped to keep them apart or get them to kill each other? But why? None of it made any sense. They'd successfully summoned the Old Ones, and they'd wanted to help.

"I don't understand," Eleden said, echoing her thoughts. "The Ayanarans aren't killers."

"They did threaten to kill you," Runa said.

Eleden shook his head. "Why would they destroy themselves? Why would they summon the dragons only to unleash them upon the world?" His face was grim, as he looked east.

"What will they do? The dragons?" Runa asked.

"What any animal feeling attacked would do," Eleden said. "Attack or flee. When they perceive the threat has passed, they'll likely feed or nest. Probably both."

"And if their rage doesn't falter? If they continue to feel the need to destroy?"

"Then the fires in Ayanar will be the first of many. Can you imagine what one of them could do to a city? To Corsicayna or Fabria? What if they burn the fields? Destroy all the crops? Winter will be here soon." Eleden looked at Sashala. "We must send word to the Gale," he said. "Warn them about the dragons."

"Serith was there," Runa said, picturing the blue dragon in her mind.

Eleden looked at her. "You saw Her?" he asked, awe in his voice.

Runa nodded. "She left as soon as she saw the Three. She

didn't speak to us. Where did she go, do you think? Was she affected like the others? Maybe she's safe because she left?"

"We must get home," Eleden said. "If Sae'shara has awakened ..." He turned, staring towards the trees and rubbed a hand over his jaw. "Sashala, take Lyric and Kell to the Talan. Hopefully the dragons left her alone. Return home, as fast as the winds allow. Tell Hali she must be swift. I'll wait with Runa until Laerdi and Teaeth return with Egan. We'll fly with Kaia aboard the Skybird. Perhaps the Gale will know what to do with the wyverns. How to fix the girls' magic."

"And if the Skybird was destroyed?" Sashala asked.

"We'll figure it out then," Eleden said. He looked at Runa, who nodded slowly.

"It seems we'll all be safer if Lyric and I stay separated for now," Runa said, "until we figure out what's going on and why our guardians think we're dangerous to each other. If the wyverns are part of Laenadara's spell, then perhaps they can be ... turned off or ..."

Raith looked at her, and Runa's loneliness whispered from the back of her mind. She was surprised that she feared the wyvern disappearing. They'd been together less than an hour, and yet the idea of being alone again bothered her.

The wyvern landed on her shoulder, their claws tugging at her robe. Runa reached up and stroked her fingers over their spine. Despite being able to see through the wyvern's body, they felt remarkably robust, the scales rough against her skin.

"Yes, Captain," Sashala said. She gave Eleden an inscrutable look then jogged back towards the trees.

"We'll leave as soon as Laerdi and Teaeth return with Egan," Eleden said.

"Will we be safe in the airship?" Runa asked, looking up into the dark sky. "The dragons are out there somewhere."

"The night should offer some protection," Eleden said,

following her gaze. "We'll have to risk it. The Skybird will be faster than the Talan, as we can fly across the land."

"And you think Kaia will take us?"

"It's what she was ordered to do," Eleden said.

"Maybe she already left, once she saw the dragons."

"No," Eleden said.

Raith's head turned to the side, and Runa followed their gaze.

Kaia was striding towards them with several Sireni at her back. Her face was a mask of fury as her eyes fell on Runa.

"What madness have you unleashed?" Kaia roared.

Raith began to glow, a dark, menacing red, and they lifted off Runa's shoulder.

"Careful, Kaia," Eleden called, holding up a hand.

Kaia slowed, her eyes snapping to the wyvern. She continued walking towards them, some of the threat leaving her body. "Why are dragons in the sky?" Her voice was muted, but no less demanding.

Runa stroked Raith's back, feeling a knot of tension between her own shoulders. *No threat*, she thought.

"The Skybird?" Eleden asked.

"Is safe," Kaia said. "We're still tethered near the beach." Her eyes took in the devastation, pausing on the bodies of Laenadara and another Ayanaran. "You said you were communing with their tree."

"We summoned the Old Ones to destroy the Taint," Runa said.

Kaia frowned at her. "The Taint," she repeated. "It's bound to the Shore. Why call the dragons now? Why risk ... this?" She gestured at the bodies. "You were ordered to leave it alone."

"It's spreading," Eleden said, "beneath the ground. Soon the Shore will not be the only place the Taint corrupts. Thousands could die."

The Sireni behind Kaia shifted uncertainly, exchanging

glances and brushing their hands on their weapons, as though drawing comfort.

Kaia stared at Runa, then Eleden, a sharp look in her eyes. "Your sister?" she asked, looking back at Runa.

"I've sent her with Sashala to the Talan," Eleden said. "They'll travel separately to the Gale. We must inform them that the Old Ones have returned."

"Separately? Why?" Kaia's keen eyes shifted to Raith, on Runa's shoulder.

Raith reared up on their back feet, nearly unbalancing Runa with the shift in weight. She followed the wyvern's gaze and saw three figures coming from the trees, visible by the bright stars overhead and the glow of fire at their backs. It was Laerdi and Teaeth, struggling with someone between them.

Raith bristled, flickers of red light gathering atop their snout as the wyvern stared intently at the approaching men.

*Don't attack!* Runa thought desperately, wrapping her hand around the wyvern's side. *My father. It's my father.*

Egan flailed between the two bigger men, grunting and hissing as they dragged him forward. As the men drew closer, Runa saw that Laerdi had long scratches across his chest, and Teaeth's left eye was bloodied.

Kaia and her Sireni sailors whirled around, reaching for weapons. "What's going on?" Kaia demanded.

"We need to sedate him," Runa said, watching her father's face contort as he bared his teeth and hissed violently.

Egan thrashed, arching his back and twisting in a way that made Runa cringe. Raith hissed, and Egan's wild eyes snapped towards the wyvern and Runa. The unnatural green glow of his eyes intensified, and he inhaled sharply. Runa sagged, feeling as if she'd been punched in the chest. She felt something unspooling out of her, draining her. She blinked, eyes blurring.

Raith roared, and Runa managed a gasped, "No, Raith!"

Then Kaia stepped forward and slammed her fist into

Egan's face, snapping his head back. Egan sagged in Laerdi and Teaeth's arms, head lolling.

Gasping, Runa felt the world flood back into focus. The terrible feeling vanished, and she tightened her hand on Raith.

*Stop!* she commanded, willing the wyvern to listen.

Raith relaxed and settled back on her shoulder, and Runa breathed out in relief. Why did the wyvern listen now but not when faced with Lyric?

"What is Egan doing here?" Kaia demanded, whirling back to Eleden. "What have they done to him?"

Eleden sighed, his eyes troubled. "It's a long story," he said. "We need to get moving. We don't know if the Old Ones will return, and Sae'shara is out there somewhere."

Kaia blinked, shock registering on her face. "Is She—"

"We don't know," Eleden said. "Runa saw Her, but She disappeared before the Three became beasts."

Kaia looked at Runa appraisingly. "You spoke with Her?"

"No," Runa said. "She left before I could. She didn't seem to want to stay with the Three."

Kaia nodded.

"We should look for kanvar root, on the way to the ship," Runa said, looking at Eleden. "I thought I saw some when I was walking in the forest earlier today. It's a sedative." She glanced at Egan, head still sagging against his chest. "We shouldn't let him wake, if possible. He was doing something to me, and to Raith," she said.

"Who?" Eleden asked. Then his eyes flicked to Raith. "Oh. Yes, I'd prefer if Kaia doesn't punch him again."

Kaia arched an eyebrow.

"You will tell us what to look for?" Eleden asked. "Will we be able to find it, in the dark?"

"Yes," Runa said. "I can make light if you fashion torches."

"We should get in the air before dawn comes," Kaia said. "The darkness is already softening."

Runa glanced towards the trees, where Sashala had fled with Lyric. They'd never been apart for longer than a day in their entire lives. Worry tightened her stomach, and she stroked her fingers across Raith's warm scales. Had she gained an uncle and father, only to lose her sister? And Mother ...

"I need to send a message to Rathgar's Hold," Runa said.

Kaia hissed and crossed her arms. "Let them burn," she said.

"To warn my mother," Runa said, glaring at her. "To find out if she survived."

"Sashala may already be sending a gull at Lyric's request," Eleden said. "But ..." He eyed Kaia. "You have a Skyrunner, don't you? The Gale wouldn't have sent you without one."

"I'm not wasting one on the Butcher!" Kaia spat.

"Sashala will have already alerted the Gale about the dragons," Eleden said, "and with the Skybird's speed, we'll reach the Sea before they do."

"Please, Kaia," Runa said, the plea bitter on her tongue.

Kaia growled and turned away, looking north. "Let's get back to the ship," she said, her voice tense. "Then we'll talk about your message."

# 31

LYRIC

*Four Days Later*

LYRIC DUCKED under Sashala's fist and swung around behind her, her arm catching the taller woman's waist. Face dark with concentration, she stopped Sashala's heel with her foot and twisted around, using momentum to pull her down to the deck of the ship.

"Good," Sashala said, slapping the deck with one hand. Her smile was wolfish, the ring through her lip glinting in the morning light.

Lyric nodded and released her hold on the woman's shirt. "Thank you, Sashala," she said.

"You're getting better," Sashala said, clapping her on the shoulder. "It's good you are training."

"Hali tells me magic is sometimes too slow when you need to react instantly."

Sashala nodded. "A Windcaller can die from an unseen knife to the ribs. Enough for today, I think. We'll meet again tomorrow."

"Tomorrow," Lyric agreed. She'd trained with Sashala for

over an hour, and though Lyric was sweat-soaked and bruised, her companion was still just as relaxed and unwinded as she'd been at the start.

They parted ways, and Lyric walked to the railing, placing her hands on the smooth wood. She lifted her face to the sky and took a deep, cleansing breath, allowing the wind to rush over her and tousle her sweat-dampened hair.

Azora flickered into existence beside her, their leafy, seaweed-like wings drifting in the air. They landed on her shoulder and studied her with one gold eye.

*You're scared*, they thought in her head, the image of a fish darting away from a shadow filling Lyric's mind.

"Yes," Lyric said.

It'd only been four days since they'd left Ayanar and her sister behind and Lyric kept turning around, expecting to find Runa nearby. *She's safe*, Lyric reminded herself. *She's with Eleden. She's following us to the Sireni fleet.*

It was odd, not having Runa close. Their separation was the longest and farthest they'd ever been apart. What if they couldn't find each other again? What if the dragons prevented Runa from coming east, or if they couldn't figure out what was wrong with the wyverns.

What was Azora anyway? Lyric knew with certainty that she was connected to the wyvern. Azora was part of her magic somehow. They protected her, acting as a shield against attack, or attacking if they thought Lyric was in danger. When she'd first started sparring with Sashala, she'd had to stop the wyvern from interfering.

Azora hadn't attacked anyone since Runa, though they watched everything intensely. The wyvern seemed intelligent and capable of free thought, but they also followed Lyric's wishes the majority of the time, like they were more an extension of her arm than a companion. Still, they had a sense of self that a beast didn't possess.

Lyric wished she could ask Gandara what she knew about the guardian, but Azora had severed the connection, and Lyric didn't know how to contact her ancestor herself. She couldn't exactly go to the Veil again.

She'd asked Hali if she knew what Azora was, but the older woman didn't know. "It's part of you," she'd said, studying the wyvern. "It feels like your magic, your summoning. Though it feels more conscious than an actual shield or sword, maybe it's a tool to give you space and time to cast spells."

*I am ... sorry, about your sister,* Azora said. A feeling of regret trickled through their bond.

"You're sorry?" Lyric asked, looking at the wyvern with surprise.

*I feel your sadness,* Azora said.

"Can you feel sad?"

The wyvern blinked, sheer lids sliding down over their striking gold eyes. *I feel your emotions.*

"But not your own?"

*I don't understand.*

Lyric sighed and looked back at the water. The day was gray, and the wind cold, which felt fitting considering her mood. "Never mind," she said. "I just want to understand what happened." Had Laenadara intended to separate Lyric from her sister? Or did something go wrong with the ritual? Perhaps the High Priestess hadn't understood the true meaning of the Velanian words she'd spoken.

"What do we do now?" Lyric said aloud.

*What do you wish to do?* Azora asked.

Lyric dug her fingers into the railing. "Fix this," she said. "Fix everything. The Old Ones said they could help; they could cleanse the Taint. Now, it seems, we have to help them first."

Azora landed on the railing beside her hand and watched as a silver fish jumped out of the water and splashed back beneath the dark waves.

"But how do we do that?" Lyric asked.

*I don't know,* Azora said.

Lyric rubbed her eyes, feeling another helpless sigh hiss from her lungs. Maybe her mother would know what to do, or maybe there was something in one of her grandfather's books in Rathgar's Hold. Now that Elaina was there, perhaps she could help.

Lyric frowned. Had her mother ever searched Rakarn's library for information about the Taint? Surely she would have. Was that why she was so certain he'd been involved? Or had she ignored it like the Sireni, even though Eleden was convinced it was spreading?

*It doesn't matter now,* Lyric thought. *We know how to heal it.*

Once the Talan was underway, sailing east back to the Sea of Screams, Lyric had asked Sashala to send a gull to Hurlen in Rathgar's Hold. She'd warned him about the dragons and asked him to respond with information about her mother. She'd also asked if he could get a message to Elaina and a reply in return.

"She has to be alive," Lyric said. "She has to."

*Your sister?* Azora asked.

"No, my mother."

*She is unwell?*

"Yes."

*I am sorry.*

Lyric smiled, tears filling her eyes. She blinked them away and reached out to Azora, running her fingers down the wyvern's silky scales. The wyvern arched into her hand like a cat and made a strange, rumbling purr.

"Let's find Kell," Lyric said. She turned away from the railing and walked across the deck to the Captain's cabin, opening the door.

Azora glided after her, slipping ahead as Lyric stepped inside.

Kell stood by the mirror with his shirt off, twisting to see his back. There was a long, angry burn from his shoulder to his left side, cutting through the intricate tangle of tattoos. His skin was charred, a mix of black and red and waxy white.

"Kell!" Lyric gasped, rushing towards him.

Azora, startled by her movement, hopped out of Lyric's way and settled on the back of a chair, eyeing Kell with large, radiant eyes.

Kell's eyes snapped towards Lyric in the mirror, and he tried to turn around, but Lyric stopped him, resting her hands lightly on his hip below the damaged skin.

"I'm sorry," Kell said. "I wanted to see it for myself, and I remembered there was a mirror in here and—"

"I didn't know you were injured!" Lyric breathed. She studied the wound, noting that someone had cleaned and covered the charred skin with ointment. The burn obliterated whole sections of Kell's tattoos, the looping black and green lines severed where the skin had melted and reshaped.

"When did this happen?" Lyric asked. She stepped back, letting him turn to face her.

"When I went to the village with Braysa, to check for survivors," Kell said. "A burning branch hit my back."

"A branch?"

"It was dragon fire. Braysa had to kick me into the water to put it out." His lips curved as Lyric stared at him with frustration, anger, and fear. "It's fine, Ly," he said.

"Fine?" Lyric said, her voice rising. "This is a serious injury! If it gets infected—"

"I'm fine." Kell reached for her and rested his hands on her shoulders. "I won't die, Ly."

She grabbed his wrists, staring at him with wide eyes. She could sense Azora shifting uncertainly, sensing her panic.

"Patho helped me," Kell said. "He thinks it will heal if I'm careful. Nothing to do about the scar."

"Patho?" Lyric asked, blinking. "How did I not notice you were wounded? When you came back to the ship—"

"You were preoccupied," Kell said. "Patho is the Talan's healer. He patched Braysa and me up. Braysa burned his hands." He smiled. "I'm fine, Ly."

"Stop saying that," Lyric said. She looked at Kell's face, assessing his health. He looked tired, more so than usual, and sweat beaded on his forehead and dampened the hair at his temples. His skin felt cold and clammy beneath her hands. "You're feverish," she said. "You may already have an infection. I need my bag. I need—"

"It's not the burn," Kell said.

"Of course it's—"

"No." Kell looked away from her, his eyes finding Azora. "Well, maybe a little, but the tattoos ... the spells are damaged."

Lyric frowned, remembering their conversation along the road to Rathgar's Hold.

"I feel different," Kell said, looking down into her face. "There are memories, old ones, older than Thenda, pressing against the edges of my mind. It feels like something is thinning. I remember a woman ..."

"A woman?" Lyric asked. She swallowed, feeling a stab of jealousy.

Kell smiled and pulled her closer. Lyric released his arms and placed her hands against his chest. His skin was too cold.

"I know her somehow like she's family or ... someone who cared for me," Kell said, "and there's this strange feeling in my chest, a tangled knot of something that I think if I could just unravel it, I could ..." His voice trailed off, and he sighed in frustration. "It feels powerful, Ly."

Kell studied her face, searching for a way to explain. "What does your power feel like? When you touch magic?"

Lyric considered and looked at Azora, who was watching her. "It's different now, with Azora, but before, when I started speaking a spell and held the runes on my tongue, I'd feel the expansion of something inside me, like I stepped into a stream of light or water. When I summoned wind, I'd feel pressure build around me, and when I released it, it'd rush away, and I'd feel this sense of—" Lyric blushed and looked down at her feet. "It feels good," she finished lamely. "Powerful."

Kell nodded, a muscle shifting in his cheek. "I suppose that's how it feels, building pressure. The knot is alive somehow like it wants something. It's almost like weight and emptiness, existing together. I don't know ..."

"You're worried," Lyric said. She thought about the nubs on his back. "You think you're going to do something, release something."

"Yes," Kell said.

"No," Lyric said, shaking her head. She stepped closer, staring up at him with a fierce expression. "I told you before. You're not evil. You decide what you are. If something happens, we'll figure it out. Don't try to protect me. I want to help you."

"I don't want to add to your burdens," Kell said, stroking his hands down her arms. "With the dragons, your mother, and Runa ..."

Lyric felt a pang at her sister's name, and she folded her arms against Kell's chest, leaning into him. She could feel his breastbone sharp against her head. He should have felt warm, not cold. Worry thrummed through her as she thought about the damage to his back. What if she lost him too? What would she do then?

"I'm sure you won't be separated for long," Kell murmured against her hair.

"I hope you're right," Lyric whispered. She raised her face, her eyes searching his.

Eyes darkening, Kell leaned down and kissed her. His lips were dry, and Lyric pushed against him. He felt strong and stable, and she felt a desperate need to claim as much time as she could with him.

When Kell pulled away, leaving Lyric breathless and worried, she rested her head against him again and closed her eyes. What if the Sireni weren't willing to set aside the war and help figure out a way to calm the dragons, and reverse whatever Laenadara and her priests did to them? What if the Gale decided to let Erith and Raendashar burn? What if Ayanar was the last time she saw Runa?

And where was Runa now? Was she safe? Was she on Kaia's airship flying to the Sea of Screams? Would Runa be there, with Eleden and their father, when Lyric and Kell arrived?

"We'll survive this," Kell said.

Lyric breathed in, drawing the scent of him into her lungs, shoving her fears aside. She focused on his heartbeat, thudding rhythmically inside his chest.

*To the end*, Lyric thought, praying her sister could hear her.

# 32

ELAINA

ELAINA STARED at her father with a tightly controlled expression. It was an effort to keep the distrust off her face, but she must have managed it for he simply studied her, his brown eyes sharp with thought.

She was propped up in her old bed, with thick pillows at her back, and she'd folded her hands together in her lap to keep from picking at the coverlet. Elaina felt weak and slow, and a glance in a mirror beside the bed had shown her how bloodless her skin looked against the deep red of her robe.

"Triktakis healed you," King Rakarn said bluntly. His hair was still cut in the same, short style from her childhood, but there was silver now that hadn't been present before. He looked older, harsher, if that were even possible, as though the harsh winds from the Sea of Screams had chiseled away all the flesh of his face, leaving just the wide bones beneath.

"Yes," Elaina said. Her voice was raspy, and it grated unpleasantly when she spoke. Though the Dragon Blessed had performed a miracle repairing the damage to her throat, her vocal cords were permanently scarred. She would never sing again or delight the Scorched Court with her voice. Her father's eyes contracted at the tortured sounds, but he said nothing.

Rakarn sat stiffly in the chair beside the bed, his focus unwavering on Elaina. He didn't shift, or fidget, just sat like an immovable statue, his hands resting palms down on his knees. "Your daughters were here, in the city," he said, watching her.

Elaina felt her heart skip but kept her face blank, controlled. She held his stare without speaking.

"I know you have children," Rakarn said. His eyes narrowed, a crack in his calm appearance. "Curious they dumped you in Ivernn. Your own children don't care if you die?"

Ivernn. That's where he'd found her? That meant Lyric and Runa had survived. Her girls were alive. She bit her tongue to keep her face calm.

"I don't know why you'd try to hide them from me," her father continued. "I could have protected them. Obviously, you failed at that yourself."

He was trying to provoke her, she knew it, but Elaina felt her blood rise and her face flush. She took a small, controlled breath. "I did not want them to become part of this," she said.

"Part of the greatest empire in the world? The strongest bloodline?"

"Part of your war," Elaina said.

Rakarn narrowed his eyes, and the barest hint of a flush darkened his cheekbones. "*My* war? Everything I do is for Raendashar. For protecting our people, for providing for them."

Elaina sneered. "Hundreds of Raendasharans are dead because of you. Women and children. For every blow you give the Sireni, they respond in kind, sinking ships and bleeding the towns along the Sea's edge."

"And thousands more are alive because I made difficult choices to ensure our survival," Rakarn said.

"I know what you've done," Elaina spat, venom dripping

from her voice. Her hands twisted the coverlet on her lap, trying to rip apart the heavy fabric. "The Taint is your fault. Thenda is gone because of you, because of your hunger for power."

Rakarn's jaw clenched, and his fingers tightened on his knees, his knuckles whitening from the pressure. "The Sireni killed my mother, my father," he said coldly.

"You killed a *young woman*! Someone's daughter."

"I prevented a massacre," Rakarn said. "The Sireni were posed to attack, as soon as negotiations began."

"There was no sign of that!"

"Because I killed their assassins on my way to the treaty signing!" Rakarn's eyes blazed, his lips drawing back in a rictus sneer. He took a breath and relaxed again, stilling his fingers atop his knees, leaving creases behind in the dark fabric of his pants. "The Sireni have always wanted to destroy us; to drown us in their damned sea. Without me, you wouldn't be alive. Your children would never have been born."

"Without *you*, my brothers would still be alive. Better you had died, and mother lived," Elaina spat.

Rakarn laughed, a harsh, brutal sound. "I will not apologize for my actions, Elaina. I do not need your absolution." He stood, staring down at her with a look of disgust, as though he found her weak and useless. "Next time you see your precious Egan again, if he's not already dead, ask him how it was he found you. Ask him why he was so far from his beloved *sea*."

Elaina stared at her father, her blood thundering in her ears. She gripped the coverlet, focusing on the feel of the fabric beneath her skin, the pain in her fingers as she twisted sharply, holding on.

Smiling cruelly, Rakarn turned and left the room.

Elaina sat, her body rigid, teeth clenched. She waited, imagining her father striding down the hall and rounding the corner, heading towards his study. She waited for another breath, and then another, and then she broke.

Covering her face with her hands, Elaina sucked a ragged breath through her lungs and felt tears spring into her eyes. It felt like her heart was breaking, trying to rip out through her breastbone. Was it true? Had her father arranged Egan's arrival in Elae's Hollow? Had their moments together meant nothing?

Despite Rakarn's hatred and disgust for the Sireni, had he conspired to have his daughter fall in love with one? Had he known then, what Egan was? His power?

Elaina tried to focus on her father's words, tried to shove aside the violation she felt, the heartbreak. Egan had wanted to tell her something after they'd first made love in the field by her house. He'd tried to ... no, no she couldn't think about that now. She couldn't imagine, *wouldn't* believe her father willingly let Sireni blood into the Raendasharan line.

But if he had, if he'd orchestrated all of this somehow, what plans did he have for Lyric and Runa? Elaina could not let her father get his hands on them, not ever. They could never come here. They must not come here.

Her hands dropped into her lap, and she stared sightlessly at the far wall. He'd said they'd been here, in the city. Been, but were no longer. What had happened? Where had they gone?

Elaina reached for a bell on the table beside her bed, nearly knocking over a glass of water. Her hands were shaking, and she took a stilling breath as she rang the bell.

A maidservant entered, adjusting her hair with a distracted expression. She was a thin woman with a narrow face and fawn skin, covered in freckles. Elaina had not known her long, but she'd quickly learned the woman loved to read. Given her disheveled appearance, Lada had probably been tucked into a chair reading in the sitting room while Rakarn sat with Elaina.

"Lada," Elaina said, tucking away her anxiety and pasting a warm smile on her face.

Lada's expression shifted to concern, and she stepped up beside the bed, looking Elaina over. "Are you all right, your highness?" she asked. "Are you in pain? Should I send for the Dragon Blessed again?"

"I'm fine, thank you, Lada," Elaina said. "I was hoping you could tell me about any attacks that happened recently. Or anything unusual?"

Lada's forehead wrinkled, and she rested her hands on her hips with a thoughtful expression. "Attacks, your highness? Well, we did have a group of Sireni get through the second gate a few weeks ago. They slaughtered several guard squads, and the city was on edge for days afterward. That's the farthest they've ever made it into the city! To think, they could have ended up here in the castle. King Rakarn raged for hours after and sent an entire cadre of soldiers to the dock. I've never seen him so—"

"They attacked the hold?" Elaina interrupted.

Lada blinked, refocusing on Elaina's face. "Yes, your highness. They got their hands on writs of passage, and several of them somehow made it through the second gate. Darin, he works in the stables, said that they killed all the guards there, but when the stone guardians were activated, they ran off." She cocked her head to the side, speculation sparking in her eyes. "Odd, isn't it? Don't the guardians only activate if royal blood is spilled? At least that's the legend. I don't remember a time when it's happened before. Can you believe it? In our lifetime! There must be another Raendashara out there! Another heir to the—"

Lada cut off, paling, her eyes flying back to Elaina's face. She twisted her hands in the folds of her apron. "Forgive me, your highness," she said quickly. "I didn't mean to suggest that there is ... I don't mean to say that ... forgive me. I ramble on sometimes. Can I get you anything?"

"Thank you, Lada," Elaina said, trying to keep her voice

even and calm. "I agree; it is strange. So my father has increased the guards at the dock?"

"Yes, your highness," Lada said, her head bobbing nervously. "There has been an increase in patrols all over the city. I doubt very much that the Sireni will manage to get inside again."

Elaina inclined her head. "Thank you, Lada. Let me know if you hear any other news about the Sireni or anything strange in the city. That's all for now."

"Of course, your highness," Lada said. "It is good to have you back with us." She blinked as if startled she'd said that aloud, then curtsied quickly and left the room.

As the door shut quietly behind the maid, Elaina leaned back into the pillows and tried to ease the knots in her muscles. She was weak from her illness, and sometimes it was hard to breathe. Elaina drew a long, exacting breath into her sluggish lungs and looked down at her hands.

The Sireni had her daughters, and likely now knew who they were. Lyric and Runa had been taken weeks ago. Where were they now, and what would the Gale do with her children? Had Eleden learned of their abduction? Had he already rescued them? Where would he take them, if he had?

Elaina closed her eyes and tried to calm herself. Giving in to worry and fear would not help her daughters. If they were with the Sireni, it was unlikely they'd hurt them, at least not right away. First, they'd try to use them. For now, Lyric and Runa were safer there than here with her father.

Eleden would see that they were safe; she knew he would. After everything Elaina had done for the Sae'kan, he owed her. Still, she had to find a way to contact him. Find out where her girls were. Make sure they were protected. She would not give up now, even trapped in bed as she was.

And perhaps Egan ...

Elaina swallowed, feeling battered. She hadn't seen Egan

for nine years. She had no idea where he was or what he was doing. What did a god-child do, when not seducing women? Her lips twisted bitterly. Had his words to her been a lie? Maybe if she'd told him about the girls, perhaps if he'd known—

No, she would not think about him. They'd been so young when they'd met, so hopeful, so naive. However they'd found each other, what they'd felt, what they'd shared, it had been real. No one would take that away from her.

Who then, had betrayed her? Who told the Sireni where to find Elaina's daughters? Only a handful of people had known, and all members of Eleden's crew. She knew them, had fought, and slept beside them. They would not have sacrificed her children. She pictured their faces, but she couldn't name anyone as a traitor. Elaina ground her teeth. Whoever it was that had put her daughters in danger would be punished. She *would* find them.

A wave of exhaustion washed over her and she sagged, closing her eyes. She had to get out of bed and find out what her father was up to, and she had to find her daughters.

The door opened, and Elaina blinked her eyes open, feeling groggy. It was Lada, carrying a tray of food. She looked excited.

"Good, you got some rest," Lada said, smiling at her.

Elaina frowned. Her eyes felt gritty, and her mouth dry. She'd just closed her eyes, hadn't she? She turned her head to look towards the window. The light seemed softer, filtered by the thick glass. How much time had passed?

"What time is it?" Elaina rasped. She reached for a glass of water by the bed.

"You slept an entire day, your highness," Lada said.

"A day?"

"Yes, your highness." Lada set the tray down on the bedside table, moving aside the water-filled jug, and uncovering a bowl of orange broth and slices of dark spice bread. "There've been reports of dragons, your highness!" Lada flushed, laughing nervously. "I know it sounds ridiculous, no one has seen a dragon in thousands of years, but a merchant coming from Elesieayn sent a Skyrunner to Lord Yaender, claiming he'd seen one west of Lisos! The poor bird arrived half-dead from exhaustion with a singed wing! Can you imagine? The merchant claimed Ayanar is on fire, and a white dragon attacked one of Elesieayn's border cities."

"Dragons?" Elaina asked. Her thoughts felt slow like they were caught in heavy mud. Surely she'd misheard Lada.

"I'd say he was in his cups, of course," Lada continued, "but there have been other reports as well. I don't understand it. I thought the Old Ones were dead." Lada paused and stepped back from the table. "Begging your pardon, your highness."

"No, it's all right, Lada," Elaina said. "It does seem impossible." What did it mean? Who had brought them back?

"My father," Elaina asked, "how has he taken the news?"

"King Rakarn has called a council with his strategists, your highness. They are in the War Room. He's set to address the city, I believe. The townsfolk are clamoring for a response. People are both excited and concerned. No mobs in the street yet, but there are no dragons here. Not yet." Lada laughed nervously. "I thought the Old Ones were wise and helpful. Didn't they mediate concerns between the kingdoms, after the Demon War? Why are they destroying cities?"

Dread twisted Elaina's stomach, and she pressed her hand over her belly. "I don't know," Elaina said. "Thank you, Lada. Please let me know if you hear anything more."

Lada nodded then put a hand in her pocket, laughing. "Forgive me, your highness. I almost forgot that I have a letter for you."

"A letter?" Elaina frowned.

"Yes, it was delivered by a stable boy." Lada flushed, staring at the folded paper in her hand. "Were you not expecting one?

I'd thought you might have a ... a male friend or ..." Her face turned bright red, and she looked up at Elaina worriedly.

"Yes, yes I'm expecting it," Elaina said quickly, holding out her hand. "Thank you. This is something I'd like kept private."

"Of course, your highness." Lada gave her the letter then left the room, closing the door.

Elaina held the letter in her hands, examining it curiously. The paper was rough, not the silky parchment the highborn used, but one available to anyone in the market. It bore no seal and had been skillfully folded, the ends tucked in such a way that the letter stayed closed. Opening it with her fingernail, Elaina unfolded the paper.

*They are safe*, it read. It was not signed, the words centered in the paper.

Who had sent this? She didn't recognize the handwriting, but to who else could it refer other than Lyric and Runa? Eleden must have sent the letter, which meant someone was in the city who could tell her what had happened to her daughters.

Smiling with relief, Elaina tucked the letter inside her robe. She'd have to burn it. She could not let her father know she had an ally nearby.

Looking at the window, Elaina's thoughts returned to the dragons. She stared hard at the glass as if she could see through it to the lands west of Raendashar. Was her father involved? If anyone could summon the dragons, it'd be him. Is this what he'd tried to do, all those years ago? Had he finally succeeded?

But if he'd brought the Old Ones to life, why were they on the other side of Erith in Ayanar? Why weren't they here?

Elaina thought about Kell's mother, the Daughter of Valen she'd seen speaking with her father all those years ago. Could she be connected to Thenda or the dragons? What secrets might she have shared with Rakarn? What mysteries about death and the Veil? Why was she helping him? And why hadn't she tried to find Kell?

"I need to get out of this cursed bed," Elaina growled. She reached for her tray and lifted it with shaking hands onto her lap. She needed strength and clarity. She needed to find out what in Hel's name was going on. Lyric and Runa were out there somewhere. They needed her. She would not leave them to fight on their own.

She'd find Eleden's man in the city and learn where the girls were. She'd let them know she was alive, and tell them to stay away from Raendashar. She'd find out her father's connection to the dragons, and his plans for the Sireni, for her daughters, and for Erith itself. Her father's lust for conquest had never been confined to the Sea. Everything that now threatened her children was because of Rakarn's obsession with power, with control.

"I will find you," she said, thinking about Kell's mother. "And you'll tell me how to break my father."

Eyes blazing fiercely in her gaunt face, Elaina ripped apart a piece of bread and imagined the look on Rakarn's face when she tore his kingdom down around him.

# AUTHOR'S NOTE

Thank you for reading *Daughters of Fire & Sea*, the first book in the Daughters of Fire & Sea series. If you'd like to find out about new stories (including the next in the trilogy), you can join my mailing list or visit my website byhollykarlsson.com.

If you enjoyed the book, I'd love it if you left a review. Reviews help me craft better stories and help other readers find this book. Thank you for your support!

Lyric and Runa's adventure continues in *The Dragon Flute*, the second book in the Daughters of Fire & Sea trilogy coming in 2020.

This book would not have been possible without the endless encouragement and support from my husband Kent, who always graciously listens to my ideas and short stories, often presented enthusiastically at inopportune moments. Thank you for inspiring and challenging me. Thanks to my kids for growing old enough to entertain themselves and giving me lots of little moments throughout the day to furiously type on my computer.

I'd also like to thank my developmental editor, Kendra Olson for understanding the heart of my story and helping me see where it needed to be strengthened. A big thank you to my friends and beta readers: Amanda Alling Andrén, Allison Carr Waechter, Ashley Pfohl, Beth Okamoto, Heather Maddox, Jenn McGuill, Jim, and Tove Maren Stakkestad. Your critique and enthusiasm have been invaluable.

And thank you, my readers for taking a walk in Lyric and Runa's world. I'd love to hear from you, so please feel free to send me a message on www.byhollykarlsson.com, Facebook, or Twitter.

## ALSO BY HOLLY KARLSSON

A Wish in the Dark & Lawbringer (available on www.
byhollykarlsson.com)

Daughters of Fire & Sea (Book 1)

The Dragon Flute (Daughters of Fire & Sea Book 2) *Coming 2020*

SECRET NAME* (Daughters of Fire & Sea Book 3) *Coming 2020*

Unusual Diction: Volume One

Unusual Diction: Volume Two

# ABOUT THE AUTHOR

**Holly Karlsson** is a speculative fiction writer who roams and writes in the Pacific Northwest with her husband, children, and a dragon's hoard of journals. She's the author of *Unusual Diction Volume One* and *Two* and a new epic fantasy trilogy called *Daughters of Fire & Sea*.